THE ONE THAT GOT AWAY

DI HEATHER FILSON
BOOK 1

JD KIRK

ZERT⊕X
CRIME

THE ONE THAT GOT AWAY

ISBN: 978-1-912767-73-1

Published worldwide by Zertex Media Ltd.
This edition published in 2023.

1

www.jdkirk.com
www.zertexmedia.com

BOOKS BY J.D. KIRK

A Litter of Bones

Thicker Than Water

The Killing Code

Blood & Treachery

The Last Bloody Straw

A Whisper of Sorrows

The Big Man Upstairs

A Death Most Monumental

A Snowball's Chance in Hell

Ahead of the Game

An Isolated Incident

Colder Than the Grave

Come Hell or High Water

City of Scars

Here Lie the Dead

One For the Ages

Northwind: A Robert Hoon Thriller

Southpaw: A Robert Hoon Thriller

Westward: A Robert Hoon Thriller

Eastgate: A Robert Hoon Thriller

If you choose to read this book you will need a strong stomach.

Battersea Dogs & Cats Home is a charity
registered in England and Wales 206394

BATTERSEA DOGS & CATS HOME

Founded 1860

PROLOGUE

THE PUNGENT ODOUR scorches her airways. Sizzles and pops in her nostrils. Burns all the way to the back of her throat. Harsh. Chemical. Toxic.

She gags, not on the stench, but on the filthy rag wrapped around her head, pulled tight across the corners of her mouth so it carves painful red welts into her cheeks. Her lungs cramp. Her stomach tightens, bringing up a hot wave of acid that she has no choice but to choke back down.

Pain sears itself across her wrists. Her arms are behind her, but she knows she's torn the skin of her hands in her struggles to get free. She can still feel the blood oozing along her fingers.

There is blood above her eye socket, too, drying into her hair and what's left of her eyebrow.

There was a blindfold, but she managed to shake that off, running her forehead back and forth across the rough ground until she worked the tightly tied material free.

The skin is torn and ravaged there, from where she rubbed, and rubbed, and rubbed against the stone floor.

And why? To what end? Wherever she is, it's dark. Impossibly dark. As dark as it was beneath the blindfold.

Perhaps, she thinks, even darker still.

It's cold, too. Bitingly so. She can't see them, but she can imagine the shaky clouds of her breath as they come rasping in and out of her raw, damaged airways.

She screamed at first. Of course she did. She screamed when she roused from a sleeping nightmare into this waking one. The gag muffled the sound, but didn't block it completely. And so, she screamed, and she kicked, and she thrashed there on the floor.

In the cold.

And in the dark.

She screamed, and she kicked, and she thrashed. She cried, and she shook, and she shivered.

Nobody heard. Nobody came.

And as she lay there, trembling and alone, she thought of her mum and her dad. Thought of how worried they'd be. How frantic. They'll be out looking for her now. Her brother, too. Knocking on doors. Calling her name.

They'll have called the police. There'll be a hunt on. People will be searching.

No one has told her that any of this is happening. They don't have to. She just knows it. Instinctively. Unshakably. She knows that people will be looking for her. Friends, relatives, neighbours, even strangers will all be out in force.

They'll be coming for her, sooner or later. They'll be coming to take her home.

A crack of light appears down low. Just a thin line at first, then it spreads, becoming a faint and insipid suggestion of yellow that paints itself on the concrete floor, oozing towards her like something liquid and alive.

The sound of an engine grows louder. A vehicle is approaching.

In the cold, and in the dark, she knows that her family will be searching for her.

But, as the light creeps closer, and the engine grows louder, there is something else she knows, too.

Instinctively.

Unshakably.

She knows she will never see any of them ever again.

ONE

BETWEEN THE PAIN needling through her skull and the erection jabbing into her back, Heather Filson could tell that mistakes had been made. It was now just a question of magnitude.

She could hear him snoring away behind her, whoever he was. Snoring was good. Snoring meant she could get out of there without any awkward small talk, or suggestions of one more quickie for the road.

First, though, she'd need to find her clothes. That would involve opening her eyes, but she wasn't quite ready for that yet. Opening her eyes meant facing the reality of where she was, what she'd done, and—more importantly—who she'd done it with.

Even with her eyes closed, though, the signs weren't encouraging. The mattress beneath her felt lumpy and old, the sheet thin and bobbled against her bare skin.

The room smelled stale, like an old pair of wet running shoes. Notes of cheap beer and discarded fag ends were woven through it, along with the cloying sweetness of cannabis. The cheap resin variety, she thought. Not even the good stuff.

There was light coming from somewhere, tinting the darkness behind her eyelids. Daylight, she thought.

That was bad. It was early March in Scotland, so for the sun to be up it had to be at least eight o'clock. But the last few days had been overcast, threatening some late-season snow, which meant it was probably much later than even that.

Great. She was supposed to be at the station in Glasgow by half eight.

That would teach her to go out on a school night.

Neither the headache nor the prodding at her back seemed to be going anywhere. She couldn't put things off any longer.

Heather peeled open her eyes, grimaced at the jarring brightness, and closed them again in a hurry. She pressed a thumb and the knuckle of a forefinger against her eyelids, massaged them until the aching eased off, then tried again.

This time, she was just about able to tolerate the discomfort, and the room came into a queasy sort of focus.

The first thing she saw was a movie poster. It was sideways, so it took her a moment to figure out which film the poster was promoting. Some shite from the *Fast and Furious* franchise, she eventually concluded, which did nothing to make her feel any more positive about the night before.

There was an overflowing ashtray and a couple of *Tennent's* cans on the bedside cabinet, which went some way to explaining the smell. There was also, to both her disgust and delight, a used condom. It reminded her of some dead deep sea creature—bloated and full at one end, flat and shrivelled at the other, and with a general sense of despair permeating the whole thing.

Still, at least one of them had been sober enough to take precautions.

The smell of the lager triggered memories of the night before.

She remembered the house feeling too small for her. Too confined. She'd gone out. The pub, definitely. She remembered being in there, knocking back a few drinks and a few suggestive comments from the other punters.

Had she put someone on their arse? Did she remember that? Some grubby wee bastard with wandering hands? Had that happened? A throbbing when she clenched her fist suggested it was a definite possibility.

From there, things became a bit hazier. She dimly remembered eating at *Wimpy*, then the thunder of noise and the claustrophobia of hundreds of hot bodies around her.

She'd hit *The Garage*, then. No great surprise, really. When it came to nightlife in Kilmarnock, it was that place or the *Gala Bingo*, and getting absolutely shitfaced and shagging a randomer were both generally frowned upon at the latter.

Although, that wasn't to say they didn't happen.

The smell of the bedside table was turning her stomach. Individually, all the elements on it were bad enough. Together, with her head pounding, her mouth dry, and the room starting to undulate around her, they were unbearable.

She looked away, and her eyes fell on another poster nearer the window.

This one was of a footballer. God knew who. She only figured out he was a footballer because he was wearing a tracksuit, held a ball under one arm, and had a twatty haircut that probably cost more than her first car.

Then again, her first car had only cost her fifty quid, so that wasn't exactly saying much. It'd had mushrooms growing in the boot, and wouldn't reverse, but it had still seemed like a good deal at the time.

Her eyes throbbed in protest as she steered them down the wall until they eventually settled on something troubling.

There was a skateboard. It was propped up against a shoddily built IKEA chest of drawers, which had two of its handles missing.

The underside of the board was turned to face the bed, and Heather found herself looking into the cartoon eyes of one of the *Teenage Mutant Ninja Turtles*. The one with the purple bandana, whatever the fuck his name was. *DiCaprio*, or something.

Slowly, she craned her neck, taking in the rest of the room. There was a big telly mounted on the wall, a gaming chair positioned in front of it, and an *Xbox* on a small table between the two. Empty game cases and stray disks lay scattered around.

There was a telescope by the window, though the closed curtains would've rendered it largely useless. A pair of binoculars hung from a hook a little further along the wall, ready to be grabbed in an emergency.

Quite what such an emergency might look like, Heather had no idea. But, at least he'd be looking at it close up.

In the corner, clothes were spilling out of a laundry basket shaped like a shark, its open mouth pointing to the ceiling so it looked like it was vomiting grubby boxers and dirty white socks out onto the floor.

The pain in her head intensified. The churning in her stomach switched up a gear.

Oh God.

Oh God, she'd shagged a teenager.

Heather reached an arm out from under the covers, fumbled on the floor until she found her clothes, then rolled out of bed, already wrestling herself into her underwear.

Behind her, the steady rattle of snoring snorted to a stop, and she frantically fought her way into her T-shirt, one eye already on the door.

Maybe she could still make it. Maybe she could still get out of there before—

"Hey."

Fuck.

Caught.

She had no choice then but to face up to her mistake. She turned, teeth gritted, to look at the figure lying in the bed, his head propped up on one arm, his smooth, hairless torso exposed all the way to his belly button.

"Oh, thank Christ," she ejected when she spotted the crow's feet at the corners of his eyes, and the lines etched into his brow.

He was in his forties, at least. A grown man, despite what the room might suggest.

He smiled, incorrectly assuming the remark was a compliment. "Still like what you see, eh? Good. You certainly seemed to last night," he oozed, and Heather felt her body instinctively convulse in disgust. "And you're not so bad yourself, by the way, even without the old beer goggles."

"Eh, cheers. Aye."

She buttoned up her jeans and forced her feet into her trainers. She hadn't even bothered to look for her socks. Their loss was a small price to pay if it meant getting the fuck out of there as quickly as humanly possible.

"So, uh, right," she said, throwing a thumb back over her shoulder in the direction of the door. "I guess I'll be getting off."

"Already? You sure you don't want breakfast?" he asked. "Or, maybe something… more substantial?"

He winked at her and lifted the covers, showing off both his erection and a potbelly that lay partly pancaked against the crumpled sheet beneath him.

Bile rose into Heather's throat and burned as she swallowed it back down. She shook her head. Quite emphatically, too.

"No. You're alright," she said.

I'd rather claw out my own eyeballs.

"Cheers, for the offer, though."

"You sure?" the would-be Lothario asked. He tensed his stomach muscles, and his erection twitched. "Little Dom's awake and raring to go."

A whole-body convulsion arched Heather's back. The movement jolted her brain, shaking loose a memory from the night before.

Dom. Dominic. That was his name. She remembered his working it into a chat-up line.

"*'Hi, I'm Dom. But, if you'll let me, I'd be more than happy to be your sub…'*"

She'd laughed. Not at the line—who in their right mind would've laughed at that shite?—but at him, with his high hairline, saggy cheeks, and yellowed teeth. He was a good seven or eight years older than her, and it showed.

She thought she remembered telling him in no uncertain terms to fuck right off. And yet, here she was, full of regret, self-loathing, and blurry black holes where her memories should be.

A snake coiled in her gut. Heat prickled across her skin.

"Wait. Hang on a fucking minute," she snapped at him. "Did you spike me?"

It was more of an accusation than a question. Dom sat up, his morning glory wilting away, his eyes widening in horror.

"What? No! God, no! Of course not! I walked you home. Remember? I met you outside the club. You were a bit… worse for wear, so I offered to walk you home."

Something stirred in the murk of Heather's hangover. The surge of anger she'd felt towards him redirected itself, turning inwards.

"But when we got there, you didn't want to go in. You said we should go to my place, instead," Dom continued. He smiled self-consciously, showing off his awful teeth. "You kissed me. Remember? You, eh, you grabbed my—"

"Alright. Alright. I get it," Heather snapped, cutting him short.

"And then we—"

"I get the picture."

Dom got off the bed, still naked. He moved towards her, arms open, offering a hug she wanted to be no part of.

"I'd never do anything like that to anyone," he said. "Especially not you."

"Right. Good. Glad to hear it." Heather raised a hand to block him, her eyes scanning the room. "Is my jacket here?"

"Jacket? No, you didn't have a jacket on," Dom replied. "Were you wearing one when you left the house?"

"It's freezing. Of course I was wearing one."

She tugged at her T-shirt. It was a faded old thing from an *Aerosmith* tour that her Uncle Kenny had dragged her along to back in the late Nineties. She'd been thirteen or fourteen at the time. Her first gig. Nothing else she'd been to since had come close to matching it.

"You think I came out wearing just this?"

Dom shrugged. He didn't appear remotely put out by his own nudity, even though the coldness of the room was starting to have a visible effect.

"Maybe you left it at the club?"

Heather sighed. "Aye. Maybe," she conceded.

She put a hand on the door handle, then paused. She'd hoped to slip away without any of this, but now that they were both awake and upright, she felt she needed to say *something*.

'Let's never speak of this again,' felt like an obvious one.

But then, though her memories were hazy, she thought she remembered his hand on her elbow as he'd guided her home. She could vaguely picture him saying goodbye to her at her house. He'd shaken her hand, she thought.

In the state she must've been in, she'd have been easy to take advantage of, but he hadn't tried. She'd been the one to make the move.

Room decor aside, he'd at least earned himself some passing pleasantries.

"So, uh, thanks for…" She gestured vaguely, searching for an appropriate conclusion to the sentence. None presented itself, so she settled for, "…that."

"Anytime," he said, his voice a low, sensual purr. Or, an attempt at one, at least. "Do you want to get together later, maybe? Dinner?"

Something inside Heather cringed so hard it turned inside out. "Uh, no."

"Oh, right. Busy. No problem. Tomorrow, maybe?" He grinned hopefully. "Lunch is on me!"

"Listen, Dom. I'm sure you're a nice guy, but I don't really do that."

Still naked, and now notably shrivelled, Dominic frowned.

"Do what?"

"Dinner. Lunch. Relationships," she said, struggling a bit over that last word.

Dom laughed, but it was a forced, fake bray of a thing, and he cupped his hands in front of his crotch, suddenly vulnerable.

"No. God, no. I just meant… as friends."

"*Any* relationships," Heather said, eyeing up the exit. "It's not you, it's me. It's very much me."

But also you, she added silently.

"Oh. Right. Fair enough. Well…" He removed his hands and put them behind his head, making a display of his unimpressive nakedness. "I don't do relationships either. This could be purely sex, if that's what you're into."

One corner of his mouth tugged upwards into the sort of smirk she could imagine him rehearsing in the mirror, and Heather felt any lingering shreds of sympathy or affection evaporating.

"Nah, you're alright," she said, then she turned and opened the door.

"Wait! You sure you don't want breakfast?" he blurted. The urgency in his voice told her he didn't want her to leave. "My mum does an amazing Full Scottish."

Heather's nausea turned her stomach into a yawning pit. Pain hammered at her skull. Somewhere, deep in the fug at the back of her head, she heard the Hangover Gods erupting into laughter.

"Sorry," she said, looking back over her shoulder. "Did you say your *mum*?"

———

"Morning, hen! Kettle's on!"

The words floated aloft on the aroma of frying bacon as Heather went stumbling along the hallway towards the front door.

"Don't worry, no need to rush off. There's nothing to be embarrassed about," said a woman in her late sixties who came shuffling out of the kitchen in her dressing gown and slippers. "I put my headphones on. Noise-cancelling ones that Dominic bought me for Christmas. As soon as I knew what was happening, and what you pair were up to, I popped them on, so I didn't hear a thing! Honestly, after the first couple of minutes, there wasn't a cheep!"

The stomach acid burned up into Heather's throat again as she fumbled with the lock.

"You sure I can't get you something?" Dom's mother asked, her tone relentlessly cheerful, her smile ratcheting higher up her cheeks. "I've got bacon frying, and could stick you on a slice or two of square sausage?"

Heather whispered an, "Oh, thank fuck," when the door finally unlocked, then a louder, "I'm fine, cheers," as she pulled it open.

And, with that, she hurried out of the house, and into the bracing cold of the late-season snow that had, at last, stopped threatening, and finally started to fall.

TWO

MUCH LIKE HER SELF-RESPECT, Heather's phone had given up the ghost sometime during the evening before, and it took a few minutes of wandering before she clocked something familiar, and was able to figure out where in the town she was.

She was east of the river. Somewhere near the Dick Institute—a building whose name she usually couldn't help but find funny, but which today barely raised a smirk.

Never again, she thought, as she trudged onwards. That was it. No more drinking. She was done.

The hangover was a bad one. The worst in a long time. It wasn't just the headache, though that was grim enough. Whether aching, or throbbing, or churning, or just heavy with weariness, every part of her was suffering.

She felt like all the alcohol had been forcibly wrung out of her, like someone had picked her up and squeezed her until there wasn't a drop of the stuff left in her bloodstream.

The cold wasn't helping matters. She shivered as the cold wind and swirling snow set about her, turning her arms into gooseflesh. She wrapped them around herself, trying to hug in some warmth, even as her sockless feet froze in her trainers.

She thought about taking a detour past *The Garage* on the way home. It was barely half nine, so the club wouldn't be open, but other parts of the building would be. Maybe they'd have her jacket.

The thought of the place brought another hazy memory into focus. Standing outside, shouting at a bouncer, asking him if he had any idea who she was.

Heather felt all her muscles tighten at the thought of it, a full-body wince that made her forget the cold, if only for a moment.

No. Her jacket could wait. No way she was strolling back in there in last night's clothes, feeling like something that Death himself had shat out onto the pavement.

It took her another twenty minutes or so to get back to her house, by which time the snow had started to settle.

The house was a wholly unremarkable three-bedroom terraced place—the middle of a row of three—in the Bonnyton area of town, just a stone's throw from the community centre.

She'd grown up there, moved out at seventeen, and then been dragged back years later, after what her dad had at first jokingly referred to as his 'brain farts,' became no laughing matter.

There was a bike propped up under the living room window, snow just starting to pile up on the saddle. At this time of day, the bike could only be bad news, and she cursed herself below her breath as she hurried up the path, fumbling in her pocket for her keys.

"Hello? I'm here," she called, pushing on into the house. The warmth enveloped her like a hug as she closed the door behind her, shutting out the cold.

From through in the living room, her Uncle Kenny called back a, "Through here."

She slung her keys in a bowl on the sideboard, then checked her reflection in the mirror.

Christ, she looked rough. Her eyes were ringed with red like she'd recently been crying or was currently stoned. Her dark hair was lank and greasy, and looked like it had been styled by a controlled explosion. She was grateful she kept it a little shorter than shoulder length. Any longer, and it would be a nightmarish knot of twists and tangles.

As it was, she ran a hand through it, sweeping it into a sort of side-parted quiff, then blew into her hand and sniffed it, checking her breath for the smell of smoke or alcohol.

There was absolutely no reason for any of this, of course. She was a grown woman. She wasn't a teenager anymore, even if she still knew exactly where all the squeaky floorboards were on the stairs that led up to the bedrooms above.

Hell, she paid the rent. She could stay out as long as she liked. She could do what she wanted.

But old habits died hard, and the brevity of Kenny's reply meant his tone had been hard to judge. There was a possibility that he was angry, and it took a *lot* to get on Kenny's bad side.

Today, to her relief, was no exception. He smiled up at her from one of the two sagging armchairs that stood either side of the fireplace.

The chair was average-sized, but with Kenny sitting in it, it looked like it had been built for a child. In photographs, Kenny always looked short and stocky, appearing almost as broad as he was tall.

It was only when you saw him in real life, though, that you realised quite how enormous he actually was. He stood a couple of inches over six feet, with a barrel-like torso and limbs like the trunks of oak trees.

He had a big red beard, which was now showing flecks of white, and eyebrows that danced like marionettes up and down his forehead when he talked. He was dressed in a grey shirt and a knitted, dark green tank top. It was the classic Uncle Kenny outfit. At any point in Heather's life, had she been asked to draw the man from memory, he'd have been wearing those very clothes.

Three bars of the electric fire were burning away, and Kenny was waggling his toes in front of them, drying out the damp patches in his socks. One of his big toes stuck out through a hole, like a worm emerging from the ground to check the coast was clear.

"Easy to see you're not paying that meter bill," Heather remarked, tilting her head towards the fire.

Kenny chuckled, then put a finger to his lips, and shot a look at the couch. His brother, Scott—Heather's dad—lay under a blanket on it, his back to the rest of the room, his shoulders rising and falling with the rhythm of his breathing.

"Got a call from Bob and Sally next door," Kenny said. He wasn't whispering exactly—Scott was too deep a sleeper for that—but he was keeping his voice to a low-level murmur. "He was out wandering in his pyjamas."

"Shit. Sorry." Heather held up her mobile and gave it a waggle. "Phone died. I was… working."

"An all-nighter, eh?"

An eyebrow rose, and the faintest suggestion of a smirk tugged at one corner of Kenny's mouth. The look made Heather uncomfortable, like her uncle knew something she didn't.

"Hope you're getting paid overtime for that," he said.

"Ha. Aye. If only," Heather muttered. The guilt she felt about lying to him forced her to look away. "Sorry again."

Kenny dismissed the apology with a smile and a wave of his coffee cup.

"I found the daft old bugger over by the fence at the train tracks. He was, eh…" Kenny took a sip of his coffee, like he was steeling himself. "He was looking for you. Thought you'd been… That, you know. That something had happened."

Heather felt hot pinpricks gathering behind her eyes as she looked down at her dad on the couch. Like his brother, he had once been a big man. Broad. Strong. She remembered how it felt to be scooped up in his arms and hoisted onto his shoulder. From up there, she'd felt like she could see the whole world.

Now, there was almost nothing of him. A succession of illnesses had whittled away at him, carving a frail and shrunken figure from the giant he had once been.

"I'm sorry," she said again. "I should've been here, Kenny."

"Ach, away you go. We were reminiscing," Kenny said.

He gestured to an open photo album on the table. The images were a mix of six-by-fours and *Polaroids*. They showed Kenny and Scott as young boys, messing about on bikes outside the big family home, climbing the old oak trees out front, or surrounded by the family's cats, and their ancient, wet-eyed dog.

"We had a nice chat about the good old days," Kenny continued. "I swear, he remembers them better than I do sometimes."

Heather smiled. Obviously, she hadn't been around for those days, but she'd gone through the photo album with her dad so often that it sometimes felt as if the memories contained in its pages were her own.

"Still," she told him. "You shouldn't have to deal with this."

"Aye, well, nor should you," her uncle replied. "Not on your own, anyway. And you're not. On your own, I mean. That's what I'm here for."

He looked out of the window. The snow was still falling, and the sky was heavy with the promise of much more to come.

"Kind of wishing I'd taken the van instead of the bike, mind you. Going to be a bastard of a cycle back home in this."

"I could give you a lift," Heather suggested. She glanced upwards towards the ceiling, and the bathroom she could practically hear calling to her. "I could do with jumping in the shower first, but—"

"Eh, no. You've got quite enough of your own worries."

Heather shook her head. "Honest, it's fine. I owe you that, at least. Just let me—"

Kenny rose to his feet. The smirk was back as he presented her with the top peel-off sheet of the notepad that sat beside the house phone.

"Your work's been calling. Four times, in fact," he said. "Obviously, they couldn't have noticed you were right there on duty the whole time."

Something shrivelled up inside Heather as she accepted the scrawled list of names, times, and numbers. She forced herself to meet her uncle's eye, but saw no judgement there, only the sparkle of something bordering on mischievous.

"Kenny," she began, but he shook his head and grinned, cutting her off.

"Boyfriend material, was he?" Kenny teased. He winked, and Heather's guilt eased just a little. "Or girlfriend, this time, is it? I lose track."

"Neither," she said.

"Not settling down material, then?"

"Come on, Unc. You know me better than that," Heather said.

Kenny's smile didn't shift, but there was something in his eyes that stung her a little. A mix of sadness and disappointment, like he was still holding some hope for her that she'd long ago abandoned.

Or perhaps never even had.

"Aye, well, away you go and get showered," he told her. "Tea and a bacon roll?"

Right there and then, Heather could've kissed him.

"You're a lifesaver, Kenny," she said. She opened her mouth again, but he already knew what was coming.

"Crispy. No butter. Aye, I know," he said. His eyes flicked up towards the ceiling. "Now, away and get a shifty on. I think that nasal-sounding bastard from your work who kept phoning was starting to get pretty upset…"

THREE

THE DRIVE from Heather's house to HQ was usually just a half hour straight shot up the M77 in her Audi A4, but the snow turned thirty minutes into forty-five. Add on the shower and the hurriedly devoured breakfast, and it was just over an hour later when she went striding into the building like she owned the place.

And she had. Sort of. She'd been in charge of this particular office, at least.

Her rise to Detective Chief Inspector of the Major Investigation Team had bordered on the meteoric. To have reached those lofty heights before the age of forty had been pretty much unheard of in the UK, and certainly in Scotland.

There had been some grumbling from a few of the usual suspects about her promotions being more to do with diversity than talent. She was female and had been in an on-off romantic relationship with another woman when she'd first joined the team. Those things combined, the theory went, had resulted in her rapid rise through the ranks.

She always refuted the allegation, of course—sometimes violently. Whatever the reason, she'd done the job well. She'd been good at it. Their petty, misogynistic bullshit couldn't take that away from her.

She'd been answerable to the man above, of course—everyone

was answerable to someone—but this place, this office, had been her domain. She'd been the one running it. She'd led the investigations, and made the big day-to-day calls.

That was back before some big-mouthed rapist had gloated about getting all his charges dropped. Before he'd called his victim a slut, and laughed in her parents' faces.

Before Heather had seen red and stuck the heid on the bastard.

Before the disciplinary hearing that had seen her bumped back down to DI.

Still, it could've been worse. Had it not been for the efforts of her detective superintendent, and the good word put in for her by her former DCI, her arse could've been right out the window.

The rumour at the time had been that said former DCI, Jack Logan, was going to be dragged back down from the Highlands to run the place again. She'd quite liked the thought of that. They'd made a good team once, both on the job and off it.

He'd obviously felt differently, though, and had dug in his heels. The Det Supt up north had backed him all the way, and so the high heid yins had no choice but to go with the much less appealing Plan B.

She heard him calling across the office as she entered, his grating Invernesian whine screeching like fingernails down a blackboard.

"Well, lookie-see who I see. Her ladyship has finally seen fit to join us."

Heather slumped into her chair across from DCI Samuel 'Snecky' Grant, and tried not to let the smug wee smirk on his face bother her too much. That nauseatingly self-satisfied look was, after all, just his natural resting expression.

This was Snecky's second time heading up the Central Belt MIT. He'd been wholly shite at it the first time around, and it had taken its toll on him, both physically and mentally. He'd lost about four stone his first time down here, become a chain smoker, and kissed goodbye to half of the hair on his head.

He'd jumped on the chance to move back up north, then over to CID in Aberdeen, where he'd put on all that lost weight, plus several pounds more. The hair hadn't grown back, though, and the top of his skull rose up through what was left of it like the peak of a mountain you wouldn't want to climb.

She'd imagined that he'd fought hard not to move back down this way. That was the only positive Heather had been able to take from his appointment—Snecky hated the fact he was here even more than she did.

"What are you doing?" he demanded.

Most of the words sounded like they'd come out through his nose. Despite being bounced all over the country, his accent had remained *fiercely* Invernesian. Apparently, that was where his nickname, 'Snecky,' originated. Something to do with Inverness, though she didn't fully understand it.

According to some online dictionary she'd once looked it up in, the word also meant a person who was unpleasant to be around, so regardless of the origin, it suited him to a tee.

"What does it look like I'm doing?" Heather countered. She bumped her fists on the plastic arms of her office chair. "I'm sitting down."

"Well, don't. You don't have time," Snecky told her, his mouth puckering into a prissy little knot. He slid a sheet of A4 paper across the desk towards her, then prodded it with his finger. "Missing teenager. You're up."

Heather blew out her cheeks as she leaned over and read the studiously neat handwriting on the page. Snecky was the only adult Heather knew—the only *person* she knew, in fact—who drew the dot above the lowercase letter 'i' as a little circle. It gave his handwriting a whimsical feel, which was exactly what you didn't want in a report about a teenager's disappearance.

"Says she's fifteen and only went missing yesterday," Heather said, sliding the page back towards him. "That's CID."

Snecky placed a finger in the centre of the sheet of paper and very deliberately returned it.

"No. It's been given to us. The detective superintendent thought it would be more appropriate for us to handle it. And it's Kilmarnock, so if you'd bothered your arse to phone, you could've saved yourself a trip."

With a sigh, Heather picked up the sheet and scanned it again.

Teenagers went walkabout all the time, especially in towns like Kilmarnock. Generally, Uniform responded to those calls. By the time CID got called in, if things even made it that far, the kids had usually found their way back home.

It only became an issue for the Major Investigation Team if the worst came to the worst.

"The Gozer gave this to us?" Heather asked, eyes darting left and right across the page. Her frown deepened. "That doesn't make sense. Why would he give this to us and not…?"

She trailed away into silence when she saw it, written there down near the bottom of the page.

A name.

The name of a family member of the missing girl.

A name she'd hoped she'd never have to see or hear again.

That had been wishful thinking, of course.

Suddenly, though she very much wished it didn't, the MIT's involvement in the case made complete sense.

"Aw." Heather groaned, letting the paper fall back onto the desk. "Shite."

———

It was after lunchtime by the time Heather made it back down the road to Kilmarnock. Her stomach was growling, the two hurried bites of her bacon roll having been enough to fire it up, but nowhere near enough to keep it satisfied.

The hangover still had its hooks in her, too, and each *thump* of the car's windscreen wipers made her wince on the drive south through the swirling snow.

The house was part of a block just off MacFarlane Drive. It was a few minutes' walk from Kilmarnock Academy, and bordered the big cemetery on the east side of town. Not too far away from where Heather had woken up that morning, she reckoned, though she tried very hard not to dwell on that.

There were two police cars parked on the street near the house, one either side of a racing green *Jaguar* that had laid claim to the space nearest the gate.

Both squad cars had their engines running. Two uniformed constables sat inside each vehicle, warming their hands on the blowers. There were three guys sitting in the *Jag*, too—big lads, two in the front, and one with his head lowered so he could fit in the back.

The guy in the back was younger than the others, and with his head angled, Heather could make out a series of Chinese symbols tattooed up the side of his neck.

All three of them watched her with interest. None of them acknowledged her when she snapped off a middle-finger salute in their direction.

One of the constables sitting in the steamed-up squad cars recognised Heather as she trudged through the snow towards the house, and wound his window down to greet her.

"Detective Chief Inspector," he said, then his face paled, and he hurriedly corrected himself. "Sorry. Detective Inspector. I just... I forgot that..."

"He in there?" Heather asked, nodding up the path towards the house.

It was a boringly boxy sort of building of typical sixties or seventies construction. What it lacked in imagination, it made up for in straight lines and drab colours, its design favouring function over even the faintest notion of style. It was the sort of place that would make architects throw their hands to the skies in despair.

Time and the West of Scotland weather had taken their toll on the whole row of houses. The grey render had developed long, deep cracks, and the white-painted woodwork had seen better days.

The uPVC windows of the house Heather was heading for looked new, though, particularly when compared to those on either side. She thought the roof of this place looked in better nick than the others, too, though the piling snow made it hard to be sure.

Someone had splashed a bit of cash on the place, though.

One look at that *Jaguar*, and the three goons sitting in it, was enough to tell her who.

"He, eh, he is, aye," the Uniform replied. He and his partner both looked up the path to the house's front door. They shivered, and Heather got the impression it had little to do with the cold.

"He tell you to get out?"

The other constable nodded. "Said he wasn't talking to anyone in uniform."

Heather ran her tongue across the back of her teeth, still watching the house. "No, but really. What did he actually say?"

The first constable smiled awkwardly. "He said, 'You pricks can piss off. Get me a fucking grown-up.'" He looked at his partner. "Yeah?"

"Yeah," confirmed the other one. "Something like that."

Heather nodded. That sounded more like the man she knew.

"Right. Wait here," she instructed, straightening up.

She buttoned up her jacket. It was an old brown leather one she'd found at the back of the hall cupboard. It offered very little protection from the cold, and she had to fight to stop her teeth chattering as she turned towards the house.

"If you hear shouting or gunshots, maybe come pop your head round the door, eh?"

"Will do, ma'am," one of the constables confirmed.

"Good luck," said the other.

Heather opened the gate, eliciting a long, mournful groan from the rusted hinges.

"Cheers," she said, crunching onto the fresh snow on the path. "One of us is going to need it."

FOUR

SHUGGIE COWAN WAS RIGHT where Heather expected him to be—centre stage, making everything all about him, as usual.

She'd been met at the front door by a tall, sparrow-like woman who moved in a series of twitches and jerks. She was in her early-to-mid-forties, and introduced herself as Linda, the missing girl's mum, before ushering Heather through to a living room that was hazy with cigarette smoke.

Shuggie sat slap-bang in the centre of the couch, the cushions surrounding him squashed beneath his weight, as if he'd been dropped onto the seat from a height. He had his legs stretched out in front of him, like he was showing off the fucking awful brown leather cowboy boots that had become something of his trademark.

Glancing upwards, Heather half-expected to see a big hole he'd fallen through, but instead found only a yellowed ceiling and a dimpled glass light shade strung with cobwebs.

"Oh. It's you," he grunted, when Heather entered the room.

"Funny. That's what I was about to say," Heather replied.

Shuggie had never been much of a looker, and age had done nothing to change that. He was bulky in all the wrong places and all the wrong ways. What was left of his hair had been dyed an unnatural shade of black, and slicked backwards away from his forehead, like he was auditioning for a low-budget stage adaptation of *Goodfellas*.

His skin was saggy and pockmarked with the hangover of teenage spots. Much more interesting than the acne scars, though, was the one in the shape of a swastika, which had been carved into his forehead during one of his surprisingly few and far between stays in prison.

Some attempts had been made to disguise it, but it was still clear enough to immediately draw the eye.

Rumour had it, the guys who'd held him down and done it had been picked up the day they'd got out of prison, and had been left with some distinctive scarring of their own.

Although, not enough of them had ever been found to confirm this.

For the most part, Shuggie looked exactly like Heather had been expecting him to look, with just a couple of surprises in store.

The first was the book he held clutched in his hands. She'd never had him down as much of a reader. Although, to be fair, the book he was holding seemed to be light on words and heavy on pictures.

The second surprise was the little brown-haired girl who lay scrunched up beside him, her head resting on his upper arm, her wide eyes fixed on the book he was holding. She looked about four, maybe five, and she swung her bare feet impatiently while she waited for the story to continue.

Heather turned away from him. Her gaze settled instead on Linda, who squirmed under the sudden attention, then jumped like she'd just remembered something.

"Tea. Do you want tea? I can… I can make us tea," Linda said.

Heather shook her head. "I'm grand, thanks."

"I don't mind," Linda continued. Her hands shook as she took another cigarette from a pack on the sideboard, and looked around for a lighter. "I could do with one myself."

Heather took in the woman's red-ringed eyes and pasty white skin. She didn't look back at the man on the couch, and instead just nodded.

"Aye. If you're having one, then." Heather indicated the door with a jerk of her head. "In fact, why don't I come through and give you a hand?"

———

"Nobody was taking me seriously. I didn't know what else to do."

Linda Harrison blew the rest of the smoke from her lungs, stubbed out her cigarette in the discarded foil tray of a *Mr Kipling's Cherry Bakewell Tart*, then immediately lit up another one.

"I don't get it," Heather said. She glanced back over her shoulder at the kitchen door. She'd closed it, and the rumbling of the kettle would help mask the sound of their conversation. "What's your connection with Shuggie?"

Linda smiled. It was an anxious and unconvincing sort of thing. "He's my dad, believe it or not."

Heather very much did *not* believe it. She shook her head, her brow crumpling into a frown. "Your dad? Since when?" she asked. Then, realising this was an impressively stupid question, she hurriedly tried to clarify. "I didn't think he had kids, I mean."

"Nor did he," Linda replied. She took a draw on the cigarette like she was steadying her nerves. "My partner, he got me one of them DNA testing kits for Christmas a couple of years ago. Shuggie… He popped up on it a few months back. Fifty percent match." She blew out a long, steady cloud of smoke, then shrugged. "Turned out, my dad wasn't my dad." Her gaze flicked in the direction of the living room, and Heather couldn't help but notice there was something accusatory about it. "He is."

"You have my sympathies," Heather said.

The tip of the cigarette flared red as Linda sucked on the filtered end.

"I'd called up. Nine-nine-nine. Told them about Paula," she said. "Called five or six times. Said she hadn't come home after school, but nobody listened. Just kept saying they'd send someone round. That she'd probably gone to stay with a friend."

"I mean, I know it's not what you want to hear, but statistically, she probably has," Heather said.

"*Statistically*? Don't give me *statistically*." Linda shook her head angrily. "She hasn't gone to stay with a friend. I know she hasn't, because I've phoned her friends, and nobody's seen her." She ran a shaky hand through her hair. "And I told your lot that. I told them over and over, but they wouldn't listen. So... I didn't know what else to do. Who else to call. I know what he is. I looked him up. I know what he's done."

Heather doubted that. She couldn't know. Not all of it.

"But my daughter is missing," Linda continued, her throat tightening around the words like it couldn't bear to let them be said out loud.

Behind her, the kettle came to the boil and clicked off. When Linda spoke again, her voice sounded even more desperate in the sudden quiet.

"My wee girl's missing, and I didn't know what else to do." She turned away, fetching some mugs from the cupboard above the kettle. "He didn't want to get the police involved. Said it'd be better him handling it. But I insisted. Michael insisted. And eventually, he agreed. Told me to use his name. He said that you'd take notice then."

He wasn't wrong. The mere mention of Shuggie Cowan was usually reason enough to trigger a full-scale criminal investigation.

"Michael?" Heather asked.

"My partner. Husband, I mean. Ibby's dad. Paula's stepdad," Linda said, listing off all the possible connections. She dropped teabags into each of the three mugs she'd taken from the cupboard. "He's out in the van now looking for her. Driving around."

"How long have you been together?" Heather asked.

It was a question heavy with meaning, and though she tried to make it sound like innocent curiosity, Linda saw through it straight away.

"He's been a good dad to her. He's treated her like his own from day one."

"That's nice to hear," Heather said. She smiled, not unkindly. "But, how long? Roughly?"

Linda ground her teeth together, then sighed. "Six years. Going on seven. But Michael hasn't seen her since she left for school yesterday morning. None of us have, alright?"

"You've tried phoning her, I assume?" Heather said. The look on the other woman's face made her hold up her hands. "I know, I know. Stupid question, but I have to ask. I'm sorry. Has she got tracking on her phone or anything, do you know? Any way you can keep tabs on her like that?"

"I don't know anything about that sort of thing," Linda said, guilt flashing across her face. "I should. I should be doing that sort of thing, but I'm not technical like that, and she's never…" She swallowed, fending off tears. "I've phoned her, though. I've phoned her again and again, and it's just going through to her messages."

Her voice cracked and she gripped the edge of the worktop with both hands, her arms locked like they were taking all her weight. Outside, the back garden was thick with snow, a bright pink plastic slide barely visible beneath the blanket of frosty white.

"She's not got a proper jacket on or nothing. She'll be freezing out there."

"Like I say, I'm sure she's somewhere safe, Linda. But you were right to phone. I'm sorry you were kept hanging on."

She waited until the water had been poured into the mugs, and the teabags squished to within an inch of their lives against the side.

"That's grand. I'll leave the bag in," she said, taking the cup. "I like mine stewed."

She blew on the tea to cool it, then watched as Linda picked up the other two, one in each hand.

"Is Paula's room upstairs?" she asked.

"It is, yeah," Linda confirmed. She shifted her weight from one foot to the other. "But, eh, I think Shuggie'll want to talk to you."

"Aye, well." Heather took a big slurp of her tea. "Shuggie's just going to have to wait his turn."

———

The bedroom was a decent size, but had been split in two by a set of long curtains that ran more or less right down the centre of it, neatly bisecting the only window.

One side of the curtain had been decorated in a pale pink and pastel green. It would've looked quite tasteful, had it not been for the two-foot-tall *Peppa Pig* characters that had been amateurishly painted on all three walls.

There was a rainy day Peppa in a plastic Mac and Welly boots, a princess Peppa with a crown, and a bog-standard, garden variety Peppa holding a sign with the words, 'Ibby's Room' painted on it in sparkly pink lettering.

There was also a Daddy Pig down at the far end, but he had clearly been painted in a hurry and looked like he'd recently suffered a life-changing stroke.

The other side of the curtain had the same decor, minus the family of irritating cartoon pigs. There were a couple of posters of the various members of *BTS* on the wall alongside the single bed. Heather didn't know whether to be pleased with herself for knowing that this was a K-Pop band, or ashamed.

She decided the best thing to do, as with the band itself, was to give the question not a moment's more thought.

Paula's half of the room was messier than her little sister's, although Heather guessed Linda probably had a hand in tidying the younger girl's side. There were a couple of pairs of trainers, a few T-shirts, and some dirty socks scattered across the carpet, alongside a dinner plate with a single slice of cold pizza on it, and a couple of well-nibbled crusts.

Heather felt a sense of kinship with the kid immediately. She was a clarty bastard, too.

She could hear Linda and Shuggie talking downstairs. He didn't sound particularly impressed at being kept waiting, but then guys like him never did. They surrounded themselves with people who did as they were told. They used fear and intimidation to get their way.

Heather took another gulp of her tea. Good luck to him if he thought that sort of shite would work on her.

Besides, Shuggie Cowan had already destroyed her once. She wasn't sure there was enough left of her for him to have another go.

She poked around, checking in drawers and under the bed. Not searching for any one thing in particular, just looking in general to see what popped out.

There were plenty of books on her shelves and a small pile of notebooks teetering at the edge of her desk. Heather had a flick through, but they all contained school work, and a half-assed attempt at it, at that.

Comments had been written in the margins in red pen. 'Must try harder.' 'See me about this after class.' 'Did you even look at the homework?'

That sort of thing.

Paula wasn't a natural student, then, and appeared to have a bit of a problem with authority.

Heather was liking her more and more by the minute.

A diary would've been nice to find, but teenagers these days didn't tend to bother with them, in her experience. There was no point. Most of the time they lived their lives online, out in the open for all the world to see.

A lot of their private thoughts were shared, too, but in tighter, smaller groups, sending messages that self-destructed the moment they'd been looked at, like the tapes from *Mission Impossible*.

Rather than containing details of top secret missions, though, the messages were usually about who had been snogging who, whether anyone could secure booze for the weekend, and who in the year above would *totally* get it.

Heather made a mental note to ask Linda for her daughter's social media handles. And then, because she still hadn't fully shaken off the hangover, she made an actual note, as well.

The bed had been made, albeit in the loosest possible sense of the word, the quilt hastily chucked over the sheet, and the pillows shoved roughly into…

The pillows.

There was something poking out from under one of the pillows. It was just the edge, just barely visible, and yet it was enough to make Heather's heart start to race inside her chest.

She felt a prickly heat spreading up her throat and across her cheeks.

No. No, she was mistaken. It wasn't what she thought it was. It couldn't be.

Or, if it was, then it was a coincidence. That was all. Nothing more than that.

It couldn't be anything more.

It couldn't be anything worse.

Not after all this time.

Before she could reach for the pillow to check, she heard a creaking of floorboards from the other half of the room. After a few false starts, Shuggie found the gap in the curtains, and stepped through into Paula's side.

He was surprisingly stealthy for a man of his years and size. Either that, or Heather had been so transfixed by the possibility of what was under the pillow that she'd completely zoned out while he'd ascended the stairs.

Either way, he was here now. Standing less than two feet away. Or, as she preferred to think of it, 'within striking distance.'

"What do you want, Shuggie?" she asked. She turned away, taking in the rest of the room again, very much *not* looking down at the pillows.

"What do you think I want? I want my granddaughter back."

"Well, then I suggest you go back downstairs and leave me to crack on."

Cowan gave a non-committal sort of grunt, then ran a hand across Paula's duvet, smoothing out some of the creases.

"I know we've had our differences," he began.

Heather shut him down before he could go any further. "Differences?" She snorted. "Is that what we've had, Shuggie?"

Shuggie grunted again. "Well, what would you call it?"

Heather just stared at him for a moment. It was a glare of raw hatred, which would've made most people draw back in fear. Shuggie, on the other hand, just looked a bit bored by it.

"You done?" he asked.

She wanted to say something clever. Some pithy comeback that would put the smug fat fucker in his place. But the blankness of his stare and the smell of his sweat were too off-putting, so she kept her mouth shut rather than come out with something half-baked.

"This'll be about me, won't it?" he asked. He glanced around the room. "It'll be that Russian fuck, won't it? That's what happens, isn't it? In my line. They come for your family. Your weak spot."

Heather rolled her eyes. "You've barely known them three months, Shuggie. They're hardly your family. They're practically strangers."

He straightened, pulling himself up to his full height, and Heather was sure she felt the air between them crackle and pop.

When he spoke, his voice was low and measured, but it was taking some visible self-control on his part to keep it that way.

"That's my daughter down there. My wee granddaughter. They've been that all their lives, whether or not any of us knew it," he stated, then he pointed a fat, hairy finger down at the bed. "My other granddaughter should've slept there last night. There in that bed. She didn't. And, you'll forgive me for saying, but you don't exactly have the greatest track record when it comes to finding missing family members, do you, *Detective Inspector*?"

The words were like a knife plunging into her chest. Twisting. Opening a hole there.

Instinct made her fingers become claws, made claws become fists. Her survival instinct kept them firmly by her sides.

She would nail this fucker. Someday, she'd bring him down. Not here, though. Not now.

"So, sweetheart, here's what's going to happen," he said.

He took a sudden step closer. Heather tried not to flinch. She very nearly succeeded, too.

"I'm going to do you a favour. I'm going to do your job for you. I'm going to find out who took my granddaughter," Shuggie said, menace oozing from every word. "And then I'm going to watch all their skin being blowtorched and then peeled off them, strip by strip."

He gave her a moment to dwell on the image.

"I know that sounds like… What's the word again? *Hyperbole*. But I promise, it isn't." His anger was building now. Flecks of foam were forming in the gaps of his teeth. "I'm not exaggerating. Not one bit. Strip by strip. Every last fucking inch."

He brought up a finger to jab her on the bony plate of her chest, but Heather slapped it away, her gaze locked on his, her feet planted on the floor.

He eyeballed her for a few long, dangerous seconds, then a humourless smile crept across his face. He adjusted his tie, tucked his shirt in beneath the curve of his belly, then he turned his back on her.

"For their sake, let's hope you find them first," he said.

And with that, he pushed through the curtains, and went plodding back down the stairs.

Heather let out a breath that had got itself stuck somewhere at the back of her throat. She placed a hand flat on Paula's dressing table, taking a moment to compose herself.

When her pulse had slowed, and when she was absolutely certain that Shuggie wasn't about to put in another appearance, Heather turned her attention back to the pillows of the girl's half-made bed.

Heather tried to picture what she would find waiting for her under there. Tried to shape it into something else. Something harmless.

Something that she hadn't spent the last thirty-four years of her life living in terror of.

Part of her wanted to leave it. To not look. To pretend she hadn't noticed anything under there.

That was the same part that needed a couple of drinks to get to sleep most evenings, then woke her in the night with the covers in knots, and her whole body shiny with sweat.

That part wanted to leave this room. Leave this town. Leave everything behind, and just go somewhere, far away, to hide.

That part, though, could away and shite.

Heather grabbed for the pillow before her fear could offer up a counterargument. Her splayed fingers dug into the softness of it, and she yanked it away.

Her heart stopped.

A breath escaped her as a whimper, and then her lungs, too, seized up.

There, on the bed, lay a purple and orange feather.

Somewhere, deep in the shadows at the back of Heather's mind, a snidey wee voice whispered, '*I told you so.*'

FIVE

IT HAD BEEN ALMOST two decades since Heather had last set foot in Kilmarnock Academy, and though this was an entirely new building to the one she'd left, the smell of the place—floor polish and disinfectant mingling with whatever dark brew the canteen was cooking up that day—immediately whisked her back to her own teenage years.

This new place had been opened back in 2018, as part of the William McIlvanney Campus, named after the crime author, who —along with not just one, but *two* Nobel Prize winners—was on the roll call of famous former pupils.

The building was definitely a step up from the crumbling corridors Heather had once walked down. It was all clean lines and curves, and felt very modern, if a little soulless.

The lassie behind the front desk barely looked older than some of the sixth years Heather had passed on the way in. She met Heather with a smile and a warm welcome that could not have been further removed from the reaction she used to get when she was called to the office in the past.

After an introduction and a quick chat, Heather was given a copy of Paula's timetable, then escorted to a classroom on the second floor, where the missing girl was due to be in *PSE* class.

Back in Heather's day, this had been referred to as just 'Social

Education,' but at some point between then and now, someone had slapped 'Personal and' on the front of it.

It was being led by a young male teacher who introduced himself first as Mr Pearse and then, more quietly so the class of surly-looking fourth-years wouldn't hear, as Toby.

"Who's that, sir? Your girlfriend?" cackled a lad with a nose ring.

"His mum, more like," sniggered his mate.

Heather jabbed a finger towards them. "Shut it, you mouthy wee bastards," she snapped, and the sharpness of it stunned the boys into silence. "I'm with the Polis. Any more shite from you and I'll drag you out of here in handcuffs. Alright?"

She eyeballed them until they averted their gazes, then turned back to the teacher, who stood mute with shock behind her. With a nod, she indicated the classroom door and the corridor beyond it.

"Mind if I have a quick word out there?" She shot a narrow-eyed look back over her shoulder at the watching teenagers. "Then, I'll start working my way through this lot."

Toby snapped shut his open mouth, nodded, then fired off a quick instruction for the class to talk quietly among themselves, with heavy emphasis on the quietly part.

He followed Heather out into the corridor, and pulled the door closed with a click.

"Sorry about that. They, eh, they get a bit over-excited by visitors," he explained.

There was something a bit crooked about his smile, though in a literal sense, rather than a metaphorical one. It rose higher at one side, showing off a well-cared-for set of teeth, and forming a single dimple on his cheek.

He looked to be in his late twenties, Heather guessed, although if he had a good skincare regime he might be a little older. Not bad looking, either, albeit in a slightly Ken from Barbie kind of way.

He smelled nice, if musky colognes were your thing, and his clothes had 'cool teacher' written all over them. His shirt was a light grey, and paired nicely with a darker grey tie and matching trousers. The top button was undone, and the sleeves were rolled up. There was a faint stain where a pen had leaked in his shirt pocket, but he'd obviously got to it quickly enough to more or less salvage things.

On his feet, he wore a pair of black leather boots with a Cuban heel that would've got him eaten alive by the kids back in Heather's day. Clearly, the current generation was more forgiving of such things.

"This is about Paula, I take it?" he asked.

"You've heard, then?"

Toby nodded. "Yeah."

"And just what *have* you heard, exactly?" Heather pressed.

A look of panic darted across his face. That didn't mean much, though. Most people panicked when questioned by the police. Especially if Heather was the one doing the questioning. Her interviewing manner was deliberately confrontational, and she was proud of the fact that, throughout her entire career to date, no one had ever asked her to play the good cop.

Toby swallowed. He adjusted his tie as if it was cutting off his air supply, even though it was too loose to even touch his throat.

"Just that she's gone missing. Didn't come home from school yesterday. Her mum phoned, I think."

"That's all you know?" Heather asked, in a tone that suggested she didn't buy it.

"Yes. Yes, that's... Why? Is there something else? Has something more happened?" His concern for himself gave way to worry about his pupil. "Is she OK?"

"That's all we know so far," Heather said, letting him off the hook. "We think she's probably just run away. We're hoping one of her friends might be able to tell us something."

"Yes. Yes, of course," Toby said. "You'll want to talk to Sasha, Dawn, Suthsiri... I think those are the main ones. Of her friend group, I mean. Nice girls. Friendly. Quiet—keep themselves to themselves a bit—but they seem to get on fine with everyone. If anyone knows, it'll be them." A moment of doubt troubled his well-arranged features, just for a moment. "But..."

"But what?"

The teacher shook his head. "Nothing. No. Sorry. It's probably me. I probably picked it up wrong."

Heather sighed, making no attempt to hide her impatience. "Picked what up wrong?"

"I just…" Toby glanced at the classroom door. There was a cacophony of chatter coming from within. So much for *quietly*. "I got the impression that they'd already spoken to someone from the police this morning."

Heather frowned. "What? Who?"

"I… have no idea," Toby admitted. "You'd have to ask them. Or their first-period teacher, maybe. Mrs Hawkes. Although… she can be hard work."

"Fucking Hell. *Hawkeye*?" Heather asked. "With the big hooked nose and the squint?"

Toby had a decent stab at trying not to laugh, then nodded. "That's the one."

"Jesus. She was around when I was here, and she was no spring chicken then. I'm amazed she's still teaching," Heather said. She sucked in her bottom lip, then spat it out again. "I'm amazed she's still alive. Is she going for the record or something? *World's Oldest Teacher*?"

Toby's smile widened. "I mean, she's already got *Most Miserable*, so she might as well go for the double."

Heather chuckled at that. "Aye. Definitely the same one, then."

Toby seemed to enjoy the fact he'd made her laugh. He clicked his fingers a couple of times, announced that he'd go and get the three girls he'd mentioned, then turned to the door.

And then he continued to turn, all the way around, so he was facing DI Filson again.

"I've got a couple of free periods this afternoon," he ventured. "If you wanted to, you know, go over anything. About Paula. Or just, you know… chat, or whatever. We could go out for a drink."

The smile fell from Heather's face, and she moved quickly to shut the teacher down. "I don't drink," she said, lying to herself as much as to him.

She'd sworn off the stuff that morning, but she could already feel some part of her brain rationalising why going cold turkey would be a bad idea.

Better to take it slowly. Wean herself off the stuff.

"Coffee, then," the teacher suggested.

"I don't think either one would be very appropriate, Mr Pearse, do you?" Heather said. "So, how about you go get those girls, and point me to somewhere I can sit and talk to them? I think that's all I need from you right now."

Toby cleared his throat, fiddled with his tie again, then shrugged good-naturedly. "Oh, well," he said, turning back to the door. "Can't blame a guy for trying."

"Oh, I can, actually. I do."

The teacher stopped. He looked back over his shoulder, looking equal parts confused and amused. "Sorry?"

"A girl's missing," Heather reminded him. "A girl's missing, and yet you're here... What? Hitting on me? Asking me out on a date? Bit of an arsehole move, don't you think?"

Toby's expression rearranged itself into a grimace. "No, I wasn't... I just thought it might be useful if..." He swallowed. "And, you know, you said it yourself, she's probably just—"

"Run away. From home. Aged fifteen," Heather said, finishing his sentence for him. She pointed to one of the corridor windows. Snow was arranging itself into piles against the bottom of the pane. "In that weather."

The teacher's gaze lingered on the glass for a moment, then he dipped his head towards the detective as if offering some word-less, half-arsed apology.

"When did you last see Paula? Out of interest?"

The teacher rearranged the knot of his tie again. It was becoming a habit.

"Yesterday. No. Wait. Day before. I didn't have her class yesterday."

Heather waited just long enough for the silence to turn towards the uncomfortable. "You sure about that?"

"Yes! I'm completely... What are you implying? That I had something to do with...?"

"With what, Mr Pearse? What do you think's happened to her? Where do you think Paula might be right now?"

The teacher straightened himself up and had one last fiddle

with his tie. "I have no idea. None whatsoever. But I hope you find her."

"Aye. Me, too," Heather said. "If you think of anything else, you be sure to let me know, alright?"

Toby nodded. "Yeah. Course. In the meantime, I'd, eh, I'd better go get the girls," he mumbled, heading for the door.

"Aye, Mr Pearse," Heather replied. "I think you better had."

SIX

HEATHER SAT on a hard plastic seat, using the tips of her fingers to gently massage her temples as she enjoyed the relative silence.

She'd forgotten just how much hard work teenage girls could be, particularly when there was a whiff of drama for them to get worked up into a frenzy over.

In hindsight, she should've brought them in one at a time. On their own, they might've been easier to deal with. As a group, trying to get any sense out of them was like herding cats. And over-excited, high-pitched cats that didn't half talk a lot of shite, at that.

They'd said a lot, but told her very little.

Paula was their best friend. Not the best friend of any one of them in particular, but of the group as a whole, like they all shared one collective mind.

They reiterated what the teacher had told her, that Paula was a nice girl. They all were, in fact. They didn't smoke or drink, and they certainly didn't do drugs. Paula didn't have a boyfriend, and nor did Suthsiri or Sasha. Dawn was seeing Callum Whiteford from the year above, but it was nothing serious. Despite the age difference, he was too immature and kept asking her for nude selfies, but there was no way she was going to do that.

Laura Smythe from sixth year had sent nude photos to Callum's big brother the previous year, and they'd spread round the town like wildfire. They were apparently all over Reddit now, and Laura had dropped out before her final exams because of anxiety.

She was living with her granny in Bathgate now, where nobody knew her, or had seen her tits. Callum's brother didn't even feel guilty about it or anything. He was training to be a mechanic, and still laughed about poor Laura when he went out drinking at the end of the week with his mates, the absolute wanker that he was.

It was at this point that Heather had started to regret bringing them in as a group.

After warning the girls not to do anything as bloody stupid as sending naked pictures of themselves to anyone, and agreeing with them that most men were bastards, she tried to steer the conversation back onto the subject of Paula.

The last time any of them had seen her had been the day before, at the end of last period. It had been double maths with Mrs Salmond. Sasha and Dawn both hated maths, but Paula didn't mind it, and Suthsiri was a bit of a genius.

She'd represented the school at competitions, and everything. Won second place in a national quiz a few months back. Should've been first, but she was robbed. Racism or sexism, they reckoned, because she was better at maths than anyone.

She wasn't so keen on English, though, she admitted. Science, yes. She liked things that had a definitive answer—things that were either right or wrong—whereas subjects like English, or drama, or art were all about interpretation.

Once again, Heather had brought the conversation back around to the subject of their missing friend.

She always walked home on her own, going out the back way and cutting across the field to the housing estate behind the school. It wasn't a long walk—they'd all done it with her at various points, like for their sleepover a few months back, when—

Heather had jumped in there before they had a chance to get too far off track again.

"So, the last time any of you saw her was when she was leaving after maths?"

"Double maths," Sasha had corrected, and she and Dawn had both shuddered at the thought of it.

They'd all gone out the front to the buses, so none of them had actually seen Paula leaving the building via the back door. They hadn't heard from her later that day, either, which they'd all thought was a bit weird, since they usually pinged each other messages all evening, right into the wee small hours.

They hadn't been able to offer much more than that, besides some unrelated anecdotes about two boys fighting on the bus, and some kid from first year throwing 'an absolute paddy' after someone nicked his glasses.

Heather had asked if Paula had fallen out with anyone recently.

She hadn't.

She'd asked if Paula had been upset, or depressed, or worried about anything.

She wasn't.

She'd never mentioned the idea of running away. Sure, she argued with her parents sometimes—her stepdad especially—but who didn't?

Heather probably hadn't been as subtle as she should've been when she seized on the stepdad remark, and the girls had quickly backtracked, saying that he was a nice guy, that Paula really liked him, and that she thought of him as her dad.

"She doesn't have anything to do with her real dad," Suthsiri had said.

"Well, you wouldn't, would you?" Dawn had added.

"He's in jail," Sasha had offered, lowering her voice to a whisper. "Child abuse. Nobody knows that but us three."

"Abuse?" Heather had really sat up and taken note at that point. "Paula?"

"Naw," Sasha had continued. "Not Paula, but one of his other kids. He's got loads."

"He had loads of photos of other kids on his laptop. Horrible stuff," Suthsiri had concluded. "Proper disgusting."

As far as they knew, though, her dad was still in the nick, so if someone had taken her, it couldn't be him. Although, they usually worked in groups, didn't they? There was usually a ring. You heard about that sort of thing, didn't you? Maybe the police should look into that, just in case. Maybe she'd been trafficked.

They'd all looked worried then, and Heather had assured them that this was very unlikely.

"She'll turn up," she'd promised them. "Try not to worry."

The conversation had finished five minutes ago, when the bell for next class had rung and they'd all automatically jumped to their feet, grabbing for their jackets and bags. Heather had been grateful for the interruption and had made no attempt to stop them.

If she needed more from them, she could get it one-on-one, and save herself the headache of dealing with them as a trio.

Christ, she wondered. *Was I ever that annoying?*

She scribbled down some of the things the girls had said, before she could forget them, then pushed back in her chair, scraping the metal legs across the vinyl floor of the empty classroom.

Just as she reached her feet, there was a knock at the door—three firm raps of no discernible rhythm—followed by a pregnant sort of silence.

"Uh, yeah? Come in," Heather called.

The door was opened, and another girl entered. She was a little shorter than Paula's friends had been, and wore her dark hair cut into a boyish side-parting even more extreme than Heather's own.

The girls who'd just left had all had their own slightly varying interpretations of the school uniform. A grey jumper instead of a black one. Trainers instead of shoes. That sort of thing.

While those had more or less adhered to the spirit of the uniform, this girl followed it to the letter—black knee-length skirt, black tights, black shoes, black cardigan, white shirt, and a multi-coloured school tie which, as she got closer, Heather realised was a clip-on.

She had a pair of red-framed glasses hanging on a string

around her neck, like she was a short-sighted woman in her eighties.

"Uh, can I help you?" the DI asked.

"No. But perhaps I can help you," the girl replied.

She moved a bit rigidly across the room, like she'd learned how to walk from some instruction manual that had been clumsily translated from the original Chinese.

She took a seat on the other side of the desk, then produced her phone from her cardigan pocket, and placed it on the veneered desktop.

As she did this, Heather heard her whispering to herself, working through a mental checklist below her breath.

"Sit. Phone. Eye contact. Card."

The girl looked up at Heather. She didn't smile, or nod, or do anything else to acknowledge the detective. Instead, she just held out a business card of such low quality that it curved downwards under the force of gravity.

"What's this?" Heather asked, taking it.

"It's my business card."

Heather looked down at the card in her hand. It was printed on fairly poor quality paper, presumably on a home inkjet printer. It had been carefully cut out, but there was a slight angle to one of the edges where the scissors hadn't *quite* followed a straight path.

The slightly smudged text read:

ACE WURZEL
CrimeDeLaCrime.com

"What's an Ace Wurzel?" Heather wondered.

"I am. That's my name."

Heather regarded the girl, who was sitting with her hands folded, staring up at her, not once breaking eye contact.

"Your name's *Ace Wurzel*?"

"Well, it would be odd for me to put it on a business card if it wasn't."

"Wurzel? As in… Gummidge? The scarecrow off the telly?"

"Some people know him from the television, yes, though I

know him better from the books, written by Barbara Euphan Todd," the girl said, still staring. "And no. That's Worzel with an O, I'm Wurzel with a U. It's German."

Heather frowned. "The scarecrow?"

"My surname. It refers to someone who gathers roots and herbs. Neither of which, should you be wondering, I do."

"I wasn't wondering that," Heather said. She offered the card back, but the girl dismissed it with a shake of her head. "Keep it. It's for you. There are more where that came from."

"Uh... cheers. What's the website?"

"It's for my podcast. *Crime De La Crime*. Maybe you've heard of it?"

Heather had to admit that she hadn't. Ace sat in silence for a few moments then, like this news was taking time to bed in.

"Well, you should listen. It's a true crime series, about one of the area's most notorious unsolved mysteries. I'm sure you know the one I'm referring to."

The hairs on the back of Heather's neck pricked up. She slipped the flimsy card into the pocket of her battered leather jacket. "I'm sure I can hazard a guess. What can I do for you... *Ace*?"

The girl's relentless use of eye contact was becoming a bit creepy. Heather was starting to wonder if she even blinked.

"You don't have to say it like that," Ace said.

"Like what?"

"Like it's not a real name."

"Is it a real name?"

The girl shrugged. Like her walk, it looked like she'd learned the move through hours of study and practice. "What is a name? Isn't it just a thing we call ourselves?"

"No, I'd say it's more a thing your parents called you," Heather countered.

"Do you blindly bend to your parents' every whim?" Ace asked.

Christ, she was confident. Or maybe 'fearless' was a better way of putting it. The other girls had babbled anxiously, but this one was unsettlingly sure of herself.

Heather wondered how much of that was rehearsed, too. Or maybe the idea of being nervous just hadn't occurred to her.

"You might want to take a seat, Officer," Ace said. She pointed, stiff-fingered, at the chair that Heather had recently vacated.

When Heather lowered herself back onto the hard plastic seat, Ace finally stopped staring, looking away just long enough to hit a big red 'Record' button on the screen of her phone. She slid the phone six inches closer to the detective, then interlocked her fingers on the desk in front of her.

"I'd like to share some information pertaining to the disappearance of Paula Harrison."

Heather crossed her arms and sat back in the chair. Her eyebrows didn't share the same range of expressiveness as her Uncle Kenny's, but she managed to raise one in a suitably questioning manner.

"Would you now? Fire on, then."

"First of all, do you object to being recorded?"

"Yes," Heather said.

For the first time since she'd entered the room, the girl looked unsure of herself, like this response hadn't been something she'd prepared for in advance.

"Oh," she said, her eyes drifting back to her phone for a moment, before locking onto Heather again. "Can I do it, anyway?"

Heather shrugged. "If you like. But, depending on what you have to tell me, I might want a copy."

"That won't be a problem," Ace assured her.

"Right. So. Paula, then," Heather prompted.

"Yes. Paula. Here's my theory," Ace said. "She's run off to be with her boyfriend."

Heather blew out her cheeks, already sensing that this was a waste of time. "Except she doesn't have a boyfriend."

"Except she *does*," Ace insisted.

"That's not what her friends told me."

"Yes, well. Far be it from me to say that her friends are idiots, but her friends are idiots. They might think they know everything about her, but they don't."

"And you do?"

Ace shook her head. Another stilted movement. "Of course not. Not everything. But I know she was seeing someone."

"Are you a friend of hers?"

"No. Far from it."

Heather frowned. "Right. But, what? She told you this?"

"No. We barely ever spoke," Ace said. "I followed her."

Heather's chair gave a creak as she sat forward and rested her arms on the desk. "You followed her?"

"Yes. That's what I just said."

"And why did you do that?"

"Not sure," Ace admitted. "It's just interesting sometimes, seeing where people go, and what they do when they get there. Don't you think? Plus, I live just along the road from her, so we're usually headed the same way."

"And when did you follow her?"

"Eight days ago."

Heather took a second or two to work out what day it was today, then quickly counted backwards. "Last Thursday?"

"That's right. Last Thursday, after school. I noticed she was carrying on past her house, and my interest got piqued."

Heather blinked, processing all this. "So... you followed her and you saw what, exactly?"

"Her with her boyfriend. Older, though. Not from the school."

"How do you know he was her boyfriend? Could he maybe have just been a friend?"

"Do you kiss your friends while squeezing their buttocks like you're kneading a ball of dough?" Ace asked.

She still hadn't blinked, Heather was sure of it.

The DI shook her head. "Not generally speaking, no."

"Then he wasn't a friend."

"Right. OK." Heather nodded, sucked in her bottom lip, then spat it back out again. "I don't suppose you can give me a description, can you?"

Ace looked straight up towards the ceiling, until her pupils had all-but vanished beneath her eyelids.

"Six feet. Reddish blond hair—quite long, but tied back. Moustache and tiny little triangle beard below his bottom lip." Her eyes faced front again. "Have you heard of *The Three Musketeers*?"

"Of course."

Ace nodded her approval. "Good. Well, in that case, picture Frank Finlay."

Heather's lips moved silently for a moment, like she was doing some mental maths she had no hope of solving.

"Who the hell's Frank Finlay?" she asked.

The girl's approval soured, turning quickly to disappointment. "Porthos. From the 1973 movie adaptation? No? You said you knew it. I asked if you'd heard of it, and you said, 'Of course.'"

"Aye, I said I'd heard of it, I didn't say I'd memorised the bloody cast list," Heather replied. She saw an opportunity to be petty. She might've resisted it, had the last scraps of her hangover not still been clinging on for dear life. As it was, she said it with a smug little smirk on her face. "*Anyway*, I know them better from the books."

"Yes, me too, actually. I've read Dumas' original French version."

Heather tutted and replied in a barely decipherable mumble. "Aye, I bet you fucking have."

"I'm sorry?"

"Nothing. Go on. You were describing the boyfriend."

"Yes, that's right. Frank Finlay Porthos-like facial hair. Earring in his left ear—stud, not hoop. He was wearing a football shirt. Newcastle United. The home strip. I know nothing about football because it's tedious, but I looked it up. Grey tracksuit bottoms, and what looked like running shoes."

"Trainers, you mean?"

Ace shook her head. "No. I mean running shoes. For running in. Not fashion."

Heather felt like this was splitting hairs, but she didn't have the energy or inclination to challenge the girl on the matter.

"Impressive. You've got a good memory," she remarked.

"I do, yes. But in this instance, I don't actually need one."

She bent down, reached into her bag, and produced a glossy A4 photo. It showed a young man matching the description she'd just given, walking with one arm draped possessively over the shoulder of a girl Heather recognised as Paula Harrison.

"It's a photograph," she explained.

"I can see that, aye," said Heather, picking up the picture.

"Of them."

"I can see that, too. Did they know you were taking this?"

Ace's brow creased in a look of genuine puzzlement. "Why would they know?"

"Well, generally speaking, you don't just go taking random photos of people without their permission."

"People do it all the time," Ace argued. "I could print that on a T-shirt if I wanted. As the photographer, I own the copyright. I mean, I wouldn't, obviously. Who'd want to buy it? But I could."

"Can I keep this?" Heather asked.

"If you like," Ace said. "The paper costs around one-pound-twenty a sheet, though, and with the ink… Let's say two pounds."

Heather scowled at her. Ace stared back, unblinking.

"Seriously?"

"The card, I don't mind giving for free. It's a marketing expense, so I'm happy to take the hit," the girl explained. "But I'd rather not be out of pocket on the photo printing."

Heather sighed. She couldn't tell if the girl was trying to be so draining, or if just came naturally to her. Either way, she was hard work.

"Fine. Here."

She fished around in her jacket pockets, pulled out about three quid in coins, then dumped it onto the desk.

"Keep the change."

"How very generous of you," said Ace, picking up the pile of coins, one at a time.

The words felt like they were dripping with sarcasm, but the delivery of them had sounded perfectly sincere. Heather just couldn't get a proper read on the girl, at all.

"Well, thanks for this," she said, tapping the photograph with the first two fingers of her left hand. "It could be helpful."

"You recognise him," Ace said. It was a statement, not a question.

"What makes you say that?"

"You didn't ask me any more about him. You didn't ask if I knew his name, or saw where they went. That suggests you already know who he is and where to find him."

"Jesus Christ," Heather remarked. "Are you after my job?"

Ace gave another graceless shake of her head. "No. I'd find the politics and bureaucracy frustratingly tedious." She thought for a moment before adding, "Also, I don't enjoy running. Or sirens."

Once again, Heather found herself just gazing blankly at the girl. "Right," she eventually said. "Well… good to know."

"I'd be willing to take on a consultant role," Ace suggested. "Like Sherlock Holmes. Would Police Scotland consider that sort of arrangement?"

"No," Heather said. She shrugged. "Well, there is one guy up north, but his is a pretty unique case."

"I see," Ace said. She didn't look particularly disappointed. She didn't look particularly anything, in fact. "I assume I'm correct, then?"

"About what? About the politics and stuff? Aye, it can be a bit of a head wreck, right enough. Don't blame you for not wanting to get involved."

Ace glanced very deliberately at the photograph. "About you knowing who that is."

Heather smiled. Then, just as purposefully as the girl had looked at it, she turned the photograph over so it was facedown on the desk. "I'll ask around," she said. "Maybe someone will recognise him."

"Someone like your 'colleague' from earlier, maybe?"

Ace didn't make air quotes around the word 'colleague,' but Heather heard them loud and clear.

"He came in asking questions during first period. Just like you."

Heather sat forward again, shortening the gap between them. "Did he say he was with the police?"

"No. Not that I heard. Mrs Hawkes just seemed to assume that he was. I can't fathom why, though, since it was immediately obvious to anyone paying even the slightest bit of attention that he wasn't a police officer."

"Oh? And why's that? What was it that gave him away?" Heather asked.

"'Free egg roll with combo purchase.'"

Heather blinked. "Sorry?"

Across the desk, Ace picked up her phone, swiped away from the voice recorder app then showed the detective a photograph.

"I ran it through a translator app. I'm sure he thinks it says something deep and profound, but it's obviously taken from some menu somewhere."

Heather's jaw clenched as she looked at the picture on the screen. It showed a thick, sinewy neck with a series of Chinese characters tattooed onto it.

The thick, sinewy neck of the giant daud of shite who had been sitting in the back of Shuggie Cowan's *Jag*.

For the first time since stepping into the room, Ace smiled. It wasn't much of one, but it was enough to suggest that she found the whole thing at least mildly amusing.

"I suspect that he isn't going to be very happy about it, should he ever find out."

She craned her neck to look up as Heather rose quickly to her feet. The plastic chair the detective had been sitting on toppled backwards and hit the hard floor with a *thwack*.

"The guy. The egg roll guy. Did you tell him what you'd seen? Did you show him the photo?" she asked.

It was Ace's turn to cross her arms. "Oh please, Officer," she said. "Exactly what sort of cretin do you take me for?"

SEVEN

CONN BYRNE WAS a lot of things—a thief, a scallywag, and a neddy wee bastard, to name but three. He was twenty-one, and while the fact that he appeared to be shagging a fifteen-year-old was depressingly unsurprising, Heather didn't have him pegged as a killer.

Hopefully, then, Paula had just taken it upon herself to shack up with him. He was a good-looking lad. Absolute wide boy, but easy on the eye. She could understand why a giggly and inexperienced teenage lassie might be drawn to a guy like that. The daft buggers often were.

At least, that was what Heather told herself as she stood in the gathering evening gloom, ringing the buzzer of Conn's last known address. It was a flat his grandmother owned in an old tenement block, across the road from the hospital in Yorkhill.

Heather'd had a few run-ins with that old bastard, too, and wasn't exactly relishing the thought of crossing swords with her again.

Still, needs must. If Paula was with Conn, then it was in everyone's best interests that she return home right away.

Because, as well as being a thief, a scallywag, and a neddy wee bastard, Conn Byrne was something else, too. Something much more dangerous than any of the above, given the current situation.

He was an associate, albeit a bottom-of-the-pile one, of Karina Novikov—the woman Shuggie Cowan had called, 'that Russian fuck,' and who had been making a name for herself around Glasgow over the past year or so by moving in on Shuggie's turf.

Rumour had it that she'd once been at the other end of a supply chain bringing everything from heroin to sex workers into the UK from the former Soviet bloc. It was said that, as she'd grown older, the cold had started to affect her joints, and so she'd relocated to warmer climes.

Heather had never bought that part, though. If it was better weather you were after, why the hell would you choose Scotland, of all places?

She rang the buzzer again, then looked back over her shoulder at the falling snow picked out by the glow of the nearest street lamp.

"Aye. Warmer climes my arse," she muttered, then the security speaker crackled into life, and a voice slurred out at her, sounding drunk with anger. And, to be fair, with booze.

"Alright, fuck's sake! I'm no' Linford fucking Christie! I can't hurdle the couch to get to the fucking hing!"

Conn Byrne may have grown up with his dad in Ireland, but his maternal grandmother, Agnes McQueen, was Glasgow to the core. 'Big Aggie,' as she was better known, had chain-smoked for decades, refusing to let little things like COPD and two bouts of throat cancer get between her and her *Lambert & Butlers*.

When she spoke, it sounded like she was dragging each word across broken glass, before spitting it out through a mouthful of gravel.

Though it had been a few months since Heather had seen her, she could picture her up there in the flat now, cigarette in one hand, oxygen mask in the other, a tightly-wound fury etched in the deep, craggy lines of her face.

The woman was an explosion just waiting to happen. In every sense.

"Mrs McQueen, it's DCI—" Heather flinched, catching the mistake a moment too late. She didn't bother to correct it. "Heather Filson."

There was a momentary pause. The faint kiss of lips against the butt of a cigarette.

"The lesbian one?"

Heather just passed right over the remark. "Can I come in?"

"Have you got a warrant?"

Heather shoved her hands in her jacket pockets and stamped her boots, trying to drive out the cold.

"No," she admitted.

"Then can you fuck come in! What a stupid bloody question," the old woman rasped.

She erupted into a coughing fit that went on for several seconds. Heather listened, and heard the wheezing as she took a big draw from her oxygen tank.

Once things had settled back down again, Heather continued.

"It's about Conn. He's in trouble."

"He's no' here. And even if he was, I'd no' be handing him over to you bastards."

"He's not in trouble with us, Mrs McQueen," Heather said. "He's in trouble with Shuggie Cowan."

There was silence then. Aggie was a minor league scumbag with sticky fingers and a loud voice. She didn't move in the same circles as the Shuggie Cowans of the world, but she knew who he was. Of course she did.

And she knew what he was capable of.

There was another gasping sound as the old woman took another blast of her oxygen.

"He's no' here. I've no' seen him," she said. "What's the daft wee prick done?"

"Nothing. I think it's all just a misunderstanding," Heather said. "That's why I want to find him. Sort this all out before Shuggie catches up with him. Do you know where I might find him?"

The reply, when it came, had less of the venom of her previous responses. "Naw. I've no' seen him in a couple of days. Don't know where he's gone."

Shit. This wasn't the news that Heather had been hoping for.

"You're sure?"

"Aye, I'm fucking sure!" Aggie spat, her anger swelling again. "I'd no' be fucking saying it if I wasn't sure!"

"Right. OK. Well, it's very important that I talk to him. It's life and death, Aggie. You understand?"

"I'm no' fucking thick, hen! I know the score."

"Fine. Good. Well, if he contacts you… Do you have a pen? I'll give you my number, so you can—"

Behind her, she heard footsteps crunching in the snow. They'd been there in the background for the last few moments, she now realised, but she'd been too focused on the conversation with Big Aggie to pay much attention.

Now, though, when they came to a sudden stop just a few feet away, she turned in their direction.

There, standing in the swirling snow with his hood up and his hands in the pockets of his trackie bottoms, stood Conn Byrne.

He stared at the detective on the doorstep, his eyes widening, his jaw dropping open. Heather could see exactly what was about to happen. She raised a hand and called out to him, trying to stop him.

"Conn, wait!"

But, it was no use. Like a startled rabbit, Conn sprang into the air, spun around, and with a turn of speed befitting an early twenties professional scallywag, he ran.

"Ye wee fucker!" Heather hissed, launching herself down the short path.

She grabbed the rusted metal gate post and used it to swing herself onto the pavement, her feet sliding through the slippery snow.

He was fast. Way too fast. She thought about jumping in her car, but it was facing the wrong way. By the time she'd got it turned around, Conn would be long gone. All she could do was run, and hope that he tired out quickly, or lost his footing.

Hell, she'd take him getting hit by a bus, as long as he survived long enough to tell her where Paula was.

Besides, it wasn't like he'd have far to go to hospital.

The snow hadn't stopped falling since morning and was getting deep now. It dragged at her feet as she ran down the darkened street, her eyes locked on the much-faster younger man as he appeared and disappeared in the puddles of light from the lamp posts.

She powered on, but was already falling further behind when he turned onto Dalnair Street. He slowed just long enough to shoot a look back over his shoulder, and for her to shout out a breathless, "I just want to talk!"

But then, he was sprinting off again, lost to her around the side of the tenement block.

"Fuck's sake!" she spat, forcing her legs to move faster, churning a trench of powdery white along the pavement.

She reached the corner and repeated her quick-turn technique by grabbing one of the wrought iron fence bars and swinging herself around.

Heather slid to a stop, eyes scanning the alternating stripes of light and dark ahead. Watching for movement was pointless—the whole street was nothing *but* movement, alive as it was with the swirling, birling snow.

Looking down, she saw footprints, and set off after them, one hand raised in front of her to shield her eyes from the strengthening blizzard.

She was going to kill him, she decided. That would be one way of solving things. She'd kill the slippery wee shite herself, Paula would come home, and the city wouldn't have to find itself dragged into a gang war between Shuggie Cowan and Karina Novikov. Everyone was a winner. Even Conn, in fact, because while his death at Heather's hands would be relatively quick and painless, Shuggie was unlikely to be as accommodating.

The footprints swung sharply left, crossing the road. Heather raised her eyes to follow them, squinted through the dark, and caught just a fleeting glimpse of a hooded figure scrabbling over the tall metal fence of the hospital grounds.

He got himself snagged on one of the pointed spikes that topped the railing, and Heather hurried to close the gap between them.

But then, with a ripping sound, he tumbled free, landed softly in the snow on the other side, and went sprinting off into the glistening darkness.

Heather tried to stop, but the pavement was too slippery, and she slammed shoulder-first against the fence.

"I'm trying to help you, Conn!" she cried after him, but the only reply was a rapid *crunch-crunch-crunch* as his fleeing footsteps faded off into the distance.

EIGHT

THE CAR PARK of the police HQ at Clyde Gateway was a swamp of salty brown slush when Heather pulled up in her Audi. She grabbed her bag from the back seat, zipped her jacket right up to the top, then picked her way across the wet ground and into the shoebox of glass that was the station.

When she stepped out of the lift onto the fourth floor, she found the office in near darkness. The only light in the place came from a single computer monitor, and Heather could hear the *burring* of DS Martin Brompton's lightning-speed touch typing.

"Alright, Marty?" she said, emerging from the shadows behind his screen.

The detective sergeant jumped in his seat, let out an uncharacteristically high-pitched, "The fuck?!" then put a hand on his chest and gulped down a breath. "Jesus Christ. Don't do that!"

Heather had never been much of a team player. She hadn't been too bad at delegating, especially when it came to paperwork or dealing with members of the general public, but she had some control and trust issues that meant she preferred to see investigations through on her own.

Marty, though, was one of the few people she did trust. Give him a job to do, and he'd get straight to work. If he came across an obstacle, he'd find his way around it without making a big song and dance about it. Ask Marty to do something, and you could be sure it would get done.

He was just a couple of years younger than she was, and had recently split from his husband of three years. They wanted different things. Marty had wanted children. His husband had wanted to get noshed off by a succession of strangers in the leisure centre sauna, then vigorously gang-banged by a group of Polish truckers he'd met on the internet.

Only one of them had got what they were after.

Marty worked late most nights now. Or he sat here most nights, anyway. They'd had to put the house up for sale, and Marty's new place was apparently so depressing he'd rather spend his evenings here, reading through witness statements and updating spreadsheets.

He was still staring at her with a grimace of shock, the light of his monitor making his face look pallid and gaunt.

Heather smirked. "Sorry. Totally unintentional." She shrugged. "Or, you know, *mostly* unintentional."

"Aye, well, the joke would've been on you if I'd shat myself," Marty told her. He thumped the arms of the office chair he was sitting on. "This is your seat."

Heather raised a quizzical eyebrow. The DS responded with a sigh and a weary look.

"Snecky broke his, so he took mine. Said he needed it. He's got a bad back."

"That arsehole's got a bad everything," Heather countered. Her gaze flitted to the door at the back of the room. It led to a smaller office that had, until quite recently, been hers.

"He in?"

Marty snorted. "Course he isn't in. It's after five o'clock. He was out of here the moment the bloody clock struck, wasn't he?"

He drew up his lips in distaste. That was one of the other reasons Heather liked him. He saw through Snecky's bullshit almost as clearly as she did.

"Good. I couldn't be doing with him," Heather said. She sat her bag on the desk beside Marty, and unbuckled the straps.

The detective sergeant's eyes were drawn to it, and he watched as she worked the fastenings.

"How's it been going? Any word on the missing girl?"

"I think I'm getting close," Heather said. "You know Conn Byrne?"

Marty rolled his eyes. "That wee toad. What about him?"

"He's her boyfriend."

The DS rolled back an inch or two in the chair. "Doesn't he work for…?"

"Aye."

"And isn't she…?"

"She is," Heather confirmed.

"Shiiiiiiit," Marty said, exhaling the word as one long, worried breath. "That could get messy."

"Tell me about it."

"Any idea where he is?" Marty asked.

Heather shrugged. "Last time I saw him, he was vaulting a fence near his gran's house. Lost him after that."

Marty whistled through his teeth, then rocked back in the chair. "You think she's with him?"

"I certainly hope so," Heather said.

"And does Cowan know? That they're together?"

"For Conn's sake, I really hope not. And, I mean, he's alive, so I'd say he probably doesn't."

She finished opening her bag, then stopped and stared at the sliver of purple and orange nestled at the bottom, safely secured inside a clear plastic evidence wrapper. Even here, out of its original context, surrounded by the everyday and familiar, it had an immediate effect on her.

Without realising she was doing it, she held her breath. Then, watched by Marty, she carefully reached a hand inside the leather satchel.

"I, eh, I need you to get forensics to run this through for me," she said. She fought to control the shake in her hand as she brought out the evidence bag and placed it on the desk in front of the detective sergeant.

Marty regarded it in silence for a few moments, then frowned as he raised his gaze to meet hers. "A feather?"

"Bloody Hell. Nothing gets past you, does it?" Heather said.

The words were teasing, but the delivery was flat and hesitant. It sounded so unlike the DI that Marty frowned up at her. She was too fixated on the feather to notice, though.

It was roughly six inches long, the plumage coloured with a garish purple that tapered to an artificially vibrant shade of orange. She wasn't aware of any bird on Earth that matched those colours, and certainly none that you might find knocking around Central Scotland.

It looked more like a writing quill, or something from a dress-up kit. She could imagine it being part of a drag queen's outfit, or something one of the Krankies might wear as part of their costume at the Pavilion Pantomime.

This was good. This was different. If her instinct was right, and the feather turned out to be synthetic, then maybe she'd be able to sleep tonight.

All of the other feathers had been real ones.

"I don't get it," Marty said, still looking up at her. "Why do you need forensics to look at it?"

Heather swept her hair back with a hand. It immediately fell back into place.

"Found it in the girl's room. Under her pillow."

Marty directed his attention back to the evidence bag. "And? It's just a feather."

"Her mum didn't recognise it. Didn't think she'd ever seen it before."

"So… What? You think it was left there on purpose?" Marty asked.

Before Heather could answer, the lights of the office came on with a *clunk*. Both officers turned to see a man standing in the doorway, one hand on the switch, a look of surprise widening his eyes and his mouth.

Marty rose to his feet and to a respectful but slightly shambolic sort of attention. "Sir."

Detective Superintendent Gordon Mackenzie didn't acknowledge the detective sergeant. Instead, his gaze drilled into Heather for several long, difficult moments, then drifted very deliberately down to the desk beside her.

Lowering his hand to his side, he strode over, and Marty took a single step backwards to get out of the other man's path.

The detective superintendent stopped a foot from the desk, his head lowered, eyes fixed on the contents of the evidence bag.

Heather watched him as he stood there, not blinking, not breathing. His fingers flexed, stretching all the way to their limits, then compressing into fists.

He repeated this a few times, then let out the breath he'd been holding and shot Heather a narrow-eyed sideways look.

"Detective Inspector," he intoned. "A word in private, if I may?"

————

The Gozer's office was cast partly in shadow, the only light coming from the lamp on his desk, and the occasional headlights of cars passing on the Rutherglen Bridge. He was already back sitting at the desk by the time Heather followed him into the room, and he gestured sharply to the chair opposite the moment she finished closing the door.

He was dressed in a dark blue suit and grey tie, which he'd fastened in a Double Windsor. His hair was cropped short and grey now. It was a far cry from when Heather had first met him, when he'd sported a drastic flat top that had earned him his nickname.

Heather had been told the hairstyle bore an uncanny resemblance to that of a character from *Ghostbusters*, though she'd never actually seen the film, so she couldn't comment either way.

Age and stress had worked to push his hairline higher and higher, and he'd eventually shaved what was left of it so he could at least pretend that his near-baldness had been a personal choice, and not one that Mother Nature had cruelly forced upon him.

"Well?" he said, before Heather had even had a chance to pull her seat closer to the desk. He tapped a finger. The nail went *tak-tak-tak* against the leather desk mat.

"I don't think it's anything," Heather said.

She knew what he was thinking. There was no point in pretending otherwise.

"You don't *think* it's anything? But you don't know for sure?"

Heather shrugged. "I'm ninety-nine percent," she said. "It's an artificial feather, I'm sure of it. Nothing like the others. Probably just something she had kicking about the house."

"But her mother hadn't seen it before," the Gozer said.

Heather fought hard not to wince. "You heard that bit, then? No. She didn't think she'd seen it before, but the girl's fifteen. She could've picked it up anywhere."

The Gozer placed a hand on the desktop and fixed her with a dead-eyed look. Heather realised that one of her legs was bouncing, the knee bumping rapidly against the underside of the desk.

She clamped a hand on her thigh, preventing it from shaking.

"Sorry," she said, not quite meeting his eye.

The detective superintendent steepled his fingers and sat watching her in silence. She hated when he pulled this shite. He'd create a vacuum in the conversation that he expected whoever else was in the room to fill.

Usually, they'd become so uncomfortable, that they'd start babbling, just to fill the conversational void. Heather had seen even hardened senior detectives succumb to it. Hell, she'd fallen prey to it herself once or twice.

But, if he thought it was going to work on her today, he had another thing coming.

Her chair gave a satisfied-sounding wee *creak* as she sat back in it, enjoying the silence. It had been a busy day. She needed a break, and five minutes of peace and quiet in the Gozer's office would do just fine.

He must've seen from her face that his plan wasn't working, though, because he tutted, sighed, then kick-started the conversation back up.

"And what if it is? What if it's him?" he asked, keeping his voice low, like he didn't want anyone else to hear the question being asked out loud.

"It isn't. It can't be. It's been thirty years," Heather said. "More than that. And why would it be in her bedroom? Paula didn't even go home. It doesn't fit. None of it fits."

Across the desk, the Gozer's shoulders angled downwards a little as he relaxed.

"She'll have gone off with the boyfriend. That's all. We find him, we find her."

The detective superintendent nodded slowly at first, then with a bit more enthusiasm, allowing himself to be convinced by Heather's arguments.

"Get Uniform searching for him, then. You get home."

"I can put in another few hours on it," Heather said, but the Gozer countered with a firm shake of his head.

"You look like shite warmed up," he told her, then he twitched two fingers towards the window. "Snow's getting worse, too. Get back down the road while you still can. Get some rest. Pick it up in the morning."

"It's honestly not—"

"That wasn't a request, Detective Inspector."

His glare was packed with meaning, and Heather knew that arguing was going to get her nowhere.

Besides, he was right. It was late, the weather was worsening, and exhaustion was leadening her bones.

And then, of course, there was her dad to think about. She'd had no calls from anyone about him today, so that was something. After last night's adventures, he'd probably slept most of the day away. That would've kept him out of trouble.

On the other hand, it also meant he'd probably be awake all night.

So much for her getting some rest.

"Cheers, sir. I'll get back here sharp. Hopefully, by then, Paula will have found her way back home."

"Hopefully," the Gozer agreed.

He waited until she'd got to her feet and was almost to the door before he continued.

"But, if she isn't. And if this turns out to be..." He picked his words carefully. "...related to past matters, then you'll appreciate that you can't be involved."

Heather's eyebrows climbed up towards her hairline. "You'd take me off the case?"

The Gozer interlocked his fingers, and snapped off a single nod of his head. "I wouldn't have any choice," he told her, then his expression softened a little, and the straight line of his mouth adjusted itself upwards just a fraction at each end. "Goodnight, Detective Inspector."

"Night, sir," Heather replied, then she slipped out of the office, caught her breath on the other side of the door, then headed, with some trepidation, for home.

NINE

THERE WERE flowers in the kitchen when Heather got home.

She didn't notice them right away. The drive through the snow had taken near-supernatural levels of concentration, and had brought on a headache so severe she could feel it thumping between her shoulder blades.

It wasn't until she'd grabbed a snub-nosed bottle of cheap Bulgarian lager from the fridge and used it to wash down a selection of painkillers that she spotted the bouquet standing proudly in a vase on the draining board.

Eleven hours. That was how long she'd gone between vowing never to drink again and succumbing. Eleven hours.

Generally speaking, flowers weren't really her thing. She could tell this was an impressive selection, though—red and yellow roses, a few orange something-or-others, and some pale blue things that might have been lilies. They must've set someone back a pretty penny, so it was a shame they were now being displayed next to a sink full of dirty dishes and stagnant water.

She took a swig from her bottle while she checked for a card, and eventually found one in a tiny square envelope that was roughly the length of a business card on all four sides.

Her name was on the front, written by someone who clearly had access to a fancy pen and way too much time on their hands.

She removed the card from the envelope. The image on the front made her set the bottle down among the crumbs and the clutter of the kitchen worktop.

Most of the front was a pale pink love heart, blended at the edges so it looked like a cloud.

And, in front of it, on a perch, sat two brightly coloured little birds, nuzzling their beaks together, their plumage all puffed up and plump.

Heather placed the card on the worktop and stared at it in silence, not yet opening it. She gulped down the rest of the lager with one big tilt of her head, then fetched another bottle from the fridge.

She cracked the metal lid off with one of the three bottle openers that were usually hanging around the kitchen somewhere, still staring at the card.

The second bottle was empty before she worked up the courage to open the card and check the message inside.

It was short, and written in the same swirly script as her name on the front of the envelope. There was no signature. Nothing to indicate who it had come from.

The message was just two words, followed by a flamboyantly executed question mark.

Miss me?

Queasiness tightened her stomach, almost ejecting the fizzing mixture of painkillers and booze that currently made up most of its contents.

She slammed the card shut and shoved it forcibly back in the envelope, like she wanted no part of it, like she could undo what she'd done, and go back to the time before she'd read it.

Heart racing, she stamped on the pedal of the bin. It was almost full, and to get rid of the card, she had to shove it into a gap between the black bag and the festering, days-old rubbish.

The lid closed again with a sharp *thick* that made her flinch. She necked the rest of the lager, grabbed herself a third bottle, and was halfway through it by the time she made it through to the living room.

There was an old Western blaring out from the TV, but the sounds of gunfire, hooves, and screeching racial stereotypes didn't appear to be bothering Heather's dad, who sat snoring under a blanket in his favourite chair, head back, eyes shut, mouth hanging all the way open.

There was a note on the coffee table. Seeing her name written down for the second time that evening filled her with the same jolt of dread she'd felt in the kitchen, but then she recognised Kenny's handwriting, and some of the tension ebbed away.

She picked up the note and read it. Kenny had hung around until just after dinnertime. He'd watched over his brother until Scott had woken up, then they'd eaten lunch and played dominoes until it was time for dinner.

Her old man had been in decent form, apparently. Despite the drama of the night before, this had been one of his better days.

Those were becoming rarer now, the balance of good days tilting further and further towards the bad with each month that passed.

There was no mention in the note of the flowers. Heather retreated back to the kitchen, pulled out her mobile, and gave her Uncle Kenny a phone.

He answered on the third ring, and the echo down the line told her he was lounging in the bath, his voice booming around a bathroom that was generously sized, but drastically in need of refurbishment. Heather didn't even like to use the toilet when she went over, for fear the ancient avocado green pan dropped through the floor the moment her backside touched the seat.

"Hello! You alright? Tell me you're home," he said, all in one go.

"I'm home, don't worry," she said, and she heard the sloshing of water as he relaxed back into the bath.

"Thank Christ for that. I'm no' long in the door myself," Kenny told her. "My old bike and that bloody snow do not play well together."

"No, I can imagine," Heather said. She turned the vase of flowers, inching it around slowly, like she was checking for explosives. "Thanks for staying with him."

"Ach, away you go," Kenny said, and Heather knew that was the end of the matter. He wasn't after thanks. Scott was his big brother, and he was more than happy to share the responsibility. "You just phoning to let me know you're home?"

"Aye," Heather said. "And no."

There was the sound of more sloshing. Heather pictured Kenny sitting up suddenly in the bath. Fortunately, her imagination fashioned the scene with a lot of bubbles.

"Is there something wrong? Is he alright?" Kenny asked, concern squeezed in between every word. "He seemed fine today. He was good. Sharpest I've seen him in a while."

"No, he's fine. He's sleeping," Heather said. She stopped turning the vase when it had performed a full three-sixty, then stepped away from it. "It's just... Did you take in a delivery for me today?"

"A delivery? Like a parcel?"

"Like flowers," Heather said.

The tone of his voice changed. The concern became relief, and then something gently teasing. "Flowers? Who's sending you flowers? Did they think you'd died, or something?"

Heather laughed. It felt good. "Ha. Aye. Maybe."

"Didn't arrive while I was there. Must've been after five."

"Huh." Heather looked back at the kitchen door. "Dad must've brought them in."

"Sounds like it," Kenny said. "See, told you he was having a good day. Unless, of course, he's nabbed them from some other bugger's doorstep."

Heather laughed again, though less convincingly this time. "No. They're definitely for me. Came with a card."

"Did it no' say who they were from?"

Heather thought of the card, and the two lovebirds on the front, with their bright, colourful feathers.

"Maybe, aye," she said, looking over at the bin. "I'll have to double-check."

"Well, good luck to them, whoever they are," Kenny said. "High time you had someone to call your own."

Heather rolled her eyes. This was not the first time she'd had this conversation. "I've got Dad," she reminded him.

"Aye, well, you shouldn't," Kenny said, his tone softening, yet becoming more serious. "He's going to need more help soon. Full-time. You can't take that on."

"We'll be fine," Heather said.

Kenny hesitated. Even over the sound of the water sloshing in the bath, she could hear his sadness. "Aye, sweetheart. I suppose we will."

"I'd better go get back to him. Night, Kenny."

"Night, Heather. You know where I am," he replied.

She finished by thanking him again, then ended the call. Rather than return her phone to her pocket, she opened up the camera app, snapped off a few photographs of the flowers, then wrapped her hands around the whole bunch and hoisted it out of the vase.

The top of the outside bin was thick with a marshmallow wedge of snow that slid off as she lifted the lid. The flowers scattered as they landed inside, and she looked down at them for a second or two before letting the lid fall shut.

The snow was still falling. It streaked past the street lights like tiny white comets, existing just for that one fleeting moment before being swallowed again by the darkness.

She stood on the step and just gazed up into it for a while. It made her feel like she was on the deck of some spaceship zooming through space, stars sliding by on either side.

Lighting a cigarette, she leaned against the door frame and continued to watch the show. From inside the house behind her, the sound of gunfire, horse hooves, and whooping were all now playing second fiddle to the throaty thunder of her father's snoring.

She stepped outside and pulled the door closed behind her, keeping in the heat and silencing the racket from inside.

The sudden silence was disorientating, like the streaking star field of the falling snow had whisked her to another time and place. She closed her eyes for a while, enjoying the thought of it.

The cold was biting, though, and the alcohol, weak as it was, was starting to have an effect. Shivering, she flicked the dying embers of her cigarette across the garden, and listened to the faint sizzling sound as it sank into the snow.

It was then that she noted the footprints.

She'd looked at them—or in their direction, at least—half a dozen times since stepping outside. Now, though, was the first time she'd truly noticed them.

There were four sets of prints—two headed towards the house, and two away. The snow had covered them to varying degrees, blurring much of the detail, but providing her with a rough time-line of events.

The oldest and most obscured set headed away from the door in the direction of the gate. Although the snow had been working to fill them in, it was still possible to get an idea of their size.

Whoever had made them must've had big feet. Size ten at least, maybe more.

Kenny. Had to be. He said he'd left around five. Two or so hours of falling snow had mostly smoothed them away. Another thirty minutes or so, and they'd be gone.

The most recent footprints were her own. Those were much sharper and led in the opposite direction. She'd dragged her feet a bit on her way up the path, and most of the prints were elongated. She could still make out the imprint of her boot heel, though, so she had no doubt that the prints were of her making.

Between these two, both physically and chronologically, were a completely different set of prints. Whoever had made these had arrived after Kenny left, and before Heather got home.

He—the size and the shape of the prints suggested a man, at least, though she couldn't be sure—had walked to the house and then left soon after. The prints coming and going were practically identical, so almost no snow had fallen between him strolling up to the house and walking away again.

It had to be whoever had brought the flowers.

Whoever had written that card.

Miss me?

An icy breeze crept across the exposed skin of Heather's arms, pimpling her pores and making the hairs all rise together. Her breath formed a billowing white cloud in front of her. It hung there like a ghost for a few seconds, before dissipating away into the darkness.

There were lights on in several windows around the square, but not in all of them. Not even close. Heather's gaze darted between the darkened ones, peering into the gloom, searching for a face peeking out at her, or a figure watching her from one of the shadowy rooms beyond.

The snow that had been falling straight towards her now fractured into spirals, becoming a kaleidoscope of white on black that made her head spin and her stomach churn.

There was nobody watching. Nobody she could see, at least. Still, she stood her ground, defiantly glaring at all of the windows, into all of the houses, and the shadowy wee hidey-holes around the square.

Her every instinct was telling her to run. Fear flooded through her bloodstream, far stronger and more potent than the cheap foreign lager she'd been drinking.

But she was damned if she was going to let anyone watching see that.

She squatted by the edge of the path, snapped off some photos of the fading footprints and then, with a final glower out into the darkness, she returned to the house. Fingers fumbling, she hurriedly locked the door, flicked the kitchen light off, then leaned her forehead against the cool uPVC.

It took her a couple of long, difficult minutes to get her breath back, and to bring her heart rate down into double figures.

What the hell had that been about? she wondered, angry at herself for letting fear take over like that.

She couldn't remember when she'd last felt that scared. Fear was something that happened to other people. A luxury she didn't have time for.

But out there, though? Just then?

Heather had been afraid. Truly, genuinely, breath-snatchingly afraid.

And the worst part was, she couldn't even fully explain why.

As her panic continued to fade, embarrassment came sweeping in to replace it. It had been a long day, plagued with headaches both literal and metaphorical, and her encounter with Shuggie Cowan had shaken her up more than she'd like to admit.

Tomorrow would be a new day. Paula would turn up, she'd be hangover free, and this lingering sense of dread that was gnawing at her could away and do one.

She tried not to think about the feather, or the picture on that card.

Her dad was still fast asleep in the chair when she returned to the living room. He'd shifted around, though, and the blanket Kenny had furnished him with had slipped down onto the floor.

Heather picked up the TV remote first, and turned the sound all the way down, but left the picture playing so the sudden switch into darkness didn't jar the old man awake.

Waking him might not be so bad, though. She could ask him about the flowers. About who'd delivered them, what they looked like, what they'd said.

And maybe, by some miracle, he might even remember.

He stirred as she pulled his blanket back up and tucked it around him. There was no point trying to get him up to bed. If he fully roused now, he'd be awake for hours, and Heather was keen to put the day behind her.

"You're alright. It's just me," she whispered to him, as his eyelids fluttered.

"That you, Stewie?" he asked, the words slurred by sleep.

The sound of the name on her father's lips gave another twist of the knife that Shuggie Cowan had plunged into her earlier, further widening the wound. Her reply was barely a croak.

"Naw, it's me, Auld Yin. It's Heather."

He smiled in his sleep. A hand made rough by age, and by years of hard manual labour, gently patted hers.

"Aw, bless you," he muttered. His eyelids, which had been fluttering, grew heavier, remaining closed. "You're a good boy, Stewie. You're a good boy, son."

TEN

HEATHER WOKE first to the sound of her phone ringing then, a moment later, to the smell of frying bacon. She wasn't quite sure which concerned her most.

Her father's chair was empty, the blanket lying in a heap on the floor where it had been discarded during the night.

The sight of the empty chair dragged her out of her half-asleep stupor, so she was suddenly all the way awake. Springing to her feet, she hissed a frantic, "Shit, shit, shit!" then went racing through to the kitchen, fully expecting to find either it or her father fully ablaze.

Instead, she found him standing over the hob, holding the handle of a frying pan and eyeing up the contents with what looked to be near superhuman levels of focus and concentration.

There were two side plates on one of the worktops, and two mugs over by the kettle, which was thundering towards the boil.

"Dad?" she said, keeping her voice soft so as not to scare him.

It didn't work, though, and he let out a startled, "Wargh!" before spinning to face her.

"Jesus fucking Christ. Are you trying to do away with me?" he cried.

"Sorry, Auld Yin." She laughed. She couldn't help it. It erupted out of her so sharply and suddenly that it surprised even her.

It wasn't the jump, the cursing, or the look of sheer indignation on his face that had made her laugh, though. It was the sharpness in his eyes. The confidence in his movements. The sureness of his stance.

Today, as she'd tried to convince herself last night, was going to be a good day.

"Aye, very funny," he snapped, but he smirked as he turned back towards the hob. "You're on tea duty."

Heather crossed to the kettle and stole a look at her phone screen. She'd let the call ring out, more concerned about the potential for her father to be running in circles around the kitchen with his hair on fire.

Now that potential crisis had been averted, though, she took a moment to check who'd been calling.

It was a mobile number. Unfamiliar. Not someone in her contacts.

She felt a twinge of the same fear she'd felt out in the snow last night. It was nothing major—just an aftershock of that panic—but it was enough to leave her staring down at the number on the screen, wondering if they were leaving a voicemail message for her even now.

It was only the cry of, "Chop chop!" from her dad that made her return the phone to her pocket and get on with the much more pressing business of making the tea and coffee.

Her dad was on the tea. Coffee sent him all wrong these days, he claimed, though he'd been saying the same thing for as long as Heather could remember. She suspected he just didn't like the stuff, but didn't want to admit it.

She, on the other hand, couldn't get enough. She took it as black and as bitter as possible, and dumped two humped teaspoons of the instant granules in her mug before sloshing in the hot water.

"You're looking bright today," she said, giving her mug a stir with a spoon, while plucking the teabag out of his with a well-aimed pinch of finger and thumb.

"Aye, well, that makes one of us," Scott said. He nudged the bacon around in the pan, then looked back at her over his shoulder. "You shouldn't be kipping on the couch like that."

"And you shouldn't be sleeping in an armchair," she countered.

"Ach, I'm an old man. My back's in pieces anyway. Yours'll end up the same way, if you're not more bloody careful."

"In forty years, maybe," Heather countered. She nodded to the frying pan. "And what's this? You shouldn't be cooking for me."

"Who says it's for you?" he asked, shooting her another look.

She laughed again. He was joking with her—actually joking. This wasn't just a good day, it was the best one he'd had in months.

Lifting the pan, he brought it over to the two empty plates, spatula positioned under the bacon, ready to lift it from the sizzling oil.

Heather watched the curtain of confusion slowly start to lower as he looked down at the plates. The fact that he knew something was missing was a positive sign.

It was important to keep looking for those moments, and to celebrate them when they came, the doctor had told her. The little wins.

"Here, I'll get the rolls," she said, crossing to the bread bin. It was a big wooden thing with a lid on top, and was generally where bread products went to die. As soon as a loaf, bag of rolls, or pack of tattie scones was placed inside the bread bin, they were immediately forgotten.

Days, sometimes weeks later, Heather would lift the lid again, recoil in horror at all the blue fur that had bloomed inside the packaging, and horse the whole lot into the outside wheelie bin.

To combat this problem, instead of using the bread bin as a receptacle for holding such baked goods, it instead acted as a pedestal for them. Rather than place a loaf inside, Heather would sit it on top, so she remembered it was there.

She'd been doing this for a few months before her dad had questioned it. What was the point, he'd wondered, in having the bread bin at all? Wouldn't it be better to just put the loaf in the space on the worktop that the bin currently occupied, rather than balancing it on top?

Heather had stared at the bread bin for a while.

She'd stared at her old man.

Finally, she'd said, "Shut it, you mad old bastard," and cracked on with making him toast.

There'd been a wee twinkle in his eye as he'd laughed at that, but he'd never broached the subject again.

"The rolls!" he cried, relief flooding his features. His eyes had been starting to blur again, but they snapped right back into focus. "I was just going to ask you if you could do the rolls."

Heather didn't argue. Instead, she took a couple of floury white baps from the paper bag on top of the bread bin, split them with her thumbs, then placed them on the plates.

Usually, she'd squirt a wee dollop of tomato sauce onto the bread and let it soak in, but he wasn't giving her the chance this morning. She stepped back as he teased the hot, greasy bacon out of the pan and onto the rolls, and the look of pride on his face as he admired what he'd done made her want to scoop him up in her arms and hug him.

"Touchdown!" he declared.

Heather felt another laugh rising up from somewhere deep within her. Somewhere that had felt shut off from the rest of her for a while now. She helped her dad over to the half-moon-shaped table and eased him down into his seat.

He seemed physically a little stronger today, but he didn't resist or try to fight her. It was ironic that he only did that on his weakest days, when he needed more help than usual.

"Touchdown," she told him, and though he looked a little confused by the callback, he pointed at her and laughed, like they were sharing some old joke they both loved.

Once he was safely deposited in the chair, she fetched the rolls and the hot drinks, then took her seat beside him.

"A wee daud o' broon sauce," Scott declared, fiddling with the lid of the *HP* bottle.

Technically, it wasn't *HP*, but an own-brand alternative from one of the local supermarkets, but the taste, when applied sparingly, was indistinguishable.

Scott wasn't going for 'sparingly' though. Or, if he was, he overshot it by quite some margin.

"Jesus Christ. What are you going to do with all that?" Heather asked, eyeing up the slathering of sauce he'd applied to his bacon. "Swim in it?"

"Maybe I will!" Her dad pinched his nose, then mimed diving into the sauce. He grinned when it made her laugh, then shut the lid of his bacon buttie and took a big bite.

"Someone's in good form," Heather said through a mouthful of her own roll.

Scott could only smile. The bite had been a comically large one, and his blunted teeth were now struggling to work their way through it.

"You've got Clarissa coming in today," Heather told him. She checked her watch. "In a couple of hours, then again at lunchtime. Kenny's going to come over to get you sorted for dinner if I'm not home."

Scott nodded, though a little vaguely. His mouth was still full, and the question barely escaped through the corner of it.

"Which one's she again?"

"Clarissa? The wee ginger one."

"Oh! Aye!" Her dad brightened at that. He forced down a swallow, then helped it on its way with a swig of his tea. "I like her."

"You like Klaudie, too," Heather said, then she headed off the next question by adding, "The blonde one with the legs."

A smile spread from one side of Scott's face to the other. "Aye. Aye, I do like her, right enough," he confirmed. "Lovely warm hands, she's got."

Heather rolled her eyes. "I bet she does, you dirty old bugger."

She took another bite of her roll. The bacon was a little too well done for her liking, and the roll was dry.

But, it was the best breakfast she could remember in a long time.

"You look tired," her dad told her.

"I'm always tired," Heather said, reaching for her coffee. "It's like my superpower."

Her dad's laughter was music to her ears. "You can say that again!" he said, more animated than she'd seen him in months. "You could fall asleep on a bloody clothesline! I used to tell people. 'See my Stewie?' I used to say, 'He could fall asleep on… on…'"

The kitchen seemed to grow darker, like a cloud was passing. Heather watched the frown forming on her dad's face, the confusion descending.

"No, not… I didn't mean…" he mumbled. His eyes darted around the room, like he was searching for something he'd lost.

Which, of course, he was.

Always.

"Hey. How's your roll?" Heather asked, trying to ground him back in the here and now. "Can you taste it for all that brown sauce?"

"What? Oh. Aye, of course I can," he said, and his tone was clipped. He looked at her like she'd said something offensive. Like she'd done something terrible. "I can taste it just fine."

The cloud continued to dull the colours of the room. Heather watched her dad eating, noting the shaking of his hands, and the way his movements already seemed more hesitant and less sure.

If she was going to ask, she was running out of time.

"Did someone come round last night? With flowers?"

Scott looked up from his plate. There was a slatey greyness to his eyes, and they swam for a moment like two camera lenses trying to pull focus.

"Flowers?"

"Aye. There was a big bunch of flowers," Heather said. She shouldn't have thrown them out. She should've kept them. The sight and the smell of them—having something tangible for his mind to latch onto—might've made this easier. "Can you remember who brought them?"

He gazed at her, forgetting to chew, so the food just hung around there in his mouth.

Then, he shifted his weight and looked back at the draining board, and the empty vase standing atop it.

"That's right," Heather urged. "Flowers. You put them in the vase."

"I put them in the vase," he said, though she couldn't tell if he was remembering, or just repeating what she'd said. "I put the flowers in the vase."

"You did, aye," Heather said. She smiled at him, keeping her voice light. Pressure would make him worse. Pressure would push the memories all the way back down. "Can you remember who brought them?"

He turned back to her, his face pained with the effort of remembering. Of trying to hold onto the mist of his memories.

"The flowers," he mumbled. His eyes made a series of tiny left and right darting movements, then settled on something in the air behind her that only he could see. "I… I think I put them in the vase for you." He blinked, his eyes widening with worry, like he'd done something wrong. "Didn't I?"

Heather reached across the table and placed her hand on top of his. The skin was cold to the touch, like the life was already leaking out of him, drop by drop.

"Aye, Dad. You did. Thanks. You did good."

His uncertainty fell away again. He nodded, pleased with himself over a job well done.

"Thanks for breakfast, sweetheart," he said. He picked up his roll and took another bite. "Maybe a bit heavy on the broon sauce, though, eh?"

Heather smiled. "Aye, maybe just a bit," she conceded.

She watched him as he munched his way through the mouthful he'd taken, pausing only to occasionally wet the dry bread with a sip of his tea.

Once he'd swallowed, he glanced down at the pockets of the jeans she'd fallen asleep in.

"Who was that?" he asked.

Heather followed his gaze, frowning. What the hell was he on about now?

"Who was what?"

"On the phone," her dad said, and she leaped to her feet, almost knocking the table over.

"Shit. The phone!"

She fished it out of her pocket, tapped it awake, and studied the screen, expecting to see the office number there as a missed call.

Or, God help her, Snecky's direct line.

Instead, the number on-screen was one she didn't recognise. It was an unfamiliar mobile, and not someone from her contacts.

She checked through her texts. Nothing there from the caller, and nothing to notify her of a voice message being left.

Her pulse quickened its pace. She thought of the flowers, and the card, and that sense of being watched.

"Eh, sorry, Dad. I need to call someone back," she told him. "Just be a minute."

And, leaving him to his breakfast, she returned to the hall, took the stairs two at a time, and hit the 'Call Back' button as she threw open the door of her bedroom.

———

"Officer. Thank you for returning my call."

It took Heather a moment to place the voice on the other end of the line.

"Hang on," she said, sitting on the end of her unmade bed. "You're that kid, aren't you?"

"Ace Wurzel. The Crime De La Crime podcast. We met yesterday."

"Aye, I know. I remember," Heather replied. "What are you calling for? Have you got something to tell me?"

"No."

Heather switched her phone from one ear to the other before responding. "No? Then what are you calling for?"

"I have something to ask you," Ace said. "Two things, actually."

There was the rumble of traffic in the background, and the crunch of boots in snow told Heather that the girl was out walking somewhere. She checked her watch again.

"God. Fine. But, shouldn't you be getting ready for school?"

"I very much hope not," Ace replied. "It is Saturday, after all."

Heather winced, even more annoyed at herself than she was at the smug tone in the girl's voice. "Oh. Aye. That's right." She rubbed her eyes with finger and thumb, then squeezed the bridge of her nose. "I gave you my number in case you thought of anything you needed to tell me, not so you could—"

"Is it true? About the feather?" the girl asked.

Heather screwed shut her eyes, mumbled a barely audible, "Fuck," then ran her hand through her hair. Grease and the arm of the couch had plastered it to the side of her head, and it sprang up as her fingers wriggled through it.

"I'm going to take your silence as confirmation," Ace said. "That's interesting, isn't it? A feather. That's very interesting, don't you think?"

"No, I don't. It's nothing," Heather said. She kicked off her shoes, pulled off a sock, and gave it an experimental sniff. She recoiled at the smell from it, and tossed it into the laundry basket in the corner of the room. "How the hell did you hear about it, anyway?"

"I have my sources, Officer."

"It's Detective Inspector," Heather corrected. "And don't play bloody coy with me, princess. Who told you?"

On the other end of the line, Ace sighed. "Well, let's just say that Paula's mother isn't as adept at keeping secrets as you or I. She mentioned it to a neighbour. It spread round the estate like wildfire. Of course, nobody actually knows the significance of it. Not yet."

"But you do?" Heather asked.

There was another sigh. This one sounded positively indignant. "I take it you haven't listened to my podcast yet?"

"Obviously not," Heather told her.

"Then, I suggest you do. You might find it enlightening," Ace told her.

"Aye, well, if I ever find myself at a loose end, I'll be sure to do that," Heather said. "But, for now, I'm busy. Unless you've got something to tell me, don't call back."

"Wait!" The cry was sharp and urgent. So much so, in fact, that

Heather wasn't even sure it was aimed at her, and not at some mugger who'd just grabbed the girl's bag and legged it. "I said I had two things to ask. You said you'd answer them."

"I don't think I did."

"You did. I said I had two things to ask, and you said, 'God. Fine,'" Ace reminded her. "I have a very good memory for that sort of thing."

"Jesus." Heather scratched at her forehead, then ran her hand down her face. "OK, fine. What else did you want to ask?"

She was kicking off her other shoe when the question came. It made her freeze, locked her to the spot, held her down against the bed.

"It's you, isn't it? You're her?" Ace asked in an awed hush. "You're the one that got away."

ELEVEN

"JESUS. DO YOU EVER GO HOME?" Heather asked as she strode into the office.

She immediately felt a twinge of guilt when the expression on DS Martin Brompton's face said, *Not if I can help it.*

He'd showered and changed clothes at least, so had achieved one more thing than Heather had in her own short stop back at her house. Even then, it was only certain parts of her attire that she'd changed. Her jeans and jacket were the same as yesterday, but there was no way she could've kept going with those socks.

Snecky had called while Heather was driving up the road, but she was close enough to the station that she'd dingied it. When it came to Snecky, it was better to talk to him face to face. You could get a better sense of whether he was lying or not.

The man would not have fared well as a professional poker player.

She looked over to the door of the DCI's office. *Her* old office.

"He in there?"

"He is," Marty confirmed. "There's been news."

"About Paula?" Heather's eyebrows rose. "Good news?"

Marty gave a non-committal sort of shrug. "Just news. I'd better let him tell you. You know what he's like."

Heather exhaled. She did, of course, know what he was like. Only too well.

"Right. Fair enough," she said.

She set off towards the office, then stopped a pace or two in.

"Here. Hang on," she ventured. "What's that stuff you listen to sometimes?"

When Marty just stared blankly back at her, she tapped an ear.

"On your phone. What is it you listen to on your phone? With your pods?"

"Music?" the detective sergeant guessed.

"No. The other thing. The talking one."

"Oh. Audiobooks?"

"Is that a podcast?"

A smirk fiddled with a corner of Marty's mouth. It was fun to see Heather floundering so far out of her depth over something so simple.

"Is an audiobook a podcast? No. Not exactly," he said, deciding not to prolong her misery. "Why, what do you need to know?"

Heather placed the flimsy card Ace had given her on the desk in front of the DS. He picked it up, marvelling at its thinness.

"Christ. I've done farts thicker than this. What paper stock is it? One GSM?"

"I don't know. Is that a nerd joke?" Heather asked. "I don't know what GSM is."

"Grams per square metre," Marty explained. "It's how the weight of paper stock is…"

The look on Heather's face told him to quit while he was still marginally ahead, and he never made it to the end of the explanation.

"Some kid at Paula's school gave me it. She's got a podcast. That's the website. Can you make it so I can listen to it on my phone?"

Marty's smirk returned. "Jesus, how old are you? Ninety? Can I download it, you mean?"

"Whatever," Heather said, dismissing the jibe with a raised middle finger. "Can you?"

"Probably, aye. I'll need your phone for about five minutes, though."

Heather took her mobile from her pocket, but didn't hand it over. She looked down at it, a lifetime of trust issues painting a pained expression across her face.

Finally, with a sigh, she tapped in the PIN and handed the phone over. "Fine," she said. "Five minutes."

She set off for the office, calling a warning back over her shoulder.

"And for the love of God, do *not* look at any of my pictures."

————

DCI Samuel 'Snecky' Grant was standing with his back to the door when Heather stepped into the office, the echo of his, "Enter!" still hanging in the air.

He had his hands folded crisply behind his back, and was gazing out at the traffic passing along the M77—a picture of self-importance.

There had been some more snow during the night, but not much, and the gritters had worked their magic on the road, so Heather's drive up had been much easier than any of her trips the day before.

"Take a seat," Snecky said, not yet turning. Turning would spoil the drama of the little tableau he'd created, and if there was one thing the DCI enjoyed, it was drama.

Not *too much* drama, though. Not the sort of drama that might put him in danger, or otherwise pose a risk to his comfort and well-being. He enjoyed the sort of drama where other people were in jeopardy, and he was the one on top.

"Nah, you're alright, cheers," Heather said, puncturing the pomposity of the man. "What's up? Marty says there's been news. Has she turned up? Did she come home?"

Snecky waggled his fingers and rocked on his heels. She heard him sigh, and saw his breath paint a pale white mist on the window in front of him. Clearly, he was annoyed that Marty had said even that much.

"No. Paula hasn't come home," he eventually said. He turned, his face fixed in an expression so grave it bordered on the cartoonish. "Quite the opposite, in fact."

Heather's stomach dropped to somewhere around her knees. All of a sudden, the chair was a very tempting option. She managed to remain standing, though.

"Shit. She's dead?"

"What?" Snecky's expression became worried. "No. No, I just mean she's the opposite of home. Like... she's elsewhere."

"Jesus Christ!" Heather hissed. "The fuck did you say it like that for, then?"

"Like what?"

"Like..." She drew back her shoulders, arranged her face into something bordering on the monstrous, and delivered the words in a sinister drawl. "'Quite the opposite, in fact!' Like a fucking *Poundland* Christopher Lee."

She pushed back her hair with both hands, allowing herself a moment to breathe.

"Jesus *Christ*!" she said again, but with heavier emphasis this time. "So, she's still alive as far as we know?"

"As far as we know, yes. Paula is still alive," the DCI confirmed. He raised a finger to make a point. "But..."

Heather dug her fingernails into her palms while she waited for the bastard to finish his dramatic pause.

She didn't have the patience for it, though.

"But what? Spit it out, for fuck's sake."

"*But...*" Snecky said again.

He was determined to keep eye contact, so was forced to fumble blindly on his desk until he found the notepad he was looking for.

Once he did, he tossed it towards her. It landed on the desktop in front of her with a *thack*.

"...we did find something of interest."

———

Heather stood by the fence at the edge of the golf course, her hands in the pockets of her leather jacket, her head scrunched down into her shoulders to help keep out the snow.

The stuff falling now wasn't made up of the same fluffy flakes as yesterday. It was wetter and greyer, and burst like icy little bombs against the skin.

The ground was still white, but the sleet was steadily turning it into slush. Flashing blue lights danced across its wet sheen, while Uniforms bemoaned their sodden socks and frozen feet.

The bag had been found by a guy on his way to play golf. Heather had found that hard to believe, given the current weather conditions, but he'd apparently taken great delight in explaining to the first officers to arrive how he used special orange balls with a built-in tracking device, so he could play even on days like these.

It had become apparent, the constable had explained to Heather when she'd turned up, that the guy was only going to play golf that day specifically so he could show off his balls.

"Typical bloke then, eh?" Heather had said, but the comment seemed to go completely over the male constable's head, and she'd sent him off to join the search of the golf course and surrounding area.

The snow was going to hamper the search, of course, but the dog squad had arrived a few minutes after Heather, and the guys running it had insisted the animals could smell a dead body through six feet of the stuff.

And that was what they thought they were doing. Not just the dog squad, but the Uniforms, too. That was what everyone was looking for now.

A body.

The schoolbag was now safely stored in the back of the Scene of Crime team's van, wrapped to prevent it from being compromised any more than it already had been.

And it had been very much compromised even before the passing golfer had gone prodding at it with the dirty head of a seven iron.

Someone had tried to burn the bag. An accelerant had been

used, going by the smell, but enough had survived to be able to identify the owner as Paula Harrison.

Someone had dumped Paula's bag out here, and set it alight.

That didn't mean she was dead, though. It didn't. Not necessarily.

She could still be alive.

No. She *was* still alive. Heather was sure of it.

Or, was that just wishful thinking?

Someone had set out to destroy Paula's schoolbag. Someone was trying to destroy evidence.

The question was, evidence of what?

TWELVE

HEATHER WAS NOT PLEASED to see the *Jaguar* parked outside Paula's house when she pulled up in her Audi. She checked as she trudged past it, but this time there was nobody sitting inside the vehicle. Either Shuggie's thugs were inside with him, or he'd come on his own.

Linda opened the door before Heather had a chance to knock. It had been less than twenty-four hours since the women had first met, but Paula's mother had shrunk further during that time.

A wavy line of cigarette smoke trailed behind her as she opened the door, marking out the route she'd taken to get there.

A range of emotions all had a wee shot at being in charge of her face when she opened the door to find the detective inspector standing there. Fear took an early lead and got the strongest foothold, though, and Heather moved quickly to reassure her.

"She's not... I'm not here with bad news, Mrs Harrison," she said. "There's been a development I wanted to discuss. That's all."

The voice of Shuggie Cowan rang out from the living room before Linda had a chance to open her mouth.

"Well, then..."

He appeared in the doorway at the far end of the hall, his pock-marked features arranged into a scowl of contempt.

"…you'd best come in."

Linda averted her gaze and stepped back, practically curt-seying when the DI stepped inside the house.

"We can talk in private, if you'd prefer?" Heather said.

She wanted to talk to Paula's mother in private. She was going to have to ask about Conn Byrne, and whether Linda had been aware that her daughter was seeing him. Mention the boy in front of Shuggie, though, and she was putting a target on his head.

Or, more likely, his genitals.

But Linda just shook her head. The smile she flashed was a frantic, desperate sort of thing.

"It's fine. It's fine. Shuggie can…" Linda's gaze flitted along the hallway. "I'm happy for him to be involved."

"Hey, come on now," Shuggie intoned, shuffling his bulk along the hall and putting a hand on the woman's shoulder. "Call me Dad. Like we talked about."

Linda's smile crept higher. Her eyes weren't getting involved, though.

"Dad. Yes. Of course. I'm happy for *Dad* to be involved, I mean."

Shuggie was completely straight-faced when Heather turned her attention to him, and yet she could've sworn that the bastard was laughing at her.

"Right. Fair enough," she said, then she nodded back in the direction that Cowan had come. "Let's go sit down and have a chat, then."

"Why? What's happened?" Shuggie demanded, but Heather barely glanced at him as she elbowed her way past him in the narrow space, and led the way into the living room.

Ibby, Paula's younger sister, was sitting on the floor playing with two semi-naked *Barbie*s and a couple of plastic horses, and was far too busy to so much as look up when the adults entered.

Heather noted there were several other dolls laid out beside her, as if waiting for someone else to pick them up and join in. She wondered if Shuggie had been playing with the girl, but her brain couldn't even formulate a picture of what that might look like.

As if reading the detective's mind, Linda leaned closer and whispered, "She's waiting for Paula. They always play together at the weekend."

Heather was almost as surprised by that as she was by the thought of Shuggie doing it. An almost-sixteen-year-old playing dolls with her younger sister? Heather had barely even tolerated her little brother's existence for most of his childhood, let alone willingly entertained him.

"They're a beautiful pair of weans," Shuggie declared, looking down at his granddaughter with something that might, under very careful scrutiny, pass for real affection.

"Aye, well, I suppose apples can sometimes fall far from the tree, right enough," Heather remarked, smiling like the comment had been a friendly one.

Shuggie smiled, too, but there was danger in every curve and exposed tooth. "Take a seat, Detective Inspector," he urged, patting a pudgy hand on the couch beside him as he sat down.

"Nah, you're alright. I'm not here for long," Heather replied, her skin crawling at the thought of being sat that close to the bastard. "I just wanted to ask if you knew any reason why Paula might have been over at the golf course."

"The golf course?" Linda pounced on a packet of *Lambert & Butler* lying discarded on the mantelpiece. The lid was open, like she'd known she wouldn't want to waste the fraction of a second it would take to get access to the cigarettes themselves. "No. That's way over the other side of town. She wouldn't be there. Why would she be there?"

"And why are you asking?" demanded Shuggie, who understood the rhythms of police questioning better than many officers did. "What have you found?"

Heather hesitated, composing herself, getting ready to gauge their reactions. For all his talk about hunting for his granddaughter, and all his supposed concern, Heather hadn't ruled Shuggie out as a suspect in the girl's disappearance.

She couldn't quite figure out yet what the motive would be, but he had the means and the opportunity.

And she knew first-hand that he definitely had the stomach for that sort of thing.

Maybe Paula didn't like him. Maybe she was resisting him becoming part of the family, driving a wedge between the bastard and her mother, and protecting her little sister from growing up with a drug dealer, people trafficker, and suspected murderer for a grandparent.

Shuggie wouldn't like that. Someone talking back to him? Someone getting between him and something he wanted?

No, Shuggie Cowan wouldn't like that one little bit.

"We found her schoolbag," Heather said.

Linda's hands shook as she crammed the end of a cigarette in her mouth and lit it. Shuggie's face remained hard to read, but Heather thought she saw some light crinkling of his crow's feet and furrowing of the lines of his forehead.

"What does that mean?" Linda asked. "Found it how? What do you mean?"

"Give her a second, sweetheart," Shuggie said. He nodded to Heather to continue.

"It was hidden under a tree," Heather said. "Someone had tried to burn it, but the snow put it out. It was spotted this morning by a golfer."

"A golfer?" Shuggie's tone and his expression made it clear he wasn't buying that. "Who the fuck plays golf on a day like this? Who was it? What's his name?"

"I can't tell you that," Heather said. "As you well know."

Shuggie sat forwards on the couch. The menace in his voice made even Ibby look up from her *Barbies*.

"Aye, well, and as you well know, Detective Inspector, I've got ways and means of finding out. It's eighteen inches of snow out there. Nobody plays golf in that."

"He's got special balls," Heather said.

"Well, he won't have by the time I'm fucking through with him."

Linda pulled the cigarette from her mouth long enough to whisper a, "Please!" and to shoot a look at her daughter.

Shuggie turned to the girl, pulled a comically exaggerated, *Whoops!* face that made her giggle, then slapped himself on the hand.

Ibby went back to playing with her dolls. Linda returned to sucking on her cigarette.

"He checks out," Heather said, though she wasn't entirely sure yet that this was true. "He's a gadget guy. He bought balls especially for playing in the snow. You can find them or something, I don't know. But he's been waiting since October to try them out. He's no one."

Linda nodded. The movements were sharp and frantic. "Why would he report it if he'd left it there? You wouldn't, would you?"

"Well, I mean, that in itself wouldn't rule him out," Heather said. She glanced at Linda, but then immediately went right back to staring at the man on the couch. "Some of these bastards, they like to gloat. They like to shove it down your throat, what they've done. They don't want to get caught, of course, but they want to be part of the story. They might even want you to suspect what they've done, because they know you can't prove it. Because they know there's nothing you can do."

"Jesus Christ," Linda hissed. "So… what? It was him? Has he done something to Paula? Oh, God! Has he hurt her?"

Heather blinked, realised what she'd said, and how it must've sounded, and rushed to repair the damage.

"No. No, he isn't. Like I say, he checked out. He's just a random guy who saw something suspicious and called it in. Obviously, we'll look into him further, but we've got no reason at all to suspect he's in any way involved with Paula's disappearance. And no amount of kicking the shit out of him or threatening his family's going to change that."

She aimed that last part at Shuggie, but his face gave nothing away.

"Anyway, that's all to report so far," Heather said, turning to Linda again. "I'm assuming you've heard nothing?"

"Not a thing," Linda said. She took another long draw on her fag, turning a quarter of an inch of it to ash.

Heather's fingers twitched, like they were searching for a cigarette of their own.

"OK. Well, it's still early days. I still think she'll be with a friend or…" She didn't look at Shuggie. She didn't dare, in case he saw straight through the question. "…boyfriend, maybe?"

Linda shook her head. "I told you, she didn't have a boyfriend."

"Girls that age… She might've been keeping him a secret," the DI ventured.

She could feel Cowan's gaze boring into her. Could sense his suspicion souring the air.

"There's nobody she mentioned even in passing? Nobody from school. Nobody older?"

"Older?" Linda gasped. "What do you mean?" Her hand went to her mouth. She took another puff on the cigarette clamped between her trembling fingers. "What are you saying? There was an older man? Are you telling me she was groomed?"

"No. No, nothing like that," Heather assured her. "There's absolutely nothing to suggest that."

And there wasn't. She'd seen the update from the IT team that morning, listing the contents of the girl's laptop. Her emails were mostly spam, and a few random subscriptions, but she didn't seem to use it to communicate with anyone.

Her web history was mostly homework related, plus a lot of sites full of games designed for younger kids. She must've played those with Ibby, two sisters passing the time together.

There was nothing more suspicious to be found on the computer, although Heather hadn't really expected there to be. Laptops were left lying around. They were relatively easy to get into.

If there was anything meaty to be found, it would be on the girl's phone, and that had vanished along with Paula herself.

Before Heather could offer any further assurances, Shuggie's phone *cling-clanged* out a tuneless rhythm. He grunted with the effort of lifting an arse cheek, then pulled his phone from his back pocket and checked the screen.

There was a flicker of something on his face, but it was there and gone so quickly that Heather didn't have time to identify it.

Whatever the message said, it made him clutch a fist around the phone and heave himself up from the couch.

"Sorry, sweetheart. I need to go. Something's come up."

Heather didn't like this. Just like she'd done when she'd been trying to hide Conn Byrne's existence from him, Shuggie was deliberately avoiding eye contact. He knew something. He'd just found something out.

"Surely someone else can deal with whatever it is, Shuggie?" Heather said, inserting herself into his eyeline. "Surely your place is here? With your family."

He glowered at her, his fat purple tongue running across the front of his teeth.

"You're right, Detective Inspector," he finally said. "Getting Paula safely back home is the most important thing. Nothing else matters but that."

Brushing her aside, he leaned over to Linda, kissed her on the forehead, then lifted her chin with the knuckle of an index finger so she was looking up into his eyes.

"She's going to be alright. Trust me."

He pressed his lips to his fingertips and blew the kiss to Ibby, who was too wrapped up in her game to notice.

The smile this brought to his face positively ached with something. Regret, maybe. Or guilt.

Not love, though. No matter how much it might look like it, it couldn't be love. Heather refused to believe the bastard was capable of such a thing.

Without another word, Shuggie went striding out of the room. Heather leaned back to watch him as he headed for the front door, but he didn't turn to look at her. Instead, he took out his phone, and was tapping out a message when he stepped outside into the sleet, and closed the door with enough force to shake the pictures on the wall.

He knew something. He had to.

Shite.

"I, eh, I need to go, too, Linda," Heather said. She looked

around, a thought suddenly occurring to her. "Has a liaison been? There should be someone in uniform here."

"Shuggie—my dad—he sent them away. Said we didn't need anyone."

Heather sighed. Of course he had.

"You want me to get someone?" she asked, but Linda quickly shook her head, dismissing this as a terrible idea.

"No. No, it's fine. Don't do that. It's OK."

"Right. If you change your mind, just let me know. You've got my number," Heather said.

Through the front window, she could see Shuggie striding towards his car, the phone now pressed to his ear, the hand holding his keys gesticulating wildly as he spoke to whoever was on the other end of the line.

"Please. Just… just find her. Find my daughter," Linda pleaded.

"I will. I'm going to. I promise, I'll bring her home," Heather said. She felt a sudden and unfamiliar urge like she wanted to give the woman a hug.

Instead, she just nodded, flashed a thin-lipped smile, then turned to leave.

And then, almost immediately, she turned back again, another thought striking her.

"Where's your husband? Paula's stepdad? He still not around?"

"Michael? He's back out looking for her," Linda said. "He hasn't stopped. He's barely been home since we realised she was missing."

Heather reached up to scratch an itch that had started on the back of her head.

"What, not even to sleep?"

Linda shook her head again, but this time there was nothing but admiration to it. "He says he'll sleep when we find her. And, well…" She fiddled with the dog end of her cigarette, then stubbed it out in a brightly coloured ashtray that sang the praises of holidaying in Tenerife. "I don't think he likes Shuggie. I think he's a bit… scared of him."

Outside, the engine of Shuggie's Jaguar purred into life.

"Right. OK. Well, make sure he gets some rest," Heather urged, hurrying out into the hall. "And tell him to leave the searching to us."

And with that, she hurried out into the icy downpour, pulled her collar around her neck, and ran for her car before Shuggie could disappear around the corner at the end of the road.

THIRTEEN

COWAN WAS HEADING NORTH. Heather hung back until they reached the motorway, then matched his speed, keeping the Jaguar in sight. There was a good chance that he'd spot her—this wasn't his first time being tailed by the police—but Heather didn't care. And besides, running out of the house like that after getting a text? He was bound to know she'd follow.

Hell, there was a chance all this was a trick. A charade, designed to lead her away from Linda's house. Perhaps even to lure her into a trap.

But if so, then fuck it. Full-scale war between her and Shuggie Cowan had been brewing for years now. Maybe it was time it finally kicked off.

Even at Shuggie's above-the-limit speed, it would take twenty minutes or so to get back to Glasgow. Heather fished out her phone and, keeping one hand on the wheel and one eye on the road, searched around until she found the podcast app that Marty had set up for her.

The 1950s noir-style icon for Ace's 'Crime De La Crime' took up most of the screen when the app opened. There was a heavy block of text description below the icon, but the text was small, and the cars around her were moving at speed, so she felt it safest not to try and read.

Instead, she turned on the car's stereo, and stabbed blankly at the buttons on the screen for a while until she found the option to connect her phone via Bluetooth.

The speakers let out a series of chimes that she assumed meant the connection had been established, but just as she tapped her thumb on the podcast icon, a text message notification slid onto the screen, and she opened up that, instead.

Up ahead, some slow-moving bastard in the fast lane was forcing Shuggie to slow the Jag. Even from half a dozen cars back, Heather heard the blasting of his horn. The middle lane was packed, though, and there was nowhere for the slower driver to go. With the road still awash with slush, he didn't seem to be in any hurry to speed up, either.

Heather took the chance to read the text. It was from her Uncle Kenny, which immediately worried her. The panic didn't last long, though. He was just letting her know that he'd dropped in on her dad and was making him lunch. He was in good form, apparently.

Definitely one of his better days, then.

She couldn't type and drive, so she hit the button to call him back, and the ringing *burred* through the car.

"Hello there!" Kenny boomed, sounding as upbeat and gregarious as always. "We were just talking about you. Weren't we, Scotty?"

Heather smiled. "All good, I'm sure."

"Oh God, no. Awful stuff," Kenny laughed. His voice became muffled for a moment. "Scotty! That's no' the salt!"

She heard her dad mumbling in the background. "The hell is it then?"

"It's just a wee ornament, I think."

There was a moment of silence, then a sharp cry of indignation from Heather's old man. "It is the bloody salt!"

"Oh. Aye. So it is," Kenny said. "Sorry, Scotty. I thought it was just a wee China mannie."

Heather smirked. She knew exactly the salt cellar her uncle was referring to. It was some hideous old thing of her mother's that Scott had done nothing but slag off while his wife was alive, but which he now cherished as if, alongside the salt, it contained something of her soul.

Kenny's voice returned at full volume. "Anyway, he's grand. I brought him soup. He says it's not as good as the stuff he makes himself, but then he was always an ungrateful bastard."

"I heard that!" Scott chipped in.

"Aye, you were meant to," Kenny told him.

"All sounds like it's in hand," Heather said. "Thanks, Kenny."

"Not a problem," her uncle replied. "How are you getting on? Busy day?"

"As always," Heather said. "I'm headed to Glasgow."

"You're no' going shopping, I'm guessing?"

"Sadly not," Heather said, even though shopping was one of her least favourite activities. "I'm following Shuggie Cowan, as it happens."

She heard the change to Kenny's demeanour right away.

"Cowan? Jesus Christ, Heather. You watch yourself. You stay away from that bastard."

"It's fine, Kenny," she assured him.

"Tell me you've got someone with you. Tell me you're not going after the evil fucker on your own?"

"I'm not going after him," Heather said. "Much as I'd like to. I'm just following him. I think he might know something about this missing girl."

"Oh, I fucking bet he does!" Kenny shot back. "I wouldn't put anything past that man, family or not. But if you think he's the one that killed her, call in backup for Christ's sake! Don't confront him on your own."

A few cars ahead, the slow-moving vehicle managed to pull into the middle lane. Shuggie went roaring past, blasting his horn and gesturing furiously out of the passenger side window.

The sleet was getting heavier now, and the spray from the roads was making visibility poor. Heather was forced to speed up and close the gap, so as not to lose sight of the Jaguar.

"I don't think she's dead. And I don't think Cowan's got her. He's hunting for her, too. I'm worried about the damage he might cause and the people he might hurt along the way."

Kenny breathed out, steadying himself. "Well, just make sure that you're no' one of the people he hurts. He's dangerous, Heather. We both know that."

"Aye. We do," Heather agreed.

In the background, there was the *clunk* of something—a soup bowl, perhaps—falling to the floor.

"Ah, shite!" Scott ejected in the background. "Shaky hands."

"Och, you daft bugger, what were you even...?" Kenny's voice, which had become muffled when he turned to see what was happening, returned to full volume. "We've had some spillage. I need to go. But for God's sake, watch what you're doing, alright?"

"I'll be careful," she told him. "And Kenny."

"Aye?"

"Thank you," Heather said.

She didn't catch her uncle's reply, drowned out as it was by her dad's cry of, "It's in my socks!"

The line went dead then, and Heather swiped away the text message, taking her back to the podcast screen.

She turned up the volume of the stereo to compensate for the thumping of her windscreen wipers, which had automatically kicked into a higher gear. She immediately turned it back down a few notches when a blast of creepy, suspenseful-sounding music assaulted her from the speakers, making her jump.

"Fuck," she spat, centring her car back in the lane.

She checked her mirrors to see if any of the drivers in the next lane were hurling abuse her way, then listened to the voice that started to speak over the faded-down musical intro.

"What sort of person abducts three girls of varying ages from their homes, with the intention of murdering them?" asked Ace over the stereo system.

The question made Heather's breath catch. Something that had been lying dormant deep in her gut stirred, and lazily opened an eye.

The windscreen wipers *thunk-thunk-thunked* in time with the beating of her heart.

She knew what was coming. She'd suspected it ever since Ace's call this morning, which Heather had cut short.

Despite the cold outside, the inside of the car suddenly felt stiflingly warm. Heather turned down the heater, rolled her shoulders, and adjusted herself in her seat. Her fingers flexed, then tightened again on the wheel as the voice from the stereo continued.

"On a rainy, windswept afternoon in Kilmarnock, Scotland, on the fourteenth day of March 1988, thirteen-year-old Eilidh Howden was taken by the man the media would come to refer to as, 'The Killie Kiddie Killer.'"

Heather had started fumbling with the phone as soon as Ace had mentioned the date, her hands shaking, her breath turning sour at the back of her throat as she desperately tried to stop the podcast, to shut the girl up, to stop her saying any more.

Her heartbeat crashed in her ears, the blood surging through her veins as she stabbed at the screen, searching blindly for a way to silence the audio.

In the end, she hit the power button on the stereo itself. Silence fell, but too late for her to avoid hearing that name.

That stupid bloody tabloid nickname that tripped up most people who tried to say it, and which had turned a depraved child-killer into a fun after-party tongue twister.

The name that had haunted Heather Filson for almost her entire life. The name that still woke her up some nights, drenched in sweat and clawing at her covers.

The name of the man who had taken her.

———

Heather's hands had stopped shaking when she pulled off Clyde Street and brought the Audi to a stop.

The area had become increasingly gentrified over the years, and this street was no exception. A few old sandstone tenements still hung on here and there, but there was a lot more glass and wood cladding around these days, giving the place a more modern feel.

And then there was the *Pig & Bicycle*. It was an old-fashioned pub for old-fashioned punters. The type who liked their drink cheap, their food microwaved, and their nights out coloured by the constant threat of violence.

Service wasn't so much delivered with a smile there as with an air of calculated menace, and while the place might hide behind a wafer-thin layer of legitimacy, it was common knowledge locally that it served as a front for all manner of criminal activity.

In many ways, it wasn't just the unofficial headquarters of Shuggie Cowan, but a bricks-and-mortar extension of the man.

The outer doors were shut tight when she arrived, but she'd seen Shuggie disappear inside as she'd pulled onto the street, so she knew the bastard was in there.

She hesitated before knocking. It had been a few years since she'd last set foot in the place. A lot had changed in that time.

Herself included.

Heather hadn't listened to any more of the podcast on the drive up here. The intro had been more than enough. When she'd heard the name, it had felt like he'd invaded her private space. Like he was in there with her, breathing her air, filling the car with his scent.

Now, she found herself looking back at the Audi with something like fear gnawing away at her, as if she might see the subject of Ace's series sitting there in the back seat, peeking out at her through the gap between the headrests.

Suddenly, the thought of being face-to-face with Shuggie Cowan in his own pub didn't seem remotely daunting.

She hammered on the door with a clenched fist, shaking it on its hinges. The outer doors were thick, though. They were designed to slow down anyone trying to force their way through long enough for anyone inside to dispose of anything incriminating.

Not that anyone had taken a battering ram to any of Shuggie Cowan's properties recently. He always seemed to know they were coming, and took great delight in forcing Police Scotland to cough up for the damages.

Almost a dozen raids that had all turned up nothing had made it very difficult for anyone to get a warrant to try again.

Heather hammered on the door again, though she knew

nobody was coming. She went to one of the windows and cupped her hands to the glass to let her see inside. Cowan was sitting in his usual seat, talking to at least two men standing across the table from him. Because of the angle, Heather couldn't see, but there could easily have been several other men standing alongside those, listening to what looked to be an angry rant.

She rapped her knuckles on the window, and Shuggie's head snapped around to look at her.

He scowled as she waved, but then said something to one of the men and gestured towards the door.

Heather flashed a smile of acknowledgement, then went back to the doors and stood with her hands buried in the pockets of her leather jacket, stomping her feet to drive out the cold.

There were a series of *clunks* and *clacks* as several locks were unfastened on the other side of the doors, then a low and ominous *creak* as one side inched inwards to reveal a sliver of one of Shuggie's henchmen.

He was a big bastard—all brute force and brutality, and very little brains. Mind you, the same could be said for most of Shuggie's guys. He didn't hire them for their intellect or scintillating conversational skills. He hired them so they could hurt people.

"What?" the grunt in the doorway asked.

Heather produced her police ID and showed it to him. He didn't acknowledge it, though, which suggested either he knew exactly who she was, or he really didn't care.

"You got a warrant?" he asked with a weariness that implied he'd asked this same question a number of times before.

"No," Heather admitted.

"Well, fuck off, then."

He started to close the door, but Heather jammed her foot against it, stopping it shutting all the way. If he'd really wanted to, he could've easily forced it closed, but not without doing some damage.

He might've been as thick as mince, but even he clearly understood that breaking the bones of a Police Scotland detective inspector was unlikely to end well for him.

"Shuggie!" Heather bellowed, loud enough for everyone inside to hear. "You going to get this fuckwit out of my way?"

She couldn't quite make out the grunted response, but the guy in the doorway clearly heard it, and knew better than to argue. He stepped aside, letting the door swing all the way open, and glowered at her as she entered.

"Cheers, sweetheart," she said, winking up at him. "Coffee. Black. No sugar. There's a good lad."

Leaving the henchman fuming silently in her wake, Heather marched along the short entrance corridor, rapped the snout of the fibreglass pig standing guard at the foot of the stairs, then pushed through the second set of doors and into the heart of Shuggie Cowan's inner sanctum.

FOURTEEN

AS SHE STEPPED through the inner doors, the first thing she saw—besides the congealing mass of Cowan himself—was the weaponry. It had been gathered in the corner and piled up on the table next to the one Shuggie sat at, presumably in anticipation of his arrival.

They'd been sensible enough to avoid anything she could immediately arrest them for. There were no blades or firearms, just an assortment of wooden bats and short lengths of metal piping, alongside what looked like a blowtorch or welder's kit.

Add in the ropes and the petrol canisters, and it looked like Shuggie was planning quite the party.

"This is private property. You've got no business here," Shuggie told her. He snapped his fingers a few times, drawing her attention away from his stockpile. "What the fuck do you want?"

"I wanted to see what you were up to," Heather replied.

She suddenly sensed the presence of a man standing on her right. He was as hulking as the one who'd answered the door, but looked even less intelligent, if such a thing was even possible.

He loomed deliberately over her, his features arranging themselves into a pantomime scowl as he cracked his knuckles one by one.

"The fuck's this dopey-looking tub of shite trying to prove?"

Heather asked Shuggie, jerking her head in the henchman's direction.

Shuggie sighed, and shot his minion a scathing look. "Cut it out, son. You're embarrassing yourself."

The brute muttered an apology to his boss, then slunk across to the next table and started tucking baseball bats under his arm.

"Sorry about that, Detective Inspector. Can't get the help these days," Shuggie said. He grinned, his tongue flicking across the point of one canine tooth. "Not like in the old days. I had some good lads working for me then. Proper dependable boys." He shrugged. The grin was still fixed there, still taunting her. "Long as you knew how to motivate them."

Heather's fingernails curled so tightly into her palms she would've sworn she drew blood.

"What are you doing, Shuggie?" she asked, indicating the cache of weapons with a sweep of a hand. "What the hell's all this?"

"You know full well what it is. And you know what it's for," Shuggie replied. His smile was gone, replaced by something cold and cruel.

He sat back as the henchman who'd answered the door placed a glass of whisky on the table in front of him.

"No sign of that coffee yet?" Heather said, but the thug had already retreated behind the bar, and didn't so much as acknowledge the question. An only marginally smaller man was standing back there, too, cleaning glasses in silence.

"You knew about him, didn't you?" Shuggie intoned. He raised the glass to his lips, but didn't yet drink. "The boyfriend. That little bastard, Conn Byrne. You knew about him and Paula."

Shit.

The pub's exposed floorboards creaked beneath Heather's feet as she shifted her weight from one to the other.

"His name came up," she admitted. "But—"

"But you didn't have the common fucking decency to tell me." Shuggie raised an index finger and tick-tocked it back and forth like he was reprimanding a naughty child.

"Because I knew you'd do something like this," Heather said.

Her gaze flitted over to the blow torch, then returned to Cowan just as he knocked back his whisky. "Conn's a wee knob, but he's just a daft kid."

"No. Not true. He's twenty-one," Shuggie corrected. "That makes him an adult. An adult who's been merrily fucking my fifteen-year-old granddaughter."

"We don't know that," Heather reasoned. "It's all just rumour and hearsay. That's all. I haven't been able to talk to him."

"Don't worry about it. No need. Because I'm going to talk to him," Shuggie said. He burped, then ran the back of his hand across his bloated, frog-like lips. "Him and me, we're going to have a long, drawn-out conversation that's eventually going to end with him telling me where my Paula is. Just two grown men having ourselves a chat. Nothing for you to get involved with."

"If I thought that's all it was, and that you weren't planning on peeling the skin off him, then I might be tempted to let you," Heather said.

Shuggie laughed at that. It was a dry, mirthless croak of a thing that shook his belly and wobbled his jowls.

"Let me? I don't need you to *let me* do anything, Detective Inspector," he said. "If I want to do something, then I do it, and there's fuck all you can do to stop me."

He rose to his feet. He was nowhere near the height of his men and had only a fraction of their strength, and yet when he stood face to face with her, Heather found him infinitely more terrifying.

"I mean, let's be honest here, Heather. It's not like you haven't tried before. So, you away and take the afternoon off. Have a drink on me. Have a few, in fact." He leaned in closer, and his voice was a syrupy whisper that oozed into her ear. "It'll be just one more secret to add to our pile."

He strode directly forwards, headed for the door, forcing her to step out of his path. She could still smell the odour of his breath—something garlicky he'd eaten for lunch, then the fiery tang of the single malt he'd just thrown back.

Heather watched as his two henchmen finished gathering up the weapons. There were a lot of them for three men. Far too many.

Just as the thought struck her, she heard movement upstairs. There were a couple of pool tables up there and a second smaller bar. From the creaking of the floorboards, it sounded like there were a number of large men now moving towards the stairs.

This wasn't just about torturing Conn Byrne. This was something bigger.

"I could arrest you," Heather said.

She tried to inject enough authority into her voice to make Cowan at least take the threat seriously. From the way he laughed it off, though, she'd clearly failed.

"Like I said, talk to Adam," Shuggie told her, shooting a look at the barman. "Have a few drinks and a Shepherd's Pie. On the house."

"Where is he, Shuggie?" Heather demanded—a final desperate gambit in an attempt to stop all this escalating any further. "Tell me where he is, and I'll talk to him. I'll find out what he knows. If he knows where Paula is, I'll get him to tell me."

She tried to get in front of him, but his two goons blocked her path with their bulk. Out in the corridor, half a dozen equally imposing figures arrived at the bottom of the stairs and stood, heads lowered and hands crossed in front of them, waiting for their boss to pass.

"I can sort all this, Shuggie. I can fix everything if you tell me where he is," the DI insisted. "I'm your best chance of getting Paula back. She could be back home. Today. Just tell me where to find Conn Byrne."

Shuggie stopped so abruptly that it took the men flanking him two full paces to realise he was no longer between them. He turned to Heather, and she heard the rasping sound as he scraped his top teeth up and down on the stubble below his bottom lip.

"Adam," he eventually said.

The barman looked up from the glass he was polishing. "Yeah, Mr Cowan?"

"Make sure you stick Heather's bill on my tab. Whatever she wants."

"No bother, Mr Cowan," Adam replied.

The inner doors were pulled open by two of the guys on the

other side and Shuggie walked straight through, with the two henchmen who'd been flanking him now falling into step behind, stopping Heather getting any closer.

She wasn't going to give up that easily, though. She followed them outside, where a couple of older model Range Rovers sat idling in the road right outside the pub.

"Fine. If you won't tell me where you're going, I'll just follow you," Heather announced, fishing out her keys and heading for her car. "And I'll have backup with me, too, so if you think you can just…"

She lost the thread of what she was saying when she saw the state of the Audi. It sat low on the rims of its alloy wheels, the rubber of her tyres slashed to pieces.

"That sly, fat, fucking… *Shuggie!*" she bellowed, turning back to the Range Rovers. Shuggie hesitated halfway inside the back of one of the vehicles just long enough to give her a smile and a wave.

Then, he hauled his bulk inside and pulled the door shut just as both cars went roaring off on the hunt for Conn Byrne.

She shouted a long, drawn-out, "Bastard!" after the vehicles, then whipped out her phone, opened the contacts app, and scrolled through her list of scallywags and scumbags until she found the name she was looking for.

Conn's grandmother answered on the third ring. Her voice still had the same raw-sounding rasp, but there was a note of worry to it now. Big Aggie McQueen was scared.

"Aggie, it's DI Filson. Where is he? Where's Conn?" Heather demanded, marching back in the direction of the *Pig & Bicycle*.

"I don't… I'm no' sure," the older woman replied. "Why does everyone keep asking me that?"

"Who else has been asking? Shuggie's guys? Has one of them been asking about Conn?"

The silence from the other end of the line confirmed that the guess was bang on.

"Right, well he knows, Aggie. Wherever Conn is, Shuggie knows, and he's on his way to him now."

"I don't know, hen, I swear! If I knew, I'd tell you, I would. I know you wouldn't hurt him."

"Well, *think*, Aggie!" Heather barked. "Because Shuggie's got a lot of weapons, and a lot of guys, and…"

Heather stopped suddenly, sending salty slush spraying along the pavement.

A lot of weapons.

A lot of guys.

She knew then exactly where the bastard was going.

Shuggie Cowan was going to war.

"Jesus. The Russian."

She hung up the phone before Big Aggie could say any more, and went marching back into the pub.

Adam the barman looked up from what appeared to be the same glass he'd been cleaning for the past several minutes as Heather stormed in through the inner doors.

"You. Call me a bloody taxi," she ordered. She jabbed a finger at him. "And just to be clear, I'll be charging it to the staff account."

FIFTEEN

KARINA NOVIKOV RAN her operation from a storage unit business on Lawmoor Street on the south side of the Clyde. This was a known fact. Unfortunately, it was not yet a provable one.

Rumour had it that, while back in Russia, Novikov had ties to the KGB. Some whispers even suggested she'd once been connected to Putin himself, but that she'd fallen out of his favour and had been forced into exile.

It was said that she'd been a gymnast back in the eighties, and had then gone on to train some of Russia's Olympic hopefuls over the following decade, until a doping scandal had led to the deaths of three girls in her care.

All of that could have been true, or none of it. When it came to scandalous rumours, the Russian had them swarming around her like flies.

Moscow's loss had been Scotland's loss, also. Almost as soon as she'd settled in Glasgow, Novikov had started to make her mark. Often, the mark in question was a long, ragged scar made on the faces of anyone who challenged her, or got in her way.

Her rise up the Arsehole Charts had been nothing short of meteoric. She'd bought an existing storage business—the seller had agreed a deal far below its market value, and was presumably allowed to keep his bollocks as a result—and had begun recruiting all manner of local scallywags and vagabonds to work alongside her growing number of Russian and former Soviet bloc employees.

That had barely been two years ago. Now, she owned four other storage facilities, three laundrettes, two garages, and a number of other businesses all across the central belt, including quite a nice little shortbread shop in Cowdenbeath.

Shuggie Cowan had been a permanent fixture on the Arsehole Charts for a couple of decades, even after he'd briefly retired and handed the whole operation over to his nephew, Frankie, who was now missing, presumed dead.

But, while he was the same bastard as always, Shuggie didn't have the same ambition that he used to. He was knocking on now. He didn't have the same drive. Or maybe he did, but for different things.

Karina Novikov was no spring chicken either. Officially, she was in her late fifties, but Heather suspected she was older still. She had all the benefits of experience, but also the burning ambition of someone half her age. And that made her dangerous.

Well, that and her money, connections, private army, and willingness to do harm.

The Range Rovers were parked up outside when Heather pulled up in the taxi. Clearly, Shuggie had gone marching right in through the front door, the cocky bastard.

After checking to make sure the fare was going on the pub's staff account, Heather handed the driver five quid as a tip, alongside one of her business cards. He'd run a red light for her, after all, after she'd promised to get him off any charges or fines he might find himself on the receiving end of.

"You need me to hang about?" he asked.

"No, you're fine," she told him, then she immediately reconsidered. "In fact, aye. Stay there. Keep the meter running. If I'm not out in forty-five minutes, or if you hear things kicking off in there, call the landline number on that card. Give them my name. Tell them to send everyone."

The driver's forehead creased as he looked down at the card. "Everyone?"

"Aye. Everyone," Heather confirmed. Then, she shoved her

hands in her pockets, and set off to stop a war before it could begin.

———

The front door of the building led into a small public-facing reception area. It was here that the legitimate business of running a storage company was carried out—the bookings-in, and the checkings-out. All the day-to-day paperwork, and the tracking of what was being stored where, and by whom.

Usually, there'd be a member of staff sitting behind the desk. The last time Heather had popped in, it had been a willowy twenty-year-old Russian girl with smouldering, model-like good looks and a sneeringly condescending attitude that had very much been encouraging Heather to kill herself.

Now, the reception was empty, the single chair rolled all the way to the back wall, as if someone had stood up in a hurry.

The door behind the desk, which usually remained locked at all times, now stood ajar. This was good news in that it made life much easier for Heather, but it didn't bode well for what she might find waiting for her inside.

Things sounded calm, at least. She couldn't hear the din of battle, the clashing of weapons, or the piercing screams of the dying as she approached the door. It all sounded suspiciously silent, in fact.

Maybe she was too late. Maybe they'd all already killed each other.

Maybe it wouldn't be so bad if they had.

For better or worse, they were all upright when she nudged open the door and stepped through into the hangar-like warehouse. Both sides stood facing each other between the rows and rows of storage crates, all tooled up and ready for battle, but nobody yet making the first move.

Shuggie's guys had their backs to her when she entered, not one of them having enough sense to keep an eye on the door. They carried their bats and iron pipes, but kept them low at their sides, so as not to provoke the fifteen or sixteen men with knives and machetes, who very clearly had them outnumbered and outmatched.

The two key players in it all—Shuggie and the Russian—were nowhere to be seen.

"Alright, lads? What's the story here?" Heather called, announcing her arrival. "Another *West Side Story* remake, is it? When does all the dancing start?"

Half of Shuggie's guys turned to look at her, the others still facing front, warily eyeing their opponents.

"Oh, thank fuck," she heard one of them mutter, and she let out a short, sharp laugh that rang out through the crate stacks.

"Oh no, you're on your own with this one, pal," she said. "You brought this on yourself. I'm not here to save anyone from a shit-storm of their own making."

She strolled into the space between both sides, counting up the numbers, sizing up the risk. Confidence was key in situations like this. It was like a magic trick. Act like you were in charge, and more often than not, they'd buy it. They wouldn't challenge you.

Show even a suggestion of fear, though, and you were screwed. Let them see you were afraid, and the curtain was lifted, the trick was revealed, and there was a strong likelihood of you finding yourself sawn in half or otherwise disappeared.

Fortunately, when it came to hiding her fear, Heather had a life-time of practice.

"Is it just me, or is it quite homoerotic in here?" she asked, turning on the spot to address both sides. "All you big beefy boys with your weapons. Is testosterone flammable, do we know? Because if so, nobody light a match for God's sake, or this place'll go up like the fucking Hindenburg."

She looked around at their stony faces, then shrugged.

"No? I thought it was quite funny," she said. "Maybe too poor taste for you guys." She sniffed, wiped at her nose with the back of her hand, then gestured around at the storage facility. "So, your bosses. Where are they, then?"

She studied them, her eyebrows raised, waiting for someone to offer up an answer. When they didn't, she sighed and tapped her watch.

"Come on, lads, hurry up, eh? I've got backup on the way. I'd rather we sorted this out before fifty guys in uniform swarm this place and start asking questions about all those big shiny knives of yours."

Nobody answered.

Nobody moved, other than to tighten their grip on the handle of their weapons.

"Fair enough. Suit yourself. I'll try this way," Heather said. She walked straight for the line of Russians, heading for a door behind them.

As she passed, a hand caught her upper arm, the fingers gripping her like a vice.

She looked down at the machete the man was holding, then up into his gap-toothed, dark-eyed scowl.

Her pulse quickened and her face went hot as panic flared up inside her.

She stamped it back down before the bastard had a chance to notice.

"I'd take your hand off me, pal, or the handle of that knife's going to be sticking out of you like a tail."

His sneer widened, splitting his mouth open into a grin. He wasn't buying it. He could see right through her.

She held his gaze. It was all she could do. Saying more would only weaken her position. Trying to pull her arm free would remind him how much stronger he was. How powerless she was against him.

And so, she stared. Not menacingly—that would be too obvious, and would get her nowhere—but in a way that suggested she was rapidly becoming bored by this encounter.

His grip tightened, both on her arm, and on the handle of his machete. The tips of his fingers pressed into her flesh, hurting her even through the leather of her jacket.

She felt the fear stirring inside her, bubbling up, rising rapidly towards the surface. If he hadn't already spotted it, then he'd see it any second. They all would. The whole house of cards was about to come crashing down around her.

And then came the miracle.

Somewhere, off in the middle distance, a siren wailed. It wasn't a police car but an ambulance, she thought, although the crashing of her heartbeat made it difficult to say for sure.

Whatever it was, the effect was instantaneous on the man holding her. Suddenly, she was no longer a lone woman in a lion's den. She was part of something much bigger, and the cavalry was on the way.

He released his grip on her arm. She fought to keep her voice steady.

"Wise choice," she said. Then, before the siren could fade away, she pointed to the door ahead of her. "This way, I'm guessing?"

Nobody moved to block her way. She stopped at the door just long enough to shoot a warning look back over her shoulder.

"If I were you, I'd stash those things, sharpish," she warned. "Wouldn't want you all getting lifted before you get a chance to do your big musical finale."

She grinned at them, all bluff and bluster again, then rapped on the door, announced her arrival with a loud, "Knock, knock!" and pushed onwards into the room beyond.

SIXTEEN

CONN BYRNE WASN'T DEAD, much as he might have wished otherwise.

He lay curled up on the floor in the corner of a dark, windowless office that favoured function over style, and eschewed heating altogether. His arms were wrapped over his head, elbows tucked into his chest, protecting himself from the beating that Heather had clearly just interrupted.

Shuggie Cowan stood over him, his bear-like paw gripping a leather belt he held raised above his head. He was breathing heavily, his teeth gritted, the veins on his forehead standing out like knots of blue wool.

Behind a desk on the other side of the room, Karina Novikov sipped from a dainty cup. The scents of lemon and ginger wafted through the air, rising with the steam from the herbal tea.

She was dressed in a velour tracksuit—cream, with white piping down the arms and legs. It was a little short in the sleeves, and elasticated around the cuffs, so several inches of her bony wrists were exposed. She wore a watch on each one, a dainty gold thing on the left, and a chunky smartwatch on the right.

Her hair was long and silver, and cascaded over her shoulders like twin waterfalls. Her fringe had been cut savagely straight to just above her eyebrows, presumably by a stylist who had immediately been taken out the back and shot.

Her chair was angled so she could watch the beating that Shuggie had been dishing out. Both of them turned to look as Heather entered, Cowan's face immediately twisting up with rage.

"What the fuck are you doing here?" he demanded.

"Stopping an assault, by the looks of things," Heather told him.

"That's what you fucking think. Out. Go on, fuck off. Leave this little piece of shit to me."

He stuck the boot into the whimpering lad on the floor. Conn hissed with pain, and tightened the protective shell of his arms around himself.

"Alright, that's it, you're under arrest," Heather announced.

"Under arrest? Me?" Shuggie laughed. "Oh, fucking grow up!"

His smile fell away when she took out her handcuffs. "Aggravated assault. I'd say with intent to cause permanent damage or disfigurement. With your history, Shuggie, that's a five-stretch, easy. And a lot of digging around in your dirty laundry. Both of you, in fact."

She reached a hand across the desk for Novikov to shake, but the Russian just sipped her tea in silence.

"Nice to finally meet you, by the way. Heard a lot about you. Detective Inspector Heather Filson. Maybe you've heard of me, too?"

The Russian considered her impassively for a few seconds, then raised her shoulder a fraction of an inch in a lacklustre shrug. "Maybe," she said.

It didn't feel like a wry, cryptic response, or even a deliberate burn. Instead, Heather got the impression that the woman genuinely couldn't recall if the DI's name had ever come up. And, if it had, it clearly hadn't left any impact.

"Fair enough. Well, just to be clear, you're under arrest, too, as an accessory to…" She waved vaguely at Shuggie and Conn. "…all this shit right here. Uniform's going to be here in about… ooh, three to five minutes. I can tell them there's been a misunderstanding, or I can order them to go through this place with a fine-tooth comb."

"You don't have authority. You don't have warrant," Novikov said, unfazed by the threats.

"I don't need a warrant. One of your guys let me in, and I've just witnessed a crime being committed, so we're all good on that front. And as for the authority, love?"

Heather thumped her handcuffs on the desk, then dragged them slowly sideways so the metal carved a deep scratch into the wood.

"Just you fucking watch me."

"You're taking this rapey wee fuck's side over my Paula's?" Shuggie growled. He fired another boot into Conn's side, daring Heather to challenge him on it.

"No, I'm taking my side over yours Shuggie. Like always."

She got between Cowan and the foetal ball that was his victim, then pressed the edge of her cuffs into the centre of Shuggie's chest and pushed him back a step.

"Two things are going to happen next," she said. "First, you're going to phone someone and get new tyres for my car. Good ones, too. Not cheap shite. And have them clean it, too, while they're at it."

"The fuck?" Shuggie muttered.

"*Secondly*," Heather continued, "you two are going to piss off out of here and leave me alone with young Mr Byrne."

At the mention of his name, Conn parted his arms a little, just enough for him to peek out through the gap.

"You're going to give us fifteen minutes, during which time, he's going to tell me everything he knows about Paula's whereabouts."

Shuggie grunted. "Oh, aye? And if he doesn't?"

"If he doesn't..." Heather looked down at the man cowering at her feet. "Then you get him back, I leave, and we all go about our day in whatever way we see fit."

She waited a moment for anyone to voice any objections. When nobody did, she nodded, smiled, and grabbed hold of Conn Byrne by his hair.

"Right, then. Well, if everyone's happy with that," she said.

Conn yelped as she hoisted him up onto his feet. "We'd best get started."

SEVENTEEN

CONN, perhaps unsurprisingly, was suddenly in a talkative mood. His denials were already out of his mouth before Heather had directed him to take a seat. She held a hand up to silence him, and waited until he had stopped babbling before she half-leaned, half-sat on the edge of the desk beside him.

"Right, here's the situation," she told him, folding her arms. "You're fucked. No two ways about it. Shuggie's brought two cars full of bad bastards, a whole selection of heavy blunt objects, and a blow torch."

Conn's eyes darted from her to the door and back again. He squirmed in his seat, like there was something very unwelcome attempting to crawl its way up his arse.

"What's he brought a blow torch for?"

Heather shrugged. "I don't exactly know," she admitted. "But I doubt he's planning on doing some impromptu metalwork, so I'm sure you can use your imagination."

Judging by the look on Conn's face, he could indeed use his imagination. Vividly, too.

"Fuck," he said, the word escaping his bloodied lips as a whimper.

There was a box of tissues on the Russian's desk. Heather picked it up and offered Conn one. He took a small bundle which he used to wipe his eyes, then to dab gingerly at his bleeding nose and split lip.

He was a good-looking guy. Too young for Heather, of course, but she could see why the girls went for him. Usually, he had that Jack-the-Lad sort of charm about him—dangerous, but not *too* dangerous. A ruffian with a heart of gold, and a smile that gullible young lassies would do *anything* to have pointed their way.

Add in that Irish accent of his—more heavy than lilting, but easy listening, all the same—and Heather could see why they were putty in his hands.

They'd be less impressed if they could see him now. With his wide eyes, pale skin, and whole-body tremor, he looked one good jump scare away from shitting himself inside out.

Not that she could blame him, of course. Shuggie Cowan was a scary bastard at the best of times, let alone when he thought you'd murdered a close family member.

She might be able to bluff her way out of the building with Conn right now, but she'd only be delaying the inevitable. Shuggie would catch up with him. No matter where he went, Shuggie would find him.

And then, Shuggie would take him apart, limb by limb, organ by organ.

"The police are coming, though, right?" Conn asked, his bottom lip shaking loose a dribble of bloody spit. "That's what you said. You've got backup coming."

"That's what I said, aye," Heather confirmed. "But I was lying." She checked her watch. "They'll come eventually, but not for a while. Not before our time's up, and Cowan comes back in and… Well, again, I'm sure you can use your imagination."

She leaned back, locking her arms and supporting her weight on the desk with both hands.

"So, the fact of the matter is, Conn, I'm your only chance of getting out of here. In fact, you might be *my* only chance of getting out of here, too. I've stuck my neck out for you, and round here, that usually ends up with someone's head being chopped off." She smiled. It was a thin, resigned sort of thing. "So, let's help each other out, eh? You tell me what I need to know, and I'll see about getting us both out of here."

She held a hand out for him to shake.

"We got a deal?"

He eagerly grabbed the hand and shook it. "I didn't do anything," he said. "I don't know where she is."

Heather took her hand back, then searched her pockets until she found her notebook. She wasn't able to track down her pen, though, so she plucked one from the Russian's desk, scribbled on the corner of the pad to make sure it was working, then turned her attention back to the terrified young man in the chair.

"But you were seeing her, right? Paula? You and her were… what? An item? Winching? *At it*? What do you young people call it these days?"

"We weren't shagging," Conn said. "Honest. She wasn't old enough. I wouldn't."

Heather sighed. "Remember how I said I'm your only chance of getting out of here, Conn? That relies on you not lying to me."

"I'm not lying! I swear! We weren't. We kissed a couple of times, but that was it."

"Pretty young thing like her? Hot-blooded, self-centred wee arsehole like you? You expect me to believe you didn't try your hand?" She checked her watch again. "Eleven minutes until Shuggie comes back in. In case you were wondering."

Conn's face contorted, like the truth was trying to wrestle its way out of him.

"I didn't say I didn't try," he squeaked, his gaze flitting to the door like he might see Shuggie standing there. "But she knocked me back. She wasn't up for it. Said if I liked her I wouldn't try and push her into it."

"And did you? Like her, I mean?"

"Yeah. Yeah, I mean… I suppose I do. She's, like, she's nice and everything."

Heather gave him a nod of encouragement. "But…?"

"But, I mean, it's not like we were serious, or anything. You know? Like, we weren't going to run away together, or anything mad, like."

"You hadn't spoken about anything like that?"

"No! I mean, I've only really known her for a few weeks. We met at the Garage. Bowling, like, not the club. We've just hung out a few times, that's all. I have no idea where she is, like. I swear."

Heather drummed her fingers on the end of the desk, searching his face.

"OK, fine," she said. "Even if I believe you, that's not going to be enough for Shuggie. Nine minutes until he comes back, by the way."

Conn ran his hands through his hair, tears blurring his eyes. He drew in a big, shaky breath, then let it out as a sob.

"I thought she'd look after me, you know? Mrs Novikov. I thought if I came to her and told her what the story was, she'd look after me. Protect me, or whatever."

"But she got straight on the phone to Shuggie, I'm guessing?"

Conn nodded, his bottom lip petted like he was fighting the urge to burst into bubbling, snot-nosed tears.

"I wouldn't take it personally," Heather told him. She leaned in a little closer, sharing a secret. "What you need to remember is that these people, they don't give a flying fuck about anyone but themselves. Especially not the likes of you."

He didn't look too pleased by that, but didn't argue, either. This time, the look he shot at the door was laced with venom.

"I suppose I'm just a pawn to them."

"Christ, no. You're not even that," Heather replied. "You're not even on the chess board, Conn. You're a wee fucking house from *Monopoly*. You're one of the pointy sticks from *Kerplunk!* You're a blank *Scrabble* tile. That's all you are. Aye, you have your uses, but there's plenty more of you kicking around in the box, and those bastards sure as hell aren't going to shed a tear when you fall down the back of the couch. They won't even notice you're gone."

She made a show of tapping her watch.

"Less than seven minutes, Conn. So far, you've given me nothing I can use to get you out of this."

"I wasn't even here," he gasped. "When she went missing, I mean. I wasn't even in town."

"That's a start. Where were you?"

Conn chewed his bottom lip. The bleeding had recently stopped, but the scraping of his teeth started it oozing again.

"I can't tell you."

Heather stared at him, saying nothing. Her face did very little to give away her emotions, beyond a slight flaring of the nostrils and a thinning of the lips.

"Fine," she said, flipping her notebook closed. "Then we're done. I'll give Shuggie a shout."

"No! Wait!" Conn said, holding his hands up to stop her as she rose from the desk. "I just… I'm not supposed to say. I'm not sure it's…"

"What? Legal?"

Conn swallowed, then gave a furtive nod of his head.

"Trust me, pal, getting banged up is the least of your worries right now. If you end up spending the next few months or your life behind bars, that's a dream come true compared to what Cowan's going to do to you," Heather told him. "If there's something you can tell me that proves you weren't here when Paula disappeared, I suggest you spit it out in the next five minutes and twenty-two seconds, or you're going to be drinking your own bollocks through a very narrow straw. And, as much as we both might wish that's an exaggeration, I promise you it isn't"

"Mingey Mouse!"

Heather blinked. She didn't know what she'd been expecting the lad to come out with, but 'Mingey Mouse' hadn't been anywhere on the list of possibilities.

"What the hell is that when it's at home?"

Conn squirmed in his seat again, his cheeks blushing red. "It's not a 'that,' it's a her. It's this, eh, it's this bird. Woman, I mean. Bit older. Fifties. Sixty, maybe. She's got like a… channel."

"A channel?" Heather asked, frowning. Her instinct was to leap straight to 'TV channel' but she stopped herself before she could show her age. "A *YouTube* channel?"

Conn's uncomfortable squirming continued. "Not exactly. On *OnlyFans*."

Heather's frown went into full reverse, her eyebrows climbing up her forehead. "What, the porn thing?"

"It's not just porn!" Conn protested. "There's all sorts of stuff on there. I think there's, like, bakers, and, I don't know, mechanics, and stuff."

"Aye, but I'm assuming someone calling themselves 'Mingey Mouse' isn't making scones or changing a fucking carburettor."

"Yeah. No. She is one of the ones doing porn, right enough," Conn confirmed. "Proper dirty stuff, too. She's an ex-prostitute, I think. And she, eh, she…"

He swallowed, now wriggling so much Heather was concerned the friction might ignite the chair beneath him and burn the whole place to the ground.

"She what?"

"She, um, she lets people *volunteer*. You know, like… to appear in her videos."

"Appear in them? Jesus. I'm guessing they're not being interviewed?"

Conn shook his head. "No, they're getting humped."

Heather sighed. "I guessed that, aye."

"She puts on these mouse ears and a spotty dress. You know, like Minnie?" Conn said.

"Bloody hell." Heather winced, then she asked the only question that immediately occurred to her. "What the fuck does she do that for?"

"I don't know, she's never really explained it in any of her videos. It's just sort of her thing. Like her gimmick, you know?" Conn hesitated, like he was wary of giving away the next nugget of info. "She's got the big white hands, too. You know the ones. With the three fingers. Aye, they're gloves, I mean, they're not her actual hands. She's not, like, a mutant, or whatever."

Heather ran a hand through her hair, quietly despairing at the state of the human race. "How is that a thing?" she wondered aloud. "Who the fuck is getting themselves involved with that sort of…"

She realised then where all this was going.

"Jesus! You're not telling me you were…?"

"I didn't pay her, or nothing!" Conn yelped, like this was the bit Heather might be concerned about. "It wasn't a prozzie thing. And she didn't pay me, either!"

"I don't give a shit who did or didn't pay who," Heather shot back at him. "You're a dirty wee bastard."

Conn didn't argue. Instead, he just nodded in silence, his face a mask of deeply ingrained regret.

"I thought it'd be a laugh, you know? But then she does the squeaky voice, and everything, while she's trying to jam a big cartoon thumb up me arse, and the joke sort of wore off quite quickly, like." He pursed his lips, like he was fighting the urge to throw up. "Frankly, if I was *Disney*, I'd be suing the shite out of her."

"Three and a half minutes," Heather said, tapping her watch.

"She live-streamed it!" Conn ejected. "The whole thing! Start to finish. She put it out live for all her subscribers."

He buried his face in his hands for a moment, then ran them up through his hair.

"I thought it'd be funny, like, but I didn't think it through. I mean, anyone could've been watching. My gran might've seen it!"

"Why the hell would your gran be watching Mingey Mouse?" Heather asked, then she decided she didn't want to know. "Doesn't matter. Forget it. Are you saying this was the night Paula disappeared?"

"Yes! Exactly!" Conn cried. "She's in Stirling. I was away from about one in the afternoon, and didn't get back until the next day."

Heather raised an eyebrow. "Next day?"

Conn lowered his head, his fingers twisting together. "She, eh, she wanted to shoot some bonus content the following morning. You know, extra stuff for, like, her premium subscribers?"

"Fucking hell!" Heather rose to her feet again, shaking her head like she could shake away any mental pictures before they had a chance to form. "And she'll back you up on this, will she? She'll be able to verify you were there?"

"Yes!" Conn replied. Then, a little less enthusiastically. "Maybe. I mean, I think so. To be honest, she seemed pretty wasted. I think she sort of fell asleep at one point."

Heather massaged her temples. She wasn't in the mood for this right now. Then again, she was struggling to think of a time when she would be.

"One minute, Conn. One minute, and Shuggie Cowan's barging in here with his baseball bats and his blow torch, and there's nothing I can do to stop him."

"No, but that's the thing. You don't have to ask her," Conn replied. He tried to force a smile, but it was ninety percent grimace. "I can prove I was there."

————

Shuggie Cowan sat in front of the laptop, picking idly at the leather of his cowboy boots while wearing an expression that was pitched halfway between confusion and disbelief.

"What the fuck is this now?" he muttered as, on screen, a fifty-eight-year-old woman in a Minnie Mouse costume tried to give a three-fingered, giant-gloved handjob to an uncomfortable-looking naked Irishman.

"Oh, gee! You like that?" squeaked a voice from the speakers. "Haha! I bet that feels real good, pal!"

Shuggie, Heather, Karina Novikov, one of Shuggie's henchmen, and three Russian goons all turned at the same time to look at Conn, who stood awkwardly in the corner, his cheeks burning, pointedly refusing to make eye contact with anyone.

"Minnie Mouse," announced Novikov, in case anyone had failed to pick up on the similarities. She shrugged, then added, "I prefer *Winnie Pooh*," like she was passing judgement on the actual *Disney* characters, and not on some middle-aged ex-prostitute in a homemade costume.

"Don't give the wee bastard any ideas!" Cowan seethed. "Winnie the Pooh's a fucking beloved childhood bear. This…?" He gestured to the screen, his face contorting in distaste. "I mean, I ran an erotic entertainment video business for years, but this is just fucking weird. What's this bird's name again?"

"Minnie Mouse," Novikov said again.

"Aye, but it's no' the actual Minnie Mouse, though, is it?"

Cowan fired back. "Minnie Mouse hasnae got a face like a bulldog and a fanny like a bag of old mince."

"Well, I reckon that's between her and Mickey," Heather said. She leaned over and tapped the screen, indicating the information below the video. "It's timestamped, look. Went out live. When Paula went missing, Conn was being molested on camera by Mingey Mouse."

"*Minnie* Mouse," the Russian corrected.

Shuggie drew in a sharp, angry breath. He turned suddenly, as if going to take a swing at her. "It's no' fucking Minnie Mouse! Look at her! Minnie Mouse is a cartoon rodent, no' a clarty old cock-eyed tart with tits swinging down like the bars of a fucking trapeze!"

"She's, eh, she's not actually cock-eyed," volunteered Conn. "She, um, she just puts that on for the camera sometimes to make it look like she's, you know, like, enjoying herself."

Once again, everyone turned to look at him. He cleared his throat, crossed his hands in front of his groin, then went back to staring at the floor.

"This means nothing. This means fuck all," Cowan barked, pointing to the screen. He rose suddenly from his chair and rounded on Conn. "This little fuck could still know something. He could still know where she is!"

"I don't! I don't, Mr Cowan, I swear," the young Irishman protested. "I haven't seen her in days. I haven't heard from her. We barely knew each other, honest!"

"We've run the phone records, Shuggie. There's no sign of them being in touch any time leading up to her going missing, or afterwards," Heather said, putting herself between the ageing hardman and his would-be victim.

It was a bluff. She hoped her reserves of confidence held up enough to pull it off.

The phone records would've been requested by now, but if they'd come back, she was yet to lay eyes on them.

"That's true! Look, you can have a look!" Conn yelped, thrusting his phone in Shuggie's direction. "Check it. You'll see for yourself."

Shuggie stood scowling at him, not yet touching the phone. The silence was punctuated by some groans from the laptop, and a high-pitched, slightly slurred cry of, "I'm simply *ear-resistible*!"

"Turn that shite off," Shuggie instructed. "I've seen enough."

Sitting at the desk, Novikov smirked. "Oh, and here was I just starting to enjoy. Story *very* gripping."

Despite the protest, she shut the laptop lid, then reached into a box on her desk and took out a short, stubby cigar. She lit it, waved it like she was banishing evil spirits with it, then sat back and smoked while she watched the events unfolding before her.

The phone was still being offered out. Shuggie nodded to the lackey who'd been standing quietly in the corner, and he swooped in to take Conn's mobile.

Silence continued to hang in the air alongside the coiling trail of smoke from the Russian's cigar. All eyes watched as Shuggie's henchman tapped and scrolled through the contents of Conn's phone.

After what felt like an eternity, he looked up and shrugged. "Not much back and forth between them. Just stuff about how school's going. Some shite about his gran."

"That's it?" Shuggie demanded.

"Well, there was one thing…"

Heather caught herself holding her breath as the lackey showed Shuggie something on the screen. Cowan's eyes darted left and right as they read something, then his eyes became hooded, and his mouth formed a thin trembling line.

"What is it? What does it say?" Heather asked.

Shuggie snatched the phone, quite violently poked at the screen, then tossed it back to Conn, who had to frantically juggle to stop it smashing on the floor.

"What the hell was that? What did you just delete?" Heather was no longer asking, but demanding.

"Nothing. Nothing to do with you," Cowan growled, and the look he fired at her made it clear she'd get nothing more out of him.

He turned to the Russian, and nodded at her, dipping his head so low it stopped just short of becoming a bow.

"Thanks for calling me in. I appreciate it," he intoned.

Behind her desk, Karina Novikov shrugged, then dismissed his gratitude with a wave of her cigar.

"It is family matter," she said. "Missing child. What monster would I be if I do not try to help?"

She held out her cigar, and one of her employees appeared at her side with an ashtray for her to stub it out. Then, she cracked her knuckles, leaned back in her chair, and smiled up at the other occupants of the room.

"Now, please excuse," she said, lifting the lid of the laptop. The sound of Conn's grunting immediately rang out again. "I wish to see how the story ends…"

———

The taxi driver had his phone in his hand when Heather emerged from the warehouse with Conn, his thumb hovering over the first of the digits of the number on the DI's card.

"You're alive, then," he remarked, when she pulled open the back door and shoved the young Irish lad inside. "Was starting to get worried."

"Aye, so far so good. Thanks for waiting," Heather said. "You kept the meter running, aye?"

"Oh, aye. Don't you worry. It's been ticking away nonstop."

Heather pulled the door shut behind her and unfolded a backwards-facing seat so she was staring directly at Conn.

"Right, take me back to the pub where you got me, then you can drop this wee bastard back home."

"No bother, hen," the driver called back. He indicated, made more of a show of checking his mirrors than he usually would, then pulled away from the kerb.

"You're not arresting me?" Conn asked. "I can go home?"

"Why the hell would I arrest you?" Heather asked. "I mean, besides the massive list of things I'm sure you're wanted for questioning on? Right now, I'm only interested in finding Paula, and if you can't help me with that, you're no use to me. And besides, that footage of you being online is probably punishment enough for most things you've done."

She watched Novikov's building growing smaller through the back windscreen. Shuggie and his guys were climbing back into their Range Rovers. The war she'd feared had, thankfully, not come to anything.

Not yet, at least. But regardless of the pleasantries that had been exchanged this afternoon, Heather knew that the day was coming. The war hadn't been averted, just postponed.

"One thing you can help me with, though," she said, turning her attention back to Conn. "I want you to look very carefully at your phone. I want you to think very hard. And then, I want you to tell me *exactly* what Shuggie Cowan deleted from it."

EIGHTEEN

"SHE HATES HIM!"

Snecky finished pulling on his jacket and very deliberately pulled up the zip, making it clear his intention to leave the office. He was a big believer in sticking to schedules, particularly the one that involved him knocking off as close to five o'clock as possible.

DC Simon Wolfe was hanging around beside him, his own much more expensive jacket already fastened right up to the neck.

Simon came from money. A lot of it, too. He'd been privately educated at Gordonstoun, a school so posh that, during his time there, even the then-Prince Charles had felt looked down upon.

He'd transferred with Snecky from Aberdeen, and seemed determined to attend to the DCI's every need and whim. Simon wasn't so much a 'yes man' as a 'yes sir, of course, sir, whatever you need, sir' man. He'd done nothing to endear himself to Heather since his arrival, and quite a lot to get in her bad books.

He spoke like he had a half-chewed toffee stuck to the roof of his mouth, and whenever he laughed at Snecky's shite patter—which was often—he brayed through his long, straight nose.

Only DS Brompton was sitting at his desk. Marty brightened at the sight of her, and it was immediately clear that he'd been stuck in the office with these two arseholes all afternoon.

"What?" Snecky asked. He gave his zip another tug, in case she hadn't noticed he was getting ready to leave.

"Shuggie Cowan. She hates him!" Heather replied, tearing off her own jacket and tossing it onto her chair.

"Who hates him?" Snecky asked, throwing in an impatient sigh for good measure.

"Paula! Who else would I be talking about?" Heather cried. "She can't stand him. Doesn't want anything to do with him. And doesn't want her mum and wee sister to have anything to do with him, either!"

"Whoa!" Marty jumped to his feet, immediately grasping the significance. "That's huge!"

"I know! He finds his family. Finds the daughter he always wanted."

"Doting wee granddaughter," Marty added.

"And then this lippy teenager gets in his way and threatens to spoil it all!" Heather finished.

"He wouldn't like that," Marty said.

"He'd be raging," Heather agreed. "No saying what he'd do."

Snecky had been holding up his hands for silence during most of the exchange, but both the DS and DI had completely ignored him, forcing him to interject.

"Hold on, hold on, let's not get carried away," he declared. He puckered up his face, sucked air in through his teeth, then shook his head. "I'm not buying it."

Heather and Marty both turned to him wearing almost matching frowns.

"What do you mean?" Heather demanded.

"I mean… It's a bit obvious, isn't it?" Snecky ventured.

"It is," agreed DC Wolfe. "It's *very* obvious."

"The tough guy Glasgow gangster," Snecky continued, adding an almost comical emphasis to the words. "Killing his own granddaughter?"

"I didn't say she was dead," Heather shot back.

Snecky rolled his eyes. "Whatever. He'd know we'd suspect him. He knows he wouldn't get away with it."

"You don't know Shuggie like I do," Heather told him. "There's nothing that bastard doesn't think he can get away with. And he's usually right, too. But not this time. This time, he's going down."

DC Wolfe let out a juvenile snigger. "Dirty," he remarked.

Heather rounded on him. "What?"

"You know. *Going down*. Like…" He pointed to his crotch area and smirked.

"Oh, fucking grow up," Heather told him.

"Hey!" Snecky held his hands up again. "You can't talk like that to Detective Constable Wolfe. Or to anyone. Not in this office."

A red filter descended over Heather's eyes as her blood began to boil in her veins. She clenched her fists. It was an attempt to stop herself lamping either one of the two recent transfers, but Snecky spotted it and took it to mean the opposite.

"Right. Get in the corner," he instructed, pointing to a desk facing the furthest wall. "That's a threat of violence. I'm not having that."

"What? Don't be so bloody ridiculous! You'll know when I'm threatening violence, because you'll be carrying your nose home in a fucking paper hankie."

"Right! That's twice!" Snecky cried. "We all heard it. I'd have thought *Detective Inspector* Filson would've learned her lesson from her recent demotion, but it seems that's not the case!"

Heather had just decided that she was willing to give up her career for the sake of one joyous moment of explosive violence when the door behind her swung open, revealing Detective Superintendent Gordon Mackenzie.

"Everything alright?" the Gozer asked. He, too, had his jacket on, and must've overheard the argument as he was passing the door. "Sounds like a bit of a stramash going on in here."

"Nothing I can't handle, sir," Snecky said, adopting the much more 'proper' voice he used when addressing a more senior officer. "We were just discussing DI Filson's attitude."

Heather scowled. "I thought we were discussing you being an arsehole?"

"Sir," the Gozer said. He shot her a stern look, but she could've sworn there was a suggestion of a smirk mixed in with it somewhere. "'I thought we were discussing you being an arsehole, *sir*.'"

"Sorry. You're right. Thanks for the catch, sir," Heather said.

Snecky nodded, satisfied that Heather had been put in her place, the dig from the detective superintendent having whooshed right over his head.

"What's the latest?" the Gozer asked. He aimed the question at Heather, but Snecky jumped in before she could answer.

"Nothing much to report yet, sir. No sign of the girl. We're still following up leads. Phone's off and hasn't been used. Bank account not accessed."

"Dead, I reckon," said DC Wolfe. He rocked back on his heels, made a clicking noise with the side of his mouth, then shrugged. "Shame, but it happens, as we all know."

"We don't know she's dead," Heather insisted. "But Shuggie Cowan has reason to want rid of her."

"Oh, God. Here we go," Snecky sighed.

"This again," muttered Wolfe.

Heather shot both men a look like she was about to put them through the window. Fortunately, the Gozer spoke before she had a chance to move.

"Cowan? She's his granddaughter, isn't she?"

"Yes, sir. But she very much doesn't want to be," Heather said. "She texted Conn Byrne to say how much she hated him, and how she wanted him out of all their lives. She'd heard about him, about the things he's done. Didn't want her wee sister growing up with that sort of influence."

"And he knew this, did he? Cowan, I mean?"

"I don't know," Heather admitted. "I mean, he does now. He saw the text. Deleted it from Conn's phone before I could see it."

Snecky snorted and rolled his eyes. "So, you haven't even seen it? You're taking the chief suspect's word for it?"

"Conn's out of the picture," Heather said. "He was away shagging someone the day Paula disappeared."

"Shagging who?" the detective superintendent asked. "Have we spoken to them to verify?"

"Not exactly, sir, no," Heather said. "It was someone calling themselves *Mingey Mouse.*"

"From OnlyFans?" DC Wolfe ejected, the question coming out

before his brain had a chance to engage. He shuffled his feet and cleared his throat. "I think I, eh, I think I heard about that somewhere."

Heather flared her nostrils and shook her head, making her distaste of the man abundantly clear.

"It was live-streamed," Heather explained. "It's up on her channel now. Full video of him and her going at it."

"Conn Byrne? He's that young Irish lad, isn't he?" Marty piped up. He clicked the end of a pen and hovered it above his pad. "What did you say the name of the woman was again?"

"Mingey…" Heather began, then she tutted and pointed at the grinning detective sergeant. "You're a dirty bastard."

"Just keen to review all the available evidence," Marty replied, but he set his pen down again, and leaned back in his chair, looking highly amused at himself.

"Ugh. Gay," DC Wolfe muttered.

"He doesn't mean that in a bad way," Snecky quickly added.

"What? No. No, I don't mean in a bad way," Wolfe said, picking up on the DCI's urgent look. "I mean, people should be able to do what they want. Within reason. Even, you know, like, bumming, or whatever."

"Cheers, mate," Marty said. "We've all been waiting for your permission. It's going to be an absolute arse-fest out there tonight."

Wolfe's body went rigid and his jaw clenched, but he raised both thumbs in the detective sergeant's direction and tried his best to force a smile.

"Anyway," Snecky said, quickly changing the subject. "Even if it's not the boyfriend, there are plenty of other suspects."

"Like who?" Heather asked.

"Like…" Snecky waved a hand a few times, like he was trying to draw inspiration from the very air around him.

"The stepdad," DC Wolfe volunteered.

Snecky clicked his fingers. "The stepdad! Yes! I bet it was the stepdad!"

"And why would it be the stepdad?" Marty demanded.

"Because it usually is," Wolfe said. "Stepdads are notoriously… you know?"

The detective sergeant's chair creaked as he sat forward again. "Notoriously what?"

Snecky tried to intervene. "I think he's just saying—"

"No, no, Detective Chief Inspector," said the Gozer. "I'd like to hear the detective constable's theory. Continue, DC Wolfe. Stepdads are notoriously what?"

Wolfe seemed to shrink a good three inches under the weight of both men's glares. Heather stood in silence, just enjoying the moment. She, unlike DC Wolfe, had the luxury of knowing Marty's and the Gozer's family arrangements, which made the moment all the sweeter.

"I'm just saying that, you know, in cases like these, young girl goes missing, then *statistically*, it's probably the stepdad."

"No it isn't," the Gozer countered.

"Oh. Isn't it?" Wolfe asked, his voice taking on a thin, reedy sort of edge. "I was sure… But they're quite often a bit weird, aren't they?"

"What's that meant to mean?" Marty demanded. "I've got a stepdad."

Wolfe's expression started to suggest this had just proved his point for him, when the Gozer delivered the knockout blow.

"I am a stepdad. Two girls. Are you saying I'm inherently a danger to them, Detective Constable?"

"What? No! No, sir. No, I'm not… I didn't know…"

"OK, so maybe it's not the stepdad," Snecky said, trying to recover the situation.

"What makes you say that?" Heather asked. "We haven't even spoken to him."

"We can't rule him out," Marty agreed.

Snecky let out a groan of exasperation and threw his hands into the air. "I was just trying to… I thought you said it couldn't be him?"

"Nobody said that," Marty replied. "We just said we can't jump to conclusions, and that stepdads aren't inherently evil."

"Fine. Fine, yes, OK." He smoothed down what little was left of his hair, then smiled at the detective superintendent. "Anyway, we were just going to head home, and then come back and kick around this whole Shuggie Cowan theory tomorrow morning. Weren't we guys?"

"Were we fuck," Heather snapped.

Marty gripped onto the arms of his chair, like he was challenging anyone to try getting him out of it. "I wasn't planning going anywhere."

"Oh, well then," the Gozer said. He started to unfasten the buttons of his coat. "Jackets off then, gentlemen. And DC Wolfe, how about you make yourself useful and go stick the kettle on?"

He tossed his coat onto the back of a chair, then shot Heather a sideways look. She couldn't be sure, but she thought there was a wink in there somewhere.

"Looks like we could have a long night ahead of us," the detective superintendent continued. "Although, we'll need to have our game faces on for tomorrow morning."

"Why?" Heather asked. "What's happening tomorrow morning?"

The Gozer rolled a chair out from under a desk, then let out the faintest of middle-aged groans as he dropped into it.

"Well, assuming that Paula doesn't come wandering home during the night," he said, looking around the room. "Someone here'll be joining the family on a TV appeal."

Snecky's hand shot straight up, like the swotty kid at school. "I could do it. I don't mind being on the telly."

"Thank fuck," Heather said. "That's that sorted, then." She tapped the empty mug on her desk, the inside of it turned brown by the stains of coffees past. "Right, Simon, get your finger out your arse. That kettle's not going to boil itself."

NINETEEN

IT WAS after ten by the time Heather made it home. Her Uncle Kenny was pacing around the kitchen when she opened the door, and rushed to hug her before she'd even had a chance to close it again.

"Oh, thank Christ!" he cried. Heather felt the prickle of his beard on her face, and smelled the booze on his breath. "I was starting to think something had happened. You didn't phone."

Heather winced. "Shit. No, sorry. Totally forgot."

"I thought he'd done you in!" Kenny said, releasing her from his bear hug. "Cowan. I thought he'd done away with you, or something. I didn't know what to do!"

Heather smiled and pointed to the bottle of whisky on the kitchen counter. Technically, it was a bottle of mostly air now, with just a couple of inches left at the bottom. There was an empty glass next to it, and another in the sink.

"I think I can see what you did," she said.

Kenny scratched at his beard, looking a little embarrassed. "Eh, aye. Me and your old man might've had a wee dram or two. Just, you know, to settle the nerves."

"You didn't tell him did you?" Heather asked, suddenly on high alert. "You didn't tell him I was going after Cowan?"

"No! Jesus. Of course I didn't," Kenny said, shooting her a look that made her feel guilty for even asking. "But he could tell I was worried about something. He might be losing his marbles, but he's still sharp as a bloody tack when he wants to be. He knew there was something, so I thought a wee bevvy might distract him. Take his mind off it. You know?"

Heather nodded. "Aye. Makes sense." She took the glass from the sink and ran it under the tap. "He's not meant to be drinking on his medication, though."

"Aye, well. I'm no' meant to be drinking on most of mine, either," her uncle replied. He winked, and his smile split his beard wide open. "I've never let that stop me."

"What meds are you on, like?" Heather asked. "You've never said."

Kenny hesitated, but only for a split-second. "The contraceptive pill," he said. "Can't be too careful."

Heather rolled her eyes at him, then unscrewed the cap of the bottle and poured herself a glug of the Scotch. She steered the bottle over Kenny's empty glass, and he tipped her the nod.

"Go on, then. Since you're offering."

"He up in bed?" Heather asked, pouring the drink.

"On the couch. Refused to go up. Said he was staying awake until you got home," Kenny told her. "Then fell asleep about thirty seconds later."

"Shite. Sorry. Again," Heather said. She looked to the door leading out into the hall. "I'll go tuck him in in a minute. Let him know I'm in."

"Slàinte," Kenny said, raising his glass.

Heather clinked hers against his. "Cheers."

They both leaned against the counter and sipped their drinks. Kenny smirked at the way Heather tried to hide her wince as the liquid burned down her throat, but chose not to comment on it.

"Well?" he asked, when it was clear she wasn't about to volunteer any more information.

"Well, what?"

"Cowan! What's happening? What's going on?"

"Oh." Heather wiped her mouth on the back of her hand, then

shrugged. "Don't know. He might be involved in this missing kid case."

Kenny took another drink. "Aye, well," he muttered. "It's no' like he doesn't have past form."

"Yeah."

She felt her uncle's gaze on her as she sipped her whisky. She could guess the questions he wanted to ask, and could sense his struggle to keep them to himself. He knew she couldn't talk about it.

She did, anyway.

"I was convinced. Completely sure of it," she said. "But then, I thought… I don't know. Am I bringing my own baggage into it? Am I so sure it's him because I want it to be him? Because I want him to pay for what he did?"

"I wouldn't blame you. No one would," Kenny reasoned.

"Paula might. Her mum. Her wee sister," Heather shot back. "If I'm too focused on him to see what's really going on, they'd blame me. And they'd be right to."

She knocked back the contents of her glass. The liquid burning down her throat felt like a penance to be paid.

"This is about Paula. It's not about me and Cowan. It's not about Stewie."

The name caught in her throat. She looked over at the whisky bottle, and was disappointed to find it empty. Without a word, Kenny tipped his own glass into hers, and she felt tears pricking at the backs of her eyes.

"Thanks."

"It still sounds to me like he could be behind it," Kenny said. "All personal stuff aside. We know what he's capable of. If you think he's got a reason for doing it, then you owe it to the girl and her family to keep digging until—"

"There was a feather. Under her pillow, there was a feather."

The rest of Kenny's sentence fell away into the gulf of silence that suddenly filled the space between them.

He looked down at his empty glass, clearly regretting his recent display of altruism.

"A feather? That's not… It can't…"

Heather puffed out her cheeks, then let the air escape them in one big puff. "Probably not. Probably just coincidence. Forensics have run it through, but there's nothing on it."

"There you go, then."

"Aye, but *nothing* on it," Heather said. She looked up at her uncle, and saw her own fear reflected in his eyes. "Nothing of Paula's, either. Completely clean. Blank slate."

"It doesn't mean anything," Kenny said.

"No. No, probably not."

"At most, it's some daft bastard playing silly buggers. What do you call them? Copycats?"

"Christ, don't say that," Heather groaned. "I'm not sure which would be worse. But that's unlikely, anyway. The feather thing was never released to the public. Nobody knew about it."

That wasn't quite true, of course. Heather thought back to the call with Ace Wurzel earlier that day. She'd known about the feathers, but had refused to say how, citing 'protecting her journalistic sources' as the reason for keeping shtum.

"Well, it can't be the actual guy, can it?" Kenny said, with a little too much certainty. He glanced down at his glass, avoiding her inquisitive look. "After all these years, I mean? Surely he's long dead?"

"Depends how old he was at the time," Heather reasoned.

Kenny shrugged just one of his broad shoulders. "Suppose so, aye. I just… The thought that that fucker's still out there. That's he got away with it all this time…"

He put the glass to his lips and tipped his head all the way back, trying to get even a drop of leftover alcohol.

Heather watched him, then handed him the glass he'd topped up for her just a few moments before.

He accepted it gratefully, and slung the whole thing back in one quick jerk of his arm.

"What do you remember about it?" she asked. "About what happened?"

"Oh, Christ." Kenny put both glasses in the sink and screwed the top back on the empty whisky bottle before continuing. "Not a lot. Just what your mum and dad told me. I was working in oil and gas and was away at the time. Norway. I only heard after you'd…" He ran a hand down his beard, smoothing the wiry red and silver hair. "After you were safely home. I came back right away. Took me a few days. Press was still hanging around, though, desperate to get a photo of you. So, we snuck you out in my van one night and you all came and stayed at mine until the fuss had died down a bit."

It was his turn to study her face. Over the years, though, she'd become a master at giving nothing away when she didn't want to. Which was pretty much always.

"You don't remember any of it?" he asked, his voice coaxing and gentle.

Heather shook her head, but very slowly, like she was afraid of shaking the memories loose. Afraid of freeing them and having to relive them all over again. She'd been young. Whatever had happened to her, her brain had safely locked it away.

"Just the stories," she said. "It's weird. This huge thing in my life, and I only know about it second hand."

"Probably for the best," Kenny said.

"Aye. Probably," Heather agreed. She scrunched the heels of her hands into her eyes and rubbed them, then let out a long, jovial-sounding sigh that signalled the end of that conversation. "Right. What's your plan?"

"Cycling home," Kenny said. "Snow's just about away, isn't it?"

"Aye, but it's freezing on top, and you're half-pished," Heather said. "You should kip in the spare room tonight."

Kenny's big frame shook as he chuckled. "You're just hoping I get up first and make breakfast."

Heather clapped him on the shoulder. "I thought you were never going to offer," she said. "There's tattie scones on top of the bread bin, and bacon and square sausage in the fridge. If you can find a wee tin of beans in the cupboard somewhere, then so much the better!"

"I knew it, you're a bloody chancer!" Kenny laughed.

TWENTY

UNDER NORMAL CIRCUMSTANCES, Ace generally tried to avoid leaving the house unless she absolutely had to. Today was Sunday, which she tended to spend up in her room, working on her podcast, or adding to her Wonderwall.

She did much the same on Saturdays, although sometimes Ace's protests would fall on deaf ears, and her mum would drag her out to Asda in the afternoon.

The thought of it was generally the worst part. Once she was actually in the supermarket, browsing the aisles, filling the trolley with all the same foods she'd placed in it the last time, it wasn't so bad.

Afterwards, they'd go by the McDonald's across the roundabout, over by the Travelodge, and she'd order her usual—six chicken nuggets, a medium fries, and a large strawberry milkshake.

She'd consume them at home, one after the other—chips, nuggets, shake—fully finishing one before moving on to the next.

It had always been the same meal, the same order, the same pattern. It used to drive her dad mental. So she was told, anyway.

By and large though, on a regular weekend day, Ace would be at home now.

But this was no normal weekend.

Mr Patel had looked disappointed after she'd come into the shop yesterday, browsed through the newspapers, then left without buying anything. Today, she planned to buy a bottle of water and some chewing gum. It wasn't a bloody library, after all, as she was sure she'd heard him muttering as she'd left the shop.

It would be a few days until the local weekly newspapers were published. No doubt, they'd all have the story about Paula splashed on their front pages. It was already big news on their online editions, and Ace wondered if the editors would be hoping for the story to drag on until publication day, or to wrap up with a happy ending before then.

She suspected the former.

There was a bit in the *Sunday Mail* about Paula. Page four. There was a picture of her that had been cropped out of a larger photo. It was a bit grainy, and she wasn't looking at the camera. Surely there were more appropriate pictures of her that her mother could've submitted?

"Social media!" Ace said aloud.

Over at the counter, Mr Patel looked up from the bean cans he was marking with bright yellow 'Reduced' stickers.

"Sorry?" he asked.

His accent was fascinating—an unpredictable blend of Scotland and Pakistan that never seemed to follow the same pattern twice. Ace was usually so fixated on the sounds of it that she often lost track of the words.

Thankfully, he'd only said the one.

"Nothing," she told him.

He grunted, shook his head, and then they both went back to their respective tasks.

The picture must've been taken from Paula's mum's social media. Paula's own was locked down, the contents only viewable to her circle of friends.

Ace had tried looking to see if there were any clues hidden in there anywhere, but she didn't have access, so it all remained a mystery.

Now that she realised where the picture had been taken from, she recognised it. She'd done a deep dive into Paula's mum's Facebook over the past couple of days. This picture was from a holiday in Crete the previous summer. It was one of the few recent ones with Paula included, the rest of the photos mostly featuring Paula's sister, mum, and stepdad.

Ace wondered if that had been Paula's decision. She'd protected her own accounts, so privacy was clearly something she took seriously. Maybe she'd asked her mum not to post any photos of her online.

Or maybe they just hadn't wanted to.

There was a piece in *The Sun on Sunday*, too. It fell just short of the front cover, and landed on page two. It used the same photo but was cropped slightly differently, so you could see part of the bikini Paula had been wearing, and just enough cleavage to be titillating.

"Ugh. Typical," Ace muttered.

This drew a sigh and another questioning, "Sorry?" from Mr Patel.

"Nothing," Ace said again.

"This isn't a bloody library, you know?" he said.

His accent danced around in her ears, delaying her response by a second or two.

"No. I know. I'm going to buy a bottle of water and some chewing gum," she said, then she arranged her features into what felt like a smile, and nodded benevolently, like she'd just done him a favour.

Mr Patel muttered something, then went back to reducing the beans.

The article in *The Sun* mentioned that Paula's mum, Linda, had recently reconnected with her father, but it stopped short of refer-ring to Shuggie Cowan by name. Otherwise, the story was more or less identical to the other one.

Ace checked through the other newspapers. There was a tiny mention in *The Sunday Post* but it was barely a paragraph, and there was no photo. She tucked it under her arm, anyway, along with *The Sunday Mail*.

She returned *The Sun* as a matter of principle, and then headed to the counter via the drinks fridge, and presented both newspapers and the promised bottle of water to Mr Patel.

"What about the chewing gum?" he asked, his gaze flitting to the rack of *Wrigley's* on the counter. "You mentioned chewing gum."

"I did. That's correct," Ace said. She pointed to a pack at random. "I'll have that one."

He eyed her suspiciously as he keyed the prices into his ancient till. "Four eighty-nine," he announced.

Ace took a very small purse from her pocket, plucked out the correct change, and handed it over. Mr Patel counted it with one glance, then jabbed a button on the till that made the cash drawer eject so violently he had to lean backwards to avoid a sucker punch to the gut.

"Thank you. Have a nice day," Ace told him, picking up her water.

"Chewing gum," Mr Patel reminded her.

"Oh. Yes. Chewing gum."

Ace turned to the rack, picked up the pack she'd pointed to, then hesitated with it in her hand.

Finally, she held it out to him. "Do you want some chewing gum?" she asked. "I don't like it."

"You don't like it?"

Ace shook her head. "It makes my tonsils sting. To be honest, I'm not that keen on water, either. I prefer coffee. Well, coffee when I'm cold, milk or milk products when I'm hot."

Mr Patel regarded her in silence for a moment, before the obvious question exploded out of him. "Then why the bloody hell did you buy them, then?"

"It just felt like the right thing to do," Ace told him. She extended her arm, pushing the pack of gum closer to him. "Would you like it?"

"No."

"The water?"

"No."

"Oh." Ace looked at her outstretched hand, and the pack of spearmint gum contained within. "Right."

She put the pack in her pocket, tipped an imaginary cap to the shopkeeper, then left with her bottle of water in one hand, and her newspapers tucked under the arm on the opposite side.

Once out of the shop, she placed the newspapers down on top of the big rubbish bin at the front, tore out the two articles she was interested in, and disposed of the rest in the bin's recycling section.

"Alright, freak?"

Ace finished folding the two torn-out articles and placed them both in her jacket pocket before looking in the direction of the voice. People calling her names was nothing new, and it very rarely turned out to be an urgent matter.

Paula's three closest friends—Suthsiri, Sasha, and Dawn—were approaching along the street. They walked shoulder to shoulder, completely blocking the pavement in that direction.

"What are you doing out, freak?" Sasha asked, lunging forward slightly on the insult. "Aren't you normally locked away in the loft, or whatever?"

"We don't have a loft. It's a ground-floor maisonette," Ace replied, with absolute sincerity. "And I'm out gathering information."

"'Gathering information'?" Dawn snorted and turned to her friends, grinning. "Is she a fucking robot, or what?"

"What sort of *information* are you gathering?" Suthsiri asked, sniggering. "How normal human beings work?"

"Aye, look at her, but," Sasha sneered, assessing Ace with a disparaging up-and-down glance. "No way she's ever going to manage *normal*."

Ace didn't rise to it. She didn't see the point. It wasn't like anything the girls were saying was actually hurting her feelings. At least, not that she was aware of.

Normal wasn't something to aim for, her mum had always told her. Normal was for losers.

None of her heroes could be considered 'normal.' The author, Mary Shelley. The physicist, Stephen Hawking. James Marsters, who played Spike on *Buffy the Vampire Slayer* and then, laterally, on the spin-off series, *Angel*.

Were any of those people normal? No. No, they were not.

"I think you're right. I don't think I'll manage normal. I think I'll leave that to you," Ace said. She privately delighted in what she considered a pretty sick burn, before continuing. "If you must know, I was gathering information on Paula."

Perhaps, if Ace had been more attuned to that sort of thing, she'd have noticed the change in atmosphere. She'd have picked up on the way the other girls' faces fell, and how their muscles all coiled themselves tighter.

"What the fuck did she say?" Dawn mumbled, then she rounded on Ace, spitting the words out this time. "What the fuck did you just say?"

Ace, at last, sensed the danger. It was hard to miss. Reading faces and body language had never been one of her talents, but a blind man couldn't miss the anger writ large in Dawn's expression, or the way her hands bunched into fists.

"Do you know where she is, you freak?" Sasha hissed. "Have you done something to her?"

"Me? No. Of course not. Quite the opposite. I want to help find her," Ace said, hoping this would calm the other girls down.

She tried a smile again, but those weren't exactly her strong point, either, and this one did nothing to defuse the situation.

"I'm sorry she's missing," she said, pressing on. "I understand this must be a very upsetting time for—"

The punch came out of nowhere. At least, that's how it seemed. One moment she was talking, and the next there was pain. Several pains, in fact, each one different.

There was the blunt but shocking *thack* of the impact. The electric buzz that zapped through her eye socket. The throbbing ache that followed.

She'd barely had time to catalogue them all before fingers crawled through her hair, pulling it tight, jerking her head backwards and throwing her off balance.

Later, she'd remember Suthsiri's teeth, clenched together, breath hissing through them in rage.

She'd remember her bottle of water falling to the ground, and the angry shouts from Dawn and Sasha. The pain in her stomach, and in her ribs.

And she'd remember the panic that flooded through her, drowning her senses, shutting her down from within. The pavement rolled beneath her. The sky swooshed by overhead.

Had she fallen, or had she been pushed to the ground?

She saw the pointed toe of a boot drawing back, and followed it, momentarily transfixed by the pendulum of its swing.

And then pain exploded through her ribcage, and she heard herself making a sound so desperate and unfamiliar that it frightened her almost as much as the prospect of the beating.

Ace didn't believe in an afterlife. There was no God. There was no Heaven. None of those things stood up to scrutiny.

And yet, for a moment, she was convinced she heard the righteous roar of the Lord Himself ringing down from on high.

"Oi! Piss off, you wee shites! Leave her alone, or I'll call the bloody police!"

Ace opened an eye in time to see Mr Patel dragging Sasha away before she could deliver another kick. One of the other girls —Dawn, Ace thought, though her vision was too blurred by tears to be sure—made a grab for her, only for Mr Patel to shove her away.

"Get up, you daft bastard!" the shopkeeper urged, and Ace realised he was talking to her. "You get up now and piss off home!"

While Mr Patel struggled to restrain all three girls, Ace got clumsily to her feet.

She thought about saying something. There had to be words that would fix this. There had to be something she could say to bring this whole thing to a non-violent conclusion.

But she was fucked if she knew what it was.

And so, with her bottle of water rolling off down the street, and her two clipped newspaper articles stashed in her pocket, Ace Wurzel turned on her heels, and did something she had spent most of her life avoiding.

She ran.

Heather had swung by Paula's house to help prep Linda and Michael for the press conference, but found the place empty when she arrived. A neighbour had opened an upstairs window and shouted out that they'd gone to Glasgow for "some polis thing," and Heather had headed back to her car, which she'd parked in the only available space a little further back along the street.

She was surprised to find a fifteen-year-old girl standing by the front passenger side door. She was even more surprised to see the nick she was in.

"What the hell happened to you?" Heather asked.

"I was chased," Ace replied.

"Looks like you were caught, too," Heather said, studying the girl's face. A black eye was forming, and one side of her bottom lip was red and swollen.

"Actually, I wasn't," Ace said. "They did this before they chased me. I managed to evade them by running to the school."

"School's shut," Heather said, vaguely mimicking Ace's tone of voice from their call the day before. "It is Sunday, after all."

"Touché, Officer."

"Detective Inspector," Heather corrected.

"Not important," the girl replied.

"Who did this to you?" Heather asked. "What happened?"

"Also not important," Ace said. "I'm an investigative journalist. There are inherent dangers that come with the job. I've accepted that. The point is that, yes, I went to the school, knowing full well it was shut. I wasn't trying to get inside, I was just hiding round the back to avoid any more of…" She gestured to her face. "This."

"How did that work out for you?" Heather asked.

"Perfectly well. My pursuers got bored and left. But that's not why I came looking for you."

"Why did you come looking for me?" Heather asked.

"I'm about to get to that. I suspected you'd turn up here sooner or later." Ace continued. "Sooner would have been nicer, but I'm sure you had other things to attend to. Anyway, the point is, while I was hiding around the back of the school, I saw something. Something that I think might be relevant to Paula's disappearance."

Heather shifted her weight onto one hip and raised an eyebrow, feigning a casual disinterest. "Check out you, Nancy Drew. And what did you find that you think 'might be relevant'?"

"Graffiti," Ace announced.

Heather blinked. It lasted a fraction too long.

And to think, she'd almost allowed herself to get her hopes up.

"Graffiti? On a school building?" Heather folded her arms. "Christ, aye, that is weird."

"You're funny," Ace said, though her expression didn't back up that assertion. "I didn't mean there was graffiti in general. Of course there was. But, I was referring to one specific graffito."

"That's not a word," Heather said.

"Yes, it is."

"I don't think it is."

Ace held up a hand. "Please. Officer? It's a word. Trust me. It's the singular of 'graffiti,' but that's not important right now. What's important right now is the graffito in question. And, more specifically, what it said."

Heather had no option but to bite. "I still don't think it's a word, but fine. What did it say, then?"

"It said…" Ace raised both hands in front of her, like she was picturing the words written in lights above a Broadway theatre. "'Mr Pearse fingered Paula Harrison here!'"

TWENTY-ONE

SNECKY PRACTICALLY BROKE into a sprint when Heather entered the station, racing across the foyer to intercept her.

"Finally! Where the bloody hell have you been?!"

"At home. Why? Has something happened?"

"Yes!"

Heather waited for a clarification that didn't come. "Well? What is it?"

The DCI caught his breath, straightened himself up, then ran a hand down his shirt, smoothing the creases and flattening down his panic.

"I've reconsidered," he said.

Heather narrowed her eyes, sensing some oncoming storm of bullshit.

"You've reconsidered what?"

"The press conference. The telly," Snecky said. "I think you should do it."

"Jesus." Heather scowled. There were a lot of things she disliked about the job. Talking to the press was higher on the list than most people might expect. "Why?"

"Because you're closer to the case. You've been leading it," Snecky said. He rocked from one foot to the other. The panicked look that had just left his face returned like a monster in the final moments of a horror movie. "Also, there are a *lot* more people and cameras in there than I was expecting. In Aberdeen, you had Northsound Radio, the Press & Journal, and maybe someone from STV North, depending on how juicy a case it was."

He pointed off in the direction of the briefing room, and Heather noted the way his hand trembled.

"It's like a fucking zoo in there. There must be fifty of the buggers. Cameras. Microphones. The works," Snecky said. He shook his head—a series of brief little back-and-forth movements that continued as he spoke. "No. No, I'm not doing it. I don't want to do it. You'll have to do it. I'm ordering you to do it!"

"Ordering me?" Heather stepped back, looking hurt. "Jesus. I mean, you could've just asked."

"Sorry. Yes. Sorry, I should've…" Snecky said. He smiled hopefully at her. "Will you do it?"

"Nicely," Heather said. "You could've just asked me *nicely*."

"God. Alright. Will you do it *please*?"

Heather shook her head. "No."

Snecky tutted. "Fuck's sake! Yes, very good. Very funny. Right, well, this time I *am* ordering you. You're doing it. End of."

Heather raised a middle finger and waggled it at him as she walked past, headed for the briefing room.

"Fine, but I've had no time to prep," she called back to him. "So, if I accidentally call you a useless bastard in there, then I can't be held responsible."

———

Snecky wasn't wrong. It was a full house in the briefing room, with standing room only up the back.

This wasn't good. Missing teenagers rarely brought the pack out in force like this. There'd usually be a handful of local journos, and maybe one or two freelancers who sold stories to the bigger papers.

Heather recognised faces from *The Daily Record, The Sun, The Scottish Daily Mail*, plus a couple of reporters off the telly.

Cameramen and photographers were battling for space around

the room, staking claim to some spots and trying to muscle in on better ones.

Their chatter fell away when Heather entered, then intensified again as she took her seat, their whispers bubbling up like they were about to start firing questions at her already.

There was a sheet of paper on the table in front of her, and two empty seats on her left. All three chairs had microphones positioned in front of them, and a quick glance at the typed speech Snecky had presumably put there for himself to read before he'd chickened out confirmed that both Linda Harrison and her husband, Michael, would be joining her to issue an appeal.

Right now, they'd be through in a back room, being briefed and coached by one of the team. Hopefully Marty, and not DC Wolfe. Although, given the size of the crowd, Heather wouldn't be surprised if the Gozer himself was getting them prepared.

Heather scanned through Snecky's speech. It was long-winded and overly complicated, and yet somehow still managed to say very little.

Then again, she couldn't really blame him for that. After all, there wasn't a whole lot to say.

The murmuring from the journalists was sounding increasingly impatient. The briefing was meant to have started ten minutes ago, and presumably, they all had places they needed to be.

Tough shit.

"Give us a minute," Heather said, leaning closer to her microphone so her voice boomed around the room like the decree of some vengeful god.

She eyeballed the crowd in general, then flipped over Snecky's speech and skimmed the equally wishy-washy bullshit written on the back.

Then, she slapped her hands on the desk, got to her feet, and enjoyed the sounds of complaint from the gathered press as she left the room.

Out in the corridor, she almost walked straight into Linda Harrison, who was shuffling towards the briefing room, hanging onto the arm of a man Heather had never seen before.

Or had she?

He was older than Linda—late fifties, maybe—but with dark, shoulder-length hair that curled up at the ends. The hairstyle didn't suit him. Then again, Heather didn't think it would suit anyone.

He had a slightly lazy left eye, so the lid drooped a little, making it seem like he was squinting at her.

She felt something stirring. Something familiar.

But then, Detective Superintendent Mackenzie appeared in the doorway beside them, and acknowledged Heather with a nod of his head.

"He asked you, then."

"Aye. More or less," Heather said. She offered Linda and her husband a thin-lipped smile of encouragement. "You ready?"

"I... I think..." Linda's mouth formed the shape of a few more words, but the sound didn't come out.

Michael patted her on the hand, tightened his grip around her shoulder, then gave Heather a nod that made his weird, six-year-old girl's haircut bob up and down at the ends.

"We're ready," he confirmed.

Heather tried to keep her smile in place, but it lost some of its conviction.

That voice. There was something about that voice.

"Right then," said the Gozer, gesturing to the door Heather had just come through. "If we're all set, then let's go get this over with."

―――――

There was something about Michael Harrison that Heather didn't like. Something more than his awful hair, although that was doing a lot of the heavy lifting. It was the little sideways looks he gave his wife as she spoke to the press.

It was all the tiny touches he gave her arm as she read from their prepared statement, her eyes so blurred by tears that she struggled to keep track of her place on the page.

And it was the fact that she couldn't shake the feeling she knew the man from somewhere. Somewhere hazy. Somewhere almost forgotten.

Heather had done the briefing part, summarising when Paula was last seen, what she was wearing, and the direction she was headed at the time.

There hadn't been a lot more to add. They didn't know where she might be. They didn't know why she might've run away. They didn't know who, if anyone, she might be with.

No wonder Snecky had bottled it. The Q&A section was going to be a bloodbath. Hopefully, the Gozer would have the sense to get Paula's parents out of the room before that all kicked off.

Linda was doing well, considering. She'd struggled through the direct appeal to her daughter to come home. She'd assured Paula that she wasn't in any trouble, and that they just wanted to know she was alright.

As no doubt instructed by the Gozer, she'd laid it on thick. She'd made it clear how Paula's absence was hurting the family. How her little sister, Ibby, couldn't sleep for worrying. How they would do anything to have her back home with them.

At the Gozer's request, she'd shared a moving family moment —one designed to remind Paula of all the good parts of home, but also to make any potential kidnappers think of the girl as something more than just a victim, to force some emotional connection.

Linda had talked about the previous Christmas. About how Ibby had woken up at four in the morning, excited to see if Santa had been, and how Paula had sat huddled under the covers with the younger girl, whispering as they played and read together until the clock ticked over to a much more reasonable six A.M.

Cameras had flashed. Lenses had zoomed. But the reporters themselves had hung on every word.

This was why Heather didn't mind doing the telly stuff. Besides a short snippet of footage of her with a reporter's voice talking over the top, she was unlikely to appear much on the news. Linda made for much more interesting footage. Nobody watching at home cared about the details, they all wanted to experience the emotional gut punch of a distraught mother's cries for help. That was the money shot.

Linda had given them plenty to be going on with, too. Her breathless pleas had seemed genuine and heartfelt, although Heather couldn't help but notice that Michael's lips were moving throughout. He was silently mouthing the words as his wife spoke them out loud, like a particularly shite ventriloquist.

After first aiming it at Paula, Linda broadened the appeal, asking anyone with any information about her daughter's whereabouts to come forward.

"If anyone's seen my wee girl, or has any idea where she might be, please… *please* tell us. She's a good girl. She's kind, she's funny, she's just… She's beautiful. We miss her. Her little sister misses her, so, so much. Please, if you know anything, if you've seen or heard anything at all, please get in touch. Please."

She'd broken then, her head lowering, her sobbing threatening to shake her whole body apart. Beside her, Michael placed a hand on her arm and leaned in closer, whispering something that Heather would've given anything to be able to hear.

In an ideal world, he'd have added something. He'd have addressed the cameras himself, adding to what his wife had said. The Gozer would've encouraged that. He'd have tried to push him into it, in fact, so the MIT could sit around and analyse the footage later—pore over every word, study every look and intonation.

But, he clearly wasn't up for talking. Instead, he just looked along the table to Heather and gave her a nod, like he was the one running the show.

Did he wink? She couldn't be sure. His lazy eye made it hard to tell. But she thought so. Along with the nod, she was sure he winked at her.

In the murk of her mind, a memory stirred, but refused to take shape.

She knew that wink. She knew this man. She was certain of it.

Heather realised that not only were he and Linda now looking at her, the rest of the room was, too. She cleared her throat and turned to the wake of vultures sitting poised with their microphones and cameras in hand.

The Gozer wasn't coming to take Paula's parents away. If they couldn't get Michael talking, they'd at least study his reactions.

That meant keeping him up here in front of the cameras for as long as possible, no matter how uncomfortable things might get.

"I'll now take a few questions," Heather said. A dozen hands shot into the air, and a similar number of voices started to shout.

Heather pointed to Andrew McVitie from *The Herald*, a man she'd had the misfortune of speaking to on more than one occasion.

"You. Sorry, don't know your name," she lied, because it was important to keep these bastards in their place by treating them with the contempt they deserved.

The journalist—an older man with a growing collection of chins—quickly introduced himself, but Heather batted it away and motioned for him to hurry up.

"Do you have any evidence that Paula's still alive?" he asked. Clearly, sparing her parents' feelings was not high on his list of priorities. "Has she used her phone or bank account, for example?"

"We believe Paula is still alive. There's been nothing to suggest otherwise," Heather said.

"But her phone. Her bank. Has she used them?"

Heather felt the urge to shift around in her seat, but she remained perfectly still.

"No. No, she hasn't."

She pointed to a female journalist near the front—a waspish freelancer with blue, thick-rimmed glasses who wrote for a few of the more right-wing dailies. Heather knew from experience that she tended to seize on the replies to other questions, so decided to get her out of the way now before too much had been said.

"How does Shuggie Cowan fit into all this?" she asked.

The murmuring in the room rose a few decibels, then died away into an expectant hush.

Heather glanced along the table. Linda and her husband both sat with their heads down, her left hand interlocked with his right.

"Mr Cowan is Paula's maternal grandfather," Heather said.

The place didn't erupt exactly. Clearly, most of them had already known what the answer to the question was going to be. It was probably the reason that most of them were even here. But more hands shot up, and more questions were shouted from all corners of the room.

The freelancer with the glasses tried her luck with a follow-up question, but Heather ignored her and instead pointed to one of the few reporters not waving or shouting at her, or bouncing in their chair like an excited five-year-old.

She worked for one of the local papers, Heather thought. Kilmarnock Standard, maybe. She was in her forties, and Heather dimly recalled them crossing paths back in high school, though she was a few years above.

"Is it happening again, Detective Inspector?" she asked, and even amongst all the ruckus, the question rang out like the tolling of a funeral bell.

Before she could answer, the door opened again. Just a crack. Just enough. With one look at the Gozer's face, she knew.

God help her, she knew.

"No," she said, addressing the reply to the local woman. Then, to the rest of the crowd she said, "No further questions," and, despite her sinking heart trying to drag her down with it, she rose wordlessly from her chair.

TWENTY-TWO

THE MELTING SNOW had unveiled her—the rain having drawn aside the layer of crisp, flawless white like a hospital sheet, exposing the grubby horror of her to the world.

She lay in a dip between two trees, down among the roots and the low-hanging branches. Down in the soil, and the filth, and the mulch of last year's fallen leaves.

She was naked. Blood stained her neck from a wound in her throat, painting her chest a watery shade of red.

Her ribs were black, a succession of individual bruises having closed ranks, huddling together, forming one collective mass.

There were scratches on her face, and on her breasts, and on the insides of her thighs. Deep red welts that painted puckered lines on her skin. Lines that told a story of suffering, and pain.

She hadn't been buried. Not even that slight consideration had been afforded her. Instead, she'd been dumped, her limbs tangled awkwardly, her body twisted halfway around, her face partly buried in the dirt like she was too ashamed to look at anyone.

Heather was dimly aware that someone was speaking to her. She didn't bother to listen. Not yet. Let them wait.

Her instinct was to avert her gaze, to look away from the body of the girl, to allow Paula that modicum of dignity. But, she didn't.

Instead, she studied every line. She forced herself to look, to stare, to take it all in.

She needed to know. She needed to see exactly what some evil fucker had done to her.

Paula Harrison deserved that much, at least.

Finally, the voice that had been trying to get her attention managed to force its way through.

"...what I said, Heather?"

"What?" Heather turned towards the voice and saw a woman in a white paper suit. Her hair was tied up on top of her head, and the hood pulled over the top of it made the top of her skull look enormous, like some comic book super genius.

She was fairly new. Transferred up to the Scene of Crime team from Devon or somewhere. Heather had only met her once or twice before, and didn't know much about her beyond the fact that she had the potential to be a massive pain in the arse.

"This," said the SOCO, tipping her elongated head towards the body. "I was saying, I foretold this. Poor kid. I saw it. Last night."

Heather's eyes darted left and right, searching for a way to take this remark that didn't wind her up. When she failed to find one, she turned to face the other woman, her displeasure etched into every line of her face.

"What the fuck are you talking about?" she demanded.

"I did a reading. Tarot." The SOCO rocked back on her heels, clearly waiting for some sort of response. When none came, she added, "Cards. Tarot cards. I did a reading for her. Death came up. Although, people assume that means literal death, but it can just mean a change. The death of one way of life, and the beginning of a new one."

Her gaze crept to the body in the muck.

"Although, not in this case, I suppose."

"What was your name again?" Heather asked.

"Sidnee. S-I-D-N-E-E. It's an unusual spelling, so I always—"

"I don't give a shit," Heather said. "And I don't want to hear any more bollocks about tarot, or magic, or psychic fucking powers. Alright? A girl is dead, for Christ's sake. She doesn't need us reading her fucking horoscope, she needs us to show her some respect."

Sidnee, finally sensing danger, raised both hands in front of her, as if protecting herself from an imminent attack.

"No harm meant, Heather."

"It's Detective Inspector Filson. And shouldn't you be off somewhere doing your job?"

The other woman nodded, which made the hood of her suit shift around like there was something alive under there. She jabbed a thumb back over her shoulder and started to back away.

"Uh, yes. Yes, I think… Did someone just…? Yes. Right."

She continued backing off for a few more steps, then turned and jogged over to where the rest of her team was carefully picking through the melting snow.

Heather turned back to Paula, only to find DCI Grant now standing on her left.

"Jesus!" she hissed. "Where the hell did you come from?"

"Back there," said Snecky, taking the question at face value. "By the vans."

He wasn't looking directly at the body, Heather noticed, but rather focusing a couple of feet above it, and only occasionally flicking his eyes down to steal a fleeting glimpse of Paula's remains.

"They, uh, they need you to shift out of the way so they can get the tent up."

"Aye. Fine," Heather said, though she didn't yet make a move.

"It's her, I take it?" Snecky asked.

"Aye. Looks like it."

The DCI nodded, and clasped his hands in front of him.

For a while, they both just stood there, saying nothing. It was, Heather thought, the closest she had ever come to liking the man.

"How are you doing?" he asked.

"Fine. Why wouldn't I be?"

Snecky shrugged. "Just… I know you were convinced she was alive."

Heather said nothing. The silence compelled the DCI to continue.

"And, you know, she isn't."

"I noticed that, yes."

Snecky stamped his feet and blew on his hands. A cloud of white seeped through his fingers. The snow might be clearing, but the temperatures were still in the low single digits.

Heather, despite the relatively limited cold-stopping powers of her leather jacket, hadn't really noticed.

"Back at the station, a couple of the press guys caught me," he said. He sounded a little wary, like he wasn't entirely comfortable with the direction he was steering the conversation. "They asked about the Kiddie Kill—"

He stopped, shook his head, and tried again.

"The Killie Kill— The Kiddle—*fuck*!"

"The Killie Kiddie Killer," Heather said. She shot him a sideways look that gave very little away, but which contained perhaps an ounce or two of pity. "It takes a bit of practice."

"Stupid bloody name."

Heather didn't argue. "Some journalist came up with it. Media jumped on it," she explained. "Always hated it. Turned what he did into a joke."

"Yeah. I can imagine," Snecky said. He almost sounded genuinely compassionate, although the tut and the grave little shake of his head felt a bit too on the nose.

A voice from behind them butted in, derailing the conversation. "Here, anyone want tea or coffee? The old folks' home up the road there's doing them for us. Apparently, they've got scones on the go, too!"

Heather and Snecky both turned to see Detective Constable Wolfe standing there, his hands tucked under the armpits of his jacket, his face fixed in a look of baking-based anticipation that bordered on excitement.

"Do you mind, Detective Constable?" Snecky said, before Heather had a chance to tell Wolfe to piss off. "We're paying our respects here."

"Oh. Right. Sorry," DC Wolfe said. "I didn't realise."

"How the fuck could you not…?" Heather began, but she

stopped herself before she lost the rag completely, and turned back to Paula's body.

"Just go, Detective Constable," Snecky said. He, too, turned back, but then thought better of it. "Although, if they do fruit scones, I'll have one of them. And a tea. Unless there's hot chocolate, then I'll have a hot chocolate."

He shot Heather a slightly guilty look, which she pretended not to notice, then joined her in her silence.

"It *is* cold," he whispered after a few seconds. "You sure you don't...?"

"I'm fine," Heather said.

There was an older man in a well-tailored blue suit standing on the fringes, just inside the cordon tape. DS Brompton was talking to him, occasionally pointing over in the direction of the body while the other man nodded along.

"Who's that?" Heather asked.

"Hmm?" Snecky followed her gaze. "Oh. Consultant from one of the hospitals. He's been brought in to, you know..." He nodded to the body. "...make sure. Do all the paperwork."

"Where's Ozzy?" Heather asked, but Snecky just stared blankly back at her. "Dr Osgood. The actual pathologist."

"Oh! Him. Yes. Off sick. Herniated disk. We're going to have to see about getting someone in from Edinburgh or somewhere to do the post-mortem."

Heather chewed her bottom lip for a moment. She had a feeling she knew how the next few hours were going to play out, and she wasn't going to like it. There were things she could do, however, to mitigate the damage.

"What about Inverness?" she suggested. "Dr Maguire?"

"What, you mean Jack Logan's bird?"

Heather scowled at him. "No, I mean the fully qualified and highly experienced forensic pathologist whose relationship status isn't remotely relevant."

"Uh, right. No. No, you're right. That was... That was out of order," Snecky said, shuffling his feet in the slush. "I'll, um, I'll make a few calls and see if she's available." He looked back over his shoulder, and she saw him nodding at someone. "But, uh, but we really do need to let them in to put the tent up."

"OK. Just give me a second," Heather replied.

She stood waiting for him to leave, then took a couple of faltering steps closer, then squatted beside the carelessly discarded body on the ground.

As Heather got closer, she realised there was a smell to the body. Not of mulch, or of mud, or of murder. Something sharper. More chemical. Petrol, maybe. Or some sort of solvent.

The angle of Paula's face meant only one eye was visible. It was open, the pupil a milky sort of grey as she stared blankly at the ground below her.

There was so much Heather wanted to say to the girl. So many promises she wanted to make. How she'd find the bastard who did this. How she'd make him pay. How she'd make sure he could never hurt anyone again.

But none of those things came out of her mouth. No matter how much she wanted to believe all that, she couldn't guarantee any of it. She could make all those promises, but not one of them might turn out to be the truth.

And so, she said the only thing she knew *was* true.

"I'm sorry," she whispered. "I'm so, so sorry."

And then, with a final bow of her head, Heather launched herself back to her feet, and went to work.

———

Dr Shona Maguire wiped a slick of sweat from her brow, adjusted her grip on the tweezers, and held her breath.

The next part of the procedure was tricky. It was intensely fiddly work, even for someone of her experience.

She blinked, screwing her eyes tightly shut for a second, then brought the tips of the tweezers closer to the open wound of the figure on the table.

"Careful," whispered a voice in her ear, and her hand jerked as she jumped.

She looked back over her shoulder, where DCI Jack Logan sat in solemn-faced silence, just a few inches behind her.

"You did that on purpose," she said, her usually soft Irish accent hardening around the accusation.

"Did what?" Logan asked, his face a picture of innocence. "I was just saying you should be careful."

"I know I should be careful. I'm being fecking careful," Shona told him.

Logan held his hands up, continuing to protest his innocence, then nodded at the semi-naked man lying, eyes open, before them.

"Right. Shut up," Shona said, turning her attention back to the tweezers.

She passed them to the other hand, wiped her sweaty fingers on the leg of her trousers, then resumed the procedure.

"Steady," Logan murmured as she leaned in closer. She blocked him out. Ignored him. "Steaaaady…"

Easy does it, she thought. *No rush. You can do this. You've got this.*

On the table beside her, her phone blasted out the opening bars of the *Back to the Future* theme tune. Her hand jerked, the tweezers snagged on the edge of the open wound, and the patient's nose illuminated with a loud, jarring *bzzzzt!*

"Fucked it!" Logan cried in triumph. "You absolutely fucked it. I win!"

"You haven't won," Shona protested. "You haven't taken anything out of the bastard yet."

"Aye, well, no point now. You've killed him."

"What are you even talking about?" Shona cried. She gestured to the cartoon picture of the man on the *Operation* board. "His eyes are wide open. He's clearly already dead. He's got a full-sized apple stuck in his throat, and actual butterflies in his stomach. There's zero chance that lad's alive. None whatsoever."

Logan sat back on the couch with his hands behind his head, grinning smugly as Shona reached for her phone.

"I still won, though," he remarked as she hit the button to answer, and his smile only broadened when she fired him a double-finger salute.

"Hello?" Shona said. Then, remembering it was her work phone, added, "Shona Maguire."

She listened to the voice on the other end, a frown spreading down her face like a fast-moving rash. She mouthed, *It's Snecky* to Logan, who recoiled at even this silent mention of his fellow DCI's name.

"What the fuck does he want?" Logan whispered, but Shona shushed him with a glare and a wave of a hand.

"Oh. I see," Shona said into the phone. "Right, and… Ah. Gotcha. Sorry to hear…"

The couch cushion shifted beneath her as she leaned forward, swapping the phone from one ear to the other, like she couldn't trust what the first one had heard.

"Wait, Heather did?" she said. "As in *Heather* Heather? As in Heather Filson?"

Behind her, Logan went tense. Having his current partner and former lover interacting with each other was never something he relished the thought of. The last time they'd crossed paths had eventually ended on amicable terms, but it had been touch and go before then.

"Right. Well… OK, then," Shona said. She looked back over her shoulder at Logan, but her expression was giving nothing away. "I'll be there as soon as I can."

TWENTY-THREE

LINDA AND MICHAEL HARRISON had been driven straight home after the press conference, and now sat in their living room, flanked on all sides by uniformed liaison officers, hot, sugary teas slowly turning cold on the table in front of them.

They hadn't yet turned to the window, so they hadn't seen Heather standing outside, watching them through the rain-streaked glass while the constable who'd driven the couple home filled her in on everything that had happened.

They'd left Ibby with a neighbour that morning, and while, between her silent sobs and her hysterical screaming, Linda insisted they go and get her back, Michael had reasoned her out of it, one hand stroking figures-of-eight on her arm, the other draped across her shoulders.

There had been whispering, too. Michael had leaned in close to his wife and spoken hushed words into her ear. Whatever he'd said, it had been effective, and she'd fallen silent for the rest of the journey, save for the occasional choked whimper.

As Heather listened, the soft squeaking of brakes and the purring of a well-maintained engine caught her attention, and she turned to see a green Jaguar car pull up behind her Audi.

"Fuck. That's all we need," she muttered, marching off and

leaving the uniformed constable standing awkward and alone by the garden gate.

She reached the car before Cowan could open the door, and stood by the driver's side window, one hand on the roof, blocking his exit.

"Move," he said, his voice muffled by the window.

"What are you doing here, Shuggie?" Heather asked.

"What the fuck do you think I'm doing here? Move."

They glowered at each other through the glass for a moment, then Heather sighed and stepped back, letting the bulky big bastard open the door and haul himself out.

His face was pale, making the swastika-shaped scar on his forehead stand out even more than usual. His eyes were ringed with red, too, and Heather realised with a start that Shuggie Cowan—the actual Shuggie Cowan—had been crying.

For a moment, she didn't know how to react, her brain refusing to put what had, until then, been the warring concepts of 'Shuggie Cowan' and 'shedding tears' together in a way that made any sort of sense.

By the time it had, Cowan had already barged past her and was marching towards the house. The Uniform was standing her ground in front of the gate, but with each thunderous step from the gangster, she was becoming more and more jittery.

"It's fine, let him through," Heather said, and the constable practically threw herself sideways out of Shuggie's path, like a goalkeeper making a dramatic diving save.

Shuggie stopped when he reached the gate. From several paces behind, Heather heard his breath catching in his throat as he caught sight of his daughter and son-in-law sitting together on the couch.

Linda had her head in her hands and was rocking back and forth now, Michael pulling her in close against him, squeezing her like he could hold back her waves of grief.

"Oh. God," Shuggie whispered.

Heather stopped beside him. "Maybe you should give them some time. Let them grieve."

"What are you talking about? Paula was my granddaughter."

Cowan stabbed a finger towards the house. "That's my daughter in there. She needs me."

Before Heather could suggest that he might be overstating his importance in the family's life, he headed up the path and tried the door handle without knocking.

When he found the door locked, Heather could practically see the question mark forming above his head. He knocked, drawing the attention of the people inside.

Heather watched through the window as Linda got up and crossed to the window. Her face told a story that Shuggie wasn't going to enjoy the ending of and then, catching Heather looking in, she swished the curtains shut with one big tug.

The light came on in the hall, the pale yellow glow seeping out through the rippling frosted glass door panels like it was warding off the darkness outside.

Heather hurried up the path and stood within grabbing distance of Shuggie, just in case things kicked off.

The door didn't open far, the security chain on the inside rattling as it went tight. Linda's face appeared in the gap, all puffy and blotchy, made monstrous by her grief.

"Please. Not just now," she said. Her gaze darted between Shuggie and Heather, so it was hard to tell which of them she was talking to.

"Linda. I just heard," Shuggie began, but his daughter's features all drew themselves more tightly together, tears cascading down her cheeks.

"I can't do this. Not right now. You need to go."

"Linda. Sweetheart," Shuggie said, and if Heather didn't know him better, she'd have sworn she heard his voice cracking. "I can help. Please. Just let me in. I can help."

For a moment, her grief took a back seat, and contempt rushed in to fill the void.

"You've done quite enough," she told him.

"Shuggie, come on," Heather said. She caught him by the arm, but he pulled himself free.

"Linda! Please, don't do this."

"And *you*," Linda said, fixing Heather with a look of such

betrayal that it forced the DI back a step. "You promised me. You promised she was going to be OK. You told me you were going to find her. You told me she'd be safe. That'd you'd bring her home."

"I…"

Heather tried to reply, but the words wouldn't come. Shuggie seized on her silence.

"Linda. Please, listen, I can help. Just let me in, I can—"

"Will you just *go*?!" His daughter's scream was piercing, the narrow gap of the doorway fashioning it into something cutting and razor-like. "Both of you. I can't do this, not now! Please. Just go!"

The door slammed before Cowan could offer any further protest, leaving him and Heather out in the cold.

Shuggie brought up a clenched fist to hammer on the door again.

"Maybe don't, eh?" Heather suggested. "Maybe give her some time."

The hand remained raised, but it hung there in the air a few inches from the door, not yet making contact.

"I just want to help," Cowan said, not looking at her.

"Help who? Linda, or yourself? Because, if it's Linda, then the way you help is by doing what she asked. By giving her space," Heather said. "But if it's yourself you want to help, then go ahead. Knock. Weasel your way inside, if that'll make you feel better."

The hand hung there for a few moments more, then fell back to Shuggie's side.

Without a word, he turned and stalked up the path, headed back in the direction of his car. Heather followed with the intention of pestering the bastard with awkward questions, but before she could start, her phone buzzed, and a glance at the screen told her the moment she'd been dreading was now here.

The Gozer's voice, once she'd answered, was level and measured. There was kindness to it, even. He was doing this for her sake. For her own good. It was unfortunate it had to be this way.

"You can't take me off it," she protested, once he'd said his piece. "You can't take me off this case, sir."

"I already have, Heather," the detective superintendent replied. "DCI Grant will take over lead. You'll be reassigned."

"But, sir—"

"You're too close to it. You're far too close. The feather was bad enough. But, on its own, that was one thing. And we were dealing with what we thought was a runaway," the Gozer explained. "But it's murder now. And the body... The method... Well, I'm sure you don't need the similarities spelled out to you."

"It's been thirty years, sir. There's no way—"

"It doesn't matter, Detective Inspector." The Det Supt's tone became sharper. "Whether it's him, whether it's a copycat, or whether it's just a big bloody coincidence, it doesn't matter. You're too close. Your judgement could be impaired. It's *bound to be* impaired. How could it not be?"

Heather ran a hand down her face and groaned. She noticed that the uniformed constable was trying very hard not to look like she was listening in, so the DI walked away from the gate, and lowered her voice a little.

"But, sir, I think you're making a mistake. I think we should—"

"The decision is made, Heather. I'm sorry. It's already been communicated up the chain, and everyone is in agreement."

Heather stopped walking when she realised that Shuggie was still sitting in his Jaguar just a few car lengths along the street from where she was standing. He was hunched behind the wheel, staring blankly ahead, looking for all the world like a broken man.

"But, *Snecky*, sir?" Heather protested. "I mean, with all due respect to DCI Grant, he's fucking hopeless. Bob Hoon once called him, 'A collective noun of clusterfucks,' and, frankly, sir, I think he was being generous."

"Aye, well, Bob Hoon has said a lot of things about a lot of people. Doesn't mean they're all true," the Gozer reasoned. "And you can rest assured that DCI Grant will have the full support of myself, and the rest of the MIT."

"Just not me," Heather said.

"Sadly, no. Not you. I appreciate that may be disappointing, Detective Inspector, but I'm afraid my decision is final on it. You are to have no further involvement in this case at this time. Is that clear?"

Heather chewed her bottom lip and raised her gaze to the sky, and to the dark clouds knitting themselves together across it.

"Is that clear, Heather?" the Gozer asked again. "I need to hear you say it."

"Yes, sir," she said. Spots of icy rain had started to fall. She closed her eyes, and they felt like a baptism across her face. "You've made yourself very clear."

She hung up before he had a chance to add anything further, muttered a series of obscenities towards the heavens, then opened her eyes and faced front again.

Shuggie Cowan was still sitting in his car, his face still slack, his eyes still ringed with red.

Thanks to the Gozer, she'd been cut out. And if there was one person in the world who knew how she felt right now, it was the big ugly bastard in the flashy motor.

Cowan turned, blinking slowly, when she knocked on his side window. They held each other's gaze as the glass slid down between them, disappearing inside the panel of the driver's door.

"Come to fucking gloat, have we?" he asked, in a voice like two bricks rubbing together.

"Actually," Heather began, leaning an elbow on the roof of the car. "I was going to ask if you fancied getting a drink?"

TWENTY-FOUR

HEATHER AND SHUGGIE sat in the snug of the Tartan Sheep, each taking up one side of an L-shaped padded bench, both nursing their respective drinks.

The Sheep was an old-fashioned sports bar located just across the road from the train station, and boasted several large screens and a projector on which punters could watch all manner of big sporting events.

Right now, though, the place was practically empty, and the screens were all showing a nature documentary with the sound turned down. The promise of a karaoke later that evening had struck both of them as a threat, and they'd each made it clear to the other that this trip to the pub was a one-drink-and-done kind of deal.

Shuggie had surprised Heather by ordering a ginger beer and lime from the bored-looking guy behind the bar, who seemed to be transfixed by the plight of a baby elk on the nature programme.

"Driving, amn't I?" he'd grunted, when Heather had questioned his choice of beverage. "I'm not having you pulling a fly one and nicking me on a D and D charge."

"Good call," Heather had conceded. "I'd like to tell you that I wouldn't, but I'm honestly not sure I'd be able to help myself."

She was within walking distance of home, so had no such

concerns. She'd settled for a pint of cider over anything stronger, though. If she was going to be in Cowan's company, she needed to keep her wits about her.

"How's your old man?" he asked, like they were two old friends just shooting the shit. He pointed to the side of his head. "He still…?"

The skin on the back of Heather's neck prickled. The hairs on her arms tickled as they stood on end.

This was a mistake. This had been a bad idea.

Still, she was here now.

"That's none of your business, Shuggie," she told him.

"Huh," he grunted. "Suit yourself."

He reached into the pocket of his big coat, and Heather watched, passing no comment, as Cowan took out a jar of pickled beetroot and a fork, and sat both on the table.

It was only once he'd opened the jar and pronged a big shiny red slice of the stuff with the fork that she felt compelled to ask.

"What the fuck are you doing?"

"Eh? Oh. This?" Shuggie shoved the slice of beetroot in his mouth and chewed it noisily.

"Yes, that. Of course that," Heather said.

"I've stopped smoking." A dribble of purple-red liquid trickled down his chin, and he wiped it on the back of his hand. "Want to be around to see my grandkids grow up, don't I?"

"So… what? You substituted smoking for eating jars of beetroot?"

Cowan nodded and went in for a second helping. "Pretty much, yeah."

Heather raised her eyebrows and puffed out her cheeks, not quite sure what to say about that.

"Fair enough, I suppose," was the best she could come up with.

The heaters were on full tilt in the pub, making the place feel stifling and the air dry. The cider was refreshingly crisp and cold as Heather knocked back a mouthful.

By the time she clunked the glass down on a beer mat, Shuggie had returned the beetroot and fork to his pocket, and now eyed her over the rim of his own glass, drinking tiny sips of his ginger beer.

The foreplay was over, and he was clearly waiting for her to make the first real move.

Heather was only too happy to oblige.

"So, was this you, then, Shuggie?" she asked. "Did you kill Paula?"

She'd braced herself for some sudden and violent retaliation. Readied herself for the glass to come flying at her, or for Cowan himself to lunge at her across the table.

Instead, he took another sip of his drink, covered his mouth with the back of his hand, then belched quietly.

"I mean, I might as well have," he said. His shoulders rose, then fell back down to lower than where they'd started.

"What's that supposed to mean?" Heather asked. "You still reckon this was to get at you?"

"Course it fucking was," Shuggie spat. "Maybe not the Russian. I don't know. But some cunt did this, and they did it to get at me."

Heather hoped he was right. Heather hoped this was targeted at him. It would make Paula's death no less tragic, but it would mean that the killer was some aggrieved would-be *Goodfellas* wannabe, and not the ghost of a serial killer who was assumed long dead.

If this was aimed at Shuggie, then it was over. No more girls would be taken. No more lives would be ruined.

Nobody else needed to die.

"Aye, well, there's some speculation that you might have done it," Heather told him. "More directly, I mean. Taken matters into your own hands."

"And who the fuck is saying that?" Cowan demanded.

Heather took a sip of her pint and shrugged. "Me, for one."

Shuggie went through the motions of laughing, but he did nothing to really sell it.

"Is that a fact? Why doesn't that surprise me?"

"Well, I mean, it's not like you don't have previous for it,"

Heather said. "Mouthy teenager causing you problems. Not knowing when to shut up. Remind you of anyone?"

Shuggie's eyebrows dipped and his mouth drew up into a grimace. "Fuck me. This again. How many times have I got to tell you? I don't know what happened to your brother. Alright? He was a good kid. Aye, bit of a big mouth. Needed the odd slap, sure, but I didn't do fuck all to him."

"I don't believe you."

"Pfft. Course you fucking don't. Doesn't change the facts, though."

"I don't believe you about Paula, either."

She was poking the bear now, and she knew it. But, if that made Cowan kick off and brought everything to a head, then good. Bring it on. It was long overdue.

His side of the bench creaked beneath him as he leaned forward. "And why would I do that, eh? Why would I kill my own granddaughter? She's family."

"Family. Aye. She's family right enough." She took a sip of her cider. "How's your nephew, by the way? Frankie, wasn't it? Haven't seen him around in a while. Used to cross paths with him pretty regularly but, I don't know, it's like he's vanished off the face of the Earth."

Shuggie's only reply was a grunt and a glare of hatred.

"Mind you, at least he was happy being related to you. Paula wasn't, was she, Shuggie?" Heather said, holding his dead-eyed stare. "She didn't want you anywhere near her mum. Or her wee sister. Didn't want them having anything to do with you." She picked up another beermat and tapped out a rhythm on the table. "That must've been quite a blow. A man like you? Used to getting his own way? Suddenly told that the one thing he wants most of all—a ready-made family—he can't have? I mean, Jesus. You must've been raging."

Shuggie said nothing, so she pushed him further.

"When did she tell you? That she hated you, I mean? When did Paula tell you that she knew exactly what sort of man you are?"

Across the table, Cowan gave a single grunt, then raised his glass to his lips. Heather thought she saw a shake there, but he sat the glass back down too quickly for her to be sure.

"She didn't," he replied in a monotone. "I didn't know. Not until I saw the message on that wee Mick bastard's phone yesterday. I had no idea."

One of Heather's eyebrows raised. "I find that very hard to believe."

"I don't give a flying fuck what you believe," Shuggie told her. "It's the truth. I mean, she was always quite quiet. Shy, I thought. Didn't really get involved when we did anything together." His eyes lit up, and his bloated lips curved upwards into a smile. "Not like Ibby. My wee Ibby. She's grandpa's girl. But Paula... I just thought it was because she's a teenager. They're right moody bastards at the best of times, let alone when someone new's coming into their lives out of nowhere."

"Especially when that someone is a convicted violent criminal," Heather added.

Once again, she expected Cowan to erupt. Once again, he disappointed her.

"No. No, I suppose that probably didn't help," he admitted.

He stared down at the blue tartan carpet on the floor, idly turning his glass around and around on the mat. Heather studied him for a while, and didn't look away when he finally raised his gaze to meet hers.

"We need to find the piece of shit who did this," he announced, slamming his glass on the table like this marked the announcement as some sort of official decree.

Heather frowned and leaned in closer, like she wasn't sure she had heard him correctly. "Wait. We? What do you mean we?"

"Us. Me and you."

"Jesus Christ. *Me and you*? You can't be serious?"

"I'm deadly fucking serious. I'm no' saying we become best pals. We're no' going to be sitting up all night braiding each other's hair and talking about boys."

"Oh aye, because that's what us girlies do," Heather shot back.

Shuggie ignored the remark.

"But we can help each other. You've got your resources, I've got mine. We can pool them. Off the record, obviously. Low key. I can't have people knowing I'm collaborating with the enemy, but we can help each other. Share information. Keep each other in the loop. Whatever it takes to find this bastard."

"And what if you find him?" Heather asked. "You going to hand him over?"

Shuggie's nostrils flared. He shrugged. "Aye. I'll hand him over," he said. "Eventually. Maybe no' all at once, but I'll hand him over. Pinky swear, Scout's honour, dib-dib-fucking-dib."

Heather took another big gulp of her pint, then smacked her lips together. "Tempting, Shuggie. Very tempting. But there's just one problem with this whole plan of yours."

"And what's that?"

"I'm off the case."

"What?" Shuggie's scowl was one of genuine confusion. "What the fuck for? What have you done?"

Heather kept her glass raised in front of her mouth, partly obscuring her face in an attempt to hide her shock.

He didn't know.

She'd assumed Cowan knew everything about her, but he didn't know this. He didn't know about her personal connection to the case.

It shouldn't have been such a surprise, really. He hadn't batted an eyelid at the feather. He hadn't made that connection. The Killie Kiddie Killer had shocked and scared the general public all those years ago, but Shuggie was working his way up through the ranks of the Glasgow underworld, and would've already seen his share of violent deaths by that point, so it likely hadn't left the same impression.

"Politics. The usual shite," she replied.

"Well, who the fuck's leading it, then?" Shuggie demanded.

"DCI Grant. Not sure you've ever had any dealings with him, or—"

The look on Shuggie's face made it clear that he had, and that he hadn't been impressed by the calibre of the man.

"That useless streak of pish? Are you fucking winding me up?"

Heather shook her head. "Nope."

"Jesus fuck!" Shuggie hammered a fist so hard against the table that the TV screen above his head flickered.

The young man behind the bar turned their way, saw the look on Cowan's face, then decided it was probably best all round if he didn't get involved.

Unfortunately for him, Shuggie wasn't giving him the option. The gangster raised a hand, clicked his fingers, then pointed down at the table.

"Here. John. Couple of whiskies over here. The good stuff, none of your shite."

While the barman reached for two glasses, Heather shook her head. "No. Not for me. I'm heading off."

"Are you fuck," Shuggie told her.

The phrasing was classic Cowan. They were the words of a man used to giving orders to people acutely aware of the consequences of disobeying them.

But, while the words were standard for him, the intonation of them, and the hollow desperation in his eyes were both new.

"I just…" He ran a hand down his face, pausing a while to rub his eyes with his forefinger and thumb. "I don't want to drown my sorrows alone."

Heather studied him in silence for a few moments, poised and ready to leave.

Then, with a sigh, she relaxed back down onto the thin padding of the bench seat.

"Fine," she said. "Maybe just a quick one for the road."

TWENTY-FIVE

IT WAS over an hour later when Heather made it home. She heard the alarm before she reached the gate, a piercing peep-peep-peep that cut through the light haze of the alcohol, and propelled her up the path.

"Dad? Dad?" she cried, barging into the house. Smoke raced along the hallway to greet her, the opening of the door drawing it outwards, away from the kitchen.

Above her, the smoke alarm continued to scream bloody murder.

Coughing, Heather buried her face in the crook of her elbow and hurried for the kitchen. Funnels of black smoke rose from two pots on the stove, each racing the other to see how much damage they could cause to the yellowing ceiling above.

The substances now welded to the bottom of each pot had presumably once been food. Now, they were something charred and volcanic looking, burned beyond all recognition.

Heather hissed out a couple of expletives, grabbed the handle of one of the pots, then swore some more when pain ignited across her palm.

Grabbing a couple of tea towels that lay discarded on the work-top, she threw open the back door and, wrapping the towels around the handles, horsed both pots out into the back garden.

The smoke started to follow them outside, big grey-black swirls of the stuff rushing out into the darkening night as fresher air rolled in to replace it.

"Dad? Dad, you there?"

There was no answer. None she could hear over the wailing of the alarm, at least.

Her lungs burned and her eyes ran as she dragged one of the kitchen stools across the floor until it was directly under the little white puck of high-pitched misery fixed to the ceiling.

Clambering up, she first tried waving a hand in front of what she guessed was the sensor, before deciding that the big round button was probably a safer bet.

She pressed it, but it did fuck all.

She held it down, and after a few seconds and a final indignant sounding *beep-beep*, the racket finally quietened down.

"Thank Christ," Heather muttered.

She dismounted the stool, turned to the door, then ducked as a lampshade came swinging wildly at her. It missed her head by inches, and she moved quickly to block it before it could make contact on the backswing.

"Jesus! Dad! Dad, it's me!" she cried, holding onto her father's wrist.

He tried to pull free of her, his eyes wide with fear, his thinning hair standing wildly on one side of his head, like he'd just woken up from a long but restless sleep.

"What do you want? What are you doing here? What do you want?" he demanded, still gripping the lamp.

"Dad, calm down. It's me. It's just me. It's Heather," she soothed, injecting some levity and calm into her voice, neither of which she genuinely felt. "You're alright. You're OK."

"Heather?" There was a flicker of recognition, which soon settled into confusion as he looked around the smoke-filled kitchen. "What the hell have you done now? You trying to burn the place to the bloody ground?"

"What do you mean? It was you, you daft old bugger! Were you cooking something on the rings?"

"Me? No. Who would I be cooking for? Your mum does the cooking."

An ache twinged in Heather's chest as she watched her dad looking around the kitchen, searching for the wife he'd lost long ago.

"She'll have left the bloody ring on again. You wait and see."

"Aye. Probably. I'll maybe just clean it up before she notices, though, eh," Heather said. "Don't want her feeling bad about it."

Her dad smiled and gave her a wink. "You're a good girl, Heather. There's a couple of pound on the mantelpiece. You take it and get yourself a wee sweetie."

Heather coughed out the opening few bars of a laugh. "Thanks," she told him. "I'll do that."

Scott's grin widened, then fell away again when he noticed the lamp he was still holding. He turned it, looking at it from a variety of angles, like it was some strange alien specimen no one had ever seen before.

"What the hell have I got this for?" he wondered.

"Here. I'll take it." Heather said.

She took the lamp from him and sat it on the counter next to the sink. Scott immediately picked it up and shuffled with it to the other side of the room.

"Water and electricity don't mix. You should know that by now," he said, very deliberately placing the lamp down as far from the sink as possible.

He sniffed as he turned to her, nose raised like an animal picking up a scent.

"Here. Hang on. Is that smoke?"

He sighed and flashed his daughter a look of such disappointment that Heather was suddenly fifteen again, and he'd caught her sneaking back home in the wee small hours, reeking of fags and booze.

"Don't tell me you've gone and bloody burnt something," he said, groaning.

"It's fine, Dad. I'm sorting it. You away and sit down, and I'll bring you a cup of tea."

"Aye. Right. Well." Scott looked around the kitchen again,

shaking his head, then settled on his daughter again. "Maybe try and no' recreate *The Towering Inferno* this time. Some of us can't shimmy ourselves out a window as easily as we used to."

"I'll see what I can do," Heather said, then she took an arm and steered him out into the hall, being sure to aim him in the direction of the living room door.

Once she was sure he'd gone the right way, she opened the window up as far as it would go, turned on the main extractor and the one above the hob, then switched off both rings, which she realised she'd left burning away.

That done, she allowed herself a moment to collapse against the side of the fridge freezer, and spent the next several seconds standing with her head in her hands while the smoke continued to clear around her.

She should've been here. This was on her. Another few minutes, and…

There was something on the floor by the back door. A red square, about the size of a CD case lay there on the lino.

Had it been there a second ago? In her rush to get the door open, she hadn't noticed. She didn't remember seeing it, but then her attention had been fixed on the somewhat more pressing matter of stopping her house from burning down.

Wheezing out a final lungful of smoke, she crossed to the door, squatted down, and picked up what she realised was an envelope containing a card.

Her first name was written on the front in neat block capitals, with a line drawn underneath it.

There was no letterbox in the back door. Either someone had slipped the card beneath the door while it was closed, or…

Heather rose quickly to her feet and rushed out into the back garden. The gate was closed, and the light spilling out through the open kitchen window revealed nobody in the garden.

Beyond the back fence lay a darkness that stretched on for several metres before a street light drew back its veil. Heather took a step along the path towards the gate, peering through the gaps in the fence, searching for any sign of movement.

For any indication that someone was standing out there.

Watching.

Her breath emerged as a fine white mist that dissipated quickly in the cold evening air.

She stared into the darkness beyond the fence.

She should go out there. She should check to see if someone was lurking in the dark.

But the knot of dread that she'd carried for decades felt heavy in her gut, and she returned to the house, already telling herself that there was nobody there. Convincing herself that she was getting carried away.

But the card was still in her hand, and her name was still on the front.

She set the envelope down, took a pair of thin blue rubber gloves from her jacket pocket, and then fished a small, sharp knife from one of the drawers. She used the blade to slice open the top of the envelope, then carefully removed the card from inside.

There was a bird on the front. It was a cartoonish drawing of a chicken or a turkey, with its wings held over its face. One eye was staring through a gap in the feathers, which were splayed like the fingers of a human hand.

Beneath the image, in the same hand-drawn style, were the words:

Peek-A-Boo! I See You!

Heather glanced over at the door. It still stood open, letting the air circulate. She closed and locked it before easing open the card and reading the message.

There was nothing printed inside as part of the design. Instead, the sender had written to her in the same meticulously neat and evenly-spaced block capitals as on the envelope.

I saw you on the TV today, the message read. *You looked so tired, I wanted to cry for you.*

There was a drawing of a simple emoji-style sad face below that line, with tears falling from the dots of its eyes.

Beneath the image, the message continued.

Have you been sleeping, Heather? Or have you been lying awake, thinking about me? Thinking about our time together? Because I think about that. I think about it all the time. I hope we can do it again soon.

There was a big space below this, then at the bottom, it had been signed off with a jarringly professional, *Yours Sincerely, You Know Who.*

Most of the card had been hard to read, thanks mostly to the way her hands had started to shake after the first sentence.

She read the words on the inside again, then suddenly threw the card onto the kitchen worktop, like it had become too hot to touch, even through her gloves.

She felt the floor beneath her lurch. The kitchen began to spin around her. She reached for the counter, but it wasn't where she expected it to be and her hand found only empty space.

It was only the shout from her dad that anchored her and stopped her from falling to the floor.

"Heather! Heather!"

She heard his panic. Felt his fear. She was running before she knew it, stumbling out into the hall, skidding through the doorway and into the living room.

Scott sat in his chair, the telly remote in one hand, a frown underscoring all the lines on his face.

"What? What's the matter?" Heather gasped, her chest heaving, the blood rushing through her veins triggering the beginnings of a headache. "What's wrong?"

"Is it just me?" her dad asked. He sniffed the air. "Or do you smell smoke...?"

———

Kenny apologised. Of course he did. Unwarranted shouldering of guilt was kind of his thing.

"I should've stayed longer. But, he seemed fine when I left. Good, even. He'd had his dinner. Even helped me make it. But we turned everything off. I washed everything up. Sounds like the daft bugger got peckish again." Kenny sighed. "I'm sorry. I should've waited."

Heather lay on her bed, on top of the blankets, her head resting against the wall behind her. She hadn't gotten around to redecorating the room since moving back in, and the green walls were pitted with holes from the pins she'd used on all her teenage posters.

At the time, she'd wanted to go for a pale pastel shade of green, but her dad had come home from the pub with a big tub of something almost luminous that he'd got cheap off some random guy.

She'd spent the rest of her childhood feeling like she was sleeping inside a migraine, and while time had taken some of the edge off the colour, it still took her by surprise every time she entered the room.

It had been an hour since she'd managed to get her dad into bed, and to get enough fresh air into the house so it no longer smelled like the arse end of a furnace. The kitchen would need repainting. Maybe she'd track down her dad's guy from the pub, and get something eye-wateringly hideous, just to repay the favour. An electric blue, maybe, or a neon pink.

Then again, he probably wouldn't even notice, and she'd be the one left dealing with the headaches.

"No, it's my fault. I should've been home," she told Kenny. "I just… I got caught up in the case."

There was a moment of hesitation before Kenny replied. His voice was soft and lacked much of its usual colour.

"I heard. About the girl. It's all over town," he said. There was another pause before he asked, "You alright?"

"Me? Aye. I'm fine," Heather said. She tried to laugh off his concern, but it came out sounding almost cruel. "I mean, it's always rough. You know? Stuff like this. Everyone assumes you get used to it."

"How could you? No bugger could," Kenny said. "Well, listen, I'm here, alright? No' just for your dad. You've always been my favourite niece, you know that."

A smile teased up the corners of Heather's mouth. It was an old joke that he'd made a million times before, but she needed to hear it right now. She needed the normality of it.

"I'm your only niece," she said, fulfilling her role in the age-old exchange.

"That's neither here nor there," Kenny said, and Heather could hear he was pleased to be able to repeat the joke for the umpteenth time. The more he said it, the funnier he seemed to find it. "The point stands. I'm here if you need to talk. We could head out to the old house if you want. Get the axe throwing on the go. You used to love that."

"Ha. Aye. Maybe," Heather said, being careful not to commit to anything. "Is it not about time you sold that place, though?"

"Here! That's your inheritance," Kenny replied, all mock bluster and outrage.

Before she could tell him she'd rather have the money, a movement across the other side of the room caught Heather's eye. It was small and slow, and it took her a moment to realise what it was.

The bedroom door had inched open. Just a little. Just a crack. Just enough for her to see the strip of darkness out on the upstairs landing.

She was sure she'd left that light on. She always left it on in case her dad needed to get up to use the toilet in the middle of the night. Now, though, the gap in her door was a line of solid black.

"Eh, listen, I better go, Kenny," Heather said, swinging her legs down off the bed. "I'll give you a call in the morning and let you know how he is."

"Right, aye. Just let me know when to come over, and I'll be there. And remember, anything you need…"

"Cheers, Unc," she told him, then they said their goodbyes, and Heather tucked her phone back into the pocket of her jeans.

She eased the door open without it making a sound. The hinges used to creak something rotten until Heather, sick of being caught sneaking back in, had invested in a can of oil.

There were no windows in the hall, and the darkness felt absolute. A cool breeze came creeping up the stairs, nudging the door to the bathroom open just as it had done to hers, making it groan ominously somewhere at her back.

She knew the house so well that she found the light switch on the first attempt. The bulb in the light at the top of the stairs was one of the older energy-saving types that needed a good five-minute warm-up to reach full brightness. It didn't so much sweep away the darkness as push it back a little, but it revealed something that made Heather's breath snag in her throat.

Her dad's bedroom door was open. The bed that she had tucked him into had now been vacated, the covers thrown back.

"Dad?" she said, stepping into the room and finding it as empty as the bed.

She returned to the upstairs landing, quickly checked the bathroom, then headed down the stairs.

She descended in a hurry, and yet was careful to pick the right spots for her feet, avoiding all the squeaky floorboards.

Who was she worried about alerting to her presence? She didn't know. But, her heart was thumping, and her breath was short, and she wished, more than anything, that she had one of Kenny's old throwing axes with her right then.

The breeze was coming from the kitchen. There was a light in there, too—a dim red glow that initially made her think of fire. It was too stable to be the flickering of flames, though, and as she sidestepped through into the kitchen she saw all the rings of the electric hob were on, the four red circles burning a fierce, warning-light shade of red.

The back door stood open. Heather quickly shut off the cooker rings, pulled a knife from the block on the worktop, then rushed over to the door.

She flicked the switch for the outside light, but it failed to turn on. No real surprise, given that it had been knackered on and off for more of her life than it had been working.

The kitchen lights would have to do. As she turned them on, their weak glow pushed outwards into the garden, revealing the figure of a man standing halfway down the path.

She saw his bare arse first, the angle of the light picking out the lower half of his body in more detail than the top.

It was an arse she had once naively assumed she'd never have to clap eyes on, but which she'd become increasingly familiar with over the past year or so.

"Dad? Dad, what are you doing?" she asked, rushing out to him.

He didn't seem to notice her at first, and just stood there, fully naked, fingers wringing together, old eyes scanning the darkness beyond the fence.

She put an arm around his shoulder and almost recoiled at the coldness of his skin.

"Come away inside, Auld Yin. You'll catch your death out here."

"There was someone out here," he said, not turning to look at her. Heather followed his gaze, and saw for the first time that the back gate stood open. "I heard someone. And I thought... I thought maybe it was Stewie. Maybe he'd got himself locked out. Him and Heather are always doing that sort of thing." He looked at her then, but there was no recognition in his eyes. "Aren't they?"

Heather's voice sounded unnaturally deep, her tightening throat giving the words a low, hollow timbre.

"Aye. So I hear," she told him. She forced a smile, and gently guided him back in the direction of the house. "Now, away you come inside. Let's get you warmed up."

He allowed himself to be turned, but kept staring at the gate for as long as he could.

"And what about Stewie? What if he's out there?" Scott asked. The worry on his face when he turned to her almost brought Heather to her knees. "Will you keep an eye out for him?"

Heather pulled him in closer and kissed the thinning hairs of his head.

"Always," she whispered, then she glanced back over her shoulder at the open gate, as she led her dad back to the warmth and safety of the house.

TWENTY-SIX

DR SHONA MAGUIRE was halfway through a lukewarm sausage, baked bean, and cheese bake—and very much enjoying every bite—when the door to the mortuary swung open, and a bureaucratic nightmare in a leather jacket came striding in.

"Alright, Shona? Long time no see," Heather said. She grinned. "Although, probably not long enough, I'm guessing."

"No!" Shona said, spraying flaky bits of pastry over the desk. Even with her mouth mostly full, her Irish accent was unmistakable.

"No? Oh, that's nice. And here I thought you didn't like me."

Shona shook her head, then held up a hand, urging Heather to wait while she hurriedly chewed and swallowed her pastry.

Heather watched as the pathologist cracked open a can of *Fanta*, and took a few big gulps to well and truly force the food down.

"No, you can't be here, I mean," Shona said. "I've been given orders. You're not to know anything. I'm not to tell you."

"Who said that?" Heather asked.

"Everyone! Everyone said that," Shona replied. "Snecky—"

"Jesus, since when do we listen to that arsehole?"

"Detective Superintendent Mackenzie, Detective Superintendent Mitchell, Dr Osgood on the phone, who'd apparently been told to warn me not to say anything to you… I could go on," Shona said, then she shook her head. "Well, no, I couldn't. That's it. But that's enough."

Heather held her hands up in surrender. "Alright, alright. Jesus. I was just in to say hello. Just a social visit."

Shona's eyes narrowed in suspicion. "I find that hard to believe."

"Aye. No, that's fair enough," Heather admitted. She sat on the edge of the desk, and helped herself to a *Monster Munch* from the packet sitting open on it. "Jack down with you?"

"No. He's got a training thing," Shona said.

"Oh. Shame." Heather held eye contact as she popped the *Monster Munch* in her mouth. "Is this your breakfast, by the way? I mean, I thought my eating habits left a lot to be desired, but this is mental."

"It's brunch," Shona said, folding the top of the crisp packet closed.

"Oh, well that's much better," Heather teased.

She raised her gaze in the direction of the swing doors that led through from the outer office to the business end of the mortuary.

"You started yet?" she asked.

"Almost done," Shona replied.

"You worked through the night?"

"Yes. I thought it was the right thing to do. You know, for Paula?" Shona said. She nibbled at one corner of her pastry, not making eye contact with the other woman. "And I don't sleep all that well when I'm away from—"

"Jack?"

Shona did look up at her then. "Home," she corrected. "I don't sleep well when I'm away from *home*."

"Right. Fair enough." Heather picked up the bag of crisps. "Can I have these? Didn't get breakfast."

"And you've the cheek to slag off my eating habits!" Shona said. She waved a hand at the crisps. "Sure. Knock yourself out."

"And what about that?" Heather asked, eyeing up the half-eaten pastry. "You going to finish that?"

Shona contemplated the remaining rectangle of sausage, bean, and cheesy goodness sitting on the paper bag in front of her. Then, snatching it up like a predator seizing its prey, she forced the whole thing into her mouth while maintaining unwavering eye contact with the detective inspector.

"Yeth," she managed to say through the wall-to-wall filling in her mouth.

"Nicely done," Heather said, munching her way through another crisp.

Shona gave a little bow to acknowledge the compliment, then stood up, chewing laboriously, before helping things along with another few sips of her soft drink.

Finally, when she was able to swallow down the compacted mush, she tilted her head in the direction of the mortuary proper. "Right, come on then. Five minutes, that's your lot."

Heather jumped up from the desk and tucked the *Monster Munch* into her pocket. "Seriously? I thought everyone told you not to tell me anything?"

Shona crossed to the office door and locked it, then turned back to the DI. "*Almost* everyone," she corrected. "Oh, which reminds me. Jack says hello."

———

The shape beneath the sheet made Heather hesitate at the door. She moved again before Shona had a chance to notice, though, and took up a position down by the feet-end of the table.

X-rays and photographs shone out at her from screens, hinting at the extent of Paula's injuries before Shona had said a word.

"Right, we better make this quick. Someone from the MIT is coming in shortly to go over it all."

Marty, probably, Heather reckoned. It wouldn't be Snecky. He hated this part. He hated any part, in fact, that meant him getting up close to a victim, or otherwise getting his hands dirty.

"What are we looking at?"

Shona gestured to the body and raised a questioning eyebrow. Heather nodded, then caught herself holding her breath as the sheet was drawn back to reveal the naked remains of Paula Harrison.

Shona had been busy. The body had already been cut open, then Frankensteined back together.

Although, that wasn't fair. Shona had clearly taken time and care over the sutures, stitching the girl back together as neatly as she possibly could. But there was only so much you could do, and the damage was the first thing Heather noticed.

The second thing she noticed was the open eyes, Paula's tightening muscles pulling open the lids so she seemed to be gazing up at Shona standing over her.

"You ready for this?" Shona asked, and the tone in her voice made Heather think that maybe no, she wasn't. Maybe this had been a bad idea. Maybe the Gozer was right, and she was too close.

Maybe she should leave this to somebody else.

"Go for it," she said, rushing the words out before her internal debate could reach a consensus.

"OK, then," Shona began. She took a breath, like even she had to steel herself for what was to come. "She was raped."

The bluntness of it hit Heather like a hammer blow to the chest, but she just nodded, her hands on her hips, her gaze fixed on a random point on the poor dead girl's body.

Shona gulped down another breath, let it out, then continued.

"Going by the damage, I'd say there was an implement used. Something straight and solid. Could be a sex toy, but could equally have been something else. A broom handle, maybe."

She forcibly cleared her throat before throwing a tiny, curt gesture in the direction of the dead girl's groin.

"Front and back."

Heather felt the floor beneath her undulating like the deck of a ship. The room was suddenly warm. Stiflingly so. She pressed the tips of her fingers against the table, supporting herself.

What the hell was wrong with her? She'd done this a hundred times. God help her, she'd seen and she'd heard far worse.

But the floor continued to rock, and the temperature in the room continued to climb, and hot bubbles of bile rose in her throat.

"Jesus," she whispered.

Shona pointed to the girl's wrists with a pen. "She was tied up. A rough blue rope, nylon fibres. Thin but strong, judging by the way it cut into her, and from the angle, her hands were at her back. The cuts are deep. Lot of friction burns. She struggled to get free. She fought hard."

There was a suggestion of pride in the way Shona said it—a sort of 'atta girl,' complimenting Paula on her strength and fortitude.

Heather didn't see it that way, though. She'd have preferred no cuts. No burns.

That way, she'd have known that when the whole horrifying, terrifying ordeal was happening to her, Paula had already been dead.

But she'd been alive. She'd been awake. She'd experienced every damn moment of it.

"What else?" Heather asked, urging the pathologist to continue.

"She was cleaned up afterwards. Down there, I mean. Turpentine or white spirit. I've sent off swabs to find out which. Some sort of solvent or paint thinner, though. Lots of it."

"I smelled it at the scene."

Shona nodded. "Not surprised. She was…"

The pathologist gritted her teeth for a moment.

"She was doused in it. Inside and out. Her genitals mostly, but pretty much everywhere else, as well. Damage to the lining of the throat and stomach shows that she was, uh, she was forced to drink some, too."

The weight of it all became too much for Heather's fingertips to bear, so she rolled her fingers into a fist and leaned on that instead.

"That wasn't what killed her, though," she managed to say, despite the rising heat and the unsteady floor.

She knew how Paula had died. She'd seen the wound. She'd seen it three times, in fact, though only once in person. The other two had been in an old case file, the images immortalised in big glossy photos taken many years previously.

"No. Knife wound through the throat. Angled upwards so the

blade entered her mouth. I'd say it was kept there until she essentially drowned in her own blood."

"Fucking hell," Heather muttered.

"You OK?" Shona asked.

"No. No, I'm not," Heather admitted. "But go on."

"You sure? We can—"

"Go on. I'm fine."

Shona didn't look convinced, but after a few seconds of deliberation, she continued.

"From the angle of the wound… You sure you want to hear this?"

"Shona!"

The pathologist shrugged. "Alright. OK. Sorry for being concerned," she muttered. "From the angle of the wound, I'd say your man's right-handed. And, eh, he would've been standing in front of her when he stabbed her. Directly in front."

Heather realised what she was getting at. "He was looking her in the eye when she died."

"And making her look at him," Shona added.

Both women stood in silence for a while, both trying not to imagine the pain, fear, and suffering Paula had endured in her last hours alive.

Both failing.

"Anything else?" Heather asked, forcing the words out through a mouth that felt like it was filled with dry ash.

"There's bruising, as you can see. Arms, legs, ribs. There's more on her back."

"He knocked her around."

"Kicked her, would be my guess," Shona said. "But also held her down with force. The bruises on the arms and shoulders, and on the lower legs, they're at the points I'd expect to see if someone was being forced down onto the floor and pinned there."

Shona turned away suddenly, like she could no longer bear to look at the girl on the slab. She indicated the screens behind her with a wave of a hand.

"Otherwise, there's nothing major to report. Not yet, anyway. Toxicology will take a while. Time of death is hard to pin down because she was under the snow, but that in itself gives us a pretty good idea."

Heather had already figured that one out. Paula had last been seen leaving school just before 4 P.M. on Thursday. The snow had started on Friday morning, by which point her body had already been discarded in the woods a few miles out to the west of town.

The killer would've disposed of the body under the cover of darkness, which meant dumping her before eight-ish on Friday. That meant he had held her for a maximum of sixteen hours.

The last sixteen hours of Paula Harrison's all-too-short life.

And undoubtedly the longest.

Heather realised that Shona had turned back now. The pathologist still wasn't looking at the body, though, and was instead focused on Heather herself.

"What?" the DI asked.

Shona's face tried on a variety of different expressions, ranging from comforting smiles to concerned frowns. None of them seemed to fit what she was looking for, though, and she settled on something blankly inoffensive.

"I, uh, I hope you don't mind me saying, but… He told me. Jack, I mean. He told me. He told me why they took you off the case."

Heather's knuckles cracked under the additional pressure as her arm took more of her weight. The sound was enough to make her straighten up, and she shoved both hands deep into the pockets of her jacket.

"Did he?" she asked, her expression giving as little away as Shona's. "He had no right to do that."

"He just… He thought I should know. For context," Shona said. "And, well, to be honest, this could cost me my job, and it's not like I'm your biggest fan, so he thought if I knew why you wanted to know, I might be more willing to—"

"Fine. I get it," Heather told her. She looked down at the broken and empty vessel that had, until just a few days ago, been Paula Harrison. "And, um, I, you know, I *appreciate you doing this,* or whatever. I get that you're taking a risk. I'll make sure that nobody finds out you told me anything about—"

"Hello-o?"

Both women froze at the sound of the voice from the outer office. Their eyes met, and they both mouthed a silent, panicked, *Fuck!*

Heather pointed to Shona and made a winding motion with her hand, urging the pathologist to start talking.

It took Shona a moment to pick up on the instruction, then she replied in a slightly wobbly falsetto, "Just a minute! I'm... in the toilet."

She crammed her fist into her mouth and bit down on it until she tasted the rubber of her glove.

"In the fucking toilet?!" Heather whispered.

Shona winced and shrugged an apology, then she and Heather both turned as one of the swing doors was opened a few inches and DS Marty Brompton poked his head in.

"Sorry? I didn't..."

His gaze shifted to Heather, who stood stock still, like she thought the detective sergeant's vision might be based on movement.

Marty regarded her in silence for a few moments, then turned his attention back to the equally motionless Shona.

"Dr Maguire, is it? I'm DS Brompton. You here on your own?"

Shona's gaze shifted sideways to Heather, then quickly snapped back to the man in the doorway.

"Uh... yes. Just here on my own. Well..." She pointed to the body on the table. "...me and You-Know-Who."

"Right. Cool," Marty said. "I just need to nip out for exactly two minutes." He flicked a brief but meaningful gaze in Heather's direction. "Hopefully, you'll still be on your own by the time I get back..."

———

Heather hurried the last few steps to her Audi, fumbling with the key remote as fat slivers of sleet slammed sideways into her.

The windows of the car were steamed up when she finally slid in behind the steering wheel, obscuring her view of the world beyond the glass.

That was good.

That was perfect.

That was exactly what she needed.

Sitting there in her car, tucked away alone at the far end of the car park, Heather Filson did something that she hadn't allowed herself to do in as far back as she could remember.

Something she'd forbidden herself to do.

She cried.

She cried for Paula Harrison, lying cold on that slab.

She cried for thirteen-year-old Eilidh Howden, and eleven-year-old Abbie Blackwell, both long dead in the grave.

And though she felt guilty for it, though she felt like she was betraying the memories of those other three by doing so, she cried for the other girl, too.

She cried for her even more than the others, though she didn't deserve it.

She cried, most of all, for the one that got away.

TWENTY-SEVEN

THE FIRST THING Heather heard when the phone was answered was a theatrical sigh of irritation.

"We're busy, Detective Inspector," Snecky told her. "You know that."

"What, I can't even call in?" Heather asked, indicating right as she switched lanes on the motorway, headed south out of Glasgow. "I thought I was off the case, not off the fucking force."

"No, you're not off the force, you're not even off the team. Well, not permanently."

Snecky was talking to her like he was reading a children's story on *Jackanory*. If Heather could've reached down the phone and strangled the bastard, her hands would already be around his windpipe.

"But, right now, we've all agreed that it's in everyone's best interests if you stay as far away from this case as—"

"I think you might be right," Heather said, cutting him short.

This, she knew, was the perfect button to push. There was no way he'd be able to resist.

"I usually am," the DCI smarmed. "What might I be right about in this particular instance?"

"The stepdad. Michael Harrison. There's something about him. Have you looked into him?"

"Oh! I thought stepdads were off limits?" Snecky replied, mocking her. "I thought stepdads could do no wrong?"

"That's not what we were saying, and you know it," Heather fired back. She bit down on her lip and composed herself. Losing her temper with the bastard would get her nowhere. "I'm saying, you could be onto something. When I saw him yesterday, I just… I don't know. There was something about him. I got this, like, this vibe off him. This bad feeling."

"A bad feeling? I'm afraid we can't operate on bad feelings, Detective Inspector."

Heather bit down so hard on her lip she almost drew blood. She stretched her fingers on the steering wheel, and let the rhythmic *whump-whump* of the windscreen wipers wash over her.

"No. I know that. That's why I'm asking if you've looked into him."

"Course I've looked into him. It was the first thing I did," Snecky replied.

Heather glanced at her phone in the charging cradle. "And?"

"And nothing. He's clean. No record. A fine, upstanding member of the community, who his wife says came home as usual the day Paula went missing, and only left the house again to search for her."

"That's not an alibi," Heather said. "Grabs her after school, stashes her, comes home, then uses the search as an excuse to leave again. He was searching all night, Linda said. Perfect cover to go kill her, then dump the body before morning."

She practically heard Snecky's beady wee eyes narrowing in suspicion. "How do you know when she was dumped?"

"The snow. She was under the snow."

"Oh. Right. Aye," the DCI said, though he didn't sound fully convinced. "Well, it's an interesting theory, and I'll be sure to bring it up. But right now, bad feelings aside, there's nothing to indicate that Mr Harrison was involved."

Heather sat forward a little. "You've got someone else in mind," she realised.

"I didn't say that."

"You didn't have to, Snecky. You're an open book," she said, indicating and pulling off the motorway at the Kilmarnock exit.

"It's Detective Inspector Grant, thank you very much! And you're not on this case."

"Who is it? Is it Shuggie?"

The momentary pause was enough to confirm that.

"I don't think it's him," Heather said. "I mean, I did. And it might be. He's more than capable. But I don't think he did it. Not this time."

"Again, Detective Inspector, this isn't your concern! What part of, 'You're off the case,' is it that you're having difficulty with?" Snecky cried, his shrill voice screeching out of the speakers like audio feedback. "I suggest you go home, take the rest of the day off. Take tomorrow off, too, in fact. Then we'll put our heads together and see what we can find for you to be getting on with when you get back. OK? How does that sound? Sound good?"

Heather ground her teeth together. The man was an arsehole, she'd always known that. Sometimes, though, he went out of his way to remind her just how much of one he truly was.

"Sounds great, *Detective Chief Inspector*," she replied, spitting out the title like it was something wet and unpleasant that she'd hoiked up out of her lungs.

"And you'll stay out of it? You won't go poking around?"

Heather pulled into a car park and slowed the car to a stop.

"Don't worry, I'll be on my best behaviour," Heather replied.

She shut off the engine, and looked past the swishing wipers to where Kilmarnock Academy sat hunched against the icy rain.

"You can have my word on that."

————

Mrs Hawkes stood at the front of the class, staring at the door like she'd just been visited by a particularly unwelcome ghost.

"Alright, Mrs H?" Heather asked, grinning as she stepped past her First Year escort and into the classroom. "Long time no see."

The old maths teacher leaned a hand on the whiteboard, smudging a formula she'd been trying to drum into the pupils, who now sat in an intrigued sort of hush, watching to see how this was going to play out.

"Heather. Heather Filson, isn't it?"

Heather's grin widened. "Aw, you remember me!"

"Aye. Well, not for want of bloody trying," the teacher muttered.

There were some giggles from a table of girls. Mrs Hawkes—*Hawkeye*—turned and pointed at them with a red marker pen.

"That's enough! Shut up! Don't start!" she warned. "Heads down and on with your work."

Around half the heads in the class lowered, but almost all of them very quickly lifted again the moment the teacher turned back towards the door.

"You can go, um…"

"Devon," the First Year said.

"Yes. Devon. You can go," the teacher said, but the younger girl had already retreated out into the corridor, and pulled the door closed with a *thunk*.

Hawkeye turned to Heather then.

"Is this about *Paula Harrison*?" she asked, silently but emphatically mouthing the girl's name like she was shouting at a deaf person.

"Aye. Sort of," Heather confirmed. She scanned the class, until she settled on a girl sitting slightly apart from the other pupils, watching the detective with what might have been scrutiny, but might equally have been total lack of interest. "I'm here to talk to Ace."

An excited murmur began to run laps of the classroom, getting louder and louder as each wave overlapped the last.

"Did she do it?" called a voice from one of the other tables. It was one of the girls Heather had interviewed, though she couldn't quite remember which one. "Did she kill Paula?"

"I bet she did!" another of Paula's friends added. She fired a look of disgust in Ace's direction. "Freak! I bet she done it!"

"That's enough!" Hawkeye barked. She threw her pen down on the desk so hard it made a loud *crack,* and then bounced off onto the floor. "Settle down, all of you!"

"Actually," Heather said, eyeballing the two girls who had spoken out. "I'm here investigating an assault. A couple of witnesses saw a girl matching Ace's description being beaten yesterday. I want to find out if that's true. Then, I want to find out who did it."

Heather had been winding her way between the clusters of desks, and now stopped looming over Paula's friends. She leaned down and lowered her voice a little, knowing full well that Hawkeye's hearing wasn't what it used to be.

"And then, when I do, I'm going to fuck them up beyond all recognition."

Heather gave that a moment to sink in, and enjoyed watching all three girls sinking down into their chairs.

She smiled at them, winked, then straightened so suddenly that all three of them jumped in fright.

"You," Heather said, snapping her fingers and pointing at Ace. "With me. Now."

———

Three minutes later, Heather was starting to think this was a bad idea. She and Ace stood in the corridor along from the classroom, tucked away into a corner to avoid passing foot traffic. Most teachers and pupils were in classes, but there were always a few wandering around for one reason or another, and this was a conversation she didn't want anyone to overhear.

Assuming, of course, that she was ever able to have it.

"So, you do want my help now?" Ace asked. "Because, when I approached you with this information yesterday, you didn't seem all that interested."

"I was interested, I was just busy," Heather countered.

"You told me to, 'Do one.'"

"Well, yes, but—"

"I said, 'Do one what?' and you said, 'Are you effing serious?' except you didn't say 'effing,' you said the unedited version."

"No, I know, but—"

"And I said, 'Yes, I'm serious. *Do one* what?' and then you threatened to arrest me."

"I mean—"

"And then I pointed out that you couldn't arrest me because I hadn't committed a crime," Ace continued. "At which point, you called me a little weirdo and told me to piss off." She put her hands on her hips and drew a big breath in through her nose. "Does any of that sound familiar, Officer?"

"Detective Inspector," Heather corrected. "And, yes, OK. Some of that does, admittedly, ring a bell. I was having a bad day."

"Is today a better one?" Ace asked her. She'd made a clumsy attempt to hide the worst of her bruising with makeup, but had only succeeded in making it more obvious.

"No. No, today's worse, if anything," Heather admitted. "I take it you heard about…?"

"Everyone's heard," the girl confirmed. "They're doing an assembly. I've asked for permission to record it for my podcast."

"Right."

"They said, 'Absolutely not under any circumstances,' but I'm going to do it anyway," Ace said. "There should be a record. There should be a record of what people say about her. It's only right."

Heather nodded slowly. "Yeah. Yeah, I suppose it is."

"Anyway. Apology accepted," Ace announced.

Heather frowned. "I didn't apologise."

"Well, let's pretend you were big enough to, and move on," the girl said. "What was it you wanted my help with?"

"This graffiti you saw—"

"Graffito."

Heather tutted. "Fine. This *graffito*."

"'Mr Pearse fingered—'"

The DI clamped a hand over the girl's mouth to stop her saying any more.

"Maybe best not to say it out loud," she suggested, looking both ways along the corridor to make her point clear. "So, how about you just show me, instead?"

TWENTY-EIGHT

TOBY PEARSE WAS SITTING in the same classroom Heather had seen him in on Friday, although this time around, there were no pupils gathered around the desks.

He was leaning back in his chair, gazing out of the window at the housing estate that Paula Harrison had called home. He had white Apple AirPods in his ears, and Heather could tell from the way he was bobbing his head that he was listening to music. Something upbeat, too.

She could also tell that he hadn't yet heard her enter the room.

Holding a fist a few inches from her mouth, she coughed loudly. The teacher turned quickly in his chair, and a momentary look of confusion gave way to a thin-lipped smile of acknowledgement as he hurriedly plucked his AirPods from his ears.

Snapping them back in their case, he got to his feet and waved for Heather to shut the door behind her.

"Hello, Detective," he said. "Sorry, was miles away. It's a day of reflection, I suppose."

"Looked like you at least had some good tunes to reflect to," Heather said.

"Hm? Oh. Yeah. I got Paula's friends to tell me some of her favourite songs. I'm just vetting them for suitability before we play them at the assembly." His smile warmed up a little.

"Wouldn't want, 'Fuck the Police,' to start blasting out, or anything."

"No, I don't suppose that would be ideal," Heather agreed.

"It seems inoffensive enough. A lot of Ed Sheeran and Lewis Capaldi. Some lassie moaning about her boyfriend dumping her. That one was quite catchy. And, at least it's not that K-Pop shite. Have you heard any of that?"

Heather shrugged. "Don't know. Don't tend to pay a lot of attention to that sort of thing. My musical tastes sort of peaked in the nineties and got stuck there."

He laughed politely, then stole a glance at his watch, and confirmed the time with a quick check of the clock above the door.

"Sorry, am I keeping you from something?" Heather asked.

"Just the assembly. It's not for an hour or so yet, so it's fine, but I'm supposed to be helping set up, and saying a few words. I still need to write those."

"You knew Paula well, then?" Heather asked. When the teacher appeared confused by the question, she continued. "To be making a speech. You must've known her better than most."

"Not really. But, I was her guidance teacher, so the head decided I should say something."

"Right. Aye. Makes sense," Heather said. She ran a hand down her face. "Look, there's no easy way to ask this," she began, then she shrugged. "I mean, no, I suppose there *is* an easy way of asking it. Did you finger Paula Harrison?"

Toby stared back at her, mute with shock. The only sound in the room was the angry shouting of another teacher a few doors down as they let rip on some wayward pupil.

"What the hell sort of question is that?" he hissed, his handsome features instantly becoming ugly with anger.

"One I'd like an answer to," Heather replied. "Did you?"

"I mean..." Toby threw his arms into the air. "What are you even asking? What the hell even is this?"

"I'm asking if you fingered, or otherwise had any sexual contact, with Paula Harrison, Mr Pearse? I thought I was making myself pretty clear."

"Well, of course I bloody didn't! Jesus. She's a pupil. She's a pupil, and she's fifteen!" Toby cried. He ran his hands through his hair, scraping it flat against his head. "Has someone said something? One of the kids? Because they're lying. I haven't... I didn't... I'd *never* do anything like that. Never!"

"Someone took the time to write it on the wall around the back of the building," Heather told him. She produced her phone and showed him a photo she'd taken of the amateurish daubings in question. "See? It's right there in black and white. Well, blue and brownish."

"Graffiti? That's where you got this from?!" The teacher almost laughed at the absurdity of it. "It's nonsense. It's bollocks. It's... it's *graffiti*."

"Just because someone wrote it on a wall doesn't mean it isn't true," Heather said.

"Maybe, but it certainly doesn't mean that it is!" Toby protested. "There's graffiti in one of the toilets that says, 'Celtic is a poof.' *Celtic*—a football team—*is*, singular, *a poof*. Is that true? Is Celtic Football club a homosexual man? No! And that's in the staff toilets, by the way, so imagine what the kids' ones are like!"

Heather returned her phone to her pocket. "So, you're saying you've never fingered Paula Harrison?"

"No! I mean yes! I mean... Yes, that's what I'm saying! Of course I haven't. She's a child! Was. Is. *Christ!*"

He slumped down into the nearest available chair, his hands now fully gripping his head like it was in danger of detaching from his shoulders and flying around the room like a deflating balloon.

"Why do you think someone would write something like that?" Heather pressed.

"I don't know." The teacher sighed wearily. "Because they're teenagers, and kids are arseholes."

Heather couldn't really argue with that. "They can be, right enough. What about Paula? Was she an arsehole?"

"What?" Toby straightened up slowly, clearly sensing some sort of trap. "No. I mean, maybe. Probably. But not that I ever saw. She seemed like a nice kid. A bit..."

Heather's ears pricked up. "A bit what?"

"I don't know. Lonely, maybe. I mean, she had friends, obviously, and she was popular, but… Sometimes you'd just catch sight of her and she seemed a bit… I don't know. Not detached, that's too strong."

He took a second, trying to find the right words, then had another stab at it.

"Even in a group, even when everyone was getting along, chatting away, whatever, sometimes it was like she was miles away. I could never figure out if she was beneath it all or above it."

Heather cocked her head. "Meaning?"

"Well, like… I'm sure you'll remember, but being in high school is all about status. We pretend it isn't, we try and make sure everyone gets along, and all that stuff, but it's about status. Some people are high status—Paula and her friends were up there. Maybe not the top, but up there. And some people, for whatever reason, are low status."

Heather thought of Ace sitting alone in Hawkeye's class, but said nothing.

"Those are the ones who generally get bullied. They're also quite often the ones who go on to excel when they leave."

"You're describing every school ever," Heather pointed out. "This isn't new."

Toby got to his feet. "No, I know. But as well as the status people have, there's the status they believe they have. Some high-status kids are deeply insecure. They've got no idea how they got to that position, and they're terrified they're going to drop back down just as inexplicably.

"But the opposite of that are kids who are so rock-confident in their own high status that they look down on even those at the same level as themselves. They see through them. They're bored by them. They've got to tolerate them, because what's the alternative? Being on their own? Nobody wants that."

The teacher checked his watch and then the clock again. Heather saw anxiety darting like fish through the deep pools of his eyes.

"The point is, neither of those ever quite fit in. They're on the margins of their groups, either hoping not to get found out, or too aloof to properly connect with their peers. Paula was one of those, I'm sure of it. I could just never figure out which."

"Right. I see." Heather tucked both hands into the pockets of her jacket, then shrugged. "What I take from that, Mr Pearse, is that you've spent an awful lot of time thinking about a fifteen-year-old girl."

He didn't look shocked or start issuing denials like he'd done over the graffiti. Instead, he looked her straight in the eye and nodded.

"You're not wrong. I think about all of them. All the time. I worry about them. Because for those parts of the timetable when I'm on guidance teacher duty, that's my job, Detective Inspector. And because, let's face it, you know as well as I do—with a lot of these kids, if I don't worry about them, who the hell will?"

He looked at the clock again, and this time it was very clearly for Heather's benefit.

"Now, I really need to go. Thanks for bringing that graffiti to my attention. I'll ask the janny to paint over it. If you've got anything else you need to ask me, then…" He smiled. Sort of. "Well, you know where to find me."

He stepped past her, checked the time yet again, then immediately picked up the pace.

Heather called to him, forcing him to stop just as he reached the door.

"Mr Pearse?"

Toby let out an audible groan as he turned back to her.

"Yes, Detective Inspector? Was there something else? I really need to move."

"You said, 'for those parts of the timetable when I'm on guidance teacher duty,'" Heather reminded him.

Toby glanced around, as if searching for the detective's point. He pulled out his keys and jangled them, making his intention to lock the classroom behind him clear.

"Yes. And?"

"What are you the rest of the time?"

"Oh. Right. Sorry, I didn't quite… Art," Toby said. "For the rest of the time, I teach Art."

Heather managed to keep her face from registering her surprise. "Art? Like... painting?"

The teacher pulled an exaggerated look of confusion, like he was trying to point out the absurdity of the question without getting his face panned in.

"Well, yes. Obviously *like painting*. Among other things." He looked back into the corridor as if hearing someone calling his name, then turned back to Heather and rattled his keys again. "Will that be all?"

Heather looked around the classroom, then headed for the door, taking her time about it.

"For now," she confirmed. She stopped and looked up at him as he made room for her to pass. "Like you say, Mr Pearse—I know exactly where to find you."

————

Heather sat in her car, shivering slightly from the aftereffects of yet another icy rain shower. Her wipers were swooshing back and forth, valiantly battling the downpour, while the blowers worked to defog the windscreen.

The *burring* of a ringtone poured out of the speakers—a steady, regular rhythm that had already gone to voicemail twice.

She wasn't giving up that easily, though. And, more importantly, the poor bastard she was calling would know that. He'd be scrambling around now, trying to find somewhere to safely take the call where prying ears wouldn't overhear.

A moment before the voicemail message kicked in for a third time, the ringing cut off and was replaced by a low, breathy whisper.

"What do you want? I can't talk. We're in a meeting," DS Brompton told her.

"About the case?"

She heard Marty agonising over his reply, and decided to put him out of his misery.

"Doesn't matter. But I need you to do something for me," Heather said, and she could've sworn she heard the detective sergeant physically cringe. "It's nothing major. Nothing you're going to get into trouble for. Do you have a pen?"

"Yes, I've got a pen! I've always got a pen," Marty fired cattily back.

He clearly wasn't happy about this. She'd have to make it up to him.

"Right, OK, good." Heather looked up at the school in the direction of the classroom she'd recently left. "Because I'm going to need you to get me an address."

TWENTY-NINE

SHUGGIE COWAN SAT at his usual table in the Pig & Bicycle, working his way through a large cup of black coffee.

Once his guys had come to pick him and the Jag up from Kilmarnock the night before, he'd come back here, sent everyone home, and then alternated between fighting back tears and consoling himself with copious amounts of alcohol.

He wasn't sure which of those had taken the greatest toll, but he'd woken up with a blinding headache that painkillers weren't so much as putting a dent in.

Only adding to his headache was the voice blaring into his ear from his mobile phone.

"You can't kick off. This might be nothing," DI Heather Filson told him. "It's probably nothing. So, you can't go storming in and start throwing your weight around."

"I thought you were supposed to know me?" Shuggie replied, his hangover turning his throat into a quagmire of guttural growls. "I don't storm in anywhere. I might've done when I thought Paula was alive. When I thought it was a race against time to bring her home. Then, aye, some storming in might've happened."

He punctuated the speech with a big slurp of coffee, and a smacking of his blubbery lips.

"But now? What's the rush? She's no' getting any deader. So, I want to make sure we get the right person. I want to take my time, tick all the boxes, cross all the t's, so I know—so I have not one ounce of fucking doubt in my mind—that we've got the right man. And then?"

He ejected a mirthless laugh and swapped his phone from one hand to the other.

"Well, then the race is back on to see which of us is going to get to him first."

"Right, well, ignoring that last part, that's all music to my ears, Shuggie," Heather replied. "I'm going to need to borrow one of your guys. And, I'll be upfront with you, there's a good chance he's going to end up in the jail."

Shuggie, who had been bringing his coffee back to his mouth, lowered it back to the table again.

"The fuck are you talking about?" he demanded.

He listened, still gripping the handle of his mug, while Heather laid out her plan. It was a plan that, at first, seemed needlessly complicated, but by the time she had finished explaining her reasoning, Shuggie's mind was already rifling through a list of possible names.

"Gonad," he announced.

There was a moment of silence from the phone. "Gonad?"

"Big Stevie Ross."

"Oh. Right." Another pause. "Aye, I can see why he ended up with 'Gonad,' right enough."

"He's let himself go. Worse than normal, I mean," Shuggie said. "A wee stretch at Her Majesty's pleasure will do him the world of good."

"*His* Majesty's pleasure," Heather corrected.

"Fuck. Aye. Still getting used to that," Shuggie said. He glanced heavenward, as if offering up an apology, then he pointed over to the barman and mimed writing something down. "Well, whoever's fucking pleasure he's being held at, it'll help him shift a bit of the beef. And his ex has been giving him all kinds of grief lately."

Shuggie gave a thumbs-up to the barman as a pen and notepad were placed on the table in front of him. He leaned back and nodded, now fully convinced that his decision was the right one.

"Aye. Gonad'll no' just do it, I reckon he'll fucking thank us for it," Cowan declared. He jammed the lid of the *BIC Biro* between his teeth, pulled it off, then spat it onto the floor for someone else to deal with. "So, give me that address now, and I'll have the fat fucker down there in forty-five minutes."

———

Gonad was pretty much what you'd expect for a man who'd ended up saddled with that nickname. He was mostly round, quite hairy, and had a number of unsightly veins running just below the surface of his skin.

Like his namesake, he may not have been much to look at, but he served a very important purpose.

The purpose, in this case, being some light breaking and entering.

Trying to explain that to him was proving difficult, however, because as Heather was discovering, as well as looking like a testicle, Gonad had the brains of one, too.

"Look, it's not difficult," she said, for the third or fourth time.

She was sitting directly behind him in his beat-up old Ford Focus. Getting in had been quite a squeeze, because of how far back he had his seat, but there was no way she was letting the smelly bastard into her car.

Besides, if anyone saw them together, she'd be deep in the shit.

Heather started to run through the explanation again. "That address you've got—"

Gonad held up the sheet of paper Shuggie had given him. Even the effort of doing that took a toll on him, and his breathing, which had been whistling in and out through his nose, became even more laboured.

"This address?" he asked. His accent was from somewhere in the North East of Scotland. Some farming community or fishing village, Heather reckoned. Some stock of slow-but-deep-thinking men with stubborn streaks and strong hands.

Gonad, it seemed, had missed out on all the positive parts of that description, leaving him free to really hone in on the 'slow' bit.

"Yes! *Of course* that address! What other address would I be talking about?"

"I don't know," Gonad admitted.

"Right. Well, that—face front, don't look at me!" Heather hissed, pointing to the deserted street ahead. "That address. You're going to go there, and you're going to make sure nobody is watching, and then you're going to break in."

"What am I nicking, like?" Gonad asked.

"Jesus Christ," Heather whispered, massaging her temples. "Nothing. I told you. You're not nicking anything."

"Then how come I'm breaking in, if I'm no' nicking nothing?"

Heather glared at the reflection of his eyes in the rearview mirror. "Are you taking the piss?"

"No," Gonad replied, with absolute sincerity.

"I've told you this. I've explained all this!" Heather cried, barely holding her temper in check.

She wondered if Shuggie had done this on purpose. Was this a form of carefully orchestrated psychological warfare? Was Stevie 'Gonad' Ross some kind of Weapon of Mass Distraction?

"You're going to break in. You're going to leave the front door open. I'm going to see you, and I'm going to come in after you."

"Should I be at a window, then?"

"What?"

"Otherwise, how will you see me?"

Heather tutted. "I don't need to actually see you, though. Do I? I know you're in there."

"Oh right, aye," Gonad said, though he still seemed a bit vague about the whole thing. "But I'm no' nicking nothing?"

"No. Just go in, stick a few fingerprints around the place, then wait for me."

"My fingerprints?"

"*Who the fuck else's*—?!" Heather pinched the bridge of her nose, counted to five, then spoke again, more calmly. "Yes. Your fingerprints."

Gonad thought this over. Heather could almost hear the fleshy gears of his brain sloshing around from the back seat.

"Seems a bit complicated," he finally announced.

"Right, well, it isn't, Gonad. It isn't remotely complicated. It's piss easy. A child could do it."

"Aye, OK. OK. Fine. I think I've got it," the man in the front seat announced. He looked down at the address written on the piece of paper in his hands, then his eyes met Heather's in the mirror once more. "But maybe we should run through it one more time, just to be on the safe side…"

———

Toby Pearse's house was a compact one-bedroom place on the south side of town, with an upside-down layout that meant the living room and galley kitchen were up a half flight of stairs, while the bathroom and sleeping area were on the lower level.

The door stood ajar when Heather walked up the path, the frame splintered where Gonad had forced his way inside.

There was no way she'd have been able to get a search warrant. No chance she'd even be allowed to ask for one. She couldn't just break in—that would be illegal.

But spot someone else breaking in? Witness a crime taking place on the premises? Then, the world—and, more specifically, the home of Paula Harrison's guidance and art teacher—was her oyster.

"Police! I'm entering the premises!" she called.

The voice that replied from upstairs sounded as nonplussed as ever.

"Aye. I know."

"Shut up," Heather replied, lowering her voice. "Just stay up there for a minute."

"It's one of them topsy-turvy hooses," Gonad called down. "Living room's upstairs. Is that no' mad?"

Heather had known about the layout from past visits to houses on this block, and was already halfway down the stairs. She didn't have much time—there was less than an hour until the school bell rang—and if there was anything to be found, the bedroom was the best bet.

The bathroom was between the bedroom and the bottom of the stairs, so Heather chanced a quick detour through there. Beyond some light indication that he was a bit of a clarty bastard—multi-layered flecks of dried toothpaste on the mirror, a sprinkling of stubble scattered around the sink, and eight or nine empty toilet roll tubes lying on the floor beside the cistern—there was nothing incriminating to be found.

The bedroom continued painting a picture of a man with limited housekeeping skills. The double bed looked like it hadn't been made in weeks, and probably not changed in months. The sheet was badly creased on one side, nights of sleep sweat staining the cotton-nylon mix and marking it with hundreds of tiny ragged bobbles.

He hadn't hoovered in a while, and crumbs had been trodden into the carpet. A drink had been spilled at some point, too—something dark and reddish—and attempts to clean it up had bleached some of the colour from the carpet itself.

She pictured the guy she'd met at the school with his coordinated greys and Cuban heels, and struggled to make him fit in this room.

A TV was mounted beneath the squat window at the top of the wall, which let in some light, but offered nothing but pavement and passing feet as a view. Beneath the telly, a scuffed dressing table held a couple of games consoles, a stack of games, and an assortment of hair gels and deodorants.

In the corner of the room, tightly wedged in between the dressing table and bed, there was an easel with a blank canvas resting on it. A wooden box of paint tubes, each one spotted with colour and squeezed almost dry, balanced on top of a cardboard box beneath the wooden frame, and a white plastic palette hung from a hook beside it, so dry it was gathering dust.

Heather, hands safely inside a pair of gloves, pulled open the drawers of the dressing table and rummaged around inside. Pants. Socks. T-Shirts.

Nothing of interest.

Dropping to the floor, she looked under the bed. There were a few single socks under there, an alarming amount of dried, wadded-up tissue, and not a whole lot else.

"Bollocks," Heather whispered, then she froze when she realised she could hear a sound from above her.

It was a steady droning sound that had been there since she'd entered the room, but which she was only now picking up on. A low, repetitive hum that made her think of—

PING!

"The microwave," Heather muttered. "He's using the fucking microwave."

She got to her feet, visions of her immediate future forcing their way to the forefront of her mind.

What had she been thinking? This was madness. She'd lose her job over this. If she was *lucky*, she'd lose her job. If fortune wasn't on her side, then there was every chance she'd lose her freedom, too.

"Fuck, fuck, *fu*…"

She caught her breath as her gaze fell on a Kilmarnock Academy school blazer hanging on the back of the bedroom door. It was of a style worn by pupils in Fourth Year and above, and not something a teacher would wear.

Even if it was, this one wasn't in Toby Pearse's size. It was considerably smaller.

There was no name tag, and the pockets were empty. But, when Heather sniffed the collar, she got the faintest suggestion of some floral perfume or other. She had no idea what it was, but it was miles away from the musk of the teacher's cologne.

It was a girl's blazer.

A Kilmarnock Academy girl's blazer.

Here, in Toby Pearse's bedroom.

She took out her phone, snapped off a picture, then swiped to the dialler app to call in the burglary. She'd get the local Uniforms round, hand Gonad over to them, then helpfully point out the blazer on the back of the bedroom door.

It was going to be a stretch to get even Snecky to believe that she'd just randomly stumbled upon the break-in, but she didn't care. She didn't need him to believe her. Assuming Gonad held his tongue—and Shuggie would've drummed into him the importance of doing so—then neither Snecky nor anyone else would have any actual evidence to suggest she'd arranged this whole thing.

They might suspect it, yes. They might even *know* it. But they wouldn't be able to prove it.

However she'd obtained it, once the blazer was in their hands, Snecky would have no choice but to bring the teacher in. And, better still, she might be able to convince the Gozer to put her back on the case.

After all, Toby Pearse wouldn't have been born when the Killie Kiddie Killer was active. He couldn't possibly be connected to the original case, which meant Heather wasn't connected to this one, other than in a professional capacity.

Pearse had used the murders from the old case as a cover for what he'd done to Paula. That was all. None of this was actually connected to the other victims.

Or to her.

So, they'd bring the teacher in. She'd be back on the case. And Paula's killer would be brought to justice.

She just had to call it in.

Judging by the lack of bars on her phone screen, though, there was no signal downstairs, the upper floor of the house blocking the reception.

Heather started to tap out the numbers on her phone as she stepped out into the corridor and headed for the stairs.

She was so fixated on it, in fact, that she didn't notice the man in the hallway until she walked straight into him.

Jumping back and looking up, Heather found herself face to face with a wide-eyed Toby Pearse.

"What the *fuck*," he ejected, 'are you doing here?!"

THIRTY

THE GOZER WAS NOT HAPPY. Judging by the colour of his face, he was about as far from happy as it was possible to get without discovering an entirely new emotional spectrum.

Snecky, standing with his arms folded off to the side of the detective superintendent's desk, didn't look happy, either. But then, Heather didn't really give a shit about him.

"Sit down," the Gozer instructed, before Heather even had a chance to shut the office door.

He tapped a pen against the desk, clicking the button on the end against his leather mat while he waited for Heather to sit.

The moment her arse hit the chair, the pen was dropped and he jerked forwards, his fingers locking together like he was imagining her neck was between them.

"What the bloody hell were you thinking?" he demanded, barking out a question that had clearly been stewing for a while.

"I don't think she *was* thinking," Snecky said, ruefully shaking his head.

"Shut up, Sam," the Gozer spat, still glowering at Heather.

He could do 'angry boggly eyes' quite well. Not to the same extent as Detective Superintendent Hoon had always been able to do—Hoon was something of a black belt when it came to boggle-eyed stares—but it was a solid effort, all the same.

"Well? What have you got to say for yourself?"

Heather played it cool. It'd piss the Det Supt off, but pissing him off was one thing. Admitting to breaking into the home of a suspect in a case she'd been explicitly barred from working on was something else entirely.

Only one, for example, could land her in jail.

"At around two-forty-five this afternoon," she began, "I noticed unusual activity at a house on—"

"Oh, cut the shit, Heather!" the Gozer barked.

"Yeah, Heather. Cut the shit."

"Sam! Please! I don't need you to say anything. I just need you to stand there and be a witness."

A witness?

Shit. That wasn't good.

Snecky lowered his head, suitably chastened. "Sorry, sir."

"You broke into that house," the Gozer said, still staring Heather down. "You broke into the house of a man who, surprise surprise, has a direct connection to the Paula Harrison case."

"No, sir, that's—"

"A case, *Detective Inspector*, that I have forbidden you from being involved with. A case that is now compromised because of your stupid bloody actions!"

The redness of his face had steadily increased along with the volume of his voice, so by the time he roared to the end of that sentence, he looked like an angry beetroot.

Heather stuck to her guns. "I saw someone entering the house. I recognised him as—"

"Stevie Ross. Gonad," the Gozer said. "We know. One of Shuggie Cowan's *associates*. Another coincidence? Or did you make a deal with the devil? I mean, Jesus. Cowan, of all people! I'd have thought with your history you'd want nothing to do with the man."

"You'd be right, sir," Heather said. "Just coincidence, like you say. Or maybe Shuggie suspected Paula's teacher might be involved in her murder, and sent Gonad to grab him and bring him in. I've got no idea. You'd have to ask him that."

"Oh, we will. We are. DS Brompton and DC Wolfe are interviewing him now, and given that the man has an IQ on par with that of a burst balloon, I suspect he's going to land you right in it. Don't you?"

Heather tried not to let her concern show. The Gozer was right about Gonad—he did have all the brains of a bag of cold mince, and roughly half the charm—but while he might not understand much, he understood Shuggie Cowan, and he understood what would happen to him if he didn't stick to the script.

Still, best to be prepared.

"He's a known criminal caught in the act, sir," she said. "I'm sure he'd say anything if he thought it might keep him out of the jail."

The Gozer's eyes narrowed, like he was tightening his focus on her. He picked up his pen again and resumed the quick *tap-tap-tapping* on the desk.

"Right. I see. So, you're sticking to it, are you? You're sticking to this preposterous bloody story of yours?"

"Yes, sir. It's not a story. It's what happened."

"Come off it, Heather!"

Snecky sighed theatrically. "Yeah, come off it, Heather!"

The Gozer closed his eyes all the way for a moment, and gripped his pen with both hands, like he was trying to snap it in half.

"Detective Chief Inspector!" he snapped. "Can you *please*, for the love of God, just stand there and keep your mouth shut?"

"Yes, sir. Sorry, sir," Snecky rushed to say. "Won't happen again, sir."

The Gozer's pen gave a *crick*. His eyes were drawn down to it in surprise, like he hadn't been aware of what his hands were up to. He returned the pen to the ornate wooden stationery holder on his desk, then sat back.

"So, to be clear, Detective Inspector—and this is on the record, I should stress, and you're reminded of your recent disciplinary history…"

Heather fired a glance at Snecky, the smirking wee toad who had stepped into her old DCI role.

"To be clear, you're claiming that you just happened to be

passing Mr Pearse's house, and you just happened to spot a known accomplice of Paula Harrison's grandfather breaking and entering, *through the front door, mind,* of said house, so you decided to follow him in." The Gozer stared her down, like he was trying to hammer home the absurdity of her statement and force her to change it. "That's your version of events?"

"It is." Heather nodded. "Protect life and property, sir. That's what we all signed up for, wasn't it? Obviously, I didn't know it was Mr Pearse's house at the time, and I didn't get a good enough look at the person breaking in to see who it was, but otherwise, yeah. That's pretty much bang on."

She'd been sitting rigidly straight through the conversation so far, but now allowed herself to relax a little, hoping that the Gozer would follow suit.

He did not.

"And then you found 'the blazer,'" the detective superintendent said, and though he didn't mime the quote marks, Heather heard them loud and clear.

"That's correct, sir. It was hanging on the back of what I now know to be Mr Pearse's bedroom door. In plain sight."

"In plain sight in a room you shouldn't have entered, in a house you had no bloody right to be in!"

"As I said, sir—" Heather began, but the Gozer's hand slamming on the desk silenced her. It also caused Snecky to let out a little involuntary yelp of fright, but the other detectives had the good grace not to mention it.

"Even if I believed you, Heather—even if I'd sustained some sort of head injury, and believed a word of what you're telling me —do you think a jury will? Do you think the PF would even allow the case to get that far?"

"It wouldn't matter, sir, if we can build the case, get a confession—"

"Of course it bloody matters!"

The echo of the detective superintendent's roar took a moment to die back into silence. He was shaking with rage now, angrier than Heather had ever seen him. He swallowed it back, trying to compose himself.

"Everything we do matters, Detective Inspector. It matters that we obey the rules, that we do things properly. Because if we don't —if we fail to carry out our duties in the correct manner—then we put everything at risk, including this bloody case! This is why I removed you from it, Heather. Clearly, you aren't thinking straight."

"But the blazer, sir—"

The Gozer grunted out a groan of irritation. "Jesus. The blazer." He rubbed his forehead with one hand, then gestured to Snecky with the other. "Tell her, DCI Grant."

"Tell me? Tell me what?" Heather asked.

She kept her attention on the detective superintendent, in the hope that he'd answer, but Snecky was having none of it. Now was his chance to shine.

He leaned forwards, putting both fists on the desk as he forced his way into Heather's line of sight. She had no choice but to look at him.

"It's his sister's," the DCI said, then he straightened up suddenly and clapped his hands together, like he'd just delivered some killer punchline.

Heather blinked.

Heather frowned.

"What?"

"Didn't you know, Detective Inspector?" the Gozer asked. "Toby Pearse has a sister at Kilmarnock Academy. Sixth Year. The blazer belongs to her."

"What? No. No, that's not... I don't believe that."

"Yes, well. Whether you believe it or not is irrelevant. We've spoken to her. She's confirmed it. Also, her name is on the label inside."

Heather rocked forwards in her chair. "No. No, it isn't. I checked. I looked at the collar, I checked it, and—"

"The *other* label. In the lining. Down the back," the Gozer told her. "Which, presumably, you didn't notice?"

The soles of Heather's feet felt suddenly hot, like someone had cranked up the underfloor heating. It radiated quickly up through the rest of her body, until her shirt stuck itself to the small of her back with sweat.

"Uh, no, sir. No, I didn't notice," she admitted.

"Because you didn't want to. Because that wouldn't have fit the narrative you've built in your head," the Gozer continued. "And that's not our job, Heather, you know that. It's our job to gather all the evidence and let the story emerge, not to come up with the story and then go looking for whatever evidence might fit!"

"I know that, sir," Heather said.

She'd lost this fight, she knew it. Now, it was all about damage control. She felt like Conn Byrne had looked when he was lying on the floor, his hands over his head, shielding himself from Shuggie's kicking.

"Why the hell did you think the teacher was involved, anyway? What's the connection?"

One of Heather's eyebrows twitched upwards. Maybe this wasn't a total disaster. Maybe, now that he'd got the bollocking off his chest, the Gozer might listen.

"There was information that suggested he and Paula might've been in a sexual relationship," she said.

"Fucking hell. Seriously?" Snecky said.

The Gozer's reaction was much more muted. "Information? What kind of information?"

Heather's heart sank. She'd been hoping he wouldn't ask that. She pinned back her shoulders and brazened it out.

"There was graffiti," she began, but the detective superintendent shut her down before she could go any further.

Which was probably just as well, given that she had nothing more to really add.

"Graffiti?! Where, at the school?!"

The Gozer looked like he regretted putting his pen away, because now would've been the perfect time to throw it across the room.

"Do you know the shite we used to write on the back of the toilet door about our teachers when I was at school, Detective Inspector?" he barked.

In other circumstances, Heather would've made a joke then.

Something about being unaware that toilets had been invented back then, maybe.

Today, though, the ice beneath her was too thin to do anything but play it straight.

"No, sir."

"Vile stuff. Awful stuff. Not a bloody word of it true!" He ran his hands back over his head, like he was expecting to find hair there. "Graffiti. Jesus Christ. Now I've heard everything."

"And he's an art teacher," Heather said.

"So?" asked Snecky, and this time the Gozer didn't bother to shush him.

"So, the body was cleaned with turps or white spirit. Paint thinner. Used to clean brushes."

"How the hell do you know that?" Det Supt Mackenzie asked.

Shit.

"Uh, I smelled it, sir. At the scene. It was pretty pungent, so I guessed Paula's body had been doused in it," Heather said, then she quickly moved on in the hope she could drag the Gozer along with her, and away from anything that might land Shona Maguire in the shit. "Between those two things, I felt that Toby Pearse was worth following up on."

The Gozer's hand banged down on the table again, this time forming a fist. The shout that came out of him was so loud it cracked in his throat.

"*You're off the case, Heather!* You don't follow anything up. You don't ask questions, you don't poke your nose in, you stay out of the way and you do as you're bloody told for once. Just for once! Is that really too much to ask?"

The veins on the Gozer's temples were pulsing. Heather could actually see the blood roaring through them, expanding and contracting the tissues beneath his skin.

"No, sir."

"Oh! 'No, sir,' she says! 'No, sir.' And yet, here we are!"

"Here. We. Are," Snecky concurred, and for a moment it looked like the detective superintendent was going to stand up and take a swing at him.

Instead, he inhaled deeply and closed his eyes for a moment.

Heather watched his lips. They moved, just a fraction, as he silently counted to ten.

When he'd finished, he opened his eyes again, and the anger that had been burning there had solidified into something less explosive, but more permanent. Disappointment, lightly seasoned with a little contempt.

"Your actions don't just reflect badly on you, Heather, they reflect badly on all of us. The whole MIT. The whole force, in fact," he told her. "What's more, you've jeopardised this entire investigation. I get that you believed you were trying to help. I do. But, the fact of the matter is, as a result of your actions, our chances of catching Paula Harrison's killer in a timely manner have decreased."

That one stung. Heather crossed her arms, protecting herself.

"What happens now?" she asked.

"Now? Now, I don't know, Heather. I really don't know. Mr Pearse doesn't want to press charges. He has chosen—chosen, mind—to take your story at face value. He wishes us to pass on his appreciation to you, for preventing a burglary taking place. But do not think for a moment that he's any more fooled by this than I am."

"Or me," Snecky added, and the little veins in the Gozer's head began to pulse again.

"Right now, I want you to take some time off," the detective superintendent said. "Recharge. Reflect. And we'll reconvene next week and decide on a course of action."

"A suspension?" Heather asked.

"A suggestion," the Gozer replied. "But a firm one. You are to contact nobody in this office regarding the case. You are to have no contact with anyone directly connected to the investigation. If it comes on the news, I want you to change the bloody channel. In fact, unplug the TV. Stay offline. Read a book or something. Just stay away from this case."

He sat back, still glaring at her, and gave her a moment or two to process all that before he continued.

"I'd ask if that was clear, but you said it was the last time we spoke on the matter, and look where that's got us. So, I won't. I'm just going to assume we understand each other."

"We do, sir," Heather confirmed.

"Good. Now, get out of my sight."

"And mine," Snecky chimed in.

The Gozer rolled his eyes. "Jesus, Sam! What did I say?!"

"Sorry, sir. Just slipped out, sir."

The Gozer called to Heather just as she reached the door.

"Oh, and Detective Inspector?"

She turned, still holding the door handle. "Sir?"

"Let me be clear. If we have to have a repeat of this conversation, you're done."

Heather nodded, just once. "Got it, sir," she said.

And then, with the sound of Snecky's grovelling apologies to the detective superintendent providing the soundtrack to her exit, she sidled out of the office and pulled the door closed at her back.

THIRTY-ONE

HEATHER HAD LEFT the station determined that, this time, she'd follow orders. This time, for once, she'd do as she was *telt*.

Her resolve had weakened a little by the time she reached the front doors, and had almost evaporated completely as she hurried across the car park with her head lowered against the rain.

It was gone completely by the time she found the flower.

It was a single yellow rose, and lay on the bonnet of her car, rainwater pooling in its petals.

At first, her mind tried to come up with some reasonable explanation for it. A passing bird could have dropped it, maybe. A strong gust of wind could have carried it from somewhere else.

And deposited it here. Right on her car. Right in the centre of her bonnet.

Aye. Right.

She turned, scanning the car park, searching for any sign of movement. A steady stream of traffic was rumbling up and down the M77 just beyond the boundary of the station, but right then, nobody else seemed to be with her in the car park itself.

"Fuck," she whispered, glancing back at the building. There was CCTV, but everyone had brought their cars today, so she'd been forced to park well back from the entrance.

She didn't have to see the footage to know that her car

wouldn't be included in the video from the cameras. Or, if it was, it'd be such a blurry black blob at the top of the screen that it would be impossible to make out anything useful.

Heather paced all the way around the Audi, keeping the rose in sight for as much of the lap as she could, like she was afraid it might fly away or run off the moment she wasn't watching it.

She checked her doors. Locked.

She squatted down and looked under the car.

Nothing.

The rain continued to hammer at her as she stood up. The rose hadn't moved, though the weight of the water had made the petals sag further so those resting on the car were now flattened against the metal.

Someone had put this here on purpose. Someone had been here. Almost certainly the same person who'd brought the flowers to her house, and who'd delivered the card.

Was he watching her now?

She turned again, eyes darting across the station's wall of windows. Blinds had been drawn on most of them. Was someone standing peering out through a set of them now? Or were they sitting low in one of the parked cars? Or crouching behind one, peeking out at her?

A breeze rolled down her neck, chilling the sweat on her back. She could feel eyes on her from somewhere. She was sure of it. Someone *was* watching her, studying her, waiting to see what she was going to do.

She took the rose from the bonnet of the car, clamped a hand over the head, then crushed it. Holding the mangled flower up, she gave it a wave for the benefit of any hidden onlookers, then dropped it into a puddle at her feet.

Her hands were shaking when she took out her keys and pressed the unlock button. Her fingers slipped on the door handle, half-pulling it open, then letting it jerk back into place.

She opened it on the second attempt, and a sudden surge of panic spurred her into the driver's seat, like a swimmer exploding out of the ocean at the sight of a dorsal fin.

Pulling the door closed, Heather hurriedly engaged the locks.

Only then, when she was safely inside the locked car, did she let out the breath she'd been holding for the past several seconds. It added to the condensation on the inside of the windows, and she turned on the engine and fired up the blowers, trying to clear it enough so she could see out.

When it took too long, she wiped a circle with her sleeve, affording her a porthole-like view of the car park ahead of her.

The traffic continued its back and forth on the motorway, though she could no longer hear the rumbling of tyres or the roaring of engines. Otherwise, there was no movement beyond the sideways slanting sheets of rain, and the slow creep of the clearing mist on the glass.

"Fuck you!" Heather announced.

Quite who she was announcing it to, she wasn't sure, but it had been bubbling up inside her for a while now, and felt good to finally put it out there.

She took out her phone, tapped through to her call history, then pulled on her seatbelt while she waited for the call to be picked up.

Take a few days off, he'd said.

Stay out of it, he'd said.

But Paula Harrison's killer was still out there.

And if it wasn't Toby Pearse, then that meant…

The call being answered saved her from having to finish that thought.

"Hi. Aye. It's, eh, it's me. It's Detective Inspector Filson," she said, barely giving the person on the other end a chance to finish their greeting.

Heather closed her eyes and rested the back of her head on her seat's headrest. She hated saying the words she knew she had to say. She always had, for as far back as she could remember.

But sometimes, needs must.

Heather opened her eyes again. "So, listen, the thing is," she began, "I could really do with your help."

———

They met in the rain, exchanged a stilted greeting, then headed for the house. They were halfway up the stairs when a voice called from the kitchen.

"Alis—Sorry! Sorry! Ace? Is that you?"

"Yes, Mother, it's me," Ace called back.

"Have you got someone with you?"

Something deep in Heather's very core cringed itself into a ball when Ace replied with, "It's nobody. Just a friend."

"A friend?"

The voice in the kitchen sounded excited now. Fast-moving footsteps grew louder until a cheerfully plump woman with a beaming grin on her face rushed into the hall.

"I didn't know you had a friend coming over to…"

She and Heather's eyes met. The smile took damage, but didn't collapse completely.

"Oh! You're… old," she announced, then she desperately tried to salvage the statement by adding, "er. Old*er*. Than Aliso—" She winced and shot her daughter an apologetic look. "Sorry, sweetheart. Than *Ace*. You're older than Ace is."

"Aye," Heather agreed. Not that it would've been possible to argue the fact.

"By quite a margin," the woman said.

Again, this was beyond dispute. Heather could see worry drawing itself across Ace's mother's face like the lines of an Etch-a-Sketch. To put the woman out of her misery, she produced her Warrant Card and passed it down through the railings of the staircase.

"Detective Inspector Filson. Heather."

This didn't have quite the desired effect, and Heather watched as all the colour drained out of the woman's face.

"Oh, God. What's she done?"

"*Mother!*" Ace said, sounding shocked by the question.

"Nothing. No. Nothing at all. She's just, uh, she has some information that could be—"

"I'm helping her," Ace said, summarising the situation more neatly than Heather had apparently been capable of.

"Uh, yes. Aye. That's right. She's helping me," Heather said.

"I'm helping her to crack a case."

Heather chewed some loose skin on her bottom lip and tilted her head from side to side. "I mean, I don't know if I'd say that, exactly..."

Ace's mum looked blankly up at them both, then folded Heather's wallet closed and passed it back through the spars.

"Right. Well... that's good! I'm Catherine, by the way. Cathy. Nice to meet you. Any friend of my daughter's is a friend of mine! Even, you know, the much older ones."

"Thank you, Mother. Anyway, we're going to work now. Do you have any other questions?"

"No," Cathy said, shaking her head. Her smile returned, but there was a lot of scaffolding behind it. "Can't think of anything. Unless—"

"I thought you'd never ask," Ace said. "I'll have the usual, and she'll have..." She looked Heather up and down, then nodded as she came to a conclusion. "Coffee. Black. Yes?"

Heather's eyebrows crept higher up her forehead. "Uh, aye. Aye, that'd be great."

Ace held her head a little higher, clearly pleased with herself. She looked past the detective to the foot of the stairs, and for a moment the affectation slipped.

"Thanks, Mum," she said, and then she continued on up to the landing above, and hung a right at the very first door.

"Eh, cheers, Cathy," Heather said, feeling extremely self-conscious as she plodded up the stairs behind the girl and followed her into her bedroom.

Ace was already standing right in the middle of the room with her arms out, presenting the place for Heather's consideration.

"Officer, welcome to the nerve centre of Crime-de-la-Crime!"

"Uh, cheers," Heather said.

Judging by her face, this wasn't the reaction the girl had been hoping for, but there wasn't really a lot more for Heather to say. The room was, to all intents and purposes, just a regular teenager's bedroom, albeit much tidier than usual.

Like most teenagers, Ace had posters on her wall, although

Heather doubted there were many other people her age out there with this particular selection.

Two of them were of the actor, David Suchet, sporting the little moustache and smug look he used to wear while portraying Agatha Christie's *Poirot*.

Another was a cinema-style movie poster for the film, *Knives Out*, while the remaining two were celebrating some Japanese animated movies, or games, or possibly even books.

In the corner, there was a desk. A battered old laptop and a microphone sat next to an ancient-looking typewriter.

Between them, in a frame, sat a signed black and white photograph of the late Angela Lansbury as Jessica Fletcher from *Murder, She Wrote*.

It was quirky, yes, but really the place wasn't much different to any other—

"Holy fuck!"

Heather stared at the wall to the right of the door for a moment, then looked back over her shoulder at Ace. The girl's disappointment had been replaced by a look of satisfaction, and she rocked back on her heels, clearly pleased by the DI's reaction.

"Is this… Is this a Big Board?" Heather asked.

Confusion picked away at Ace's smirk. "A what?"

"A Big Board. Some of us use it to keep track of a case."

"Is that what it's called?" Ace asked. "Huh. I just call it the Wonderwall."

"Like the song?" Heather asked.

"What song?"

"What do you mean, 'what song?' Wonderwall. Oasis."

Ace said nothing for a moment. She stood there, frozen to the spot, and Heather got the impression that some algorithm was running a search through the archives in the girl's head.

"Never heard of them," Ace finally declared. "Are they recent? Music's not really my thing. A lot of racket for no real reason. Which is ironic, because I'm told I have a lovely singing voice." She folded her hands behind her back and her mouth formed a thin, sorrowful smile. "The world's loss, I suppose."

Heather waited for some punchline to arrive. When it didn't, she said, "Still, I'm sure we'll all cope." Then she turned her attention back to the wall.

On the one hand, it did look a lot like the sort of Big Board Jack Logan had always used when working cases. While, on the other hand, it more closely resembled a full mental breakdown.

There had to be upwards of a hundred different sticky notes. They were scattered across the whole wall like someone had fired them out of a shotgun. Between them were dozens of pinned-up printouts of old news articles, emails, photographs, and at least one school report card dated from the 1980s.

None of it was arranged into any sort of discernible pattern. As far as Heather could tell, had all this stuff been thrown into the air, the end result, once everything had landed, would be much the same as what she was looking at.

Strands of red thread ran back and forth across the wall, joining together things that didn't seem in any way connected. A sticky note containing just the word 'Feathers,' and a question mark was connected by a thread on one side to a cartoon drawing of a fish, and on the other to an old magazine article about the Michael J. Fox US sitcom, *Family Ties*.

On and on it all went, a random tangle of thread, and paper, and possibly madness.

"Well?" Ace asked, stepping up beside the detective. "What do you think?"

"What do I think?" Heather sucked in her bottom lip, considering her response. "I think it's fucking mental."

Ace tutted. "Please, Officer. Nowadays, we say *neurodiverse*. And it is, yes. Although, I'm sure you've noticed the pattern."

Heather cast her gaze across the wall again. It lingered, just for a moment, on a blurry photocopied picture of thirteen-year-old Eilidh Howden.

The first victim.

"Is it, *explosion in a fireworks factory*?" Heather guessed.

The sigh from the girl beside her was so quiet as to almost be imperceptible. To Heather's surprise, she felt a twinge of embarrassment at not cracking the code.

"Well, I won't lie, that's rather disappointing," Ace said. "Have you heard of the Snowflake Method?"

"Is that a sex thing?" Heather asked, the joke coming out on autopilot before she remembered she was talking to a child. "Sorry. No. What is it?"

"It's a writing technique. Well, a plotting technique." Ace pressed the tips of her fingers and thumbs together, forming a rough circle. "You start with a central spoke. A premise. A murder, let's say, if you're writing crime fiction. Or investigating one."

Heather turned back to the wall. The photo of Eilidh Howden sat slap-bang in the middle of the chaos.

"From there, you build outwards. Imagine the spokes of a wheel, or the numbers on a clock. Each one spreading from that central hub. And from each of those spokes, at right angles, another spoke. From that one, another. And then repeat, until what you're left with—"

"Is a snowflake," Heather concluded. "Bloody hell."

She could see it now, the shape of it, an impossibly complex fractal of information spreading and growing across the wall.

It still didn't make any sense, of course, but at least she had now grasped the basic concept of it.

There was a cautious, almost timid knock at the door, then it opened to reveal Ace's mum carrying a tray with a couple of drinks and a small mountain of biscuits. She had her shoulders hunched like she was trying to make herself invisible, and was smiling as if in apology for not being able to.

"Sorry, sorry. I hope you weren't recording, or anything."

"Don't worry, Mother. No harm done," Ace said. She intercepted her and took the tray, then set it down on the desk between the laptop and the Jessica Fletcher photo.

"You looking at her wall, then?" There was a sense of trepidation to the way Cathy asked the question, like any judgement of her daughter's work would be a direct reflection on her parenting skills. "I keep telling her she should leave it for a bit and maybe, you know, go outside. Meet up with friends. Friends her own age, I mean."

Heather realised that Ace was still standing over by the desk, still clutching the tray, her back to both adults.

"I think it's pretty amazing, actually," she said, and Cathy's face bloomed with relief. "I mean, it's a lot, obviously. I don't understand it, but… yeah. It's pretty good."

Over at the desk, Ace finally let go of the tray, then returned to the Wonderwall with a coffee in one hand, and a pint glass filled to the brim with milk in the other.

"Thank you for the refreshments, Mother," she said, passing Heather the coffee.

"Aye, cheers," Heather said.

"There's biscuits. Don't forget the biscuits," Cathy said, pointing to the plate as she backed towards the door. "Anything you need, I'm just downstairs. Just shout. You know where to find me. I won't be—"

The rest of her sentence was muffled by the door closing in her face. Ace turned back to Heather, and for a moment the detective thought she saw some flicker of embarrassment crossing the teenager's face.

So, she was human, after all.

"Sorry about that. I don't have many visitors. Or, well…" Her eyes rotated, doing a full sweep of the room. "…any, actually. You're the first person other than me or my mother and father to be up here."

"Right. Eh, fair enough," Heather said, not quite sure what to do with that information. "Where is your dad? Is he around?"

Ace didn't reply to that. Instead, she started to drink her milk. Heather watched with a growing sense of awe as the girl necked the full pint.

"Right, then, Officer," Ace said, plonking the empty glass back on the tray. "I suggest we get to work."

THIRTY-TWO

IT WAS the feathers that she didn't understand.

"I mean, what's the link? What's the point?" Ace asked.

She was pacing back and forth in front of her Wonderwall while Heather sat on the end of her bed, polishing off her third chocolate-coated hobnob. The question didn't seem to have been aimed at Heather, so she continued enjoying the biscuit while she waited for the girl to answer it herself, like she'd done with most of the others she'd already asked.

"I mean, it's a calling card, obviously. But… why? It's not like he's a bird-themed killer, is it? It's not like he flies down and snatches up girls, then carries them off to his nest."

"Unlikely," Heather conceded through a mouthful of chocolatey crumbs.

"So, what's the feather for?" Ace asked, and this question did feel like it was looking for an answer.

Heather swallowed, then shrugged. "If killers leave a calling card, it's usually because they want to take credit for their work. They want people to know—"

"Please, Officer," Ace said, cutting the explanation short. "I know all that. I meant, why a feather in particular? Why leave those?"

"It's just…" Heather frowned. "I don't know. It's just his thing."

"We'll put a pin in it," Ace said. "I have a theory. We'll come back to it."

She went back to pacing again. Heather helped herself to another biscuit. She'd missed both lunch and dinner, and it had been a long time since breakfast, which hadn't been anything to write home about.

"On the podcast, I've been discussing the original case of the Killie Kiddie Killer. Which, as I've put on record here…" She pointed to a note on the wall without stopping to look for it. "…is a terrible name."

"I agree."

"It makes a mockery of what happened to those two murdered girls."

"It does. Yes. I've said the same thing," Heather replied.

Ace stopped and tucked her hands behind her back. "And to you."

Heather stopped, mid-chew. She felt a flush of heat rising from the collar of her shirt.

"I'm not here to talk about that," she said.

Ace cocked her head to one side, studying the detective. "Huh. Not yet, maybe," she said, although this could also have been directed at herself.

She returned to walking back and forth in front of the snowflake of information on the wall.

"The big question we need to grapple with right now, of course, is more urgent. Who killed Paula Harrison? The way I see it, we have two suspects."

"Two?" Heather swallowed the mush of her biscuit and leaned forward as Ace raised an index finger towards the sky.

"One. The original killer. Two." She raised a second finger. "Somebody else."

Heather sat back again. "Right. Aye, it's probably one of those two, right enough."

"What's the evidence for it being the original? Well, the feather you found. So what? It's a feather. People have feathers. Not biologically, obviously. But they have them in their houses. Decoration. Fancy dress. Dusters. Tickling. There are all kinds of reasons for being in possession of a feather. If it was just a feather, then I'd say any talk of the Killie Kiddie Killer is at best premature, and at worst a deliberate and calculated attempt at media-induced hysteria."

She stopped directly in front of Heather, and pointed straight at the detective's face.

"Except, you're here, so it's more than that. You only need my help because you can't get it elsewhere. You want access to all the information I've gathered, because you're unable to do so in the usual manner, which means you've been taken off the case."

Heather was too surprised to say anything. Which was just as well, because Ace was already talking again.

"The only reason they'd take you off the case is because you're connected to it. The only way you'd be connected to it would be because evidence has come to light linking Paula Harrison's murder to the original killer."

"Jesus Christ," Heather muttered. "Are you psychic or something?"

Ace put her hands on her hips. "No. But my cousin is."

Heather blinked in surprise. "Eh?"

"Her name's Mesmerelda. She lives in a caravan. It's not important," Ace replied with a tut and a roll of her eyes. "So, I assume from your remark that I'm correct? There's more than the feather. Isn't there?"

"I can't tell you that," Heather said.

Ace drew a breath in through her nose, wriggled her mouth from side to side, then nodded as she came to a decision.

"OK," she said, picking up the plate of biscuits. "Thanks for calling round. I'm sure you can see yourself out."

"Jesus! OK. Yes, there was something!" Heather confirmed. "But I can't tell you what."

Ace sat the plate back down on the bed beside the detective. "Cause of death? Knife through the throat, angled upwards in the mouth, like Eilidh Howden and Abby Blackwell? If I'm right, just sit there and look suitably impressed."

She stepped back from the bed and studied her Wonderwall for a moment, her head tilting as she followed the fractal's angles.

"Can that be all? Surely not? The cause of death has been in the public domain for years. A journalist found out and published it. Anyone trying to emulate the original killer would know that."

"Aye, but the feathers weren't public knowledge," Heather said. "So, combining the two…"

"I knew about them," Ace pointed out.

"Well, maybe you killed her, then," Heather said.

Ace glanced upwards, as if giving this theory some serious consideration. "It would be an effective way of promoting the podcast, that's for sure. Maybe my subscribers would finally reach double digits."

"The podcast," Heather mumbled, the words triggering a thought. "You ever mention the feathers on there?"

"No. I thought it best not to. Some of us still have some journalistic integrity."

"Right. Good," Heather said. "But, how do you know about them, anyway?"

"Are you asking me to reveal my sources, Officer?"

"Detective Inspector," Heather said, for the umpteenth time. "And yes."

Ace shrugged. "Fine. I spoke to Elizabeth Howden. Eilidh's mother."

Heather's eyes widened. "You spoke to Eilidh's *mum*?"

"Yes. I told her I was doing a project on her daughter's death for school, and asked if she would give me a few minutes of her time."

"Bloody hell." Heather ran a hand down her face. "And, so, what? She told you about the feather?"

"No. She threw a plate at me and had her three big dogs chase me out of the garden," Ace said. "Abby Blackwell's mother, on the other hand, was much more accommodating. She talked for hours. Showed me photographs of Abby growing up. She cried quite a lot, which was uncomfortable, but all in all the whole thing was… oddly pleasant. I think she just wanted a chance to remember her with someone, if you know what I mean?"

"Uh, yeah. Yeah, I do," Heather confirmed. "I know what you mean."

"So, you think there's a chance?"

Heather hesitated. "A chance of what?"

"That it's him. That Paula Harrison is the latest victim of the Killie Kiddie Killer?" She flinched. "God. It's *such* a terrible name. You can't even shorten it, to 'The KKK' either, because the racists have already taken that, haven't they?"

Heather confirmed that they had, but Ace continued talking over her, regardless.

"Anyway, my theory. About the feathers. Do you want to hear it?"

"Sure," Heather said, glancing surreptitiously at her watch. There was no need for the subtlety, however, as Ace was back to marching again.

"OK. Good. Because I'm hoping you've had access to information I have not, so you can either confirm or deny my thinking."

She took a deep breath, and Heather got the impression the girl had been building up to saying this for a long time.

"It doesn't mean anything."

Heather raised an eyebrow. "What do you mean?"

"The feathers. The ones left at the scene, they don't mean anything. They're a distraction. A deliberate one. They're not even a calling card. Although, I suppose they *are* a calling card, but they weren't. Not to start with."

"What are you saying?" Heather asked.

Ace came to a sudden halt and held her hands up, like she was inviting the detective to picture what she was describing.

"I'm saying that there was only one real feather. The first one. The one found on the body of Eilidh Howden. It *was* found on the body, yes? Not at the abduction site, like the others?"

After a brief wrestle with herself over how to reply, Heather surrendered to the girl's stare and confirmed the information with a nod.

"I *knew* it!" Ace cheered, and suddenly she was off and walking again.

The carpet beneath her feet, Heather noted, was flattened and worn. Clearly, the girl did a lot of her thinking on the move.

"OK, so it's obvious then, isn't it? The other feathers aren't a calling card. They're not even clues. Not really. They're a distraction from the real clue. The first feather was left by accident. The others were an attempt to make that one look like it was left on purpose!"

She snatched one of the few remaining biscuits from the plate, held it up as if in salute, then took a big celebratory bite, rewarding herself for a job well done.

"Aye. We know," Heather said.

Ace's fast-paced chewing slowed to a halt, like the biscuit was sticking her teeth together.

"You know?" she mumbled, depositing a little avalanche of crumbs onto the carpet.

"Well, I mean, it's definitely come up," Heather said. "We've had thirty years to work on this case, remember? Every theory's been gone over, torn apart, put back together, then kicked around the office by dozens of different detectives. Hundreds, maybe, if you include the specialists brought in from other areas." She grunted. "For all the good they did."

"Oh." Ace deflated a little. "Right. And?"

"And what?"

Ace was walking again. "The original feather. Once they knew what they were dealing with, I assume they ran forensic tests on it? Techniques and technology have come a long way since the eighties. There must have been something on that first feather that could—"

"They lost it."

"Beg pardon?" Ace said, and this time she stopped so suddenly it was like she'd walked into a pane of glass.

"The feather. The first one. All of them, in fact. They got *misplaced*."

"Misplaced?"

"Aye."

"The feathers?"

"The feathers," Heather confirmed.

Ace flopped down onto the end of the bed so she was sitting side-by-side with the detective, both of them facing the Wonderwall.

"But that..." Ace's gaze became glassy and far away for a moment, like all her body's power supplies were diverting to her brain. "That's a problem. The feather was the key. That's what I was hinging everything on. Not having it is going to make things a lot more difficult."

They both fell into matching silences then, sitting together on the bed, the explosion of thoughts and theories and data taunting them from the wall.

Was the answer in there somewhere? Probably not, Heather realised, and the thought sat heavy on her.

"Why did you come here, Officer?"

Heather turned to find Ace scrutinising her, close-up, with one eyebrow raised, and her lips pursed tightly together.

"Well, because..." Heather began, but she stopped there, not quite sure how to answer the question.

Why had she come? Because of a flower on her car bonnet? Because that one tiny thing had rattled her to the point where she'd felt she had to do something—anything—to make this all stop.

She looked back to the wall, and for the first time, she spotted three sticky notes amongst the madness of it all. They'd been lost in all the colour and noise, but now they jumped out at her, like they were forcing their way to the front.

Three notes, each with a name and some other details carefully written on them in black marker pen.

Each one hit her like a punch to the gut.

'Eilidh Howden. Aged 13. (Murdered)'

BAM!

'Abbie Blackwell. Aged 11. (Murdered)'

THUMP!

And then, on the third *Post-it*, another name.

A name she rarely thought of now.

A name that had once belonged to her.

'Hayley Wilson. Aged 5. (Survived)'

KA-POW!

"I figured it out," Ace was saying, but the sound of the blood pumping through Heather's veins was like an army on the march, making it impossible to focus on anything else. "Your family didn't move house. The surname is practically the same. Age-wise, it fits. I knew you had to be her."

The room felt stiflingly hot again. Chokingly hot. Heather grasped for another subject, for a way to switch topics, for a way to make the girl *stop fucking talking*.

"The teacher. Toby Pearse," she blurted, the words rushing out of her like some emergency valve had been opened in her voice box.

Ace's raised eyebrow lowered to join its partner. "Mr Pearse? What about him?"

"I spoke to him. And looked into him. Sort of."

"Because of the fingering thing?"

Heather rose to her feet, the closeness of the kid beside her making her uncomfortable.

"Yes. No. I mean, that was part of it," she said.

She found herself pacing, just like Ace had, her heart crashing against the inside of her chest as she passed those names on the wall. The room was too small, though. She couldn't walk far enough to stop the rising panic squeezing the air from her lungs.

"He had a school blazer in his bedroom," she announced. "It smelled of perfume."

"Oh? That's interesting," Ace said, perking up.

"Right?! That's what I thought."

"Was it Tanya's, though?" Ace asked. "His sister? I think she's in Sixth Year."

Heather felt something shrivel up and die inside her. "I mean, aye," she admitted, her shrivelled lungs providing only just enough air to force out the words. "It might have been. But, still…"

She realised then that the Gozer had been right all along. She was too close to this. Far too close.

She'd wanted it to be the teacher. She'd *needed* it to be the teacher. If it was the teacher, then it couldn't have been *him*. He couldn't be back.

Still pacing, Heather turned to look at the wall again, like she might find some crucial piece of evidence there that would bring this whole thing to a swift and happy ending.

Instead, she saw a list of names she knew off by heart. Names that had etched themselves into the walls of her brain.

Six men, all former suspects, all released without charge.

Four of them were dead now. One was in a care home in Dundee. The other had lived in Australia since the mid-nineties, and was now pushing eighty years old.

Most of them had been brought in simply because the public needed to see the police were actively working on the case. All of them had then had every aspect of their lives torn apart and pawed through by the press.

Two of them had eventually committed suicide, leaving wives and children to pick up the wreckage that had been left behind.

Two more lives lost to the killer. Countless more ruined. And nobody would ever answer for any of them.

"This was a mistake. I… listen, thanks. This was… I shouldn't have come here," Heather babbled. The heat was stinging her face now, burning her cheeks, slicking her back.

The names and the dates and the data on the wall felt like it was swirling now, becoming a real snowflake, one of a billion spinning in circles around the room.

The room itself felt small, but the door was miles away. Heather set off for it. Her feet felt like she was dragging them through deep snow. Every step was agony. Every inch of progress made her muscles scream.

The names of the girls on the wall followed her like the eyes of a painting. Watching. Staring. Accusing. Blaming her for all the many failures that had prevented them from being avenged.

"I think I know why you came."

Ace's voice rang out like the back of a knife tapping against the rim of a glass, cutting through the din in Heather's head.

She stopped, and her burning thigh muscles howled their gratitude.

When she shuffled around, Ace was back on her feet, the Wonderwall behind her, all three girls' names visible over her shoulders.

"And why's that?" Heather asked.

"You didn't need my help. Not really. That's not why you came," Ace said. "You came here because you have nobody else you can talk to about what happened to you. You came because you needed someone to listen."

Heather snorted out the beginnings of a laugh, but the girl didn't react. Instead, she pulled the swivel chair out from under her desk, planted herself in it, then placed her hands on her knees and sat back.

"Well, I'm sitting comfortably, Officer. I'm listening," Ace said.

She carefully and painstakingly arranged her mouth into what was presumably meant to be an encouraging smile. It looked like she learned it from a book, and not necessarily one written in a language she understood.

"Shall we begin?"

———

There was nothing to tell her. Heather had nothing to say. The truth was, she couldn't remember. It had been over thirty years ago, she'd been just a child. Who remembered anything that had happened to them when they were five years old?

And then, of course, there'd been the nature of the memories. Her developing brain would've worked hard to suppress them. That's what all the therapists had said.

Even in the statements given in the days following her return, she'd been able to tell the police very little, and each statement was less structured and more vague than those that came before, like the whole experience had been a dream she had struggled to hold onto.

Heather had read through the statements one night when she was alone at the station. It was something she had been planning for years, but she'd always found some excuse to put it off for another day or so.

Just until next week. That was all. She'd definitely get to it then.

When she had finally forced herself to read them, she'd felt nothing for the girl she'd once been. There was nothing familiar in the description she'd given of the van she'd been taken in, or the room where she'd been kept.

Or the things that had been done to her.

She couldn't remember any of it. Not the abduction. Not the abuse. Not her escape.

But she *had* escaped. She'd been sure of that much in the statements she'd given.

'The man'—that was how she referred to him throughout every interview—had forgotten to lock the door one night, after he'd left her alone. The door opened onto darkness, and it was only the cold on her face that had told her she was outside.

She'd run then. She'd run as fast as she could, stumbling through bracken and weeds, until the morning had started to creep across the sky, and a bin lorry had almost ploughed into her while she'd been staggering across a road a couple of miles to the west of Kilmarnock town centre.

Heather couldn't remember any of that. She'd tried to. She'd closed her eyes and searched the darkest recesses of her mind, hunting for the memories, but they weren't there.

Or perhaps they were, but she didn't want to find them.

"That's it?" Ace asked, making no effort to hide her disappointment. "That's all you can remember?"

"I don't remember anything. That's the point," Heather replied. "I've heard all that stuff secondhand. From my dad. From my uncle. From reading reports and statements. None of it is... mine. None of it."

"I know exactly what you need," Ace announced. She got up from her chair, and the momentum of her movement swung it back into place beneath her desk.

"And what's that?"

"Hypnosis!"

Heather frowned. "Why, so I can bark like a dog? No, thanks."

Ace rolled her eyes. "Not that rubbish. Proper hypnosis. By a trained professional. They can help you access what's in your head."

"I don't think so," Heather said.

"But it might tell us what we need to know!" Ace protested. She stared at Heather's forehead with an intensity that might well eventually bore a hole straight through the detective's skull. "The identity of the Killie Kiddie Killer might be locked up in there!"

"I doubt that."

"My cousin does hypnosis. We could talk to her."

"Your cousin? Mesmerelda?" Heather guessed.

"Yes."

"The psychic one? Who lives in a caravan?"

"Yes!"

Heather shook her head. "Nah, you're alright."

Ace sighed. "Look, I know how she sounds, but she's properly trained. She studied clinical hypnotherapy in Glasgow. She completed the course in less than a month, so she obviously knows her stuff."

"Or it was a shite course," Heather countered.

"Either way, she's good. She'll be able to help you unlock all the secrets in your head."

"No." Heather waved a hand, dismissing the idea. "I'm not doing it."

"But you have to!"

"I really don't," Heather snapped.

Ace's voice climbed sharply in urgency and pitch. "She'll be able to help you remember!"

"But what if I don't want to remember?!"

The raw ferocity of the reply stopped Ace dead in her tracks. She backed up a pace or two, looking Heather up and down like she was only now seeing her properly for the first time.

Only now seeing the real her.

Ace may not have been all that good at reading people's emotions, but this one was coming through loud and clear.

"OK. Well… fine," she said, dropping the subject. "If you're not going to do it, then… I guess I'll have to find some other way."

Heather forced her muscles to relax, and unclenched the fingers that had balled themselves into fists. "What do you mean?" she asked.

"I mean someone has to do what's necessary to find Paula's killer. And if you won't, then…" Ace hesitated, then drew herself up to her full height and nodded. "I'll have to."

"No, no, no, no," Heather said. She raised an index finger and pointed it in the girl's face. "You have to do nothing. You stay out of this now. It's being dealt with. They're going to find who did it. You do *not* get involved. And, if anything we've spoken about tonight winds up on that bloody podcast of yours, you and I are going to have some serious words. Is that clear?"

For a moment, it looked like Ace was going to argue, but the steely coldness of Heather's expression made her see sense.

"Fine. Yes. It's clear, Officer."

"It's Detective Inspector," Heather shot back. She picked up the final biscuit from the plate Ace's mum had brought in, and took a big, messy bite. "Sorry for getting crumbs on your bed," she said, spraying more of them as she spoke. "You stay where you are. I'll see myself out."

Then, with a final glance at the Wonderwall, Heather turned and marched out of the room without looking back.

And those three names on the wall followed her, like the eyes of a portrait, every step of the way.

THIRTY-THREE

IT WAS after eight when Heather kicked the sleet from her shoes and announced her arrival back home with a loud, "Hey, Auld Yin! Just me!"

The snow was almost completely gone now, with just a few disparate patches scattered in grassy areas like garden lawns. Even then, the marshmallow whiteness of it had long given way to a thin, depressing shade of grey.

Still, at least the rain had stopped for long enough for her to make it to the house from the car without getting drenched.

Her dad was dozing in front of the telly, the big woolly blanket tucked up under his arms, his head lolling down around his chest. From the looks of things, he was wearing a pair of clean tartan pyjamas, and his cleanly shaved face and fluffy hair told her that he'd had one of his better days.

A note on the coffee table from Kenny confirmed this. Scott had showered himself, with only minor intervention needed when he couldn't find a towel with which to get soap out of his eyes.

Kenny had helped with the shaving, but even that had gone pretty smoothly.

Not *perfectly* smoothly, judging by the two little patches of blood-spotted toilet paper Heather could see on the side of her old man's jaw, but otherwise, it was a pretty decent result.

It was too late for coffee, so Heather cracked the top off a snub-nosed bottle of beer, and knocked most of it back in one swig. She ran her sleeve across her mouth, burped, then leaned on the kitchen counter, searching the room for anything out of the ordinary.

Tonight, though, there was nothing obvious to be seen. No surprise bunch of flowers. No colourful envelopes. No sign that anyone but her dad and her uncle had been anywhere near the place.

Thank God. After Ace's house—after seeing those names, and wading through those memories—she wasn't sure she could cope with anything more tonight. She just wanted today to be over and behind her. She'd deal with tomorrow when it came.

She'd get her dad up to bed. She'd make sure the house was locked up, grab something to eat, and then she'd fight herself to sleep for at least a few hours. An early night would work wonders. Everything would look better after some rest.

But first…

Opening the fridge, Heather grabbed another of the stubby beer bottles, banged the lid off on the edge of the worktop, and knocked the chilled contents back in two big gulps.

"Right, then," she announced to the room at large, then she dumped the empty bottles in the bin, and headed through to wake her dad.

Sylvester Stallone's voice was blaring out of the TV when Heather returned to the living room. Gunfire erupted, an explosion boomed, and a number of presumably bad men let out agonising death screams.

Scott, sitting with his head down in his armchair, didn't so much as flinch.

Annoying as the racket was, Heather left the telly's volume up. From past experience, she knew she'd need all the help she could to wake her dad up, and the explosively violent shenanigans of John Rambo certainly couldn't hurt her chances of rousing the old man.

"Alright, Auld Yin?" she called, squatting down beside his

chair so the TV was at her back. She laid a hand on his knee and gave it a jiggle. "Wakey wakey!"

Nothing.

"Hey. Dad. Time for bed!"

Behind her, something erupted into fire, and a handful of bad guys howled as they burned.

But the old man in the chair didn't react to any of it.

Heather marvelled at how deep he was sleeping tonight. How still.

How silent.

She gave his leg another shake, more firmly this time. More urgently.

"Dad? Dad, it's me. It's Heather. Wake up. Come on."

Her heart skipped over a couple of beats. The shock of it made her gasp out a sharp, sudden breath.

The speakers of the old TV vibrated as they churned out the booms, and the bangs, and the stirring musical score.

Heather gave up on the leg and reached for the old man's shoulder. Even through the towelling of his pyjamas, she felt the ridges of his bones rising up like a mountain range through his paper-thin skin.

"Dad? Dad? *Dad!*"

He woke with a snort, and a start, and a bellowed, "*Howazafuck*?!"

The suddenness of his shouted nonsense, and the jerk of his body sent Heather tumbling backwards, and by the time her arse hit the floor, she was laughing with shock and relief.

"Jesus Christ, Auld Yin! I thought you'd carked it!" she cried.

Scott's face was contorted into a deep scowl of confusion, his head twisted awkwardly as he rubbed at the back of his neck. A barrage of gunfire from the TV gave him some cause for concern, before STV mercifully went to an ad break.

"You're alright, Dad. You're OK. It's just me. It's Heather."

"Heather?" Scott grunted. He had been squinting with his left eye, but now he switched to the right, in case that one proved to be more effective. "That you?"

"Aye. It's me," Heather confirmed, picking herself up. She

spoke to him calmly and clearly, in the voice he best responded to. "You fell asleep in front of the telly again and didn't look comfy. Thought I'd get you up to bed."

"Eh?"

"I said will we get you up to bed?"

He continued to squint at her for a while, then an advert for sanitary towels proved too fascinating for him to resist. He shifted his attention to the TV, and his frown deepened.

"That woman said something," he muttered.

Heather checked out the screen, then shook her head. "No. She's just roller-skating."

Scott tutted. "Not her. The woman. The other woman. A minute ago. Her with the teeth. She was talking shite."

"Was she, aye?" Heather asked, humouring him.

She moved into position beside the chair, and attempted to hook one of her arms under his. He shrugged her away, still focused on the screen.

"She shouldn't be bloody doing that. News people. They shouldn't be lying like that. I said to…" He jolted, like something had startled him, then he looked around the room. "Where's…" His lips searched in silence, but the name eluded him. "…my brother? He was here."

"Kenny's gone home, Dad. He got you showered and made you dinner, remember?"

"Kenny." Scott said the name out loud like he was trying it out, but then the lure of the television proved too strong. "She was on. A minute ago. She was a bloody liar! A bloody liar!"

He was fidgeting now, his bottom lip and his hands trembling in harmony. He shook his head, shaking loose a single tear that tumbled down his blotchy cheek.

"They're no' meant to do that. They can't say that!"

"Can't say what, Dad?" Heather asked, crouching beside him and rubbing his arm. "What did she say that upset you?"

He continued to shake his head, his lips pursing together, his eyes shining with the threat of further tears.

Before Heather could say anything else to console him, something on the TV caught her attention. Still smiling at her dad, she tuned her hearing into the telly, and caught the tail end of an advert.

"For service with no comparison…"

That voice. She knew that voice.

Fortunately, she didn't have to wait long to find out where she knew it from.

"You can trust Michael Harrison!"

Heather looked back over her shoulder, and there he was, standing in front of a big white van, staring back at her, his long hair tumbling over his shoulders, his smile applied awkwardly for the camera.

Michael Harrison.

Paula Harrison's stepdad.

The man she had recognised, but couldn't remember why.

"Jesus. Of course."

How many times had this ad played in the background while she'd been lying on the couch, dozing fitfully, too drunk or too wired to completely pass out? How many times had she seen and heard him in her half-awake state, while she'd dipped in and out of the usual nightmares?

No wonder the guy had made her uncomfortable. He'd been the backing track to her bad dreams.

Once again, it seemed that the Gozer was right. She was too close to this. To all of it.

Still, the reason for Michael Harrison's familiarity was one mystery solved, at least.

The advert concluded with an animated logo and a phone number. Heather was about to turn back to her dad when the text drawing itself across the screen below the logo made her stop.

"Painter and decorator," she mumbled, and the shape she'd been building in her head since Paula had vanished shifted around as parts slotted into place.

"She said that bastard's back," Scott announced, totally oblivious to Heather's moment of realisation.

"Sorry, Dad?" she said, tearing her eyes away from the telly. The advert was over now, and a promotion for the *House of Bruar* had taken its place. "Who said what?"

"That lying cow on the news. She said that bastard's come back."

Heather searched the old man's face. His eyes were making tiny micro-movements, like he was following a bug zipping around in the air right in front of him. His mouth was gnashing at the air, chewing on nothing, while his dry, liver-spotted hands were twisting themselves into knots in his lap.

"Who's come back?" Heather asked him.

The news couldn't be running with it. Surely not. Not yet. The papers, maybe, but not the TV news bulletins.

"That *bastard*. The bastard who took my wee girl," Scott sobbed.

He was looking straight at Heather now, but she had learned to read the signs, and she knew he didn't recognise her. Not fully, at least. On some level, he'd be aware that he knew her, but he wouldn't be able to say who she saw, and she'd learned not to ask him.

"They're saying he's back. They're saying it's him," her dad continued, his voice drying out, becoming a whisper. "But it's no' him. They're lying. It can't be him, can it?"

Heather laid a hand on his forearm. He stiffened, then relaxed a little when she rubbed her thumb back and forth, stroking his wrist.

"No. Don't worry. It's not him. The woman on TV was talking shite."

"That's what I said! That's what I told her, but she wouldn't shut up. She kept going on."

"Aye, well, she's gone now. No need to worry."

"It can't be that bastard, I told her that. There's no way it can be that bastard," Scott said. He smiled, but it was a vacant, glassy-eyed thing, and Heather could feel him staring straight through her. "There's no way it can be that bastard, because he's dead."

Heather leaned back a little, trying to place herself in the right focal range so Scott would see her.

"Dead? How do you mean?" she asked. "What are you talking about?"

"He's dead. I know he is," Scott said.

He relaxed deeper into the chair, and much of the tension that had been building up left him in one slow sigh. He smiled, his eyelids fluttering closed.

"I know he's dead, because we made sure of it."

The rising and falling of Heather's chest stopped. A cool breeze blowing in from the hall prickled across her skin.

"What do you mean?" she asked. "What are you saying?"

She shook his arm, but his eyes remained closed. The words came out of a soft, sleepy slur of syllables.

"I know he's dead, because me and my wee brother Kenny killed him."

———

Ace didn't like being out this late. She didn't like being out at all, if she could possibly help it, but particularly not after the street lights had come on.

And especially not when there was a killer on the loose.

But needs must. Officer Filson hadn't proven to be particularly useful, and Ace was having serious doubts that the police were going to crack this case anytime soon.

Someone had murdered Paula Harrison. Someone had abducted a girl her age from the same housing estate Ace was marching across now.

And that was something she wasn't prepared to let stand.

Her bag was heavy with the weight of her recording equipment. The laptop was an old, clunky thing that her dad had sent her a few years ago, back when he'd still feigned interest. He'd included a couple of game disks, too, but the processor hadn't been powerful enough to even run the setup, let alone play them.

Ace hadn't minded. Games weren't really her thing, anyway. Especially games with names like *Call of Duty* or *Total War*. She'd mostly just used it for the internet.

Then, for an intensive two-month period, she'd used it to make complicated spreadsheets about nothing in particular. They'd had colour-changing cells and complex filters, allowing her to very efficiently refine a lot of unimportant data for no real reason whatsoever.

After that, she'd dabbled in *Microsoft Powerpoint*.

And, once the novelty of that had worn off, she'd discovered audio editing. She had zero interest in music, so a podcast had been the obvious next step.

She'd used some birthday money to buy her first microphone, and then significantly more birthday money to buy one that didn't make her sound like she was shouting from the bottom of a well.

That was the day she'd become a journalist.

It was a week later, once she'd decided on the subject of her podcast, that she'd become an *investigator*.

And investigators investigated, even when they didn't want to.

Even when it was late, and the street lights had come on.

Even when they were scared of what they might find.

Ace stopped outside the garden gate, took a breath, then whispered a series of reminders to herself.

"Knock. Wait. Say hello. Introduce yourself. Say sorry. Ask to come in."

She ran through them again, then repeated them below her breath a couple more times as she made her way up the path.

Arriving at the door, she raised a hand, and rapped her knuckles on the frosted glass. Beside her, a blue circle appeared around a chunky black button, and she saw herself reflected in the fish-eye lens of a doorbell camera.

Ringing a bell hadn't been part of the strategy she'd rehearsed all the way here, but while she wasn't keen to break from the plan at this early stage, she pressed the button and listened to the faint *ding-dong* chime from somewhere inside.

A light came on in the hall, and Ace smoothed down her school blazer. She'd worn it deliberately so she wouldn't be mistaken for a member of the mainstream press and told to sling her hook.

The uniform was her Trojan Horse. It would mark her as one of Paula's friends. It would get her inside. From there, a certain degree of improvisation would be required, but she'd cross that bridge when she came to it.

Footsteps approached cautiously up the hall, and a blur of

colour became increasingly solid and human-looking as it approached the bubbled glass.

Ace could see the light of a phone screen in the person's hand. She angled her Kilmarnock Academy badge towards the camera on the wall, and then listened to the sound of a lock being undone.

She started to speak as soon as the door began to open.

"Hello. I'm Ace Wurzel. I was in school with Paula. I'm so very sorry for your loss," she said, more or less in one big breath. "Would you mind if I came in?"

Just inside the door, standing in the hallway in a dirty T-shirt and saggy jogging bottoms, Michael Harrison slowly looked the girl on the doorsteps up and down.

"Please," he said, opening the door wider. "In you come."

"Thank you," Ace said.

She stepped past him into the hall. Michael peered out into the evening gloom, and looked along the street in both directions.

And then, without a word, without a sound, he closed and locked the door.

THIRTY-FOUR

ACE WAS MOMENTARILY STARTLED by her own reflection in a big circular mirror on the wall directly across from the front door. For a second, she'd thought it was someone else—another girl in a Kilmarnock Academy uniform, looking just as anxious and apprehensive as she felt—before the reality had filtered through.

She felt her breath falling out of its usual rhythm. The quickening of her pulse. She centred herself by studying the place, focusing on all the things she could feel, see, and hear.

She felt the swirling outside air, dragged inwards by the closing door, pushing its way deeper into the house.

She saw a bowl on the sideboard beneath the big mirror, full of coins, keys, and other random stuff.

She heard… Nothing. The inside of the house was silent, aside from the creaking of a floorboard as Michael Harrison stepped up close behind her.

"Go through," he said, pointing to a door on the left. It stood open, and Ace saw a couch with a crumpled blanket spread over the seats.

Light danced across the walls. The TV was on, with the sound turned all the way down.

"Please," Michael urged. "Do you want a drink?"

"I'm only fifteen," Ace said.

Michael smiled, though it was a hollow, painted-on thing. "I'm sure I was drinking at that age," he said. "But I meant juice, or tea, or—"

"Do you have milk?"

"Uh, yeah."

"I'll have milk, please," Ace said.

Michael pulled a face that suggested he approved of the choice, then motioned through to the living room again.

Ace centred herself with one more look around the hallway, then she pressed on through to the front room, and gave herself a moment to take it all in.

Someone, presumably Michael, had been sleeping on the high-backed couch. A couple of pillows were propped up at one end, and had been squished down by the weight of someone lying on them.

There was an almost empty bottle of wine on the coffee table, alongside a glass with a tiny puddle of red at the bottom. On the floor between the couch and the table, a plastic tray of half-eaten microwave curry sat on a dinner plate, steam rising gently from the congealing mush of reddish-brown contained within.

Some sort of action movie was playing on the TV. A muscleman with a headband was doing an astonishing amount of damage to what was presumably private property. This was much to the apparent dismay of the owners, who were all either, A) shooting at him, or B) getting stabbed in the head and throat.

"Milk."

Ace lunged further into the room and turned to find Paula's stepdad standing there, holding a glass of milk in one hand, and another bottle of wine in the other.

He was smiling. Sort of.

The rest of his expression wasn't immediately familiar to Ace, though, and she struggled to place it. Was he confused by her being there? Annoyed?

Amused?

"Thank you," she said.

She accepted the glass, drank the whole lot in a oner, then passed it back.

"Thank you," she said again, because manners cost nothing, then she took a seat on the armchair across from the couch, and placed her bag on the floor beside her.

"Uh… OK," Michael said.

He looked at the glass for a moment, like he wasn't quite sure what had happened, then he set it down on the table and unscrewed the cap of the wine bottle.

"You're a friend of Paula's?" he asked, perching himself on the very edge of the couch, so he was only a couple of feet away across the table, directly facing Ace.

"No," Ace admitted. "I mean… We were in a lot of classes together. We went to primary school. We were friends then. I think. But, people grow apart in secondary school. It's perfectly normal. It happens all the time."

The way she recited the words, like she was repeating them parrot fashion, made him glance up, mid-pour. "I suppose they do, aye."

He filled the glass to the brim, set the bottle down, then ran a hand across the blanket beside him. His sigh was so soft as to almost be silent. "Then again, people grow apart all the time."

Ace looked around the room. "Paula's mum…"

"Staying with her sister. Her and Ibby. Just for tonight," Michael said. He forced a laugh, but it stuck somewhere in his throat. "Couldn't be doing with the bloody press watching our every move. Hounding us."

Ace shot a glance to the window. The curtains were drawn, but through a crack she could see the darkened empty street beyond.

"They must have all left," she noted.

Michael carefully raised his over-filled glass to his lips and slurped noisily. "I'll drink to that. About fucking time," he said, then he grinned like a mischievous schoolboy and touched his three middle fingers to his mouth. "Whoops. Sorry. Bad language."

"That's alright, I've heard most of them before," Ace said. Something about the response made him laugh, though she had no idea why. She hadn't been joking. She had been privy to a lot of swearing over the years, the majority of it aimed at her.

Michael took another sip of his wine, though there was less theatre about it this time. As he did, he carefully considered the girl sitting across from him.

"I've seen you, haven't I?" He ran a hand through his long hair, pushing it back off his face and over his shoulders. "I've seen you passing. You live on the estate."

"I do," Ace confirmed, though a little nagging voice at the back of her head made her regret confirming this information.

"You're always on your own, aren't you?"

The nagging voice intervened then, and stopped her from replying. Unfortunately, it didn't offer any alternative responses, so she just sat there, saying nothing.

"I was like you when I was young."

"I highly doubt that," Ace said, but Michael's expression didn't change.

He swirled the wine around in his glass. "Always on my own. A lonely kid. Never any mates. Not real ones." He sipped at the wine again. "No one looking out for me."

"I prefer my own company," Ace said.

"Ha. Yeah." Another drink of wine. A gulp, this time. "That's what I used to tell myself, too."

Ace had no idea how to respond, so she returned to the mental checklist she'd made on the way here, and moved on to the next part of the plan.

"I want to help find Paula's killer."

On the other side of the coffee table, Michael almost managed to hold his face steady. "Do you?" he asked, a hoarseness creeping into his voice.

"Yes. I do," Ace confirmed.

"Why?" Michael gestured to her, a quick up-and-down wave of his hand that indicated the girl as a whole. "You said you weren't friends. You prefer your own company, you said. Why do you care?"

Once again, Ace found herself at a bit of a loss. This was a question she hadn't prepared for, and one she now realised she hadn't given any thought to.

Why was she so concerned about finding Paula's killer? Would Paula have tried to do the same if the roles were reversed? Almost certainly not. They'd barely spoken in years.

Her last memorable interaction with Paula had been soon after the start of First Year, back when Ace had just been plain Alison. A couple of boys from one of the other schools had cornered her around the side of the school building one break time. There had been name-calling. Pushing. The threat of further violence.

Ace hadn't been able to work out what she'd done to draw their attention and rile them up like that. Then again, she never could figure that one out. She'd eventually put it down to pheromones, believing she was inadvertently giving off some kind of scent that turned people against her.

Keeping her distance from people cut down on the number of times such altercations happened, which she believed proved this theory correct.

On that day, though, back in First Year, Paula Harrison had come swooping in like an avenging angel, elbowing the boys aside, barking at them to, "Fuck off and leave her alone!"

She'd grabbed Ace by the wrist—something Ace usually hated, but was happy to tolerate on this occasion—and pulled her away from the jeering boys.

The bell had gone before Ace could even thank Paula for her intervention, and they'd headed off to their respective classes.

Paula had become friends with Suthsiri, Sasha, and Dawn soon after, and while Ace was sure she'd spoken to her in the months that followed, she had no recollection of anything that might have been said.

And, when the bullying happened again, Ace had always hung onto the hope that Paula might come charging in to save her.

She never did. But she did that one time. And one time was more than anyone else.

For some reason, though, Ace didn't want to share any of that with the man sipping wine on the couch across from her.

"Because it's the right thing to do," she said, which seemed enough to satisfy him.

"Fair enough. Well, good luck. I hope you find out who did it." He took another drink, and this one seemed to taste unpleasant, judging by the way his lips drew back over his teeth. "Police don't seem to have a fucking clue. Sorry. Language."

"What do they think happened to her?" Ace asked.

Michael frowned. "Well, she was murdered, wasn't she?"

"I meant before then. How did the killer get in the house?"

"Well, he didn't. She didn't come home. Didn't make it." Michael cleared his throat. Forcibly. "The bastard grabbed her before she could get here, didn't he?"

"Huh." Ace sat back in the chair until her weight was resting against the cushions. "Are you sure?"

"Yes," Michael said, quite emphatically. He shrugged, playing his certainty down. "I mean, that's what the police reckon. Her bag was found miles away."

"Is anyone else home when Paula gets back after school?"

"Some days. Not Thursday, though. Not that Thursday, anyway."

"And do you keep your doors locked?"

"In Kilmarnock? On this estate? Course we do," Michael confirmed.

Ace sat forwards suddenly and unzipped her bag. "Do you mind if I record this?"

Michael's frown deepened further, until his eyebrows were a single straight line that underscored his forehead. "Record what?"

"This conversation. For my podcast."

"Uh, no. I mean, yes, I mind. I'd rather you didn't."

"Oh."

Ace remained frozen with one hand on the bag. This was not the plan. This wasn't how it was supposed to go. He was supposed to agree to being recorded. This was going to be her best episode yet.

"Why were you asking if we keep the doors locked?" Michael asked, and the question snapped her out of her trance.

"The bowl."

A few moments of silence passed while Paula's stepfather tried to figure out what the fuck that was meant to mean.

"The bowl?"

"In the hall. Under the mirror. There were coins, batteries, a plastic bag full of what looked like screws, and a set of keys. They're Paula's. Aren't they? They have the little windmill keyring on them that Sasha brought her back from Amsterdam."

She spoke most of the sentence to Michael Harrison's back as he leaped to his feet and went running out into the hall.

A moment later, he ejected a sharp, "Fuck!" before reappearing in the doorway. "I'm just... Give me one second, alright? I'll be right back. I just... I need to do something."

"That's fine. Take your time," Ace told him.

He disappeared out of the room again, and pulled the door closed. Ace sat drumming her fingers on the arms of the chair for a little while, listening to the faint but urgent-sounding murmur of Michael's voice from somewhere beyond the door.

After a while, Ace took out her phone, and tapped out a quick text to Officer Filson.

That done, she returned the phone to her pocket, and went back to waiting.

Elsewhere in the house, out beyond the door of the living room, Michael Harrison's voice became a low hiss of anger, rose to a shout, then stopped abruptly.

The floorboards creaked under the weight of his footsteps.

The door opened and Paula's stepfather returned. He looked more dishevelled than he had when he'd left, and he was pushing his long hair back from a face that was more red than Ace remembered.

"Now," he said, exhaling as he took his seat across from her. "Where were we...?"

———

Heather's phone *thudded* against her bedroom wall, crash-landed on her dressing table, then lay there, face-down, among the scattered deodorant canisters and dry shampoos.

Kenny wasn't answering. That wasn't particularly unusual—he'd often be sleeping by this time, and would always call her back in the morning—but tonight, she needed to talk to him.

Tonight, she needed to know why her dad had said what he'd said in the living room.

She could hear the old man snoring in the room next door. He'd clammed up after his announcement, and had insisted he go to bed. When she asked him what he'd meant, he claimed to have no idea what she was talking about, and while Heather suspected he was lying, she didn't want to force the issue.

Not when she had someone else she could ask.

Assuming the bastard ever answered his phone.

She'd considered driving over there and confronting him, but she'd been four or five beers in before she'd had the thought, and a drink driving charge on top of her current work troubles would be a career-ender.

Besides, her dad had been just agitated enough that she didn't like the idea of leaving him alone, in case he decided to rustle up something in the kitchen again, and burn the whole house to the ground.

Over on the dressing table, Heather's phone buzzed, rattling one of the spray deodorant cans so the sound was amplified around the room. She jumped up from her bed, crossed the floor in two big spaces, and snatched up the mobile, hoping to see Kenny's name and awkwardly smiling photo filling the screen.

Instead, she found a text notification from a number she'd stored under the name 'Nancy Drew'. She groaned and swiped the message away. She had quite enough shit of her own going on without a dollop of teenage angst being heaped on top. She'd read it tomorrow, and deal with it then.

Returning to her list of recently made calls, she tapped the top name, listened to it ringing, then hurled a mouthful of abuse at her Uncle Kenny's voicemail.

THIRTY-FIVE

HEATHER WAS in her car outside Kenny's house when she remembered Ace's text from the night before.

It'd have to wait, though. She could see Kenny standing by his living room window, mug in hand, a worried expression ageing him more than the greying of his beard ever could. He nodded to her when she got out of the Audi. She slammed the door, and didn't nod back.

"I can explain."

He was standing by the bottom of the stairs when she barged in. There was no sign of the mug now, and both Kenny's hands were raised as if to ward her off.

"Listen, just listen. I can explain."

"Oh, I'm fucking listening, Kenny. I'm all ears!" Heather seethed.

Her anger had been honed and sharpened by the long, restless night, and was now a razor ready to cleave her uncle clean in two.

She crossed her arms and stared into his soul, a foot tapping, a leg shaking, her whole body electric with rage.

Kenny leaned back on the bannister. The wood was marked with a thousand tiny scratches left by the cats he'd inherited when his and Scott's mother died. They had been big, heavy-set bastards that were used to roaming the farm, and had even been known to scare off the odd fox.

They hadn't settled well in their new house, and in the few years between their arrival and their deaths, they'd made a point of well and truly fucking up all the woodwork.

"Well?" Heather barked. "You going to tell me then, or what?!"

"Aye. Aye, of course," Kenny said. He looked a decade older. Half a foot shorter. "But, eh, not here, eh? Come away and sit down."

He put a hand on her arm to guide her through, but she jerked away from him. "I don't want to sit down, Kenny! I want you to tell me what the fuck my dad was on about!"

Scott had been bright and on good form when Heather had left him, but he appeared to have forgotten everything he'd said the night before. He'd looked taken aback by her questioning, then had more or less laughed off the very suggestion that he or Kenny could've hurt anyone, much less killed them.

He'd been lying, though. His confusion had been forced, the gaps and hesitations all the wrong lengths in all the wrong places.

Kenny had no illness to hide behind, though. Kenny would tell her the truth, like it or not.

"Right. Well, I'm going to the living room," her uncle announced. "If you want to talk, that's where I'll be."

"Jesus fucking Christ, fine!"

Heather led the way into the room and was standing in front of Kenny's chair when he followed her in. She stabbed a finger at the chair and ordered him to sit. Kenny shuffled his feet, like he was thinking of doing a runner, then plodded over and lowered himself into the chair.

"Right. Explain," she said.

Kenny smoothed down his beard, his eyes glancing up at his niece, then quickly darting away, like they couldn't bear to look at her.

"What did he say? What did he tell you?"

"What I said in my message. One of my *many* fucking messages, Kenny," Heather spat. "He said the Kiddie Killer couldn't possibly have got to Paula Harrison because he's dead. Because you pair killed him."

She let the enormity of the statement sink in, and watched her uncle squirming in the chair.

"Tell me that's bollocks, Kenny. Tell me he's confused."

Kenny's wandering eyes locked on Heather's for a moment, and the look that passed between them made Heather fall back a step.

"Jesus. Jesus Christ," she whispered, running both hands up through her hair. "I mean... Jesus fucking Christ, Kenny! What are you saying?"

"Look, I know. I know. Alright? I *know*," Kenny said, holding both hands up again. "But listen, I'll explain. Alright? I'll explain, just sit down. Sit down, and I'll explain."

Heather stood there, feet planted on the floor, staring down at a man she no longer knew. Then, with a grimace, she dropped down into the other armchair, and gestured to him with both hands.

"Right. I'm sitting. Tell me. Go on. *Explain*."

Kenny grunted as he leaned his weight forwards, reaching for his mug on the coffee table. Heather lunged for it, swiping the mug across the room, spraying milky, lukewarm tea across the carpet.

"Do not piss me around, Kenny! Start talking!"

Kenny sat, head turned, observing the mug on the floor for a moment, before he sat back and nodded. "You're right. I owe you this much. How much do you want to know?"

"Everything. I want to know all of it."

Kenny's face was pale beneath the reddish-grey of his beard. "I'm not sure you do."

"Aye, well, I'll be the judge of that. Go. I want to hear it."

A few seconds passed while Kenny considered this, then he let out a sigh that seemed to come from somewhere impossibly deep within him.

"OK," he said. "But don't say I didn't warn you."

Heather fidgeted as she listened to her uncle relaying the story.

"By the time I heard... By the time I made it back from overseas, you were back home. We thought you were safe. We thought the whole bloody ordeal was over."

He looked up at her. His face had aged ten years in as many seconds.

"We were wrong."

The physical injuries healed quickly, he explained. The bruises. The rope burns. The damage to her privates.

The mental scars she had been left with, however, continued to worsen as the days went on. She'd sit on the toilet for hours, screaming and clawing at herself when anyone tried to get her off. She'd spend her nights sobbing uncontrollably, and her days in mute silence, flinching at sights and sounds that only she could see and hear.

She refused to be touched, not even by her mum, and the sight of any man, from the postman to the journalists outside—and even her dad and Kenny himself—reduced her to a gasping, snivelling mess on the floor.

Meanwhile, the police were out hunting for the man the papers were calling the Killie Kiddie Killer, and the town was in mourning for the lives of the two victims who hadn't been *as fortunate* as the one that got away.

"It was about a month later. After you got back," Kenny said. "It'd all gone quiet with the polis. You still weren't looking at anyone, still not sleeping, still didn't want to be touched. Me and your dad, we didn't know what to do, so we were out looking, you know? Digging around for information. Not to do anything, mind, to help the polis. We just wanted the bastard caught and put away. That was all."

Heather was already growing impatient. "But?"

"We, eh, we got word of a guy," Kenny said. He was looking out of the window now, like the past was a wide vista stretching off beyond the garden gate. "He had previous with that sort of thing. Not murder, I mean. Just, you know, kids?"

"Who was he? What was his name?"

"Cyril Carter," Kenny said. His tongue flitted across his lips, then his teeth scraped them dry. Even after all this time, the name clearly left a bad taste in his mouth. "He was from Kent, or somewhere. Done a stretch down south for fiddling with his sister's weans. Sick fuck."

The name wasn't familiar. It was nowhere on the list of suspects the police had pulled together over the years.

"Anyway, he was sleeping rough around Glasgow. Nobody knew he was here. Not officially, like. But he talked. To other lads, I mean. Word got out, and a couple of bad bastards—old school guys, pre-Shuggie Cowan, even—got their hands on him and got him to confess."

"What, by torturing him?" Heather asked. "Aye, because that's always so fucking reliable!"

"I don't know," Kenny admitted. "I don't know what they did to him. I don't know, and I don't want to. But these guys, they knew that the polis had nothing on him. They knew if they let him go, he'd run off somewhere and do it again."

Kenny swallowed. He was gripping his hands together, trying to stop them from shaking. He managed to look at her, though only for a moment before the pain of it became too much.

"And they knew that me and your dad were looking for him."

Heather realised she wasn't breathing. Her whole body was poised, waiting to see what her uncle was going to say next.

"So, you killed him?" she asked when Kenny didn't offer up anything more.

"He'd confessed. He admitted it. He knew things he couldn't have known otherwise. It was him, Heather. It was him. That bastard, that sick piece of scum, he did it. He killed those girls. He… did those things to them. To you."

"You could've gone to the police. You could have told them!"

"I said that. I did, I swear. But your dad, he was… There was a wildness to him. When he saw the guy, when he heard what he'd admitted to, all the things he'd done."

"You're blaming him for it?" Heather demanded.

"No! God, no! It was both of us. We both did it! He was right. They all were. What would the police do? What did they have on him? They might bring him in for questioning, but what evidence did they have to hold him? That confession was hardly going to stand up, was it?" Kenny shook his head with a level of conviction

Heather almost admired. "They'd have to let him go. He'd be free. And you were the only real witness. You were the biggest threat to him. If we let him go, what then? Would he come after you? Would he finish the job?"

"They could've done something. He could've been in breach of parole. They could've found a way to hold him."

"Maybe. But that's a lot of 'coulds.' Lot of uncertainty. Lot of risk. Risks we weren't prepared to take." He forced himself to look at her, and didn't shy away from the heat of her glare. "And, I know you don't want to hear this, given where you've ended up, but sometimes the police aren't the best option. Justice and the law, Heather, they're not always the same thing. Sometimes, they're mutually exclusive, in fact. Sometimes, to stop evil—true evil—you have to do a bad thing. Even if you don't want to. Even if you know it's wrong. Even if it eats you up for the rest of your days, sometimes, good people have to do bad things.

"And it does, Heather. Believe me. It eats me up. It ate us both up. Even with what he was. Everything he'd done, it eats me up, Heather. Every bloody day." He sat forwards in his armchair, his eyes wide and pleading, like they were begging her forgiveness. "But the killings stopped. They stopped, there and then. No more girls went through what you did. No more girls died. That's what I remind myself. That's how I sleep at night."

"Why didn't you tell me?" Heather asked. She was holding onto her anger, but it was losing some of its grip on her. "All this time, I thought he was still out there. I thought he'd got away with it. You didn't tell me."

"We wanted to. We planned to, when you were old enough," Kenny told her. "But then, typical bloody you, you go and join the polis! How could we tell you, then?"

Heather scowled at him. "Aye, like I was going to bloody arrest you."

"But don't you get it? That's the problem. You wouldn't. We knew you wouldn't. It'd be your job to. It'd be your *duty* to, but you wouldn't. You'd be risking your career. Everything you worked for. You'd be risking it all because of something we'd done. Us, me and your dad, not you. How could we put that on you? After everything, after all you've been through, how could we let you carry that, too?"

Heather's head felt like it was fit for bursting. She fell back into the welcoming embrace of the armchair, buried her face in her hands, then ejected a guttural, "Christ!"

"We were just trying to protect you. I wasn't here to look out for you when that bastard took you, and I just... Me and your dad, we just..." He sighed. It was a slow, weary thing, that weighed heavy on the room around them. "You can take me in for it. I'll say it was all me."

"Jesus, Kenny."

"We'll no' mention your dad. He doesn't have to be—"

"Kenny, shut the fuck up!" Heather barked. "I'm just... Give me a minute, alright? Just give me a minute to think."

"Right. Aye. Sorry." Kenny quietly cleared his throat, then tapped his hands on the arms of the chair.

He sniffed.

He scratched his beard.

"Do you want a coffee or anything, while you're thinking?"

"No!" Heather snapped. Then, "Yes. Aye, fine."

Kenny got to his feet, picked his way between the wet stains on the carpet, then retrieved his mug.

"I'll maybe just get some kitchen roll and..."

Heather's eyes glared up at him from beneath her furrowed brows. He got the message, and continued through to the kitchen in silence, leaving his niece to process her thoughts.

But where was she supposed to start? What was she supposed to think?

And, more importantly, what was she meant to do?

If Kenny was telling the truth, then he and her dad had murdered a man in cold blood. Leaving aside who the guy was, that meant she had a responsibility to report this. To investigate. To gather all the evidence and present it to the Procurator Fiscal.

But then, *who the guy was* was everything. It was the crux of the whole thing.

And the murders had stopped. The Killie Kiddie Killer's short but terrifying reign had been brought to an abrupt end.

Sometimes, good people had to do bad things.

Heather took out her phone to search for the name 'Cyril Carter,' but was stopped in her tracks by a reminder that she had an unread message from Nancy Drew.

Irritated, she tapped the notification with her thumb, and read the message.

> Paula came home. Her keys are here.

It was the last word that propelled the detective up off the chair.

'Here.'

'Her keys are *here.*'

A memory rushed in from the night before—one that had seemed important until her dad's confession had blown everything else apart.

Michael Harrison. Painter and decorator.

He had a van. He'd use turps or white spirit to clean his brushes, just like the killer had cleaned the body with.

And Ace must've gone round there after Heather had left the girl's bedroom.

———

"Right, here we are. Coffee, black, just as you like it," Kenny said, returning to the living room.

He stopped when he saw that the room was empty, then his eyes were drawn to the front window as, outside, the engine of Heather's Audi roared into life.

THIRTY-SIX

"ACE WURZEL. She's in fourth year. Is she there?"

The voice that came from the speaker sounded tinny, but that didn't stop Heather picking up on the secretary's impatience.

"I'm sorry, I'm afraid I can't give out that information."

Heather jerked the steering wheel of the Audi, and the tyres screeched their objections as the car skidded sideways onto a ninety-degree junction.

"This is Detective Inspector Heather Filson. I've been to the school. You've seen me. I need to know if she's there."

"Like I say, I'm afraid I can't—"

"Look, shut the fuck up!" Heather barked. "She could be in danger. Her life could be in danger. Is she there, yes or no?"

"Please hold."

"Wait, no!"

It was too late. An upbeat Salsa-style number began to tinkle from the stereo system. Heather slammed both hands on the wheel, cursed loudly, then blasted her horn at a slow-moving car in front.

"Get out of the fucking road!" she bellowed, before realising that someone was talking to her.

"Hello? Detective Inspector Filson?"

It was a man's voice. One she, regrettably, recognised.

"This is Toby Pearse. What seems to be the problem? You're not calling to ask where I keep my spare key, are you?"

Heather didn't have time for this. "Ace. Is she in? Is she in school?"

There was a momentary pause, the urgency in the detective's voice forcing the teacher to recalibrate his tone.

"No. No, she didn't come in," he said. "We called her mother. She's very upset. Ace wasn't in her bed this morning. She doesn't know where she is. She's called the police, but—"

Heather stabbed the button that ended the call, furiously slammed both hands on the steering wheel several times, then gripped it so hard her knuckles went white.

"No, no, no, no," she hissed.

And then, with a sudden swerve that earned her half a dozen angry horn blasts, she pulled off the main road, and onto the housing estate that backed onto Kilmarnock Academy.

––––––––

There were a few journalists out front of the Harrison household, lingering around like a bad smell in the hope of a quote, or a candid photo, or a whiff of scandal. When they started firing questions at Heather, she shot back with a curt, "Fuck off," and shouldered past them, hands shoved deep in her jacket pockets, sights locked on the front door.

She hammered twice, then tried the handle. It was unlocked, and she entered without waiting for an invitation. Ibby, Paula's little sister, stood in the hall, motionless aside from a slight shifting of her throat as she gulped down a carton of orange juice through a straw.

The girl was wearing a puffy pink jacket, like she was either about to go out, or had just come back in. Judging by how alert and lively the vultures outside had seemed, Heather guessed the latter.

Linda appeared from the kitchen, peeling off her jacket, and let out a cry of fright when she saw Heather in the hall. Had she not been here, in this house, in this context, Heather might not have recognised the woman.

She'd aged a decade in the past few days. Her skin seemed thinner somehow, like she was fading away, becoming invisible. Even her hair was changing colour, it seemed. Or turning to straw, maybe.

"What are you doing here? What do you want?" Linda demanded. There was a wobble to her voice that sounded more frightened than angry, like she expected Heather to attack her.

"Where's your husband, Linda? Where's Michael?"

Linda's eyes were drawn to the kitchen. Heather barged past her, and found Michael Harrison standing with a knife in his hand. A big bugger of a thing, too.

Heather stopped at the door and raised one hand, fingers together, thumb splayed.

"Put down the knife, Mr Harrison."

Michael just stared back at her, his expression giving nothing away.

"The knife, Mr Harrison, put it down!"

"What?" Michael looked down at his hand, and then reacted with surprise. "Oh! God. Sorry."

He turned to the counter and set the knife down beside a small mound of mushrooms he had been in the process of slicing. Picking up a tea towel, he gave his hands a rub, then slung it over his shoulder and removed a sizzling frying pan from the heat.

"What's wrong? What's happened?" Linda asked. "Have you found something?" She swallowed, barely daring to think it. "Someone?"

"What? No. I mean…" Heather looked at the knife, then at the frying pan, then at the family standing around her. "A girl came here last night."

"Ace. Yes. She knew Paula. Nice girl. Bit odd, but seemed nice," he replied without any hesitation. "She said she wants to help."

"What did you do with her, Michael?" Heather demanded.

"*Do* with her? I didn't do anything with her!" he replied, partly amused, but mostly horrified by the implied accusation. "What do you mean? What's she said? We just… we just talked. She found the keys. Paula's keys. They were in the bowl. Nobody else noticed. Not us. Not you lot. She saw them, and I called it in."

"And then what?" Heather asked.

Her heart was racing, that familiar sheen of sweat forming on her lower back. She didn't want to start doubting herself. She wanted to *know* that Michael Harrison had the girl. She wanted it to be true.

Because, if it wasn't…

"Then we spoke for a bit about how Paula had been in recent weeks, whether she'd mentioned anyone new, and then she went home."

"I don't believe you," Heather said.

She did, though. Part of her did. God help her, part of her knew he was telling the truth.

"She'll be on the doorbell cam," Linda said.

"That's right, she will!" Michael agreed. He smiled at his wife, and though she returned it, the rest of her face remained clouded by sorrow.

It took a minute or so for Michael to call up the video on his phone. He scrubbed through it to make sure it was clear, then held it out for Heather to watch, and tapped the play icon.

On-screen, a light appeared on the darkened front path. A door opened. A figure stepped out, too close to the camera to identify at first, but then it moved further away, and became the girl that Heather had come here searching for.

"Thank you for your time," Ace said. "I'm going to do my best to find her. My condolences to you and Paula's mother and sister."

Michael's mumbled thanks were too quiet to fully make out, but loud enough for Heather to get the gist. The light dimmed as the door was closed. Ace continued walking along the path, then opened and carefully shut the gate behind her, before turning right in the direction of her house.

The footage stopped then, but not before something deeper in the frame caught Heather's eye.

"Wait. Go back."

"To the start?"

Heather grabbed the phone from his hand and rewound a few seconds. She stood there, staring at the screen, her index finger poised and ready to strike.

There. She jabbed at the pause icon a split second before the video stopped playing. Only part of Ace was still in frame—a blur of black school blazer on a dark background.

But further into the estate, fifty yards away, maybe less, a set of car headlights had just illuminated.

It wasn't him. It wasn't Michael Harrison. He hadn't done it.

Unless…

Heather stepped away from him, frantically tapping and swiping at his phone, searching for his call history.

"Did you phone someone? Did you call someone to come and grab her? Are you working with someone?!"

"What the hell are you talking about? No!" Michael cried. He looked into the hall, where his daughter was watching, still drinking her juice. "Ibby, honey, why don't you go watch cartoons in the living room, eh? *Peppa* might be on."

Ibby continued to drink in silence for a few seconds, until a rasping from the juice carton signalled she'd finished. She held it out for her mum to take. Then, without a word, she headed for the living room, fiddling with the buttons of her jacket.

Michael nodded to Linda, who closed the kitchen door. Neither of them made any attempt to stop Heather searching through the phone.

"Has she…" Linda's voice wavered worse than usual. She didn't want to ask the question, but she had to know. "Is she missing?"

There was nothing obviously incriminating about Michael's call history. He could've deleted it, though. She'd have to get access to the call history somehow. Maybe Marty could help.

"Detective Inspector?" Michael's voice forced its way into her thought process. He looked worried, not too much, and not too little. Just enough. Just enough for it to be real. "Is she missing? Ace? Is that what this is about?"

Her lack of response told the couple everything they needed to know. Linda's hand flew her to mouth and she grabbed for the worktop to stay on her feet. Her husband quickly moved to support her, but the colour was draining from his face like someone had pulled out a plug somewhere, and he looked a little unsteady himself.

Heather knew how they felt. The walls of the kitchen seemed to pulse and throb around her, pushing towards her, closing in.

It wasn't him. He didn't have her. She wasn't here.

Which meant that Heather had absolutely no idea where she was, or who she was with.

Or what was happening to her.

She'd sent her a message the night before. Had Heather read it, had she done something about it, had she raced over here right away, then the girl would be at school now. She'd be safe.

But Heather had done none of those things. And now, whatever happened was on her.

She handed Michael Harrison his phone. He took it without a word, one arm still wrapped tightly around the shoulders of his sobbing wife.

"Send that video to the MIT," Heather instructed. "Tell them they're going to need it."

Her voice sounded like it was held together by sticky tape and spit. It felt that way, too.

She buried her hands back in her pockets, and turned for the door.

"Where are you going?" Michael asked. "What are you going to do?"

Heather stopped, but didn't look back.

"Something I should've done a long time ago," Heather said. "I'm going to go look for a caravan."

THIRTY-SEVEN

THERE HAD BEEN two police cars parked out the front of Ace's house, and a Volvo Heather had recognised as Snecky's. No doubt, Ace's mum would be telling the DCI about Heather's visit the evening before. She'd be hauled over the coals for that. Hell, she might even be treated as a suspect.

She didn't care. Right now, none of that mattered. Right now, a girl was missing, and it was all her fault. If she'd spent more time with her in that bedroom, if she'd done the interview for that stupid podcast, Ace might never have left her house last night.

If she'd stopped thinking about her own problems—about herself—for two fucking seconds, she'd have read that message. She'd have rushed round there. She'd have taken the girl home herself.

Whatever Ace Wurzel's fate was now, whatever happened to her—*was* happening to her—Heather bore the brunt of the blame.

She had to find her. She had to bring her home. But she'd run out of suspects now. She'd hit a dead end. Half a second of head-lights on a grainy video was all she had, so all she had was nothing.

She'd texted Marty, asked him to look into Michael Harrison's story about calling in the discovery of the keys. Marty hadn't replied, but it didn't matter. It was going to check out, her gut had already told her that.

That left Heather with only one option. She had to open a door that she'd kept locked shut for most of her life. A door behind which, the nightmares lay.

When searching the internet had proved fruitless, and with Ace's house and the police station off limits, Heather had resorted to paying a visit to the one man who knew everyone.

Shuggie had been surprised to see her. Like his daughter, he'd hoped she was coming with news of the killer, so when she instead told him that another girl was missing, he'd knocked back a drink and suggest that she do the same.

She'd declined, and instead asked him to help find the person she was looking for. The request had seemed so odd, so out of the blue, that he'd laughed.

Heather hadn't. And, when Cowan asked her why she wanted the address, she'd told him. She had no idea why, but she'd told him.

She'd told him about Hayley Wilson, the girl who once was. About all the terrible things that had happened to her. About all the lengths she'd gone to, to bury the memories of them somewhere deep.

She laid it all bare, laid it on thick, watched as his eyes had widened, and his mouth had gone taut, and he'd looked at her in a way he'd never looked at her before. In a way that made her hate the bastard even more than she already had.

He'd looked at her with pity.

And then, with a couple of phone calls, he'd got her an address for a council-run Traveller site in Larkhall.

Flashing her badge had got her through the front gate, though it had earned her a few wary looks, too. A couple of men so large they looked like they'd been over-inflated sat in deckchairs outside a caravan, smoking rolled-up cigarettes, and watching her as she got out of the car.

She ignored them, having already spotted the caravan she was looking for. The picture of the unicorn on the side—painted by someone with no discernible artistic talent whatsoever—would have been giveaway enough, were it not for the wooden sign above the door bearing the name of the woman residing within.

Mesmerelda.

———

It took twenty minutes to convince the woman in the caravan that she wasn't in any sort of trouble.

Mesmerelda—Heather had tried to get her real name from her, but had eventually given up—was short. That had been the big takeaway the moment Heather had first seen her.

Or... no. The big takeaway was the third eye she had tattooed on her forehead. The height thing followed closely on its heels.

She stood bang on five feet tall, and her frame would've once been childlike, before the onset of middle age had scuffed up the edges a bit.

The caravan was small and cluttered, although it probably felt more spacious to Mesmerelda than it did to Heather. Dream catchers and wind chimes hung from the ceiling, so anyone over five foot six either had to duck their head or *cling-clang-clong* every bloody time they stood up.

Incense cones burned at each end of the caravan, going some way to mask the smell of damp that infected the ancient vehicle. Some way, but not all the way. Not by any means.

When Heather had finally managed to explain why she was there, Mesmerelda had put a quick call through to Ace's mum, and had made appropriately concerned and saddened noises while Cathy had sobbed down the line to her.

Mesmerelda had said something about her phone credit then, and had ended the call, before turning back to Heather, her face alive with excitement, her hands rubbing together with glee.

"You want my help!"

"Uh, aye," Heather said. She tried to nod, but the angle of her head made it impossible.

"You want me to tune in to her frequencies. Reach out to her through the ether. Use my powers to find out where she is!"

"What? No. No, none of that shite," Heather said.

Mesmerelda's hands, which had been up near her head, her fingers pressed against her temples, fell to her sides.

"Oh," she said, obviously disappointed. "Well, what are you here for, then?"

Heather took a deep breath. This was it. No going back now.

"Ace told me about you," she said. She pulled at the neck of her shirt, suddenly feeling warm in the freezing caravan. "She said there's some things you might be able to help me remember…"

———

She is five years old. She is cold. She is alone.

And she has never been more afraid.

There were tears, she thinks, though she's run out of them now.

There were screams, too, muffled by a hand on her mouth. Rough. Strong. Wet.

She feels his arm around her waist. Sees the back doors of a van. A dirty rug on the inside. Blood on the walls.

She's on another rug now. Or is it the same one? She doesn't know, but it's just as rough. Just as dirty. Smells just as bad.

It's a different room now, she thinks. Not the van, but the walls are still metal, a pattern of frost painting itself between the corrugated valleys and ridges.

There's a gap where two walls meet. Thin. Narrow. Letting daylight sneak through from the world outside.

She remembers an eye there, she thinks. Staring through, watching her.

Or… no. Was that her? Was she watching?

Was she the one outside, staring in, watching some other girl? Some older girl she didn't know.

Watching the man in the mask moving on top of her. Hurting her. Holding her down.

The girl had seen her. She'd turned her head. She'd stopped crying, just for a moment.

Just for a moment, their eyes had met.

Just for a moment, the whole world had gone silent, gone still.

And then, shouting. Movement. Panic.

Had the man seen her, too? Was that what had happened? Was that why she was here? She didn't know. She couldn't remember. Those corners of her mind were dark. Empty. Everything that had once been there had been cleared out long ago.

She wants her mummy. More than anything. Even now, after all these years, she wants her mummy.

Back then, today, she wants her mum.

She's alone now. Always alone. She's where the other girl was, hands and feet tied, a smelly gag tied across her mouth. It hurts. It all hurts. Everything hurts. The ropes, and the gag, and the cold, and all the parts of her that he's touched. That he's pawed at. That he's leered over and photographed.

And her heart. Her heart hurts, most of all.

There is a thud from somewhere nearby. She holds in the steam of her breath, sniffs back her tears, and listens as it comes again. Slow. Rhythmic. Several seconds between each one.

Thud.

Thud.

Thud.

She hears a voice. Low. Angry.

The man. The man in the mask.

And beyond that, further away, she hears something else. Something that makes her even more afraid. But not for herself this time. Not just for her.

In the distance, far away, she hears the sound of babies crying. Screaming, like their worlds are ending, like all they know is pain.

And the man's voice is still muttering, but the thudding has stopped.

She hears footsteps crunching on pointy, jagged stones. Growing louder. Getting closer.

A metal wall dongs like the tolling of a bell that echoes all around her. Flakes of frost fall on her from above, and slide down the trenches of the walls, soaking into the dirty rug beneath her.

An eye appears in the gap. Watching. Staring.

The eye disappears.

The tears come again.

With the crying of babies still ringing out in the distance, the door opens, and the man in the mask is there. Right there. Right beside her.

The sudden burst of light from outside blinds her. It makes her eyes hurt.

Her eyes, and her wrists, and her ankles, and all the places he's touched.

And as he closes the door behind her and his voice scratches her name in the air, Hayley Wilson's heart hurts.

Her heart hurts most of all.

————

Heather was screaming as she rose from the couch. Screaming as she grabbed the woman beside her by the throat. Screaming as she pinned her to the chair.

Screaming as the memories that had just assaulted her went slithering back into the shadows.

"What the fuck was that? What did you do?" she hissed, her hand tightening around Mesmerelda's throat.

Mesmerelda gagged and choked, slapping at Heather's arm, grasping for something around her to use as a weapon.

She found a copy of *Psychologies* magazine, which she slapped firmly but harmlessly against the side of the detective's head.

It wasn't enough to hurt, but it brought Heather to her senses. She leaped back, releasing her grip, clambering quickly to her feet.

The wind chimes and dream catchers *clonked* and *tinged* as she stumbled backwards through them, her arms swinging, ripping the decorations down from the ceiling.

"Hey, watch what you're doing!" Mesmerelda protested.

"Who the fuck has wind chimes inside?" Heather spat.

She didn't hear the reply. Instead, she threw open the door and practically fell onto the patch of muddy grass outside the caravan. Her hand pressed against the painting of the skelly-eyed unicorn as she steadied herself, and then she marched back to her car, fighting back tears, swallowing down the urge to vomit.

One of the fat fuckers in the deckchair shouted something to her. She ignored it and picked up her pace so she was running now, powering back to her car as fat drops of rain began to tumble from the sky.

She returned to the cocoon of the Audi. Slammed and locked the door.

It was all churning inside her—the memories, the pain, the fear, the regret.

And the realisation.

The stark, horrible realisation that she'd done it all for nothing.

That none of the nightmarish memories she'd churned up were going to help her.

Nothing she had seen or experienced was going to lead her to the missing girl.

Nothing. It had all been for nothing.

Heather smacked her hands on the wheel until her palms turned red.

She pulled at her hair, gripping it with both hands, tangling her fingers in it.

She drove her elbow against the glass of the side window until pain ricocheted up her arm and exploded from her as some primal, animal roar.

What he'd done to her. All those things. He'd done them to the three other girls, too.

Eilidh Howden.

Abbie Blackwell.

Paula Harrison.

And now, he had another one. Now, he had Alison Wurzel. Ace. The girl who had come to her. Who had helped her.

Who had needed her.

Heather's hands stung. Her scalp ached. Her elbow, where she'd driven it against the window, throbbed in pain.

But her heart…

Dear God, her heart.

Her heart hurt, most of all.

THIRTY-EIGHT

IT WAS one of the liaison officers who answered the door. Christina something or other, though Heather knew her as 'Teeny.' Her big sister, Alanna, had been in the year below Heather in high school. If memory served, she'd been somewhat of an arsehole. Teeny, however, was cut from different cloth.

Alanna had fucked off to London and married a banker.

Teeny had joined the police, and quickly discovered a talent for helping people deal with grief.

"Heather? Uh, DI Filson, I mean. Hi," Teeny said. She had opened the door all the way, but now closed it a little, holding it in place. "Sorry, DCI Grant's orders."

"Is Cathy there? Ace's mum. I need to talk to her."

Teeny grimaced. "I'm really not supposed to let you in. I'm not even meant to be talking to you. I'm supposed to call it in if I even see you."

"OK. Do that," Heather said.

The constable in the doorway blinked. "What?"

"Call it in. Tell them you've seen me."

Teeny's laugh was plagued by uncertainty. "I don't need to do that. I don't want to get you in any trouble. We can pretend that this didn't happen."

"Call it in," Heather said. She hopped up onto the top step and gave the door a shove, throwing it open and forcing the constable to retreat further into the hall. "I mean it. Go call it in. I won't stop you. I just need two minutes with Ace's mum. That's all. Two minutes."

"It's fine."

Heather looked past the constable to where Cathy Wurzel was standing in the living room doorway, a dressing gown pulled tightly around her. Like Linda Harrison, she'd been aged by worry. Already, her fear and her grief were shrinking her, whittling her away bit by bit, piece by piece.

Teeny looked from Cathy to Heather, then back again. Finally, she groaned. "I'm going to the shops to get milk. I didn't see any of this."

Heather thanked the constable with a nod as they squeezed past each other in the hall. The door closed behind her, and Cathy half-heartedly beckoned her into the living room.

"Actually," Heather said, stopping at the foot of the stairs. She pointed to the floor above. "Can we do it up there?"

————

Cathy sat on the end of Ace's bed, her elbows on her knees, her head in her hands. Heather had been braced for the other woman to attack her, to blame her—rightly—for what had happened to her daughter.

But she hadn't. She'd hugged her, in fact. Completely out of the blue, completely unbidden, Cathy had put her arms around Heather and they'd hugged on the landing outside Ace's bedroom.

And, though she couldn't explain why, Heather felt like she was the one being comforted.

Then, without a word, Cathy had led the way into Ace's bedroom and flicked on the light, chasing away the evening gloom that was creeping its way into the corners.

The Wonderwall was unchanged from the night before. It was still a mad fractal of printouts, and photos, and sticky notes, and scribbles, all connected by a web of red thread.

The only difference Heather noticed was that another name was now added up there, on a similar yellow *Post-it* as the others.

'Paula Harrison. Aged 15. (Murdered)'

"I didn't know she'd gone out," Cathy said in a voice barely louder than a whisper. "She never goes out. Not on her own. Not at that time of night. But they told me she went round to Paula's. Told me she found something that might help. Keys, or something."

Heather turned her back on the Wonderwall, shuffled uncomfortably for a moment or two, then took a seat on the bed next to Cathy.

"She did, yeah. It'll help them build a better picture of what happened when Paula was taken."

Cathy sniffed. "That's good," she said, though there wasn't a whole lot of conviction behind it. "She always likes to be helpful."

She was sitting up now, twisting her fingers together like she was tying them into complicated knots.

"I think she wanted to impress you," she said. "I think... I think that's why she went."

There could've been venom in her words. Should have been, probably. But there wasn't. Quite the opposite.

"It was nice to see," Cathy whispered. "Nice to see her engaging with someone. She, um, she doesn't have many friends. She doesn't have anyone, really."

"She has you," Heather pointed out, but Cathy tutted and swatted the suggestion away.

"I mean, yes. She's got me. She'll always have me. But I just wish..." Her voice betrayed her and it cracked, and the wall she'd built to hold back her tears crumbled, too. "I just wish people could've seen her like I did. Like *I do*. She's smart. Funny. She's got a huge heart—a *huge* heart. And now... Oh, God. I'm sorry, I'm sorry, I shouldn't..."

She buried her head on Heather's shoulder, and she broke. Her body heaved, and trembled, and shook. Heather put one arm around her, then the other, holding her like she could stop the shaking, force it back inside her, bring it back under control.

In the end, though, it was Cathy herself who stopped it. One long sniff, one abrupt gasp, and she pulled free of Heather's arms and purposefully got to her feet.

"You didn't come here to listen to me whining." She gestured to the Wonderwall. "You came for this, didn't you? You think there might be something on it that can help."

"Maybe," Heather said.

"You think it'll help you find my daughter?"

"I don't know," Heather admitted.

"But it might?"

"It might."

"Well, then," Cathy dabbed at her eyes with the back of a hand, sniffed again, then tightened the belt of her dressing gown. "You'd better get a move on."

She headed out of the room then, stopping only to run a hand down the cardigan that was hanging from the hook on the back of the bedroom door.

Heather felt a pang of guilt—one more to add to the pile—as she watched Cathy stroking the fabric, lovingly caressing the sleeves, and rubbing a thumb across the plastic buttons.

Not wishing to intrude any further on the woman's grief, Heather turned her attention back to the wall. There was no way she could go through it all before someone from the MIT came back to check in. Even if she had time to look through all the information pinned in place there, she had no hope of figuring out how it all fit together, or what most of it meant.

If you believed Ace, the data was arranged in a very deliberate pattern. To Heather, though, beyond the first victim's photo being slap-bang in the middle, it was all just a hodgepodge of randomness.

Heather took out her phone. She worked her way from the top left to the bottom right, snapping off photographs, capturing the information, covering the whole wall one area at a time.

By the time she'd finished, she had a dozen overlapping pictures saved to her camera roll.

By the time she had checked them, Cathy Wurzel was gone. In her place stood Teeny, the liaison officer.

"Just had word," she said. "DCI Grant's on his way." She

nodded at the Wonderwall, a suggestion of panic creeping across a face well practised in appearing calm. "Whatever you're doing, you need to finish up quick!"

THIRTY-NINE

HEATHER SAT cross-legged on her bed, her phone on the blanket in front of her, a notepad balanced on one knee. On the bedside table, the remains of a microwaved lasagna sat congealing in its plastic tub, next to an untouched mug of cold black coffee.

She'd instinctively reached for a bottle of beer while she'd waited for the microwave to *ping*, but had decided against it at the last second. She wanted to keep a clear head.

Her dad, to her relief, had been dozing in his chair when she'd eventually returned to the house, and he hadn't roused when she'd put a blanket over him and tucked him in, other than to snore a little louder and mumble in his sleep.

She'd nuked the frozen pasta dish, made herself the coffee, then retired to her bedroom with the notebook and phone to see if she could find anything useful in the photos of Ace's bedroom wall.

That had been two hours ago. She had pages of scribbled notes, but had no idea which of them, if any, might actually be helpful.

It was the lack of focus that was the problem. Following the photos from left to right, Ace hadn't seemed to be able to stick to any one topic for more than a few inches of wall space.

A theory about the feathers became Eilidh Howden's school report, which led directly on to a list of cities and countries.

Scroll on a few photos, and 'Chicken or duck?' was scribbled on a *Post-it* and repeatedly underlined. It was flanked by a hand-drawn map of Abbie Blackwell's street, and a photocopy of her obituary in one of the local papers.

She'd been a keen swimmer, apparently. Heather hadn't known that. In fact, she realised, she didn't know much about the girls at all. She'd only ever known them as victims. As crimes to be solved. She knew everything there was to know about their deaths, but almost nothing about their lives.

Another swipe of the phone brought her face-to-face with Abbie herself. The photo wasn't the clearest, and she was smiling in it, but the sight of her jolted Heather back to the caravan, back to the memories that had been dredged to the surface.

A girl on the floor of a metal shack.

A man in a mask on top of her.

She swiped quickly to the next photo, but Abbie's picture was in this one, too, just visible at the left of the frame, smiling out at her from all those years ago.

Continuing through the photos, Heather still couldn't spot the pattern. She felt there must be information here she could use, but it was too fractured and disjointed, and would take far too long for her to figure out.

It was like a puzzle with a missing piece. A code that needed a key to decipher.

Heather sat up very straight, very quickly, making her notebook slide off her knee. She grabbed her phone with one hand, while angling herself with the other so she could reach into the left pocket of her jeans.

When she flipped open the lid of her AirPods, it showed only sixteen percent battery. Hopefully, that would be enough.

Shoving in her earphones, she opened up the podcast app and scrolled back to the first episode of *Crime De La Crime*.

After a moment, Ace started talking, telling the listener about Eilidh Howden, and the fate that had befallen her.

Heather listened as she returned to the photos. She swiped to the end, then back to the beginning, then flicked onwards to the middle picture.

Eilidh's photograph sat in the centre of the frame. In Heather's ears, Ace described a girl who loved horses, who wanted to be a vet, and whose laugh was described by her parents as being so infectious it was like 'smallpox for the soul.'

Which sounded pretty fucking awful, Heather thought, but she got what the girl's mum and dad had been going for.

Ace began describing the events of December 9th, 1989. The day that Eilidh Howden went missing. Two days before she'd be found dead and naked at the side of the road between Kilwinning and Beith.

Six days before Abbie Blackwell vanished.

Eight days before the then Hayley Wilson would be snatched from outside the Nursery she attended every morning by a man whose face she had never seen.

Three victims more than three decades ago.

Was it really him now? Was he back? Or had someone taken up his mantle?

He had seemed old in the memories that Mesmerelda had helped summon—a vast and ancient and terrible creature who wasn't truly of this world.

Even if he'd been in his thirties, he'd be pushing seventy now. He'd be weaker. Slower. In theory, easier to catch.

On the other hand, maybe he'd been quietly planning all this time. Maybe those three victims had just been a warm-up. Maybe he was finally ready to start his Magnum opus.

But Kenny and her dad had killed him. Hadn't they? Her uncle had seemed sure of it. They'd dealt with him, and the killings had stopped.

Unless…

With Ace's voice still droning in her ears, Heather returned to her phone and swiped backwards through the pictures she'd taken.

She settled on the list of place names. There were around a dozen of them, from all over Europe, including a couple of places in England and one in Wales.

A line of red thread stretched down and to the right. Heather flicked back and forth through her photos until she reached what she was sure was the other end of the line.

Dates. Eighteen in total, beginning in March 1990 and continuing through until 2006. They were bunched together in groups of ones and twos. Heather quickly jotted them down in her pad, then returned to the list of places.

She counted them up. Eleven towns and cities.

Eleven groups of dates.

Heart racing, she went back to the picture with the dates in it, and saw a second length of thread trailing almost straight down. She plotted it out, swipe by swipe, until she found a page on which Ace had written girls' names.

Eleven of them.

'Ingrid Olsen. Aged 17. (Murdered)'

'Daisy Walker. Aged 14. (Murdered)'

'Béatrice Toussaint. Aged 13. (Murdered)'

On and on it went. All girls in their teens. All dead.

All eleven.

Eleven places. Eleven dates. Eleven victims.

Spread across the continent, across seventeen years.

Heather's hands shook as she wrote the details in the notebook.

She'd have to check them out, of course. She couldn't take a fifteen-year-old's word that any of these deaths were connected to the attacks here in Kilmarnock.

But if Ace was right, if the deaths were all linked, then the Killie Kiddie Killer had been active far longer than anyone had previously suspected. He'd been killing for years after everyone had assumed he'd stopped.

Which meant that her dad and her uncle had murdered an innocent man.

Silencing the podcast, Heather tapped through to her phone app, called up Marty's number, and sat with her thumb hovering over it. It was late, but he'd almost certainly still be in the office. Would he answer, though? She had no idea how much shit he was in for helping her last time.

But this was different. They needed to have this information. They needed to check to see if it was right. Maybe there were clues to his identity out there. Maybe the other investigations had found bits of the puzzle that could all be slotted together to find—

The rest of the thought was shattered by the exploding of her bedroom window. Heather ducked, covering her face to protect it from the flying shards of glass.

A rock, roughly the size of an orange, thudded against her bedroom wall, punching a hole in the plaster before dropping heavily onto the floor.

"Jesus Christ!" she cried.

She grabbed her trainers from beside the bed, shook the glass out of them, then forced her feet inside and hurried to the broken window.

Her bedroom looked out over the back garden and there, in the pool of darkness beyond the fence, she saw a figure looking up at her.

A man, his face mostly obscured by shadow, standing there on the road, surveying the damage he'd caused.

"Right then, you fuck," Heather hissed.

And with that, she ran.

———

Had she stopped to think about it, she might've grabbed a weapon. A knife. A rolling pin. A can of fucking hairspray and a lighter, even. But her urgency and her rage were such that she raced outside without a thought, launching herself from the warmth of the house into the bracing cold of the world beyond.

The tall gate at the end of the path was locked. It had been many years since Heather had attempted it, but adrenaline propelled her towards the gate and, using the centre bracing as a footing, she launched herself up and over the top.

Pain seared through her ankles and knees as she landed on the pavement on the other side, but a glimpse of a figure running away in the middle distance drove her onwards, giving chase.

He wasn't particularly fast, but then neither was she these days. His head start was insurmountable in a straight race, but Heather had roamed this estate for years, and knew every turn and alleyway. If she could figure out where the fucker was going, she could head him off at the pass.

Unfortunately, the fleeing suspect didn't seem entirely sure where he was going himself. He swung right towards what Heather knew to be a dead end, then aborted and continued straight on, throwing panicky looks back over his shoulder as he went clattering past the entrance to another cul-de-sac.

The sky had darkened all the way into night now, and only the street lights picked him out as he ran. He'd appear in the pool of orange light for a few moments, then vanish again into the darkness beyond it, only to be picked up again a few seconds later, a few dozen metres down the street.

He was slowing, Heather thought, but the pain caused by her ill-advised fence jump was making itself felt now, and the shock of adrenaline that had sent her thundering out of the house was being chipped away by the cold night air.

Up ahead, illuminated beneath a lamppost, the suspect banked to the right, and a sudden realisation surged through the chasing detective, buying her a few more moments of resistance against the pain in her legs.

The garages. The bastard was going to run down past the garages. If he made it to the road at the end, he'd be home and dry. There'd be no way of finding him in the maze of alleyways.

He wasn't going to get that far. There was only one route past the garages—a straight sprint down the road the metal-fronted concrete blocks stood on, with nowhere to hide.

But while there was only one way past the garages, there was more than one way *to* them. There was the long way that the man leading the chase was taking.

And then there was the short way.

Heather shifted her trajectory sharply to the right, darting between two rows of houses and then swinging into a left turn. There was a smaller fence ahead of her, but she cleared that with only some light grumbling from her joints, and then she was running on the path alongside the graffiti-covered backs of the garages.

She could hear him clattering and wheezing on the other side of the row of dilapidated buildings, a little behind her, but almost running parallel.

Fifteen metres ahead, the row came to an end. Beyond it, just out of Heather's line of sight, lay the mouth of an alleyway that led into the twisting network of passageways that would spell escape for the man Heather was chasing.

Right now, he'd almost be able to taste freedom.

Right now, he'd be thinking he was home and dry.

The thought of his impending disappointment was the happiest moment of Heather's week.

She reached the end of the row of garages, listened to his footsteps, then timed her launch perfectly.

She hammered her shoulder into him. Hard. He went springing off like a pinball in a machine, crying out in fright as his world upended and he crashed down into an icy puddle of manky brown slush.

He was whimpering by the time she was on him, squealing, "No! Don't! Don't!" as she twisted an arm, drove in a knee, and pulled at the hood that covered his head and hid his face.

"You!" she hissed. Mostly because she couldn't remember his name.

The guy from the club. The guy she'd woken up with. The guy whose mum had offered her breakfast on her way out the door.

"Yes! Yes, it's me! I'm sorry, I'm sorry! I didn't mean it!"

Heather shoved him back down into the puddle, and then stood over him as he dragged himself out of the cold and filthy water.

"Stay down," she warned when he tried to get to his feet. He nodded quickly, eager to demonstrate his compliance.

"I'm sorry. It was an accident."

"An accident? You threw a fucking brick through my window."

"It wasn't a brick! It was a stone. I was just trying to get your attention!"

Heather put her hands on her hips and stared down at him. Off in the distance, late-night traffic rumbled towards the town centre, and a couple of bams started singing at the tops of their voices.

"Well, you've got my attention, *Dom*," she said, his name

popping into her head just in time to round off the sentence. "Though you're going to wish you fucking hadn't."

"I just… I did it all for you. Everything. I wanted to get your attention. I did it all for you. For us."

The sounds of the traffic and the singing faded away into silence. The cold night breeze wrapped itself around Heather, ejecting a little gasp of shock.

"What do you mean? What are you talking about?" She heard a scuffing sound, and realised she had taken a backwards step. "You did what for me? What the hell did you do?"

"I tried phoning you. The day after we made love. I was going to leave it, play it cool, but Mum said it's best to show interest. If you like someone, go after them. Tell them."

He got slowly to his feet, one hand held out to keep Heather at bay. She didn't make any move to stop him, though. She needed to hear this. She needed to know.

"And I thought, yeah. That's good advice. If you like someone, go after them. Tell them. And if they don't listen…?"

Dom wiped the back of the black jogging bottoms he was wearing, but the water had well and truly soaked in, and so he quickly gave up.

"Then *make* them listen."

He took a step towards her. She drew back a fist, warning him off.

"What did you do, Dominic?" she whispered. "What have you done?"

"I tried phoning you," he said again. "But you must've made a mistake with the number, because it went to some guy in Exeter."

"That wasn't a mistake. I gave you a fake number."

Dom frowned, confused by what she'd said. "What?" He laughed. "What do you mean?"

Heather tutted. "It's not fucking difficult. I didn't want you contacting me, so I gave you a fake number."

He tried to smile through this revelation, but the hurt in his eyes betrayed him. "Oh. Oh. Well, that's just… That's just mean."

"What did you do?" Heather demanded again. She looked him

up and down, sizing him up, getting the measure of him. "Was it you? Did you do it?"

"I thought you might phone me after the flowers," he said. "They weren't cheap. I went to a lot of trouble and spent a lot of money on them. I thought you might at least have the decency to get in touch then. Even a, 'Thanks, but no thanks.' But, no. Nothing."

He pushed his hands back through his hair. They were dirty from the ground, and left muddy brown marks on his forehead and up onto his scalp.

"You put them in the bin," he said. His voice shook with anger, or outrage. Some mix of the two. "You took them outside, and you ripped up the card, and you shoved it all in the bin."

"You were watching," Heather realised. "You were watching me."

"Well, of course I was watching you, babe! I wanted to see your reaction. I wanted to see the big smile they put on your face. I delivered them myself, thinking I might be able to hand them over. Thinking maybe we could go upstairs, you know? Have some fun like we did last week. But it was just your dad." Dom shrugged and smiled at her. "He seems nice, by the way. I think he and my mum would get on like a house on fire."

"You stay the fuck away from him," Heather spat.

"When I saw you binning them, though, I thought that was the end of it. That hurt, Heather. It really hurt."

"Good."

"I was going to give up on you then. Move on to someone else. Someone who deserved my attention. But then, I saw you on TV, and I felt so bad for you. You looked so sad. And I thought, does she miss me? Is that it? Should I give her another chance? So, I wrote you a lovely card. Put some thought into it. I drew it myself. Thought the message was cute, but apt, given that I was standing ten feet away when you picked it up."

He grinned at her, and his voice became a thin and reedy sing-song.

"Peek-a-boo, I see you!"

He spotted the colour of his hands for the first time, tutted, then wiped them on his jacket. Heather took another step back as he began to pace back and forth in front of her.

"I shouldn't have done that in your kitchen. With the pots on the rings. I shouldn't have done that," he said, shooting her an apologetic look. "But I was angry. You tore the card to bits. The card I'd made specially. You ripped it to pieces. You *discarded* it, no pun intended. You discarded it, just like you'd done to me."

He was growing in confidence now, his panic replaced by some misplaced sense of righteous indignation that was buoying his confidence.

"But the kitchen. The pots. I shouldn't have done that. It was petty, I know. I'll help pay for any damages. Although, I think you need to take some of the blame, too, Heather, because—Jesus Christ! I just wanted to get your attention! I just wanted you to notice me. That's what all this has been about!"

"Paula Harrison." The name came as a croak from way back in Heather's throat. "Did you kill her? Was that you?"

His growing sense of confidence sputtered and died. He stopped pacing, and instead took a slightly staggered backward step.

"What?" he said, snivelling out a laugh. "Jesus. No. No, of course not! God. Why would you even say that?"

"Because you're exactly the sort of sad, creepy little fucker that would rape and kill a girl," Heather told him. "Did you do it? Did you kill Paula?"

"No! Fucking hell! Is that really what you think of me?!" Dom cried.

"The birds. On the card and the flowers. There were birds. What were they for, if you didn't kill her?"

"What the hell have birds got to do with anything?" Dom asked. "I like birds. I'm a twitcher. I've got a telescope and binoculars. I watch them in the trees. Plus, double meaning, you're *my* bird."

"Am I fuck," Heather shot back. She shook her head, refusing to accept it. "No. I'm not buying that. I'm taking you in."

"I was with you!" Dominic squealed, thrusting his hands above his head. "Remember? The night she went missing. Paula.

Remember? We were in the Garage all evening, then you stayed at mine all night. I didn't do it. I mean, of course I didn't do it, but I couldn't have done it, even if I'd wanted to. Which I didn't!"

Oh, God. He was right. The timings didn't work. It couldn't have been him. He'd been shagging a Police Scotland detective inspector at the time.

Alibis didn't come much more cast iron than that.

The sounds of the night came rushing back to the fore. The traffic. The singing. A car alarm a few streets over.

And another sound, too. A sound that rose up like the fin of a shark through the murky water of her memories. A sound she thought she must surely be imagining.

The same sound she'd heard all those years ago, tied up on that filthy carpet, locked in that frosty room.

The sound of babies crying.

"Do you hear that?" she whispered. Her eyes darted around, searching for the sound, but it seemed to be coming from all directions at once.

"Hear what, babe?" Dom asked.

"Don't fucking call me *babe*!" Heather warned. She pointed with her eyes into the darkness. "That. That noise. The crying."

"Oh. Yeah," Dom said. "I hear it."

She stared at him like he'd lost his mind. How could he be so relaxed about it? So casual?

"You hear it? You can hear them crying? The babies?"

Dom frowned. It was an exaggerated thing, designed to make anyone seeing it feel stupid. "Um, babies? No. I mean, it does sound a bit like babies, I suppose," he said. "But it isn't, *obviously*."

Heather glanced around. The cries were still ringing out across the estate. It sounded like four or five infants all screaming at once.

"Well, what the fuck is it, then?" she asked.

Dom's smile was as patronising as the satisfied little head wobble he gave before replying.

"Well, it's obvious, isn't it?" he said, milking his big moment. "It's cats."

"Cats?" Heather felt hot bile rising in her throat, and a sudden urge to scream, though she didn't know why. Not then. Not yet. "But that's… They sound…"

"They do that. My mum has four of them. That might even be hers we're hearing!" Dom said, laughing at the thought of it. "When they're in heat, or hungry, or trying to scare something off, or just want to be a pain in the arse, they cry like that. Have you seriously never heard it before?"

She had.

She'd heard that noise. That *exact* noise. She'd thought it was the sound of crying babies.

She'd been wrong.

Her trainers splashed in the puddle as the enormity of it spun her around, turned her in a circle. The icy cold water seeped through, soaking her socks, chilling her feet.

She didn't notice.

Instead, she thought of the cats.

She thought of the feather.

She thought of a list of eleven girls, on eleven dates, in eleven different places.

"Hey, you alright, babe?"

Heather felt Dom's hand stroking her back, and realised that she was bending over, her hands on her thighs like she'd been about to throw up.

His hand followed the curve of her back, creeping down until his fingers brushed against the bottom of her spine, and continued on towards her arse.

She straightened, spun, then laid the fucker out with a single punch that burst open his nose and sent him spluttering and squealing to the ground.

"Stay the fuck away from me and my dad!" she warned.

Leaving Dom there to choke and gag on his blood, Heather ran back to her house and grabbed her phone and her keys.

She checked on her dad to make sure he was still sleeping, put a call through for backup, then jumped in her car.

She knew where Ace was. She knew who had taken her.

God help her—God *damn her*—she knew.

FORTY

THE TREES CAME alive as the headlights of Heather's car sliced across them, sending sharp, spindly shadows scurrying away like insects into the woods.

She cut the engine and shut off the lights. Her destination was still a quarter of a mile away, but she daren't announce her arrival. Not yet. Not until Ace was safe.

There was a torch in the boot—a big, long-handled, heavy bugger of a thing that could blind a man at twenty paces, and bludgeon him unconscious at two. She held it low at her side, angled downwards so its beam illuminated the forest floor a few feet in front of her, and no more.

She'd made this trip a dozen times before, though never in the dark.

No. That wasn't true, she now realised.

Only once in the dark.

The ground was damp from all the recent snow and rain. Her boots squelched into the moss, squeezing pools of greenish water from it with every hurried step.

The vapour of her breath trailed behind her, falling behind as she hurried on, weaving through the trees, picking her way through the darkened forest until, many minutes later, she arrived at a clearing.

She arrived at the house.

It had been a bustling family home once, though that was before Heather's time. Her dad had grown up here, and even now —especially now—he spoke of it like it was some wondrous, magical place where the sun had never set, and the rain had never come, and anything had been possible.

It must've seemed that way to a child. A big stately farmhouse, a few acres of land and sky, and more trees than a young boy could ever hope to climb.

Heather couldn't remember those times, of course. She couldn't remember a time when this place had been occupied at all, in fact.

Her grandmother, who owned the place, had died soon after Heather was born. Her only memory of the woman was a fiction she'd put together from old photographs and stories. Her grandfather had been gone years before that, killed in an accident at a mill in Kilbirnie.

Heather's dad had brought her to see the place countless times through her childhood and teenage years. She'd never been keen. Something about the place had unsettled her.

At least now she knew why.

Heather clicked off the torch. There were no vehicles parked in the overgrown driveway, and no lights in any of the windows, but no need to take any stupid risks.

Well, no more than were necessary. Backup would still be a while, but there was no way Heather could sit and wait. Not when the girl could be in there somewhere. Not while anything could be happening to her.

The light from the moon guided her towards the farmhouse, and the smattering of outbuildings scattered across the grounds in front of it like pieces on a chess board protecting the King.

Years of neglect through the hard Scottish winters had taken its toll on the buildings. Those made of brick had partly collapsed, while the wooden ones had been almost entirely eaten away by the passing of time.

It was through a hole in the side of one of the brick buildings that she saw the glint of corrugated steel, picked out by the pale light of the waning moon.

She thought of frost forming in the ridges and valleys of the walls.

Of a filthy old rug on the cold hard floor.

Heather glanced up at the darkened house, then changed direction. The outbuilding was about the width of a car trailer, and longer than it was high. Even before part of it had caved in, it would've stood lower than six feet at its highest point, with an opening for a window at one end, and a rusted mesh gate at the other.

Rainwater had flooded in through the hole in the roof, but not enough to wash away all of the mounds of long-dried chicken shit that had congealed on the poured concrete floor.

And there, standing in the centre, still shining like a beacon after all these years, was a metal box around five feet square.

A heavy bolt had been fastened across the door and secured with an industrial-grade padlock. Heather flicked on the torch just long enough to check the brickwork as she ducked inside, hoping to find a key hanging on a hook nearby.

No such luck.

The smell of turpentine lingered in the air. A solvent. A paint thinner.

And just the very thing for cleaning an oily old bicycle.

She crept closer. Listened at the door. It was cold to the touch when she placed her hand on it, making her think of things long dead.

"Hello?" She rapped her knuckles on the metal, softly at first, then more forcefully. "Ace? Are you in there? Hello? Is anyone there?"

Silence. The only sound was the ragged rasp of her breathing.

Shit.

Heather remembered the eye at the crack in the wall, watching her. She felt along the sides of the metal box, ran her fingers down the joins at the corners, but there were no gaps to be found.

Through the hole in the roof, she saw something that made her blood ice up in her veins. A light. In one of the upper windows of the house. A light had come on.

She thought, for a moment, that she saw movement there, but then it was gone.

"Officer?"

The whisper was so quiet, so raw and hoarse, that Heather dismissed it as the wind. It was only when it came again—"Officer, is that you?"—that she pressed her hand against the metal and stifled a sob of relief.

"Yes! Yes, it's me. Are you OK? Did he hurt you?"

The length of the delay curled Heather's fingers into claws.

"I want to go home," Ace whispered, and her voice echoed unnaturally inside the box.

"We're going home. I promise. I just need to get you out," Heather said. She checked the bolt. It was riveted in place, so a screwdriver wouldn't help.

The padlock was old, but heavy. Bolt cutters might do it, but not without a long set of handles and a big heavy bastard on the other end.

What she did have was a torch with a handle designed for smashing people in the face. It would be noisy, though. She'd have to work fast.

"OK, I'm going to try and break the lock," she whispered. "When I get the door open, can you run?"

"Yes," was the only reply from inside the cell.

"Good. Because we're going to run, OK? You're going to take my hand, and we're going to run." She turned the torch around and rested the bottom of it on top of the padlock where it secured the bolt. "I'm getting you home."

Heather jerked the torch upwards, but before she brought it down she stole another glance through the hole in the roof at the house.

The light in the window was out. The place, once again, was in darkness.

"Shit," she whispered.

"What is it?" Ace asked, panic bubbling up through the gaps between the words. "What's wrong?"

"Nothing. Just be ready," Heather said. She brought the torch down. It *thunked* against the lock just as a footstep behind her went *crunch*.

She saw a shadow. Heard a gasp.

Before she could turn, an explosion against the side of her head sent her sprawling sideways into the moss-covered brick wall.

She swallowed down copper. Blinked in the blinding light.

And then, she choked on the pain as a hand caught her by the hair and jerked her backwards, and a fist struck her face like a hammer blow.

FORTY-ONE

FOR A WHILE, her whole world was sick, and blood, and spit.

It pooled in her lap, oozed down her front, hung as stringy strands from her burst lips.

For a while, she didn't remember. For a while, she sat there, silent.

And then, it all rushed back. The trees. The house. The girl in the box, alone and afraid.

Heather jerked, but the ropes around her tightened her arms to her sides and pulled her against the back of the old wooden dining chair she'd been tied to.

The kitchen was lit by candles. It made the light an ethereal thing, always moving, never still. Damp had gotten a grip on the place, infected the corners, then spread across the ceiling and down the walls, consuming the plaster and blackening the wood of the rustic old cabinets. Rotting it away like the soul of the man sitting on the matching chair directly across from her.

The man who had killed all those girls.

The man who had sexually assaulted her.

Her uncle.

"Shh, shh, shh, shh," he soothed, holding out a hand to calm her as she thrashed and raged against the ropes. "Chill out.

Alright? Calm down. Let's talk about this, alright? It's me and you. Let's just talk."

"Let me out," Heather spat. She twisted violently, until the ropes burned her through her shirt. "I swear to fucking God, Kenny, let me go!

"No. I can't. Not yet. Not when you're this…" He gestured at her. "Wound up. You need to calm down first. You need to—"

Heather became stock still. She spat out the blood, and swallowed back her rage. "I'm calm. There. I'm perfectly calm. Untie me. You want to talk, we can talk."

Kenny laughed, but it only lasted for a moment. "Nice try, kiddo," he said. "But I know you too well for that one!"

"Aye? Funny. I don't know you at all."

Her uncle winced at the comment, then rested his hands on his thighs and nodded. "Fair. No, that's fair," he said.

"It was you. All along. Right from the start. It was you."

"You were never meant to get mixed up in it, Heather. You were never meant to be involved. I hated that you were. Hated it."

Heather's eyes narrowed to slits. She spat her response at him. "What, you accidentally abducted and raped me?!"

"Jesus! I didn't rape you!" Kenny protested.

He squirmed in his chair, clearly uncomfortable with this part of the conversation. Beside him, lying on the table, Heather saw a throwing axe. There was blood on the flat of the metal. The same blood she could feel matting the hair on the side of her head.

"We… you know. We fooled around a bit. That was all. We didn't go all the way."

Heather's stomach spasmed, ejecting acid up into her throat. "Fooled around?! I was five! I was terrified! I thought you were going to kill me."

"But I didn't!" Kenny cried, and that big gregarious smile that she knew so well lit up his face. "I could've, but I left the door open. I let you escape! Do you have any idea how worried I was about that? You say you were scared, but what about me? Did you ever think about that? That could've been the end of me! I could've been caught!"

"My heart fucking bleeds for you, Kenny," Heather said.

"Come here and untie me, and I'll give you a hug. We'll let bygones be bygones, eh? No harm done."

"Oh, I wish," Kenny said. He groaned and rubbed his eyes with a finger and thumb. "I wish that could happen."

"So, you killed those girls. Back then. You killed them?"

Kenny pulled an apologetic sort of face, then nodded. "Afraid so."

"And that was just the start. Germany. Denmark. Down south. That was you, too."

Her uncle's eyes had started widening when she'd mentioned Germany, and were now two saucers of surprise.

"Wow. Someone's been doing their homework! I'm impressed," he said. "Although, not quite right. The girls here, they weren't the start. Newcastle was the start." He clapped his hands together and laughed. "You didn't know about that one, did you? July nineteenth, nineteen-eighty-seven. Eleven-seventeen P.M., give or take a few seconds."

He sat back in the chair, smiling wistfully, gazing out through the big kitchen window that looked onto the dark, empty driveway.

"Never caught her name. Not her real one, anyway. She was a prostitute with an attitude problem. I was a young man full of testosterone and drink. One thing led to another, things got a bit out of hand, and, well…"

"You killed her."

Kenny jumped to his feet, excitement blazing behind his eyes. The sudden movement made the candles judder and dance, sending shadows scurrying up the rotting walls.

"You've got no idea what it's like, Heather. There's nothing that compares. The exhilaration of it. The power!"

His hands formed two letter Cs, like they were wrapping around someone's neck.

"I was sure they were going to catch me. That I'd get locked up for it. I kept waiting for the knock at the door. For them to take me away." He frowned, like he still couldn't quite believe his luck. "But nobody came. Nobody. I kept checking the papers, but I don't think it ever even made it to print. Poor cow. Dead in a hotel room, and nobody gave a shit."

He ran a hand down his beard, then tugged on the bottom of it, shaking his head, like he was saddened by the callous nature of society.

"What then?" Heather asked.

She looked to the window behind him, where the moonlight coming through the clouds picked out the shapes of the outbuildings. Was Ace still out there? Had he left her alive?

"I kept thinking about it. Day, night, when I was working, when I was home. I tried not to, tried to forget about it, but I couldn't. It just… it kept calling to me. Like one of them fucking mermaids you hear about. Singing to me."

He licked his tongue across his lips and studied Heather in the chair, like he was debating how much to give away.

"So, I went back."

"To Newcastle?"

He nodded, just once. "To Newcastle. I found someone else. Another girl. Nobody that mattered. Not really. And this time, I planned it. I knew what I was doing. My hands were shaking I was that excited. She shoved them down the front of her skirt. 'To warm them up,' she said. 'No charge.'"

He laughed, suddenly and sharply, delighting in the memory. The sound of it rattled around inside Heather's injured skull, bringing a wave of pain with it.

"I fucked her, and then I cut her throat," he said, and the bluntness of it, the brutality, forced a sob to burst unbidden on Heather's bloodied lips. "You do want to hear all this, right?" he asked, still smiling. "The details? Because, honestly? You have no idea how long I've waited to tell someone. I mean, I tell *them*. The girls. Before. I tell them what I've done. What I'm going to do. But they're always too fucking concerned about themselves to listen. They don't *listen*, Heather. No one really *listens*!"

"I'm listening, Kenny," she told him. "I want to hear it all."

"It all?! Ha! Christ, even I don't know it all. I mean, your dad's memory's fucked, but mine's not what it was, either. And you forget them, after a while. All their faces. All their screams. All their *tits*. They blur together. One big, sobbing, naked, bloody fucking mess. That's all most of them are. A homogeneous fucking mass of flesh."

"Eilidh Howden," Heather said, thinking of that sticky note on the Wonderwall. "Aged fifteen. Murdered."

Kenny pointed to his niece like she'd just got a question right at a pub quiz.

"Now, Eilidh, Eilidh I *do* remember," he said. "She was the first one I brought here. Not to the house—I never did anything in the house. This, in here, this was home—but out there. Out in the shed."

He gestured to the window. A wind had got up now, and a movement over by the trees drew Heather's eye.

"She was young. I liked them young. Not like you. You were too young. But fourteen, fifteen, maybe? Sweet sixteen?" He inhaled deeply through his nose and smiled, like he'd just picked up on some delicious aroma. "That's the stuff. That's spot on. Old enough to know. To understand it all."

He let out a low moan of pleasure at the thought of it, then scratched at his beard and gave himself a shake. He rested his arse on the edge of the table, within easy grabbing distance of the axe.

"I thought I was done for with her, though. Thought I'd given the game away."

He raised an eyebrow, like he was trying to tease a response from Heather. She refused to give him the satisfaction.

"The feather. It was from the hen house. See, I had a mate at the station. Reg Gardner. Way before your time. We used to go out drinking, and he let slip that they'd found this feather on the body. I was sure that was me fucked. Nearly turned myself in, would you believe? And then I thought, you see all these American guys and stuff, don't you? The Zodiac Killer. The Night Stalker. That other one. What's his name? Scorpio."

"He's from *Dirty Harry,* you fucking idiot."

A flash of anger crossed Kenny's face, but then he chuckled. "Aye, right enough. Creepy bastard. Weird laugh. Anyway, the point is, they all had these gimmicks. And I thought, what if I did that? What if I made it look like I'd left the feather on purpose? Make it a calling card, sort of thing. I knew I didn't have a lot of time, and so, a couple of days later, I followed another girl."

"Abbie Blackwell."

"Abbie Blackwell," Kenny confirmed.

"Aged eleven. Murdered."

Her uncle regarded her with confusion for a moment, then shrugged. "Aye. Her. I was still worried they might be onto me, so I told everyone I was going away."

"You said you were down south when I asked you a couple of days ago," Heather said. "When you were telling me about what you and my dad did, you said you'd been overseas. That got me thinking."

It had, though she'd been quick to dismiss it as a slip of the tongue, the alternative—this alternative, here and now—being too awful to even contemplate.

"Did I? Fuck. Getting careless in my old age." He smirked, and gestured to Heather in the chair. "I mean, obviously. But, aye, I said I was going away. Instead, I rented a room, hid out, and then waited a few days until I saw someone who just, you know, *did it* for me.

"Because that's the thing. Back then, there was never any one particular reason for me choosing the girls I did. It could be anything. Any wee simple thing. The way they smiled. The way the light caught their hair. Their voice. How good I thought they'd look when they were scared."

"You're fucking sick," Heather said, and she followed it up with a wad of blood that she spat at him.

"I know. God. Do you think I don't know that? Do you think I haven't beat myself up about that for years? This isn't normal, Heather. None of this is normal. I get that. But I couldn't help myself. I wanted to give it up, but it was the only time I felt awake. Alive. How do you quit that?"

"Maybe start by not raping and killing children!"

"Hmm." Kenny put his hands on his hips. "That's a bit of a simplistic view of it, if you don't mind me saying. See, what I do, Heather, this thing, it's like any other addiction. It's an illness. *I'm more to be pitied than scolded,*" he said, though he smirked when he said it.

"And what about me? Why did you *choose* me, Kenny? What did I do to earn your attention?"

Kenny ran his hand along the handle of the axe, then smacked his lips together and stood up.

"We'll come back to that. The point is, I did stop. Eventually. I went cold turkey. Quit while I was ahead. I'd got away with it. I'd had my fun, and I'd got away with it. And I was too old. When you hit forty, the urges just sort of fall away. You know? You've not got the same drive. You'll find that out in a year or two. The fire's not there, not in the same way."

"So why start again now? Why kill Paula?"

Kenny looked up to the damp-stained ceiling and let out a long sigh that had clearly been brewing for a while.

"I wish I hadn't. Cards on the table? Between you and me? I really wish I hadn't. It wasn't about her. Not really. It was about him. That evil fucker, Cowan."

He began to pace around the kitchen, scratching furiously at his beard, his movements becoming increasingly agitated.

Heather watched him get further from the axe, before he spun around and marched back again.

"When I heard he'd found a family… A daughter. Grandkids. It turned my fucking stomach. Why should he get to have a life? A family?" Kenny asked. "That bastard killed Stewie."

"We don't know that."

"Aye, we fucking do!" Kenny roared, and motes of dust and plaster rained down from the ceiling. "We might not be able to prove it, but we do! We know, Heather. You and me, we know he did it!"

He gulped down a few desperate steadying breaths, one hand on his chest like his heart was racing out of control.

"But we've no evidence, have we? We know he did it, but we've no proof. So, it's like I told you this morning, sometimes, justice and the law aren't the same thing! Sometimes, you have to take things into your own hands."

"You were telling me about getting my dad to help you murder an innocent man. That's not justice, Kenny!"

"I had to. It was to cover my tracks. And I wanted out. I thought, if someone took the fall for it, I'd stop. I'd quit. But it's not that easy, Heather. It gets its hooks into you. The killing." He held his hands out, as if he could see the blood on them. "I'm as much a victim as anyone."

Heather bit her lip to stop herself screaming at him. She bit so hard that the blood started to flow again, trickling down her chin and drip-drip-dripping into her lap.

"You killed Paula to get at Shuggie Cowan," she said, steering him back to the matter at hand.

"Yeah. I think so. Mostly," Kenny said. "But, OK, cards on the table. It wasn't just that."

"What, then?"

"I'm dying, Heather."

The bluntness of it caught her off guard, and she could only stare at him in shock.

"I should've said weeks ago. I'm dying. Cancer. Prostate, but I've left it too late. It's spread. I'm dying. I've got six months. Maybe less."

"That's the best news I've heard all night, Kenny," Heather said.

He winced, like this was some unwarranted attack. "Aye, I suppose you might see it like that, right enough, considering."

"So, what? This was one last big hurrah, was it?"

"Maybe, aye," Kenny conceded. He chewed his bottom lip for a moment, before spitting out what he'd been holding back. "At the hospital. One of the wee nurses. Red haired. Tattoos. Pretty wee thing. She rubbed my arm."

Heather waited for more, but it didn't come. "She what?"

"She rubbed my arm."

"And what, you thought that was a come on?" Heather scoffed. "You sad old fucker."

"No. No, that's it. That's it exactly. She looked at me like I was a fucking joke. Like I was this old, dying waste of fucking space. Like I was nothing. She looked at me, and all she saw was this decrepit *thing* waiting to die. Me! After everything I've fucking done!"

He crossed to the window and pointed out at the moon-dappled landscape beyond. Heather froze. From there, he'd be able to see where Heather had been twisting her wrists in her ropes. All he had to do was look.

"It's the same out there, day to day, on the street," he ranted, still oblivious to what she'd been up to. "They don't know I'm dying, but they look at me, and they see an old guy. Grey beard. Overweight. Someone to be dismissed. Laughed at. Someone to feel *sorry* for."

"If it's any consolation, I don't feel sorry for you at all," Heather told him.

Kenny stormed back to stand in front of her. For a moment, he looked angry, like he might physically lash out at her.

He chose to do it mentally, instead.

"But when I was on her, Heather... When I was *in* her..." Kenny closed his eyes, savouring the memory. "Before then, even, when she knew what was going to happen. When she realised what I was going to do next. Aw, Heather. It was something else. It was something new." He snapped his eyes open, and smiled at her. "It was a fucking tonic, is what it was. I felt twenty years younger, I swear to God."

He raised his hands, palms facing her, like a magician showing the audience they were empty.

"That was going to be the end of it. I just wanted to prove to myself that I still had it in me. One and done. One for old time's sake. One for the road. But, like I said, it's a sickness, Heather. It's an addiction, and when I saw that other girl, saw how nervous she looked, how out of place, I just... I couldn't help myself. I couldn't not. But she's the last, I promise. Once I've finished with her, I am done. No more."

A sad and distant look settled across his face. He returned to the table, and to the axe resting on it.

"I hope that's some consolation for you. There'll be no more after her. Ever. I'm going to try *so hard* to make her the last."

Heather's attention became laser focused on the axe. He had a hand on it, but hadn't yet picked it up.

"And what about me?" she asked.

Kenny huffed out a groan. "I don't want to kill you, Heather, but what choice do I have? What choice have you left me here? My hands are tied. It's going to break your old man's heart when he hears, but, hey, tomorrow he won't remember. So, you know, silver linings."

"I meant back then. You were going to tell me why you picked me then."

"Oh. Aye. Sorry," Kenny laughed, like he was about to launch into one of his usual funny wee anecdotes. "Just bad timing. You saw me."

Heather blinked. "What?"

"You saw me. From the garden at your nursery. I was meant to be away. Everyone thought I was out of town, and you saw me sneaking about. Shouted to me. Gave me a big smile and a wave."

He grinned goofily at her, and waved one hand from side to side.

"I fucking waved back, too. That was my big mistake. If I'd just ignored you and kept going, I could've denied it was me. Kept them thinking I was out of town. But like a fucking div, I waved back. And then, well, then I had no choice, did I?

"So, I grabbed you and took you with me. Here. Chucked you in the van. I put the mask on, though I was sure that horse had well and truly bolted. But I put it on, and I kept it on when I came in to see Abbie. Some of them, they go for your face. Sharp fucking nails. Hence the mask."

"I got out," Heather said. "I got out of the van, and I saw you. I saw what you did. What you were doing to her."

Kenny looked her up and down, like he didn't quite recognise the woman sitting there before him. "I didn't think you remembered that."

"I didn't."

He continued to stare at her for a while, then shrugged. "But, aye. You saw. You were watching while I fucked her."

Heather swallowed down her bile and her hatred. He was trying to get a reaction from her. And he would. He'd get one.

Just not yet.

"When I'd finished with her, when everything was done, I put you in there. I had to. Just like today, you left me no fucking choice. I was going to kill you. I was. I knew I'd hate myself for it, but I had to. It was too risky not to."

He flopped back down onto his chair, and his hands clasped together between his knees.

He was two feet from the axe. Maybe a little less. Not enough.

"But I couldn't. I couldn't do it. Not to you. Not to Scott, or your mum. Call me a big fucking softy if you want. I'll take it. But I just could not bring myself to do it! So I... messed around with you for a while. Scared you a bit. Got you so worked up that you weren't thinking straight. But believe me, Heather, I took no pleasure from any of it. None. You weren't like them other girls. With you, it wasn't like that."

"What the hell am I meant to say to that?" Heather asked. "Are you looking for a fucking *thank you*?"

"I'm just explaining. That's all. I'm just telling you what happened," Kenny said. "I just, I wanted to give myself a fighting chance, that's all. I wasn't going to kill you, but I didn't want you telling everyone what had happened, so I just kept you a while. And then, after a few days of that, I left it in the lap of the gods. I let you go."

"You didn't let me go. I escaped," Heather corrected.

"'Escaped,' she says!" Kenny roared a big booming laugh that grew to fill the room. "Fuck's sake. Seriously? You really believe that? You were five years old. And, I mean, no offence, but you're hardly the sharpest knife in the fucking drawer. You're tenacious, aye. You're persistent. I like to think I gave you those qualities, by the way. But you were never exactly a child prodigy."

He leaned forward in his chair, his thighs squeezing his hands together. The laughter died in his throat.

"Escaped? Jesus fucking Christ, Heather. But that's you all over, isn't it? You've lived your life thinking you're so fucking capable. That you can do anything on your own. 'I don't need nobody, I'm the big fucking I-Am.' It's wound me up sometimes, I won't lie, because it's a load of pish. I mean, look at you trying to take care of your old man. Without me, he'd be dead in the fucking road, or have starved to death on that couch."

Heather felt sick at the thought of this bastard looking after her dad.

And sick at the thought that he was right.

"You didn't get away from me on your own, Heather. I allowed you to live. Me. Not you." A thin, insidious smirk manipulated the lines of his mouth. "The only way you could've ever escaped was because I *let* you escape."

"Want a fucking bet?" Heather hissed.

It was now or never. She kicked herself upright, shrugging her shoulder, wrenching the loosened ropes up over her head.

The chair clattered to the floor behind her before Kenny had a chance to react. He howled, a deep, guttural, animal noise, like the sound of a nightmare being forced through a straw.

Heather was closing in, but his hand was on the axe now, gripping the handle, swinging in a wide horizontal arc. She aborted the attack, ducking and dodging as the blade sliced through the space she'd just vacated.

He spun to face her, wheezing heavily, the axe raised and ready to hack or to throw.

"Sit the fuck down," he barked. "Sit the fuck down, or I'll hack your hands and feet off, and keep you in that fucking box!"

"It's over, Kenny! Put it down."

"Over? I say when it's fucking over, *Hayley*," he spat, the name seething through his teeth with a foam of hot spit. "And it isn't. It won't be. That stuff I said to you earlier, about me being finished? Being done?" He shook his head, all fast and angry. "No. I'll keep going. Right till the end. Till either your lot catch me, or the cancer does."

Heather stole another look at the windows, and the shifting shadows on the overgrown driveway.

"I've got backup coming, Kenny. They'll be here any second."

"Bullshit! You wouldn't have brought the fucking polis here. Not here. Not for me. Because you know what this would do to your old man, don't you? If he found out what his wee brother had done to his little girl. This would kill him. And if I go down, I'm taking your dad with me. They'd find out about what *he'd* done, too. Poor old Cyril Carter. How do you think Scott'd cope in court, Heather? In prison? What do you think all that would do to a man in his condition?"

Heather said nothing, just kept her hands raised, and took a step further into the kitchen, away from the door.

"And for what? For *what*? So I can be punished for my crimes? I'm knocking on now, Heather. Not got long left. And if I think for one minute that I'm going down, once I've ratted out your dad, I'm taking the fucking coward's way out. I'll be dead before I see a fucking courtroom. You'll have blown up your whole life, destroyed your old man, and for what, Heather? For nothing!"

He laughed, shaking his head. "No. No way. No way you did it. No way you called the polis."

"No," Heather admitted. "I didn't."

"I *knew* it! What did I say? I can always tell when you're lying, Heather. I know you better than you know yourself!"

"But, I'm not lying, Kenny," Heather said. In the confused silence that followed, she let her arms fall back to her sides. "I said I'd called for backup. Nobody mentioned the polis."

From out in the hall, there came the creaking of a floorboard.

From out by the back door came a scuffing on the step.

Car headlights flooded the inside of the kitchen. Both doors, inside and outside, were thrown open, and suddenly the room was wall-to-wall with gun-toting big bastards.

Kenny swung at one with the axe, but it was blocked. A fist half the size of his head cracked him across the jaw, sending him crashing to the floor.

He landed beside a pair of brown leather cowboy boots.

"No. No, Heather, no, no, please, no," he pleaded, before four hands caught him by the arms and heaved him up onto his feet.

They dragged him into position so he was standing before Shuggie Cowan. The gangster was smiling at him, all dead-eyed and shark-toothed.

"Long time no see, Kenneth," Cowan said. "High time you and me got ourselves reacquainted."

Kenny struggled pitifully against the hands holding him. He managed to twist his head just enough to find his niece standing by the back door, edging towards the dark night beyond.

"Heather. No. Please. You can't. You can't do this! Don't do this. Call it in. Arrest me. Take me in, I'll tell them everything! Please. *Please.* I did bad things. Bring me in. You're the police. You're the *law*, Heather."

The sight of him there, so helpless, so scared, made an ache spread through her chest.

He was her uncle.

Her funny, dependable, kind, generous uncle.

"It's like you said, Kenny." She stooped and picked up the axe. "Justice and the law aren't always the same thing. Sometimes, for evil to be properly punished, good people have to do bad things."

She met Cowan's eye, just long enough for him to give her a nod.

Then, with her uncle screaming her name, she stepped through the door into the cold night air, and ran as fast as she could to the crumbling brick building halfway along the garden.

"Ace? Ace? It's me! I'm here!"

The axe made it easier. She swung it down. Once. Twice. Sparks flew and metal clanked, then the padlock bounced on the concrete, and Heather pulled the door wide open.

She saw a girl in a school blazer on a damp, filthy rug.

She saw frost on the walls, between the ridges and the valleys.

The axe hit the ground with a *thunk*. Heather ignored her instinct to turn and run, and instead ducked through the door of the metal box, and dropped to her knees on the mat.

With a long, throaty cry, the girl on the floor put her bound hands over Heather's head and hugged her with every ounce of her strength.

"You're OK, Nancy Drew," Heather whispered. "I've got you. Everything's going to be just fine…"

FORTY-TWO

FIVE DAYS LATER

"AND SO, that's the conclusion to this mystery. The story of the Killie Kiddie Killer—which, I'm sure we'll all agree, is still a terrible name—ended in an old family farmhouse, filled with secrets and…"

Ace frowned, trying to think of something else the house had been filled with.

"Spiders?"

The girl shot a sideways look at the grinning woman in the chair beside her, rolled her eyes, then leaned in closer to the microphone.

"That'll have to do, I suppose," she said. "Thank you for listening to this first season of Crime De La Crime, and thank you to today's special guest, Officer Heather Filson, formerly known as Hayley Wilson, and now and forever to be known as the woman who saved my life. Probably. I mean, I might've escaped."

"You wouldn't have escaped," Heather said.

"I might have."

Ace side-eyed the detective again.

"Anyway, Officer. Would you like to say a few words?"

"Just that—"

"Into the microphone, please."

"Sorry." Heather leaned closer to the mic. "Just that it's 'Detective Inspector.' It's not 'Officer.'"

Ace raised her eyebrows like she was waiting for more, but Heather sat back in her seat, clearly done.

"Well, food for thought there. So, on behalf of Crime De La Crime and any sponsors we may get in the future and go back and add in—please email me if you'd like to advertise, rates are very reasonable—I'm Ace Wurzel, announcing *case closed*."

Heather removed her headphones and sighed. "Well, that was—"

"Hang on! We're not done!" Ace told her. She sat poised with a finger over a button on the laptop for a few seconds, then she stabbed at it and nodded. "*Now* we're done."

"About bloody time!"

Cathy's voice came from a narrow crack she'd opened in the door to her daughter's bedroom. She stuck an arm through and tapped at her watch.

"You're going to be late for school!"

Ace looked up at the clock on her wall, said the word, "Eep," like it was the most normal thing in the world to do, and then jumped to her feet.

Heather sat watching the girl go buzzing around the room, muttering below her breath as she grabbed her brand new blazer from the back of the door while scanning the floor for her shoes and bag.

"Get changed, three minutes. Brush teeth, two minutes, thirty seconds. Toilet…" She stopped walking for a moment, and looked upwards in thought. "I can hold it. Running to school, four minutes. But I can't run. Walking, six minutes."

Heather stood up. "It's fine," she said. "Calm the hell down, get yourself organised, and I'll give you a lift."

Ace looked up at the detective. Her expression, like almost always, was mostly blank, but there was a suggestion of surprise written across it.

"You will?"

"You *will*?" Cathy gasped, pushing the door open a little further.

"Aye. Sure. It's no bother," Heather said. She shrugged, masking the embarrassment she could feel prickling its way up her neck. "I mean, what are friends for?"

———

The journey to school was pleasant enough, even with Ace criticising Heather's driving at what felt like every available opportunity.

They arrived in good time, although Heather realised that a few minutes after the bell may have been better, as the sheer number of pupils gathered outside the school building had taken Ace's breath away when they'd pulled into the car park.

"Is it weird that I'm nervous?" the girl asked, staring wide-eyed at the mass of bodies.

Heather shut off the engine. "No. It's not weird."

"Yes, it is," Ace insisted. "I was never nervous before. Now I am. Nothing has changed, though. Nothing bad happened here. None of these people did anything to me."

Heather nodded slowly, her hands gripping the wheel. "It doesn't work like that. You don't get to choose when it hurts, or when it scares you, when you want to curl up and cry, or just scream. You don't get to choose any of that."

Ace turned to look at her. "So, what do you do? How do you deal with it?"

Heather shrugged, and summoned the most reassuring smile she could for the girl. "You just deal with it. And... you talk to people. People who've been there. I'm, uh, I'm told that helps."

Ace considered this very carefully for a few moments.

"Well, if you'd ever like to talk to me, I'd be more than happy to listen."

It was the look of absolute sincerity on the girl's face that brought hot pinpricks to the back of Heather's eyes.

"I might just take you up on that," she said.

From outside, there came the sound of the school bell ringing.

Ace immediately drew in a breath so large it made her grow several inches in the seat.

"Right, then," she announced. "I'd better go."

She opened the car door, hauled her bag out of the footwell, then shot Heather one last look. "Thank you, Officer."

Heather smiled. "Good luck, Nancy Drew."

Ace left the car, slammed the door far too hard, and then waved a quick apology. Heather ushered her towards the school entrance, then held her breath as she watched the girl go marching towards the doors with her head down.

Halfway there, a couple of girls stepped in front, blocking her path. Heather grabbed for the door handle, ready to run in there swinging, when one of the girls put her arms around Ace and pulled her in close. The other girl followed suit, and though Ace remained completely motionless, she showed no signs of pulling away.

From elsewhere in the crowd, there came a shout. A boy this time. He pushed through the throngs towards her, his hands raised above his head, clapping.

Others joined in. That one boy clapping became a ripple, became a roar. There were whoops and cheers. A few people called Ace's name.

Over by the door, Toby Pearse appeared and started to usher everyone inside. He spotted Heather in her car, raised his hands as if surrendering, then smiled, clearly amused by his own joke.

"Knob," Heather muttered, but she didn't fight back a smile of her own.

As the pupils started to file through the door, Ace turned back to the car. She looked bewildered, but happy, and when she shrugged her shoulders, Heather laughed.

She wiped away the tears that had sprung to her eyes, and fired up the engine.

"Get it together, you soppy great shite," she told herself.

And, with a wave and a toot of her horn, she headed for home.

———

The sight of the green Jaguar parked on her street sent the upwards trajectory of Heather's morning into a nosedive.

She hadn't seen or heard from Shuggie Cowan since that night at the house. She'd called 999 the moment he'd left with Kenny, and put a direct call in to the Gozer at home. The detective superintendent had *not* been happy, but when she'd told him that Ace Wurzel was safe and well, he'd quickly changed his tune.

There was still another disciplinary meeting looming in the not-too-distant future, but the Gozer seemed to be on her side again, and he'd help absorb the worst of it.

The police now knew almost everything. They knew that Kenny had been the Killie Kiddie Killer. He'd been other killers, too, all over the continent, his murder spree reaching as far as Germany and the Netherlands. Maybe even further, though they'd probably never know for sure.

He'd escaped. That was the official story. He'd caught Heather trying to free Ace from the shed, he'd attacked her, and then he'd run off. There was a manhunt on for him now. They were confident he'd be found soon.

And he would, Heather knew. He'd be found in the Clyde. Maybe it would look like a suicide, though knowing Shuggie Cowan, she doubted that very much.

But, he'd be found. The case would be closed.

Finally, this would all be over.

She pulled up behind the Jag, and could see Cowan watching her in his wing mirror as she approached.

The passenger side window slid down, and Heather bent so she could look the gangster straight in the eye.

"What are you doing here?" she demanded. "What do you want?"

"Well, that's fucking charming, that is," Shuggie retorted. He tilted his head towards a box file sitting on the cream leather of the passenger seat. "Brought you something."

Heather regarded the box with suspicion. "What is it? It's not a severed hand or something, is it?"

"Jesus Christ. What sort of fucking maniac do you take me for?" Shuggie scowled. "Course it's no' a fucking hand!"

"What is it, then?"

Shuggie sighed and picked the box up. It didn't look particularly heavy, and when he passed it over, Heather felt some paperwork sliding around.

"It's everything I've got on your brother."

Heather's eyes were drawn back to the file in her hands. "Stewie?"

"He owed me money. Fifteen grand. But I don't know where he is. Wherever he's wound up, whatever state he's in, it's fuck all to do with me. But I've asked around. I've called in a few favours, and pulled together what I can. It doesn't tell you where he is, but it might help."

Heather pressed the button that unfastened the clasp of the box. Inside, on top of the pile of paper, she saw a list of names and addresses. A couple of toerags she recognised. Some she didn't.

"Why are you giving me this?" she asked.

"Fuck knows," Shuggie admitted. "Call it a rare attack of conscience."

Heather looked into the car again, and this time she spotted a child's booster seat set up in the back, a teddy with its tags still on sitting there all strapped in.

"And, listen, if you find him," Cowan continued. "Tell him we're square. His debt's been paid in full."

"Eh, aye. OK. I'll be sure to pass that on."

A look and a nod passed between them. The window slid up, and Heather stepped back as the Jaguar purred away from the pavement.

She watched until she was sure the bastard was gone, then tucked the box folder under her arm and headed into the house.

"That you, Heather?"

"Aye, it's me," she called along the hall. She set the box down on one of the bottom stairs, then continued through to the living room.

Her dad sat in his usual chair, under his usual blanket, watching the TV. Heather had retuned the satellite receiver to block out the news channels, but she needn't have bothered. Scott had gone straight to one of the old movie channels, and was watching some black-and-white war film where every member of the British Army spoke like they were members of the aristocracy.

"You alright?" she asked, planting a kiss on his head.

"Aye." His head shook as he turned to look at her. His tremors were getting worse. "You?"

"Not bad, aye. Not bad at all."

He smiled at that, and his pale, empty gums revealed he'd forgotten to put his teeth in.

"Is Kenny coming over the day?" he asked, and the note of hope in the question twisted like a knife in her heart.

She put a hand on his arm. Looked him in the eye, and smiled as best she could.

"Not today, Auld Yin," she said. "Not today."

"Maybe tomorrow, though?"

She nodded. Something stuck in her throat. "Aye. Maybe."

Her dad's eyes searched her face, like he was committing it to memory, forcing it to stick this time.

"Ah well," he said, smiling back at her. "Looks like you're making breakfast, then."

Heather laughed. The sound of it took her by surprise, and brought a big gummy smile to the old man's face. She put an arm around him and pulled him in close to her.

"Aye," she agreed, planting a kiss on his wispy-haired head. "It looks like I am."

AFTERWORD

I did it again.

For some reason, I decided to write a book about a character in the DCI Logan universe that a lot of people didn't like.

That a lot of people positively *hated*, in fact.

When I first mentioned that, following my Robert Hoon Thrillers series, I was writing another spin-off from the Logan books, people started trying to guess who it would be about.

Would it be a prequel series with DI Ben Forde back in his younger days, walking the beat and catching scallywags?

Would it be a dystopian, future-set Neo-noir with a grizzled, hard drinking, now-Detective Chief Inspector Tyler Neish solving murders with an artificially intelligent robot sidekick?

Or, perhaps it would be the Shona Maguire solo series that everyone seems to love the idea of, judging by the number of emails I get about it every week.

But, no. It was none of those. Instead, I picked a relatively obscure character who has only made fairly minor appearances in three books, and in that time, has managed to alienate half my readers.

Why? Because I love a challenge.

And also, very possibly, because I hate myself.

It's Bob Hoon all over again. Although, to be fair, that turned out quite well, and he won over a lot of people who previously couldn't stand him.

I have no idea if Heather will do the same. Heather isn't as outrageously over-the-top as Hoon. Nor is she as likeable as Logan. She's a strong, no-nonsense thirty-something woman with a list of troubles a mile long, and zero interest in making anyone like her.

She wouldn't give a shit if you liked reading about her or not. Unfortunately, I do, as I became very attached to DI Filson while writing this book.

I became even more attached to her sort-of sidekick, Ace, who was only supposed to appear in one scene, but quickly grew into the version of the character you've just read about.

Like I did with the first Hoon book, I'm painting a target on myself and inviting you to get in touch and let me know what you thought of Heather's solo outing. I'd love to hear your thoughts, whether they be positive, negative, or somewhere in-between.

Drop me an email to jd@jdkirk.com, and let me know what you thought. I'll be bracing myself.

Best wishes,

JD Kirk - 2nd April, 2023

PS - I'm taking my family to Disneyland in October, and am fairly certain I won't be able to look poor Minnie Mouse in the eye...

ALSO AVAILABLE

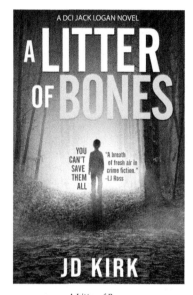

A Litter of Bones

Meet DCI Jack Logan in the first bestselling book from JD Kirk.

JOIN THE JD KIRK VIP CLUB

Want access to an exclusive image gallery showing locations from JD's books? Join the free JD Kirk VIP Club today, and as well as the photo gallery you'll get regular emails containing free short stories, members-only video content, and all the latest news about the author and his novels.

JDKirk.com/VIP

(Did we mention that it's free...?)

ABOUT THE AUTHOR

JD Kirk is the author of the million-selling DCI Jack Logan Scottish crime fiction series, set in the Highlands.

He also doesn't exist, and is in fact the pen name of award-winning former children's author and comic book writer, Barry Hutchison. Didn't see that coming, did you?

Both JD and Barry live in Fort William, where they share a house, wife, children, and two pets. You can find out more at JDKirk.com or at Facebook.com/jdkirkbooks.

Printed in Great Britain
by Amazon

23145064R00199